WHERE THE BUFFALO ROAM

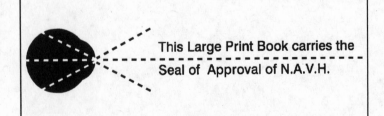

This Large Print Book carries the
Seal of Approval of N.A.V.H.

WHERE THE BUFFALO ROAM

MICHAEL ZIMMER

WHEELER PUBLISHING
A part of Gale, Cengage Learning

GALE
CENGAGE Learning

Farmington Hills, Mich • San Francisco • New York • Waterville, Maine
Meriden, Conn • Mason, Ohio • Chicago

GALE
CENGAGE Learning®

LIBRARY OF CONGRESS CATALOGING-IN-PUBLICATION DATA

Names: Zimmer, Michael, 1955– author.
Title: Where the buffalo roam / Michael Zimmer.
Description: Large print edition. | Waterville, Maine : Wheeler Publishing Large
    Print, 2017. | Series: Wheeler Publishing Large Print western
Identifiers: LCCN 2016051247| ISBN 9781410496683 (paperback) | ISBN 1410496686
    (softcover)
Subjects: LCSH: Large type books. | BISAC: FICTION / Historical. | FICTION /
    Westerns. | GSAFD: Western stories.
Classification: LCC PS3576.I467 W47 2017 | DDC 813/.54—dc23
LC record available at https://lccn.loc.gov/2016051247

Published in 2017 by arrangement with Michael Zimmer

Printed in the United States of America
1 2 3 4 5 6 7 21 20 19 18 17

WHERE THE BUFFALO ROAM

ONE

From the shelter of a sagging jack-leg tent, Clay Little Bull stared bleakly at the falling rain. Thunder rumbled across the low, rolling hills, and the autumn-cured grass glistened sleekly.

The rain had started just after dawn the day before, a steady drizzle wrung from sullen, fast-moving clouds. As the day progressed, the temperature had fallen steadily, until by nightfall Clay could see his breath puffing like steam from an idling sidewheeler as he unsaddled his pinto and pulled the packs off the three shaggy-haired Indian ponies he had hauled with him all the way from Iron Hand's village of Wichitas, far to the southwest. The mustangs were carrying — in addition to the tent, some cooking utensils, a leather sack of dried meat and squash, and an assortment of personal gear — twenty-two beautifully tanned buffalo robes traded from the Wichitas, plus a mixed bale of wolf, skunk, and beaver pelts — maybe two hundred dollars worth of robes and furs, if he could get them to market without damage from the rain.

Pulling his sleeping robe up until the long, tawny shoulder hairs of the tanned buffalo hide tickled his nose, Clay stretched luxuriously. Despite the wretchedness of the weather, he had slept comfortably wrapped in his heavy bedroll, and he dreaded relinquishing its warmth to start another day. Yet he knew he couldn't lie there forever. His bladder was full, his stomach empty, and maybe, just maybe, he had men trailing him. He wouldn't put it past Moses Gray to sic a posse on him.

With a weary sigh, Clay began to dress under his robes. He had dried his clothes as best he could the night before by hanging them over the smoky flames of a buffalo chip fire during a brief break in the rain, but they were still damp and difficult to slip into. He pulled his mackinaw and hat on last, then gritted his teeth and ducked into the rain, dragging his saddle with him.

Clay Little Bull was about nineteen-years-old that fall of 1858, give or take a year. He was of average height, though broad through the shoulders and chest, strong and wiry.

His complexion was almost the same weathered shade as the oil-darkened leather of his saddle. Only his eyes, a curious pale green in color, and hair that was more curly than kinky, worn to his shoulder in the fashion of the plains, revealed the mixed blood of his heritage.

He wore hard-soled moccasins he'd traded from the Wichitas after his boots wore out, gray wool trousers patched at the knees, and a soft buckskin shirt beneath the red-and-black plaid mackinaw. His hat, once the color of fresh-churned cream, had darkened with age to a gloomy gray, its band sweat-stained and dented, its broad brim starting to sag in places, but with a quick upward curl in front that gave it a bit of dash. He had fastened a cinnamon-hued turkey feather to the leather band while with Iron Hand's people, although the plume had quickly lost its luster in the driving rains of the past twenty-four hours.

Clay stood quietly outside his tent, scanning the flat plain to the south, along his backtrail. For as far as he could see through the slanting veils of misty rain, the land appeared empty and desolate. For a moment his thoughts ebbed backward to Simon Little Bull, and the life they had shared in the heart of the Indian Nations. He wondered what the old Choctaw would say if he could see the way things had turned out for his adopted son. He suspected Simon would have been angry at Moses Gray's treachery, but doubted that he would have been surprised by it.

Clay saddled the pinto, then led his pack string in and quickly cinched the sawbucks in place. The robes and pelts he'd traded for over the summer were bundled inside a double layer of oilcloth, but he knew even oilcloth had its limitations. He eyed the dull, reddish brown canvas worriedly, yet didn't dare pull back a corner for a quick peek.

Working alone, it took him the better part of an hour to pack up. When he finished, he walked out along his backtrail until he was clear of the camp, away from the creaking leather and stomping, blowing horses. The rain fell heavily now, and the tracks he'd made coming in the night before had been all but obliterated. It gave him a measure of comfort to know that if men *were* following him, they'd have the devil's own time of it today.

The pinto snorted and tossed its head as Clay gathered the reins and heaved into the saddle. He settled his heavy plains rifle, sheathed in a well-oiled, fringed elkhide case, across the saddlebows, then shook out the lead rope to the first pack horse in his string. Heeling the pinto's ribs, he called, *"Hup!"* in a voice grown scratchy from disuse, and led out to the northeast, keeping his left shoulder to the blustery wind and peppering rain. He ate on the trail, chewing doggedly on pieces of jerky carried in the pocket of his mackinaw, and washing it down with swigs of water from his canteen. The rain continued unabated as he slogged his cavvy across the muddy landscape, through rain-swollen streams and a thickening gumbo that clung to the horses' hooves like iron weights. He halted only twice to rest the stock and clean their hooves, walking to the rear of the string each time to scrutinize his backtrail. It was mid-afternoon before the rain finally let up and the clouds lifted.

Just before dusk, Clay came in sight of a grove of trees growing in the middle of a broad, shallow valley, and his spirits rose for the first time that day. Halting his horses on a small rise about a quarter of a mile away, he studied the woods intently for some sign of habitation — wood smoke or a corral or a chimney. His shoulders ached beneath the mackinaw's sodden weight, and his eyelids felt heavy as lead. He was wet clear through, and chilled to the bone. But mostly, he was tired . . . tired of the loneliness and isolation, of the endless, butt-numbing days in the saddle. He hadn't realized until that summer, while trading among Iron Hand's people along the mid-waters of the Washita, how much he missed the trappings of civilization, even if all he had known of it for nearly half his life were the crude settlements of a frontier society. That he longed for even that had surprised him, and saddened him in a way, too, for he had spent most of his years among the Choctaw of the Indian Territory dreaming of someday returning to the wild lands of his youth, to a people he now only vaguely remembered — the Kiowa.

It would be good to find a cabin down below, Clay thought as he eyed the woods, even if its inhabitants would be white-eyed Kansans.

Wisps of fog clung to the treetops, and the narrow trunks of oaks, hickories, and maples looked dark and oily in the fading light. The once vivid colors of autumn were now drab and lifeless, as if the rains had sponged away the more brilliant hues of yellow, orange, and red. A stream ran out of a notch in the hills to Clay's left, curved through the woods like a dull pewter ribbon, then disappeared through another gap to the south. But there was no sign of human activity, no hint of cabin or camp. Glumly, Clay booted the pinto's ribs and rode on down.

He let the horse pick its own path through the trees. His gaze shifted constantly, missing nothing. A deep silence shrouded the woods, broken only by the occasional squeaking of tree limbs rubbing together in the breeze and the steady dripping of water.

It was the silence that finally caught Clay's attention, that made the flesh on his scalp crawl.

He stopped the pinto less than half a dozen rods into the trees and sat quietly for several minutes. Then, without lowering his eyes, he slid the elkhide cover from his rifle, running his thumb over the copper cap on the nipple to make sure it was still in place.

He felt better with the rifle free and butted to his thigh. With his fingers curved around the forestock and his thumb pressed lightly to the smooth, brown iron of the heavy octagon barrel, Clay slitted his eyes, attempting to absorb the silence around him, to let his other senses reach out among the trees and thick brush. He could hear the soft purling of the stream just ahead, and after a few minutes he eased the pinto toward it.

The creek was running full-tilt after two days of rain, its opaque waters filled with silt and debris. The tall grass growing along its banks had been beaten down by the storm, the tops closest to the runoff bent into the stream, swaying and bouncing with the current. Cautiously, Clay dismounted and knelt on the bank, dipping his fingers into the icy waters. His gaze lifted to the opposite shore, where a small, grassy clearing opened invitingly. For a moment he envisioned his tent set up at the rear of the clearing, a crackling fire with coffee warming in a pot beside it, fresh meat dripping and spitting above the flames.

The vision faded almost as quickly as it had appeared, and Clay rose and wiped his fingers dry on his coat. The light was fading rapidly now, the deepening shadows inking out large sections of the woods. Soon it would be too dark to make a thorough search of the grove. Clay stood by the pinto's head in indecision. Logic told him to abandon the woods for another cold camp on the open prairie, miserable perhaps, but safe. Yet his chilled, wind-wrung body begged for the comfort of a real fire, fueled by wood instead of soggy buffalo dung, with tall grass to cushion his bed and maybe a rabbit or squirrel for supper. He tried to convince himself that this sudden jumpiness was the result of his imagination, a product wrought from weariness and solitude, but he couldn't do it. Regretfully, he turned back to the pinto. His toe was reaching for the stirrup when a taut voice broke the fragile silence.

"Drop the rifle! Now!"

The command came from a thicket of brambles downstream, punctuated by the crisp ratching of the sear snapping into place — a weapon being cocked.

The pinto snorted and tossed its head. Clay's fingers tightened around his rifle, but he resisted the instinct to bring it up or swing around to face the voice. Fright scurried up his spine like icy claws, but he kept his voice calm as he replied, "I'm just passing through." He turned slightly for a better view. "If this is your property, I didn't mean to trespass."

"I said, drop that rifle," the voice barked, and there was no mistaking the sound of a second barrel being cocked, a rifle, perhaps, but more likely a shotgun. Judging from the sound of the voice, he couldn't be more than thirty feet away — close enough, Clay thought, that the blast from those twin barrels would cut him in half. Carefully, he lowered his rifle to the wet grass.

"Now your pistol," the voice demanded.

"I'm not carrying a pistol."

A second voice, this one from Clay's left, said, "Boy, if you're lying, I'm gonna take it real personal."

"I'm not lying," Clay replied tersely.

"Then throw your knife down," the man with the shotgun said. "I know darn good and well you've got a sticker on you somewheres."

He had two, counting the throat knife with its three-inch blade, carried in a sheath hanging from a braided buckskin cord around his neck; the sheath rested against his chest under his shirt, solid but concealed. His other knife was a common Green River butcher, carried in a brass-tacked sheath above his right hip. With the tips of his fingers, Clay pulled the blade and let it fall to the grass beside the rifle. He took a deep breath, but left the throat knife where it was.

"All right, now step away from that spotted pony," the man with the shotgun said. "Move on over toward Ezra there."

Clay looked to his left. A shape had emerged from behind a hickory on the near bank of the stream. Clay saw a tall, lanky individual with sloping shoulders beneath a dirty, knee-length coat. A bushy beard

16

concealed his neck and the upper half of his chest, and a recently waxed mustache stood out on either side of his narrow, hollow-cheeked face like small wire cornucopias. His hat was medium-brimmed, the crown tall and flat, flared slightly outward near the top. He carried a carbine in both hands that he kept leveled on Clay's stomach.

"Over here, boy, and be easy about it," the man named Ezra instructed. Dropping the pinto's reins, Clay moved to obey, stopping only when the bearded man gave a quick, upward jerk of his carbine.

"By God, we got 'im, Ezra," the man in the brambles crowed, his voice suddenly young and full of enthusiasm. "Caught 'im slick, we did." Clay heard the rattle of branches and the rip of cloth as the man extracted himself from his thorny hideout.

Ezra was smiling crookedly. "You did fine, Jake, real fine. Now search him, and make a good job of it. He looks like the kind who might sport a hideout knife or a belly gun under his coat."

"Hell, I know that," Jake replied, sounding put out. He jammed the shotgun muzzles into the small of Clay's back. "I'm gonna search you for hideout weapons. You just rest easy while I do it. Nobody wants to shoot you, but we will if we have to."

17

Jake took the shotgun away from Clay's spine. A second later, Clay felt Jake's hands patting the tops of his moccasins, moving swiftly but ineptly upward. He reached under the mackinaw to explore Clay's waist, then under his arms to feel for a shoulder rig, but he missed the throat knife completely. Yanking the shooting bag and powder horn for the rifle over Clay's head, Jake tossed them aside, then stepped back and brought his shotgun up. "Nary a thing," he proclaimed.

Clay risked a sidelong glance. Jake was even younger than he'd expected, certainly no more than seventeen or so. He stood about five-foot-six, which was only a couple of inches shorter than average, but was so skinny he appeared frail. He had long, auburn hair that flared wildly from beneath a wide-brimmed sugar-loaf hat, and a fuzzy upper lip that would someday support a fair-haired mustache. He wore boots that were rundown at the heels, striped pants that were splotchy with mud, and a claw-tailed black preacher's coat that had been tailored for someone taller and with far more girth than Jake would ever pack.

Jake met Clay's gaze evenly, but without animosity.

"Get the shackles," Ezra told Jake; his dark

18

eyes glittered savagely. "Looks like we've caught ourselves another runaway."

"Runaway?" Clay echoed. Suddenly a fresh new fear gripped him, and his head jerked up and his throat constricted. "No," he croaked. "I'm not a —"

Ezra stepped in before Clay could finish, swinging his carbine in a short, wicked arc. The iron buttplate slammed into Clay's stomach. Bright lights exploded before his eyes as he staggered backward, then collapsed in the wet grass, retching violently. As if from a long way off, he heard Jake say, "Dangit, Ezra, there weren't no call for that."

"You just get the shackles," Ezra snarled. "Let me handle the prisoners. Bring the horses, too, and the girl."

Clay lay motionless for a long time. Tears of pain ran down his cheeks, and a clammy sweat sheeted his forehead. After several agonizing minutes, he managed to twist his head up off the spongy ground to look at Ezra. "I'm not a runaway," he said weakly. "I'm a free man — a Choctaw."

The greased tips of Ezra's mustache twitched against the purpling sky. "Boy, I've got a Sharps carbine here that says different. Now, if you're of a mind to question Mr. Sharps' authority, then I reckon it'll be your funeral. Not that I'd take time to bury your sorry ass way out here."

Clay lowered his face to the cool grass, his pulse pounding in his ears. Jake returned a few minutes later, mounted and leading a pair of horses. Straining his eyes against the backdrop of trees, Clay could just make out the shape of a rider on the second mount — a small, huddled figure, like a distant mountain seen at sundown. From the tilt of her head, he knew it was a woman; from her silence and immobility, he suspected she was a prisoner, the same as he.

Jake dismounted with a rattle of chains, and Clay's pulse quickened. He put his hands under him, palms flat to the ground, and cocked his knees. The dark timber beckoned. He wouldn't have to go far at all before the black woods swallowed him whole. But Ezra must have read his thoughts. With a quick rack of his carbine, he said, "You just forget that idea right there. Go ahead and stand up, if that's what you have in mind, but try anything stupid and I'll blow a hole through you big enough to run a fist through."

Stifling his frustration, Clay struggled to his feet. Jake stepped behind him, shaking out a length of chain. He pulled Clay's left arm behind his back and clamped the cold

20

iron bands around his wrist. A key grated, and the cuff was locked.

"Give me your other hand," Jake ordered, grabbing Clay's free arm.

With Ezra's carbine pointed at him, Clay had little choice but to comply. A moment later the task was completed. Ezra lowered his weapon and stepped forward, digging into his pocket.

"Let's have a look," he said, striking a lucifer with his thumbnail. Clay wrinkled his nose as the pungent odor of sulphur mushroomed in his face. "Hold still," Ezra growled, shoving the match close. His lips curled into a sardonic grin. "I knew it," he chortled. "By damn, soon as this buck said he was Choctaw, I knew it."

"Knew what?" Jake asked, puzzled.

"Take a look at those eyes," Ezra said, his own dark eyes gleaming in the dancing light of the match.

Jake stepped closer, squinting nearsightedly. "So?"

Giving the younger man a disgusted look, Ezra said, "It's the nigra Moses Gray told us about. The one with the green eyes." As the match burned down near his fingers, Ezra slid back a step and shook it out. In a barely audible voice, he added, "That's who we've caught, Jake. Clay Little Bull, of the

21

Choctaw Nation, and damn if the Captain don't already have the paperwork filled out on him." He laughed, poking the muzzle of his carbine into Clay's stomach. "Your luck just ain't worth a shit, is it, boy?"

Two

Clay lifted his face to the icy drizzle. The rain had started again around midnight, as near as he could tell, coming down hard at first, like a thousand tiny, pummeling fists, then softening to a gentle, half-frozen spray. Closing his eyes, he listened to its patter on the oilcloth covering his robes and furs, a simple sound, yet reassuring in its familiarity. Lowering his face, Clay blinked the wetness from his eyes. With the storm's return, the darkness was complete. He couldn't even see the ghostly outline of the pinto's ears, let alone the tail of the horse in front of him. If not for the heavy shackles dragging at his arms, he might have imagined the whole thing as some sort of bad dream. But there was no mistaking the solid weight of the iron cuffs chewing at his wrists, or the ache that throbbed between his shoulder blades from riding all night with his arms trapped behind his back.

It hadn't surprised Clay to learn that Moses Gray had posted a five hundred dollar reward for his arrest. Clay had learned a long time ago that there were things even the greediest person valued above money. In Moses Gray's case, it was power, and in an ambiguous kind of way, Clay had pirated some of that the night he'd sold most of the furnishings and farm implements from Simon Little Bull's farm, just before leaving the Choctaw Nation early last summer. The catch was that he'd sold it *after* Moses had foreclosed on the property, and sent a couple of members of the Choctaw Lighthorse Police out with an eviction notice for Clay. Clay, who had been neither Simon's legal heir, nor Choctaw, had been forced to relinquish the land without contest.

"It is a raw deal," Weed Jackson had commented on the day he and Lyn Broken Horn rode out to the Little Bull property to serve Clay his notice. "I'm glad you did not fight us over this. I was afraid you might, and that I would have to shoot you. I did not want to do that."

Eyeing the holstered revolver Weed kept his right hand close to, Clay said, "I see you would have, though."

Weed had shrugged and followed Clay into the cabin. As Clay gathered his personal

24

effects and shoved them into a warbag, the lighthorseman's eyes roamed the cabin's interior, taking in the smooth-planed, whitewashed log walls, the gingham curtains hanging over the glass-paned windows, the braided oval rug protecting the polished hardwood floor. The furnishings were spartan but well-made, the white bone china and hand-carved wooden utensils washed and stacked away, the hearth swept clean of ashes.

"You know, everyone said old Simon was crazy to free his slaves and let the land go fallow like he did, but I always kind of admired the old coot." Weed looked at Clay without embarrassment. "No offense."

"No," Clay replied darkly. "No offense." He took his bedroll and warbag out to the barn and saddled the pinto. Weed Jackson followed him out there as well, chewing on a toothpick whittled from a sassafras root.

"Leave the mules and the milk cow," Weed said. "They belong to Moses Gray, too. He is going to send somebody down tonight to take care of them."

"But not Moses Gray," Clay pointed out.

Weed laughed, but didn't reply. They walked back to the porch where Clay had left his rifle, and where Lyn Broken Horn was attaching a large latch and padlock to

25

the cabin's door. Clay watched silently as the lock was snapped closed, then glanced at Weed.

"Like I said, it is a raw deal, but they say old Simon owed Moses Gray a lot of money," Weed remarked.

Clay swung into the saddle without comment, settling the rifle across his lap. Coming to the edge of the porch, Lyn added, "Don't do anything stupid, Clay." He pocketed the key. "I hate hunting down men I've fished with."

Clay nodded curtly and reined away. Bitterness created a sour taste in his mouth, but he held his anger in check as he rode across the weed-choked fields and into the woods. He was aware of the two lighthorsemen watching him. They were good friends, and he knew they worried that he might try something foolish.

Clay rode only as far as the little hunting shack he and Simon had built a few years before, when Simon's legs started hurting him too much to allow him to make the trek from the cabin to the rear of his property and back without a place to rest. There, Clay settled in. He hunted a little and fished a lot, spending the time alone with his thoughts. It rankled him that a man like Moses Gray could so effortlessly move him off what he had come to consider his own, even if Simon was dead. In the weeks following his eviction, Clay often rode into the town of Jack's Fork, at the foot of the Winding Stair Mountains, to speak to the Choctaw Council about paying off Simon's debt and reclaiming the Little Bull farm. But although most of the council members agreed with Weed Jackson that it was a raw deal, they said the law was the law, and their hands were tied.

Then one evening in late April, after another futile session with the council, Clay was heading for the trees where he'd tethered his pinto for the day. On his way he spied Moses Gray and a council member named John Bear standing on the back porch of the council house, sharing cigars and an animated conversation, laughing frequently. Clay froze in his tracks. John Bear stood with his back to him, but Moses had a clear view of the path that led to the trees. At one point, Moses took the cigar from his mouth and looked pointedly at Clay, a smug expression on his face. Then Bear made some comment, and Moses turned his attention back to the council member, chuckling politely.

Clay quit riding into Jack's Fork after that. Spring was well advanced by then, the trees leafed out and the days warm and muggy. He ran his trotlines in Red Creek and sold some of his catch in the town that bore the stream's name. He ate catfish stew and turtle soup until he grew sick of them, and simmered in anger when he thought of the slabs of pork and beef that had hung in Simon's smokehouse, and of the corn, beans, and squash that had been put up for the winter. Most of the provisions had been carted away to Moses' plantation south of Red Creek, to feed his fieldhands, but a lot of it had been shoveled out to rot on the garden patch, or to feed the wild hogs that roamed the area. Finally Clay's anger got to be too much. On a Saturday in early May he bartered his fish and a couple of big snapping turtles for a bottle of illegal whiskey, then got roaring drunk. Toward evening, reeling in his saddle, he rode into Red Creek to kill Moses Gray. But Moses was away at the time, and Weed Jackson and Lyn Broken Horn got Clay back on his horse and out of town before he caused any trouble.

Two days later, Lyn and Weed rode out to the shack where Clay was skinning a pair of opossums he'd trapped the night before. The two lighthorsemen sat down beside the fire while Clay skewered the rodents on a green stick and hung them over low flames.

Clay's drunk had been the first really big one of his life, and he was still feeling its effects. He was edgy and not in much of a mood for talk, which seemed to suit Weed and Lyn just fine. They dug out their pipes and smoked while the meat roasted. Weed eventually commented on the weather. When that failed to elicit a response, he brought up the annual green corn dance that would be held in a few weeks. When that also failed, Weed blinked a few times and took to examining the face of a turbaned Arab, which was cast into the bowl of his pipe.

Clay split the opossums evenly between the three men, and they ate in silence, peeling off fatty strips of meat with their fingers and stuffing them into their mouths. Afterward, they sat back and relit their pipes. It was only then that Lyn let his gaze slide toward Clay in a meaningful way.

"Moses Gray is doing some talking around Red Creek," he began hesitantly.

Clay looked up but remained silent.

"He's claiming Simon Little Bull didn't legally free his slaves," Lyn went on. "At least, not according to the letter of the law. Moses is saying that just telling them they're free ain't good enough. He's also saying that

29

maybe the law ought to consider you a part of the foreclosure on Simon's property — either that or send you back to your rightful owners in Texas, if they can be located."

Clay's face hardened. "Is that a fact?"

"Now, that ain't gonna happen," Lyn went on quickly, "and Moses knows it. But what he's doing is putting a lot of bad ideas in the heads of folks who seem to take naturally to bad ideas."

"And easy money," Weed added. "Old Simon never did properly register you. He was already going a little soft on his niggers when he came back from the plains with you. No offense."

"Half the Negro population in the Choctaw Nation isn't registered," Clay pointed out.

"But they should be, which is Moses Gray's argument." Lyn's gaze dropped to the fire. He clicked the stem of his pipe against his teeth a couple of times, thinking. "You know, Clay, you ain't gonna get this farm back. Likely you wouldn't even if you had some kind of legal fingerhold on the place, which you don't. You don't even have a neighbor remembering what old Simon said he wanted done with the place after he died. And Moses Gray ain't a man to tangle with. Folks turn up missing when they push

30

that old money-grubber too hard."

"Sounds to me like you ought to arrest Moses Gray," Clay said. "And leave honest people like me alone."

Lyn looked perturbed, but it was Weed who took up the thread of conversation. "You are a young man, Clay," he said. "How old are you? Nineteen? Twenty? You are strong and quick. I have seen you wrestle at the green corn dance, and won good money betting on you against men who were bigger but not nearly as slippery. Someone like you would fetch a good price at a slave auction, especially over in Tennessee, where they got more rich people."

Clay's anger was still building, but something in Weed's words struck a note of warning. Studying the lighthorseman closely, he asked, "Why Tennessee?"

"Because Moses Gray sent a letter to Colonel Carry, over in Memphis," Lyn replied bluntly.

Everyone in the Nations knew that Colonel Douglas J. Carry ran a profitable auction house in Memphis, dealing in horses, mules, cattle, real estate, and slaves — slaves rumored to have been abducted from Kansas and Nebraska Territories, then marched south in chains over owlhoot trails to the Colonel's auction barn.

Clay's gaze shifted quickly between Weed and Lyn. He considered both men his friends, but he knew they'd sworn an oath to uphold the laws of the Choctaw Nation, as well as those of the United States. It was an oath the two lighthorsemen took seriously, and the laws being what they were, if Moses Gray came up with paperwork proclaiming ownership and Clay couldn't counter them with documents of his own, then Weed and Lyn would be legally bound to turn him over. It wasn't fair by any stretch of the imagination, but it was the way things were in the Nations, and everyone knew it and accepted it and hoped that someday it would change.

"I'm a free man," Clay said tautly. "Maybe Simon didn't tell anyone what he wanted done with his farm, but he sure as hell told folks what he was doing with his slaves."

Simon had owned four slaves at one point — a man, a woman, and their two children — but he'd sent them on their way while Clay was still a boy, giving them a wagon and mule, and two hundred dollars in greenbacks to make a start on their own.

Lyn nodded sympathetically. "I know, but Moses is a cantankerous bastard who's used to getting his way. He didn't like it that you went to Jack's Fork to raise a stink with the

Council, whether it came to anything or not."

"He does not like it that you are still on his place, either," Weed contributed.

Lyn's mouth turned down in distaste. "Moses Gray has a lot of influence in the Nation, Clay. He's a powerful man, and a mean son of a bitch, to boot. It's something to think about."

"Maybe you ought to go hunt buffalo for a while," Weed suggested in an offhand manner. "I hear a bunch of Chickasaws from over around Ada are going out with wagons."

"That wouldn't be a bad idea," Lyn agreed quietly, studying the puckered toes of his moccasins. "Let things settle down around here."

Clay didn't reply. He felt overwhelmed by the information Lyn and Weed had passed along to him. The two lawmen finished their pipes. Then, without further comment, they mounted their horses and rode out. Clay barely acknowledged their departure. He spent the rest of that day stewing in the juices of indecision, facing, for the first time in his life, the consequences of his color.

THREE

Clay barely remembered his place of birth or his natural parents. From those earliest years of his life he had salvaged only a handful of dim memories: a conglomeration of thatch-roofed shacks set amid low, sandy hills; chasing a blacksnake with other children, all of them dark-skinned like himself; a straw-filled mattress on a freshly swept dirt floor, covered with a tattered patchwork quilt that was old and threadbare, but clean-smelling all the same, and warm to snuggle under.

Of the people who may have been his parents he had only the vaguest recollection — an image of riding in a jolting wagon piled high with loose cotton that made his eyes water and his nose itch, sitting between a man and woman who had no faces in his memory, but who had given him a sense of being at the center of their world.

His most vivid memories before coming

34

to the Little Bull farm in the Choctaw Nation were from his years among the wild tribes far to the west. Plucked like a cotton boll at the end of a freshly plowed furrow where he had been playing with twigs, Clay had been swept westward with a retreating war party of Kiowas, thrust unceremoniously into a culture as foreign to him as travel among the stars.

Even the practice of slavery had its distinctions. Although the Kiowas embraced the institution with a philosophy every bit as dehumanizing as that which existed among the whites. Clay had quickly discovered that within the Plains tribes slavery hinged upon factors other than a person's color. Clay, despite his darkness and the obvious caste from which he had been abducted, had been assimilated into the tribe, rather than made its drudge.

Not that he was untouched by slavery. His village had for many years owned two — a Mexican male of about forty, who had been castrated to increase his docility, and a snowy haired white woman who bore her captors' insults and fury with a chillingly vacant stare. During Clay's first few weeks among the Kiowas he had been drawn to both individuals, recognizing in them the same detached mannerisms he had observed in his own parents when in the presence of their white masters or the Creole overseer with his well-oiled coil of whip. But Clay's affinity for the Kiowa slaves soon dissipated. By the Moon of the Berries Ripening he had become one with the People, an equal in all regards.

He was adopted by a woman whose husband had been killed by Texas Rangers, and tutored in the art of warfare and horsemanship by the woman's brother-in-law, who became Clay's adoptive uncle. At an early age, Clay learned to manage his own small horse with a skill that matched any other boy his age. Riding at a full gallop, he could slip down along the pony's neck, all but hidden from an imaginary enemy, or stand with his toes digging into the mount's rocking withers, his arms stretched wide to catch the wind. He learned to shoot the small bow and arrows his uncle made for him, and became proficient at driving the blunt wooden tips through pieces of rawhide or buffalo dung rolled along the ground. And with the other boys, he had become adept at stealing meat off the drying racks of the women. This stunt would have earned him a sound scolding had he been apprehended, but it also taught him the stealth he would need on his first horse stealing raid.

Clay's was a boyhood of freedom and acceptance that would have been unimaginable to those children with whom he had once chased blacksnakes. His days were filled with roughhousing and mock warfare with other boys his age, and his nights rang with laughter and stories told within the warmth of his uncle's lodge. He had been called Night's Son, and as the pain of separation from his birth parents lessened, his world became complete.

The Osage came when he was nine, while the men were away hunting. Although the older men and boys, and many of the women, fought bravely — Clay himself had seen his best iron-tipped hunting arrow buried in a shaved-head's thigh — the People, as the Kiowa called themselves, were no match for the superior numbers and better weapons of the Osage. With the glancing blow of a war club, Clay's life once more changed irrevocably. He became a captive again, this time in the purest sense of the word.

It was among the Osage that Clay received his first real lesson in slavery. If he had been too young to understand the concept on an East Texas cotton plantation, or too far removed to give it much consideration while growing up a Kiowa, it was brought home vividly now.

For three months he lived a life not quite as dignified as that of a village cur, for a dog could roam at will, while Clay barely roamed at all, and never without the watchful eyes of the shaved-heads or their women on him.

The Osage had enjoyed strong bonds with the white communities of the South for generations. They understood the worth of Clay's color, the riches it would bring them in rifles and powder and shot. But first they would have to break him, a task that would increase his value tenfold.

Simon Little Bull arrived near the end of summer, driving a rattletrap buckboard laden with trade goods. Clay was hauling firewood into the village — his young back bent under the awkward load, his buttocks stinging from the lead-tipped quirt of the flint-eyed squaw who owned him — when the old, white-haired Choctaw arrived. Simon *whoaed* his team as the woman and boy passed, propping a bony elbow contemplatively on one sharp-jointed knee. The woman scowled, but Simon's eyes were on the boy. Clay risked a glance, and for his trouble received a snapping pop from the woman's quirt and a quick wink from the Choctaw.

Two days later, in exchange for a pair of used J. Henry trade rifles, four cheap swords, twenty pounds of powder, fifty of bar lead, and a couple of .50 bullet molds, Clay left the Osage for Simon's cabin outside of Red Creek, in the Choctaw Nation.

It took time for Simon to weed the ways of the high plains out of the boy. The traits of the People were deeply ingrained by then. Some, the old Indian knew, would probably never be fully erased. But others could be reshaped, redirected. And Simon had the time. More important, he had the patience.

For months Clay schemed over plans to escape back to the People. He would steal a horse, a rifle, provisions from the smokehouse. He would take the old Choctaw's scalp as a trophy, and cut off his ear to mark this the work of a Kiowa. He would return to the People a hero, and songs would be sung in his honor.

All this Clay dreamed of nightly, yet the days passed one after another without any attempt to break away. August — the Moon of the Berries Ripening — waned. Then the Moon when the Buffalo Calves Lose Their Color came and went. Clay became restive. Deep, emotional stirrings ran through him. During the Moon of Leaves Falling, his turmoil deepened.

The days turned shorter, the evenings chillier. Ice filmed the water barrel in the mornings, and frost grew like whiskers atop the fence rails. Clay began to wander farther and farther from the cabin. He knew Simon often watched him as he plunged into the woods, always in a westerly direction. Clay also knew the old Choctaw feared he might someday run off to rejoin the People, but he never came after Clay. He never asked where he had been or what he had done, never called him back or turned a suspicious eye on him.

As the Moon of the Geese Going South rolled around — Simon called it November — Clay knew his resolve to return to the high plains was weakening. He grew angry, and chastised himself daily for his waffling. Soon the cold, blue northers of winter would sweep across the land, locking the long, hostile country that separated him from the People in ice and snow. Travel would become dangerous, if not impossible, for one who had yet to count his tenth summer. Is that what he waited for? he asked himself. Unable to make the decision himself, did he tarry so that winter would take the problem out of his hands?

Clay's thoughts raced as he wandered the

forests surrounding the cabin in ever shortening circles. To be sure, the life Simon
Little Bull offered was more sedate, yet in
many ways, it seemed more fulfilling. He
could still hunt and fish when he wanted to.
He could ride Simon's ponies with the same
reckless abandon that had thrilled him
among the People. But here in the Choctaw
Nation, Clay noticed, there were never any
starving times, periods when buffalo
couldn't be found, meat couldn't be made.
Simon raised a garden that included corn,
squash, and beans; apples and cherries grew
in a small orchard behind it, and nuts and
wild berries were abundant along the creek.
Deer, bear, wild boar, and turkey flourished
in the deep woods. There was bread every
day, and coffee made syrupy with molasses.
There were other boys his age to run with,
and a snug bed in which to retire each
night. And when the icy winds of winter at
last swooped down out of the north, there
was the cabin with its large stone fireplace,
rather than a thin hide lodge and a fire
everyone huddled around to keep warm,
eating smoke until their lungs burned.

Clay gave up much when he finally accepted his home with Simon, not the least
of which was the family he had left behind
on the plains. But if had lost a mother and

uncle among the People, in Simon Little Bull he had gained a father.

And then the old Choctaw died.

Ten years had passed since Simon had driven out to the Osage to trade for buffalo robes and hump meat, and returned instead with a half-wild, curly haired youth of the plains. He was on his way to Red Creek with a keg of hard-earned honey to trade at Moses Gray's store when witnesses said he pulled off the road at the outskirts of town, found a shady spot under a sycamore tree leaning over the creek, and settled down against its white bark trunk, as if he knew death was approaching, and wanted to await its arrival in comfort.

Moses Gray gave it a month, then drove into Jack's Fork to inform the Council that Simon Little Bull owed him more than seven hundred dollars in unpaid debts, some of which Moses had purchased from other merchants around the Nadon. Two days later, Moses was back in Red Creek, and the day after that Weed Jackson and Lyn Broken Horn arrived at the Little Bull farm with Clay's eviction notice. Moses Gray wasn't a man to waste time.

Moses Gray's tribal name had been Gray Boy before the Removals of the 1830's, when Andrew Jackson forced many of the

Southern tribes out of their homelands east of the Mississippi and into the land of the Osage, which had since come to be called the Five Nations of the Civilized Tribes by the white eyes. The move had been hard on the Indians — the Choctaws, Creeks, Cherokees, Chickasaws, and Seminoles — the old and extremely young, in particular. But Gray Boy had been hardy enough to adapt. He had embraced a budding culture that had already taken on many aspects of the white culture, including the ownership of slaves.

Moses was about forty-five now, Clay figured, a portly, hard-eyed man of cunning intelligence and ruthless ambition. He already owned the largest plantation around Red Creek, plus twenty odd fieldhands to run it, and look out for his other enterprises as well. In addition to the plantation and the trading post in town, Moses also owned stock in a watermill in Poteau, and a flatboat operation that ran goods down the Red and Canadian Rivers to the Arkansas, and from there to Fort Smith.

Moses Gray was a busy man, but not so busy he couldn't keep several pretty, young, black women who kept the plantation house neat and sparkling, or so the wags claimed. He also had a wife, Sally, who lived in a two-story log home in Red Creek, and never ventured out to the plantation.

It was easy to envision what Moses Gray had in mind, Clay thought the day he watched Weed Jackson and Lyn Broken Horn ride away from Simon's old hunting shack, their bellies heavy with roasted opossum. Moses intended to turn the Choctaw Nation against Clay by destroying those ties that had bound him to them, that made him a member of the tribe. By casting doubt on the legitimacy of his freedom, Moses was slowly stripping away a heritage that Clay had come to consider his own.

It wouldn't be easy. The Choctaw, as a tribe, lacked the deep-seated prejudices of many Southern whites against interracial contact; it already had a large population of Negroes within its ranks, mostly through marriage. But Clay knew such a task wouldn't be impossible, either, especially for a man of Moses' unique talents.

The bitterness that had simmered in Clay for so many weeks finally boiled over. If he weren't Choctaw, if the last ten years were nothing more than a thin-skinned dream that a man like Moses Gray could burst with a single visit to the tribal council, then what had his life amounted to?

That was the night Clay saddled his horse

and returned to the cabin. The livestock had been taken away long before, but the buckboard was still in the barn, its yellow spokes laced with spiderwebs, its worn seat coated with dust and pigeon droppings. Clay wheeled the small wagon into the moonlight, then threw in all of the hoes, shovels, pitchforks, rakes, and axes he could find. He added the steel traps and fish nets he and Simon had used, and a fifty pound grinding stone, then hitched the pinto between the shafts and drove to the cabin. The lock on the front door gave with the single whack of an ax. Without lighting a lamp, Clay quickly ransacked the cabin of everything of value, dumping it all into the buckboard's bed. He was sweating heavily by the time he finished, his heart pounding with the zeal of action, of reclaiming a part of his past. Climbing into the seat, he drove to the dilapidated trading post of a half-breed who had built his cabin on a swampy bend of Red Creek, well off the beaten path. The man's name was Red Deer Carter, and he was used to getting up in the middle of the night to dicker over property a man might not want to try to sell in daylight.

By dawn Clay was far away from Red Deer's post, following a back country trail that took him west toward the Chickasaw

Nation, and the wild tribes beyond. Behind the pinto trailed a long-legged sorrel mule, its canvas packs crammed with provisions and an assortment of trade goods and gifts. Although he hadn't gotten nearly as much as he should have for the merchandise, Clay was satisfied. From Red Deer's stores he had stocked up on tobacco, tin arrowheads, knives, and tomahawk heads — all prime trade items on the plains. And with any luck at all, he'd be well into the Cross Timbers — that wildly tangled forest that separated the Civilized Tribes from the savage lands to the west — long before the plundered cabin was discovered.

Clay went in search of the wandering bands of the People, but never found them. After three weeks of solitary rambling, he finally came across a village of Wichitas, their thatched houses and vast gardens established in a broad, oxbow loop of the Washita. It was there he spent the summer, trading, hunting, gambling, horse racing, napping, swimming, and flirting with girls — dark-skinned women who wore skirts of cloth or buckskin but often neglected blouses during the sultry months of summer. Though not an especially promiscuous people, Clay soon learned they weren't all that much different from anyone else. As a trader from the East, he was, by Wichita standards, an opulent and honored guest. In that role, he had no trouble at all finding women who were willing to slip into the bushes with him.

Although the Wichitas raised *maize,* beans, squash, and a variety of spices, they were only partly agrarian. Living so close to the buffalo ranges, they had developed a kind of low-keyed hunter and warrior mentality that sparked in Clay half-forgotten memories of the more aggressive Kiowas.

It was a profitable summer, and an enjoyable one, but by September — with his robes and pelts baled and his packs of trade goods empty — he was ready to leave. He traded the sorrel mule and a double-barreled pistol for three small mustangs, and arrived back at the hut at the rear of Simon's farm less than two weeks later.

Weed Jackson and Lyn Broken Horn rode out to talk with him that first night. Both men, Clay noticed, looked grim and wary, and kept their hands close to their revolvers.

"Did you come to fight, or share a meal?" Clay asked with friendly caution, squatting beside the fire where he could tend his supper. Neither man smiled or dismounted.

"Clay, you tell me one thing, right up

47

front," Lyn said, putting his hand on his pistol. "Did you shoot Moses Gray in the elbow last spring?"

"Shoot Moses Gray?" Clay looked from Lyn to Weed, then back again. "You're serious?"

"As a toothache," Lyn replied.

Clay stood, letting the wooden spoon he had been stirring his rice with hang limp at his side. "No," he answered solemnly. "I didn't even know the old skinflint had been shot."

"I told you he didn't," Weed said to Lyn.

"His denying it ain't enough, Weed, and you know it. Clay, someone shot Moses Gray last spring, not forty-eight hours after you stole all that stuff out of Simon's cabin and sold it to Red Deer Carter. Damnit, man, you stirred up a hell of a stink around here."

Clay's eyes grew angry. "I lived with Simon from the time I was a kid. I helped him build most of that furniture, and I helped him collect the honey and fish he sold in Red Creek to buy the rest."

"You were his . . . property," Lyn replied coldly. "Helping didn't entitle you to anything. Moses had clear and legal title to that land and the contents of the cabin and barn. He's signed a complaint with the Council, which has issued a warrant for your arrest for attempted murder and theft. Moses also put up five hundred dollars, as a reward for your capture."

Clay's anger quickly vanished. Lyn and Weed were watching him closely, although Clay took it as a good sign that neither man had drawn his pistol.

Finally Lyn sighed. "Moses was at the plantation when it happened. The bullet came through a window and struck him in the right arm. Tore the elbow up pretty bad. He was right-handed, and now he's got to learn to do everything all over again with his left — write, eat, drive a buggy . . ."

"Wipe his ass," Weed put in. "Unless he has one of his darkies do it for him."

"That ain't funny, Weed," Lyn said. He studied Clay intently for several seconds. "He was shot with a big-bore rifle, Clay, like that bear gun of yours. I don't know. I'd like to think you didn't do it, but everyone in Red Creek remembers how you came into town drunker'n a skunk last spring, threatening to kill him. Plus you did a lot of bad talkin' on him at Jack's Fork. Nobody's forgetting that, either."

"Lyn, I didn't shoot Moses Gray, but you know as well as I do there isn't any shortage of men who'd like to. There isn't any shortage of bear guns in this part of the country, either."

"Me'n Weed have already discussed that. We went out to Moses' place the day after he was shot, but by the time we got there half the population of Red Creek had already trampled the ground looking for sign." He shook his head sadly. "You'd think a bunch of Choctaws would know better, wouldn't you?"

"Maybe that's why they went out there," Clay suggested.

"Yeah, we thought of that, too," Lyn admitted glumly. "But it's worse than that. A couple of men from Tennessee showed up here last June and went straight to Moses' place. They pulled out when they learned you'd gone West, but Moses said they'd be back. He put the word out that it's worth a ten dollar gold piece just to hear when you've returned. You know the Nation, Clay. Ten dollars will buy a lot of drink for some of these whiskey heads. Moses probably heard you were on the way as soon as you left the Cross Timbers." He shrugged. "We did."

"Damnit, Lyn, I grew up here. This is my home."

Lyn Broken Horn looked away. "If I were you," he said softly, "I'd take those robes to

Kansas, or maybe all the way to Chicago. Find yourself some free soil, Clay, because if you don't, I'm afraid Moses Gray will see you in chains, just for spite."

"Moses Gray is mad," Weed added. "Very mad. They say a little crazy, too, from the pain and the morphine. He says he will not rest until you are either hung or sent back to Texas, but everybody knows he means Tennessee, and Colonel Carry's auction barn."

Clay shook his head in disbelief. "Moses has my land," he said in exasperation. "What else does he want?"

"He wants his way," Weed replied quietly. "He is like a spoiled child who demands candy every time he goes into a store. If he does not get his peppermint stick, he throws a fit. That is what Moses Gray wants, to throw his fit, then get his way."

"If it wasn't you, it'd be something else," Lyn said. "Trouble is, right now it's you, and me and Weed will have to come out here in the morning and arrest you for stealing those things from the farm, plus trying to kill Moses Gray . . . if you're still here."

Clay felt a cautious hopefulness. "You're letting me go?"

Lyn straightened in his saddle and pulled his horse partway around. "Nobody'd better find out about this, Clay, whether you get caught or not. Me and Weed ain't never done anything like this before, and I won't do it again. Not even for you."

Clay walked over to shake Lyn's hand, then Weed's. He knew he would probably never see either man again, or any of his old friends. Moses had won, and Clay would have to hightail it out of the Nations immediately, and never look back. "Thank you for the warning," he said to Lyn. "You, too, Weed."

Lyn shook his head. "I haven't warned you of anything, Clay. I haven't even seen you." He reined his horse around and rode into the trees.

Weed Jackson held back though. "It is a shame we never got to go fishing one last time. I always enjoyed fishing with you."

"So you've said."

"Yes, many times. I even told Moses Gray, but Moses Gray is not a fisherman. He did not understand." He gathered his mount's reins, adjusting them so that they hung evenly along both sides of the horse's neck. Finally he looked up, flashing a sad smile. "You watch yourself in that north country, Clay. I have heard some bad stories about that land." With that, he pulled his horse around and spurred after his partner.

Clay watched until both lawmen were out of sight, then kicked out his fire and packed his mustangs. By sundown he was on his way north, pushing his string of ponies as hard as he could into the twilight.

FOUR

After what seemed like an eternity of riding blindly through the starless night, a thin, chalky glow began to honeycomb the clouds over Clay's left shoulder; as it grew stronger, it pushed back the darkness to reveal a soggy landscape of rolling hills, patchy with fog.

Exhausted, Clay lifted his face to the cold morning drizzle. His eyes felt like sandstone pebbles rolling around in the gritty sockets of his skull. His legs and hips ached, and there was a knot of pain between his shoulder blades that was like a crowbar gouging into his spine. Despite the rain, thirst raked maddeningly at the back of his throat.

The man named Ezra led, dragging Clay's pinto after him on a long lead rope, with one of the Indian ponies tied to the pinto's tail. Jake led the woman's mount, plus the other two pack horses. Clay glanced back at the woman. There wasn't much to see, even in the strengthening light. A bulky greatcoat, patched in places and needing it elsewhere, concealed most of her body; a floppy brimmed hat, together with her bowed head, hid her face. Clay caught a glimpse of rain-swollen shoes below the muddy hem of the greatcoat, and thin, scratched shins the color of milk chocolate.

Ezra gave the lead rope a sudden jerk, causing the pinto to snort and move ahead at a jarring trot. Clay grunted in surprise and pain, his knees tightening on the pinto's ribs. "Keep your nose up front," Ezra growled.

"She's tired," Clay said. "We all are. Why don't we rest a while?"

Ezra cocked a brow. "Boy, you have been a free man, haven't you?"

"All my life," Clay replied evenly.

Guffawing, Ezra said, "You ever hear the like, Jake?"

"Shoot, what's wrong with taking a breather?" Jake asked. "My butt's dang near rubbed down to my tailbone."

"Take a look around you," Ezra said contemptuously. "You see any place to hole up?"

Jake shook his head. "Uh uh," he replied in a woeful voice.

"Let's jog a spell," Ezra said abruptly.

"The Captain can't be too far ahead now."

They put their horses into a shuffling trot. Although the pinto had an easy gait, the shackles bit deeply into Clay's wrists with every step. He tried glancing over his shoulder a couple of times to see how the woman was faring, but it was impossible to see much under such circumstances.

Full daylight gradually flooded the rolling prairie, chasing away the last of the shadows. After an hour of steady travel, they came to a grove of trees in the middle of a shallow valley. Ezra called a halt, eyeing a thin column of smoke curling above the upper limbs.

"That them?" Jake asked.

"Now how the hell would I know that?" Ezra snapped. "We'll just sit tight a couple a minutes. If it's the Captain, he'll —" He shut up as a man stepped out of the woods and waved them in.

"Hey, that's Seth," Jake said, perking up. "Damn, Ezra, we done caught up."

"I reckon we have," Ezra agreed, tickling his mount's sides with his spurs.

Looking back, Clay was startled to see that the woman had finally raised her head. He studied her as best he could from the pinto's swaying back. She might have been his age or a little older. She had a slim face, a firm jaw, and high, smooth cheekbones beneath almond-shaped eyes. But fear had marked her badly, drawing her features taut. She kept her eyes on the woods, and refused to return Clay's look.

The man called Seth was waiting for them at the edge of the trees, a short, muscular man who, with his feet planted firmly in the rain-matted grass, looked as if he might have been carved from seasoned oak. "Where the hell have you boys been?" he demanded as they rode up. He was eyeing Clay curiously.

"The gal gave us a run for our money," Ezra replied flatly. He hooked a thumb over his shoulder. "We caught this one last night, on our way back. It's the buck the Indian in Red Creek told us about."

Seth gave Clay a dubious glance. "You sure?"

"I'm sure."

"Well, damn," Seth said. "The Captain's gonna like this. Come on, let's get 'em into the trees." He stepped out of the path to let them file past, then brought up the rear on foot.

They stopped at a simple camp pitched deep in the woods. Clay saw horses scattered among the trees, and piles of saddles and gear stacked beside a small fire. A canvas fly was stretched beneath the sprawling limbs of a massive oak about thirty feet away, with a number of dark, featureless forms huddled beneath it.

Two men stood before the fire, and Clay had no trouble picking out the Captain. He was a stocky man of medium height, with a neatly trimmed mustache and a Vandyke gone to gray. Thick silver hair was brushed back behind his ears. He wore a good hat, with sturdy, custom-made boots visible below the flowing hem of a gum poncho. Even without any obvious insignia of rank, the man's rigid demeanor and dark, boring gaze commanded attention.

His companion was skinny and long-featured, reminding Clay of a starving hound dressed in ragged clothes and taught to stand upright. He held a long-barreled squirrel rifle butted to the mud between his feet, his elbow draped over the muzzle in a way that would cost him his arm if the rifle went off accidentally. The man's lantern jaw was covered with a stiff bristle, framing a lumpy nose and thick, slack lips.

Ezra dismounted and nodded to the Captain. "Howdy, Eugene," he said.

"Good morning, Ezra," the Captain replied cordially. "I see you've picked up some additional merchandise." He eyed Clay speculatively. "A fine specimen, it appears. Have you had a chance to examine him?"

"Not close. We just snared him last night."

"And the girl?"

"Caught up with her early yesterday." He shook his head in what might have been admiration. "That gal runs like a deer."

A look of disapproval crossed the Captain's face, but all he said was, "Were you spotted by anyone?"

"Nary a soul."

"You're sure?"

"Yes, sir," Ezra replied, and the Captain looked satisfied.

"Then it was a job well-executed, and a worthwhile delay if it brings us another body. Seth, you and Hog take care of these runaways while Ezra and Jake have their breakfast — or supper, as the case may be." The Captain's gaze rested briefly on the man standing next to him. "Need I remind you of the importance of properly shackling your charges, Mr. Waller?"

The skinny man's eyes dropped quickly to the leafy forest cover in front of him. He shook his head. "No sir, Cap'n. It won't happen agin."

"If it ever does, Hog, I can assure you the consequences will be severe. Is that understood?"

Hog Waller nodded without raising his head, then started for the woman. The Captain's arm flashed from beneath the poncho, stopping Waller with the light touch of a braided leather quirt. "Not her," the Captain said softly. "I don't want you taking out any petty revenge on a helpless Negress."

Hog hesitated, then nodded and headed toward Clay. Ezra handed him the pinto's lead rope as he passed. Stopping at the gelding's shoulder, Hog finally lifted his eyes. His face blazed with fury, his lips drawn into a tight, bloodless slash. "Ya git down real easy like," he grated just loud enough for Clay to hear. " 'Fore I drag ya down."

Clay dismounted awkwardly, his hands still trapped behind his back. On the ground, Hog stepped close and hissed, "Ya try anything funny, nigger, and I'll cave yer head in like it were a melon. Savvy?" He gave Clay a shove. "Over there," he snapped, jerking his head toward the canvas fly at the base of the giant oak. He slammed the heel of his palm against Clay's spine, propelling him forward. The Captain observed Waller's roughness with a veiled glance, then resumed his quiet conversation with Ezra. Clay thought he heard Moses Gray's name mentioned as he and Hog passed, but couldn't be sure.

The fly was stretched about four feet above the ground, with a shallow peak that ran the rainwater off to either side. Within its skimpy shelter Clay counted five Negroes — three men, a boy of thirteen or fourteen, and a middle-aged woman with close-cropped hair.

Hog stopped Clay at the edge of the fly. He could feel the dark, questioning eyes of the Negroes on him, but couldn't meet their gazes. He stared into the trees until Seth arrived with the woman in the greatcoat. There was a stirring among the prisoners as she came up, then a sharp, indrawn cry from the middle-aged woman. Seth eased the younger woman down on the far side of the fly, and for the first time Clay noticed the heavy chain that connected the entire group, fastened to large iron collars locked around the neck of each prisoner.

"Jesus Christ," Clay breathed thinly. He heard Hog's cackling laughter as if from a long way off, then felt the ramming blow of the squirrel rifle between his shoulder blades. Even then, it was as if someone else's body tumbled forward, someone else's face smacked the leafy floor of the shelter with a sharp rap. Hands grabbed his shoulders and rolled him over. He saw Hog grinning broadly as he bent forward with a collar in hand. Clay, his arms still manacled behind his back, drew his knees up in an almost childlike position of defense. An older man on Clay's left touched his shoulder, murmuring. "He be a waitin' for that, son. It won't get you nothin' but a whuppin'."

Waller's eyes darted between the two men. Then he jumped back and snatched up his rifle. "Ya thinkin' of tryin' somethin', boy?" he shrilled. He remained motionless for what seemed like an eternity, his finger taut on the trigger, his thumb curled around the hammer. No one moved or spoke, and after a time Hog's lips peeled back in a sneer. "I got ya though, didn't I? Damn black bugger ain't been born yet what kin fool ol' Hog."

"You should've let him shoot you," a young man on Clay's right said.

"Mistah Hog here mighta kilt 'im, Sammy Lee," the older man admonished gently.

Sammy Lee snorted. "He'd have been better off."

Numbly, Clay realized both men thought he'd intended to strike out with his feet when he'd pulled his knees up, kicking Hog in the stomach and maybe making a break for the trees. Clay took a deep, calming breath and forced himself to sit up. Waller watched uncertainly, the dark bore of his squirrel rifle an unblinking eye six inches in front of Clay's nose. Hog licked his lips nervously, doubt clouding his eyes. "Don't be tryin' anything funny," he told Clay. "I could just as easy blow yer head off. It's yer choosin'."

"No, it ain't his choosing," Seth said curtly, crabbing forward under the fly. "Put that rifle up, before the Captain sees it."

Hog threw a glance over his shoulder. The Captain was still conversing with Ezra, his back turned to the prisoners.

Kneeling at Clay's side, Seth picked up the collar Hog had dropped. "Son, I don't know if Ezra or Jake has explained anything to you yet, but you are now the property of Captain Eugene Carry, brother to Colonel Douglas J. Carry, of Memphis, who I reckon you have heard of, even if you ain't heard of his brother." He placed the collar around Clay's neck, careful not to pinch any skin between the hinges, and deftly locked it in place. Swaying back, he said, "We're gonna return you to your rightful owners if they can be found. If not, you'll be put on auction and sold to new masters. It's over now, do you understand? Ain't nothing to be afraid of any more." He patted Clay's shoulder reassuringly. "Be for the best in the long run, for you as much as anyone. You just wait and see."

Seth scooted out from under the fly and stood up. "The Captain's rules are simple," he added. "Just don't cause any trouble and you won't break any." He nudged Waller's arm with his elbow. "Come on, Hog. Plato can fill him in on the particulars, and the Captain will talk to him later, if he wants to."

The two white men walked away, and the older man on Clay's left shifted carefully, mindful of the short length of chain between them. His unshackled hand came up to rest on Clay's shoulder like a knotted chunk of coal. "First you be in chains, son?" the old man inquired kindly.

Clay swallowed hard, trying to dislodge the lump that had formed in his throat. "Near about, I reckon."

The old man's fingers squeezed sympathetically. "Seem like the end of the world, don't it? Yes, sir, it can now. I reckon I felt that feelin' a time or two myownself. But it ain't. That what you gots to 'member. It ain't no end of the world, son. It just be more white folk trouble, and they ain't never been no shortage of that for a black man. Or woman." He held out his hand. "Folks

64

call me Plato. You got a yourself a name?"

"Clay. Clay Little Bull."

"Little Bull?" Plato's eyes sparked with sudden interest. "You one of them nigger Injuns I always heerd talkin' 'bout? That what you is, one of them Seminoles?"

Clay shook his head. "No," he said, "No, I'm not Seminole."

"But you a Injun, ain't you? Name like Little Bull, you gots to have some 'gator blood in you somewheres."

Slowly, Clay shut his eyes and took a deep, ragged breath. The man on Clay's right, Sammy Lee, said, "A name doesn't mean anything, old man. Do you have any idea who you're named after? Beside your grandfather, I mean."

"My granddaddy be 'nough," Plato replied with quiet dignity, giving Clay the impression that this exchange had occurred before.

Sammy Lee said, "You're a simpleton, old man. Unlike your namesake, your *true* namesake."

"Mebbeso I am," Plato acknowledged. "Don't know nothin' 'bout no ol' Greek thinker, but I do know this be a mighty fine shelter we got us here." He looked smugly at Clay. "Was my idea, you see? Them white folks figure it was theirs, but it warn't. That be a trick you gots to learn, son. That be how you get along with white folk. You get what you want easy 'nough, you just know how to do it."

"Like your freedom?" Sammy Lee ridiculed. "Or don't you want that?"

"No, I wants my freedom 'gin, same as ever' man and woman here. I figure now maybe I get it, too."

"We're done for, old man," Sammy Lee said. "We're prisoners of a madman, and less than four days away from slave territory. It's too late, *too damn late!*"

The hopelessness in Sammy Lee's voice was almost palpable. It was the same hopelessness Clay felt, and that lined the faces of the others. Of them all, only Plato appeared unaffected by Sammy Lee's outburst.

"Well, mebbe we is, but mebbe we isn't, either." Plato looked at Clay and smiled. "Sammy Lee be what you call an educated nigger, see? He done been to college, up there in Canada. But what Sammy Lee don't know is, ol' Plato's been to college, too."

Scowling, Sammy Lee said, "What college did you ever attend?"

The smile vanished abruptly from Plato's face; his voice turned hard as stone, and his eyes burned. "Boy, I been in chains since I was born, one kind or 'nother. That's what

66

college I been to, and that's how come we got us this here piece of canvas to sit under, and that's how come you been sleeping under blankets at night, too, which I noticed you wasn't doin' 'til I got here." His voice mellowed as he turned to Clay. "Now, Missy — that be her down there on this side of Jenny, the gal you come in with — well, Missy there took to coughin' one day something fierce. I waited till that stack of shit what calls hisself Cap'n was within hearin', then I says, 'How you doin', Miss Missy? Sure hopes you don't ketch you no ague.' I says, 'You be too young by a mite to die on us now.' Ten minutes later, the Cap'n has them white boys riggin' us up this here shelter and passin' out blankets like we was kings and queens."

"Shoot," Missy said, comforting the girl, Jenny, in her arms. "Wasn't nothing but a piece of dried up old meat got stuck in my windpipe. But you done it, Plato, right enough, and a whole passel more'n Mr. Sammy Lee did."

"Blankets won't break these chains," Sammy Lee replied bitterly. "And canvas won't buy us horses or guns, or train tickets out of here. So what else have you got, old man? Was that the extent of your college training, or are you planning to conjure up something like a knife or a pistol? Is that it? Are you going to mojo us a brace of pistols apiece?"

"I believe pistols be outta my reach jus' yet," Plato replied mildly. "Though don't you go sassin' things you don't know diddly squat 'bout. I seen things, boy, turn a man's hair white. But no, I ain't got that kind of magic. Never did. But I do mind a knife might help the cause." He looked at Clay, and his voice dropped a notch, "That is, if our new friend here wouldn't mind partin' with his'n."

FIVE

Tyler Calhoun knew there was going to be trouble as soon he saw the Indian at the door.

Ty was sitting near the side wall of the Tiger's Eye Saloon in Leavenworth, Kansas Territory, sharing a table with Virgil Nash and the Burdette brothers, Matt and Keith. He was nursing a beer and not saying much when he spotted the absurdly tall, dented crown of a stovepipe hat, hovering above the scooped batwing doors of the Tiger's Eye like some magician's chicanery. Ty blinked, not quite believing what he saw. Then a current of air momentarily parted the haze of tobacco smoke, and a feeling of dread settled in the pit of his stomach. He exchanged a glance with Matt, who had also spotted the hat. As if on cue, both men looked at Virgil.

Virgil Nash was sloped loosely in his chair, his back to the door, his legs stretched out under the table. He was a tall, lanky man with a slim face and heavily lidded blue eyes. Like the others at the table, Virgil wore his dark brown hair long, combed back over his narrow shoulders like a true plainsman; as did Ty, he sported a full mustache that drooped down on both sides of his mouth.

At five-ten, Ty wasn't quite as tall as Virgil, but he was broader through the shoulders and chest, stouter in his legs. He had deep hazel eyes that could appear almost golden in a certain light, and a strong, angular face. He was twenty-years-old, four years behind Virgil, the same age as Matt, and two years older than Keith.

Of the four, only Virgil was drinking whiskey. He had a bottle of rye on the table in front of him, with less than two inches remaining in the bottom. Virgil had been drinking slowly but steadily all afternoon, a pattern Ty recognized with foreboding. There was no humor in Virgil's approach to his bottle. While the rest of them drank to be sociable, Ty knew Virgil was only screwing himself up for trouble.

They had arrived in Leavenworth just before noon, and driven straight to Christian Lobenstein's tannery at Third and Cherokee. There, with the help of their three hired men and a couple of Lobenstein's warehousemen, they had quickly off-loaded the big Hamilton and Finn freight wagon of its cargo of hides, tallow, and meat. The second wagon, a canvas-hooped prairie schooner, had taken less time to unload, it being smaller and carrying their personal outfits, as well. With an advance from the hide dealer, Ty had quietly paid off the hired help while Matt and Keith took the empty wagons and the livestock to a corral behind Becker and Mile's Mercantile, a few blocks away. Afterward, the three young hunters converged on the Tiger's Eye, where they found Virgil already at a table, the bottle of rye freshly opened at his elbow.

Except for dried slabs of cold buffalo roast and some pickled eggs the Tiger's Eye kept at a table near the end of the bar for its customers, the four men hadn't eaten anything since breakfast. Nor had they taken time to bathe, to peel away with hot water and strong lye soap the six months of sweat, dust, dried blood, burnt powder, and the stink of green hides that impregnated their clothing and grimed their skin. For the four partners, friends since childhood, there was a death to be mourned, a passing that, because of the rigors of the trail and the threat of another attack, they hadn't been able to acknowledge until today.

71

They had made the long haul in from Salina in just under two weeks, after burying Virgil's brother, Wade, under an elm tree on the bank of the Saline River. Wade had been killed by Indians — Cheyennes, they figured — who had mutilated the body and taken the scalp. Wade had been riding alone, a couple of miles in advance of the rest of the party. They'd all heard the distant boom of Wade's rifle, fired once, but no one had been especially alarmed. It being late in the day, Ty had assumed Wade had found some fresh meat for the evening's meal. Being so close to the little frontier settlement of Salina, he hadn't even considered the possibility of Indian trouble, despite the rumors of growing unrest among the Cheyenne.

It was Ty and Virgil who first came upon Wade's naked body. Wade's torso had been quilled with more than a dozen arrows. The flesh of his thighs and arms had been slashed to the bone, his fingers and tongue hacked off and tossed aside in the tall grass, his severed testicles and penis shoved into his bloody, gaping mouth. The gruesome discovery had sickened Ty, and he'd stumbled away to heave his guts out in the grass. But Virgil had reacted differently. Since that day, he'd grown quiet and withdrawn, his jaw constantly knotted, his temper short and violent. Like an open keg of gunpowder set too close to a spitting flame, Ty knew it was only a matter of time before Virgil erupted.

The Tiger's Eye had been almost deserted when they arrived that afternoon, but as the day progressed that changed. Stevedores and deckhands came in from the levees. Soldiers and a couple of noncoms made the two mile trek down from Fort Leavenworth. As the afternoon waned, muleskinners, bull-whackers, 'smiths of numerous kinds, store-keepers, clerks, and farmers began to appear. Timber cutters lined the long mahogany bar alongside honey merchants and carpenters. Bricklayers rubbed elbows with speculators in land or livestock or hardwood. Weathered plainsmen and buckskin-clad mountaineers moved easily among pale-skinned gamblers attired in brocade vests and light frock coats.

The whores turned out shortly after the swamper made his rounds lighting the hurricane lamps along the saloon's walls. There were five of them, all obvious veterans of the trade. They strutted through the crowd like gaudy birds of prey, their sharp eyes missing nothing as they circled in on the more promising patrons.

As the evening lengthened, the air inside the saloon grew close and uncomfortable.

The steady hammering of half a hundred conversations seemed to pound at the back of Ty's head. He finished his beer and set the empty mug on the table. The Tiger's Eye was located so close to the river that earlier in the day he'd caught an occasional whiff of the Missouri's wild, damp odor, drifting in over the batwing doors. Now, staring at the dented crown of the tall stovepipe hat at the saloon's front entrance, it occurred to Ty that he hadn't smelled the dank aroma of the Missouri in at least a couple of hours. Pulling his legs under him, he said, "That's it for me. I need some fresh air."

Matt looked at Ty with relief. "Mind some company?" he asked.

"No, I sure wouldn't." He glanced at the door just as one of the batwings swung inward, away from the stovepipe hat. A short, bowlegged Indian stepped inside. Keith saw him then, and his eyes widened. All three men looked immediately at Virgil, but Virgil was staring into his glass, unaware of the tension that rippled through the saloon as the Indian paused with one hand on the door.

The Indian's name was Francis Duck, a Delaware from the newly relocated reserve to the west. Although Ty had never met him

74

personally, he knew him by reputation, and had seen him around town a few times. The word was that Francis Duck had been a troublemaker from the days when the first crude shacks of Leavenworth City had gone up, just five short years before. Of course, back then Leavenworth had still been a part of the Delaware reservation, and Francis Duck had claimed title to a good part of the land that now made up the bulk of the main business district — title he had lost when politicians in Washington decided to move the reserves farther west to make room for the white settlers pouring into the lands of the Delawares, Kaws, Kickapoos, and other small tribes.

Ty had his doubts regarding the validity of Duck's claims. He'd heard a lot of outlandish tales regarding Indians in the two years he'd been on the frontier, and had learned to discount most of them. The only thing he knew about Francis Duck with any certainty was that he had been horse-whipped twice in the empty lot behind the sheriff's office — the first time for stealing chickens, and the second time for killing the sheriff's favorite hunting dog. A lot of people said Duck was also responsible for the fire that gutted the sheriff's house six months later, but if that were true, then

Duck had made considerable progress along the white man's road by then — he'd had an airtight alibi for the night the sheriff's two-room home on the upper end of Fourth Street was torched, including some of the town's leading citizens as witnesses.

If Duck was a troublemaker, there was nothing in his manner that night to suggest it, other than his coming into a saloon in the first place. The laws concerning Indians and alcohol were explicit, if not always strictly enforced. When no one shouted for him to leave, Duck let go of the door and headed for the Negro section at the back of the room as quickly as his bowed legs could carry him. He made a comical figure in his baggy, bibless overalls and ratty calico shirt. His dark, coarse hair flowed from beneath his hat like a river of dried ink, and a heavy silver earring stretched the lobe of his left ear. Offsetting his greasy hat was a pair of beautifully beaded pucker-toed moccasins.

Silence followed Duck's passage down the bar, although Ty heard a few cutting remarks. "Watch your horses tonight, boys," and, "Watch your sheep, too. No telling what they'd whelp with that redskin around," were a couple. If Duck understood any of them, he pretended not to. He breezed into the segregated portion of the saloon like a Great Lakes frigate into berth, looking neither right nor left until he was well within the dimly lit corner partially shadowed by the stairs that led to the second floor. There he lifted his elbows to the bar and waited patiently for one of the Tiger Eye's two bartenders to saunter down and take his order.

For the first time that evening, Ty took notice of the two black men who shared the lower bar with Duck. Although both were strangers, he sensed that here was a different breed of Negro than those he had become familiar with since his arrival in the Territory. Both men wore dark, broad-brimmed hats and long wool coats. They sported small-roweled brass spurs on their boots, and had a bulkiness around their waists that suggested weapons concealed just out of sight. Neither man appeared openly hostile, yet there was a menacing aloofness about them, a honed wariness in their manner.

Ty and Matt exchanged glances, and Ty said, "I think I'll take that walk now. Who's coming with me?"

"Let's go," Matt replied.

Keith straightened and put both hands on the table. Looking at Virgil, he said, "Come on, Virg, let's take a walk, maybe grab a bite to eat."

"You go ahead," Virgil said without looking up.

"Aw, come on," Keith prodded, giving Virgil's elbow a nudge. "Let's go get something to eat before we all get so drunk we can't stand up."

Virgil gave the younger man a surly look. "Why don't you just trot along?" he answered sarcastically. "Getting falling-down drunk sounds fine to me." He looked around the crowded saloon, as if noticing it for the first time. "Where the hell'd all these peckerwoods come from?" he grumbled, brows furrowed in annoyance. Then his gaze settled on Francis Duck, and his scowl deepened. "Ain't that that little sawed off redskin runt who got his ass horse-whipped by the sheriff a couple of years ago?"

Ty watched Virgil carefully, waiting to see what he would do.

"It wasn't him, Virg," Matt said mildly. "He didn't kill Wade."

"You just shut up about Wade," Virgil said. "Besides, how the hell do you know who it was?"

"Oscar said it was Cheyennes. He'd know."

"Oscar Garrett is a drunken old whoremonger, and a simpleton, to boot," Virgil retorted. "I wouldn't trust him to tell me which way the sun travels."

Matt pushed away from the table. "The hell with this," he said, standing. "Let's get out of here."

Ty started to rise, then sank back in his chair. As much as he wanted to leave with Matt and Keith, he knew he couldn't abandon Virgil — not tonight, not after what had happened to Wade out on the buffalo range. "Let it go, Virgil," Ty urged. "Duck didn't kill your brother. You know that."

"A redskin is a redskin," Virgil answered sullenly, drawing his legs under him.

"You're wasting your breath," Matt said.

Ty gave him an annoyed glance. "You aren't helping matters. How would you feel if it had been Keith we buried out there?"

"I wouldn't be blustering around Leavenworth looking for trouble." Matt shook his head. "The hell with it," he said. "Let's go, Keith." He started for the door, and after a moment's hesitation, Keith followed.

Virgil drew the back of his sleeve across his lips. His face darkened in anger as he struggled to push his chair back, then climb to his feet. Even then, he had to hang onto the table to keep from falling.

Ty stood and let his fingers brush the

smooth black leather of his holster, as if to reassure himself that the Navy model .36 Colt still rode there, carried butt-forward on his left hip. He watched as Matt and Keith disappeared into the night. Only Keith looked back, pausing at the door as if in regret, but he didn't stay.

Virgil let go of the table, waited until he was sure of his balance, then picked up his hat and the bottle of rye and started for the bar. Grimly, Ty followed.

Francis Duck spotted the two white men while they were still some distance away. The Delaware's eyes narrowed suspiciously as he straightened from his slouched stance, moving his hands back until only the tips of his fingers rested on the edge of the smooth mahogany bar. Turning slightly to face them, Duck artfully exposed the gracefully curving butt of a single-shot muzzle-loading pistol, carried in the waistband of his trousers.

Virgil stopped a couple of feet away and reached out to carefully grab the bar with his right hand. His movements were slow and slightly exaggerated, as if the whiskey he'd consumed that afternoon hadn't fully kicked in until then. Ty slid into the bar at Virgil's side. The larger of the two black men standing with Duck leaned back to stare past the Indian's tall stovepipe, his stubbled face void of concern. "Can we help you gentlemen?" he asked in a voice that rumbled from deep within his chest.

"Yeah," Virgil said, swaying slightly. "You can keep your ugly black puss outta this."

The black man smiled amiably. "We are in the colored section," he pointed out. "There shouldn't be any trouble."

Virgil frowned. "Boy, you just keep your mouth shut and your eyes to the front. This is between me and the redskin here."

Ty glanced over his shoulder. It seemed as if everyone in the saloon was watching them, eager for some kind of diversion. Sweat popped out on Ty's forehead. He felt half sick from all of the beer he'd drunk, the cold meat and pickled eggs stirring it up all the more.

Calmly, the black man said, "We ain't causing trouble, and me and the Indian have some business to discuss."

"I do not even know you," Duck said to Virgil, confused.

Virgil's cheeks reddened. "I say you're a backstabbing sonofabitchin' redskin who doesn't have enough sense to get in out of the rain when you're about to drown in it."

For a moment no one spoke or moved, and Ty could feel the tension mounting.

Then, unexpectedly, the black man burst into laughter. Virgil jerked as if slapped. "Just what the hell do you think you're laughing at?" he raged.

"I ain't laughing at nothing," the black man said. Then, still chuckling, he added, "And that's the God's honest truth."

Virgil's hand came out to settle like a claw over Francis Duck's bony shoulder. He shoved the smaller man aside, causing Duck's stovepipe hat to tip dangerously toward the floor. Glaring at the black man, Virgil said, "Just who the hell do you think you are?"

"The name's Buford Hart," he said casually, then jerked a thumb at his partner. "This here's Ross Lake."

Virgil licked nervously at his lips. If either Hart or Lake was nervous, neither showed it. It was obvious their lack of concern worried, Virgil, though. He said, "I've never heard of either one of you."

"No, I don't expect you have," Buford agreed.

Duck had straightened his hat while Virgil and Buford spoke. Now, giving Virgil a withering look, he stepped back to the bar. Sensing that things were quickly slipping out of control, Ty put a hand on Virgil's arm. "Come on, Virg. Let's get some air."

Virgil shook off Ty's hand, but the fight seemed drained out of him. He stared silently at Hart, clearly puzzled by the black man's lack of intimidation. There was some scattered laughter from the rest of the saloon, and Virgil whirled and moved clumsily down the bar, shoving a couple of white men out of his path. "Get outta my way," he snarled. "It smells back there."

A white man, a muleskinner with a thick black beard and a coiled bullwhip tied to his belt, snorted derisively. "I'd say he's right," the muleskinner stated loudly, "but it ain't them colored boys or the redskin that's doin' the stinkin'."

Virgil came to an abrupt stop, but Ty grabbed him and ushered him past the glaring 'skinner. "Come on, Virg," he said. "Let's get out of here."

"I ain't afraid of that sonofabitch," Virgil muttered thickly. "I ain't afraid of any of 'em."

"Hell, I know that, but you're in no condition to fight anyone right now."

"I could take him," Virgil asserted loudly. "Drunk or sober, by God, I could take 'em all." He tried to pull away, but Ty kept him walking, and trying to free himself of Ty's grip and keep his feet straight at the same time was more than Virgil could handle in his present condition.

Several men laughed openly as Ty guided Virgil toward the door. More than a few stared after them in angry disgust. Since Kansas had been opened to white settlement back in '54, there had been a lot of ambivalent feelings toward Indians. And the sentiment toward Negroes, and the tangled issue of slavery, was as volatile as old, sweating gunpowder. Ty had little doubt that a lot of men in the Tiger's Eye that night would have liked to have seen Francis Duck and his two black companions stomped into the sticky sawdust; he had even less doubt that, had Virgil started a fight, he would have soon had all the help he needed to finish it. It struck Ty suddenly that Buford Hart had taken a big chance laughing at Virgil the way he had. Hart was either one of the bravest men Ty had ever met, or one of the stupidest.

Outside, Ty guided Virgil to the littered alley between the Tiger's Eye and a dry goods store. A misty rain was falling, and the ground where Virgil sank to his knees was slick with mud. Virgil leaned weakly against the cold brick wall of the dry goods store and gulped air. His face looked pale and panicky in the dim light. Then he leaned forward and vomited. Ty found an empty crate upwind of Virgil's mess and sat down. His own stomach was churning dangerously, and he felt lightheaded and chilled; the sweat that had tracked his forehead inside quickly vanished in the cool breeze flowing through the alley.

It was several minutes before Virgil quit heaving and put his back to the wall. He lifted his face to the fine drizzle and took a couple of deep breaths. "I could've whipped 'em," he said finally. "Damnit, Ty, you shouldn't have pulled me away like that. You made me look like a fool."

"You goddamn idiot," Ty said wearily. He stood up. "I'm going to find Matt and Keith and get something to eat. Do you want to come along, or not?"

"In a little while. I don't feel very good right now."

Ty gave him a suspicious look. "You aren't thinking of going back, are you?"

"Naw, I ain't going back. Go on, damnit. I think I'm gonna puke again."

Ty shook his head. "Yeah, likely you are," he agreed, then started for the alley's mouth. Although he still felt woozy, the cool mist on his face was soothing, and he realized he was ravenous. Spotting an eatery across the street, he made his way toward it.

As he negotiated the broad, muddy street,

it occurred to him that he was tired of the person he had become. Wade's death had changed something for him. Maybe it had changed everything. Either way, he knew he couldn't go on the way he had, always looking out for others, and generally at the expense of himself, one way or another.

He'd come to Kansas seeking adventure and a fortune, and although he'd found the former in abundance and not much of the latter, he'd made a legitimate start on it by hunting buffalo for market. And it could be done. A man determined enough — willing to set aside his fears and take the plunge feet first — could make a good living as a hunter and trader, and maybe a good name for himself in the process.

Ty stopped in the middle of the street, his excitement growing. The others had talked of returning to Ohio all the way in, but that didn't mean he had to, did it?

Did it?

Maybe, he considered, it was time he made up his mind about what he wanted to do. Maybe it was time he got serious about the economics of a hunter's life, and shoved the adventure part of it into the background for a while. Maybe it was time he found his own way, rather than letting the whims of Virgil and Matt and Keith bounce him around like a cork bobber in a Lake Erie surf.

Maybe, by God, it was time for Tyler Calhoun to let the wolf howl.

Six

It was coming onto dawn when Captain Eugene Carry brought his party to a halt. As the haggard coffle limped to a stop, Clay pulled the collar of his mackinaw closer around his neck. A stiff wind was blowing out of the west, buffeting the huddled prisoners. But with daylight approaching, Clay figured the Captain would soon lead them into hiding. There would be food then, and rest, and if the Captain deemed it safe enough, a fire to leach some of the chill from their bone-weary bodies.

Clay stood with his hands shoved deep in the pockets of his coat. He was only vaguely aware of the Captain and Seth speaking in hushed tones. Never in his life had he felt more tired, more cold, or miserable. Yet as exhausted as he was, he knew the others had to be suffering much worse. This was only his third day in bondage; some of them had been marching in chains for more than a week, trudging steadily southward toward slave territory.

Although the Captain had expropriated Clay's pinto and the three pack horses with their loads of furs and robes, he refused to let any of the prisoners ride. Not even old Plato, whose swollen knees popped and creaked with every step, was allowed near the horses. Chained one behind the other, the seven blacks could only stumble blindly through the long, cold nights, the wind a lash that never let up.

Clay knew their brief respite now was only to await Ezra's return. The Captain had sent the bearded scout ahead more than an hour ago to find a place where they could hole up for the day. Even as they waited, Clay could hear the rapid drumming of an approaching horse; against the paling sky to the east, he could just make out the shadowy form of a rider galloping across the featureless prairie.

"Mistah Ezra who that be," Plato announced authoritatively. "Shore 'nough he done found us a place to get outta this ol' wind."

Minutes later, Ezra pulled his mount to a stop in front of the Captain's horse. "About an hour straight ahead, Eugene," he said. "There's a fair-size grove of trees, and nothing close by that I could see."

"Then we shall make for that," the Captain replied. "I want to be off this prairie before full light. We're too close to the end of our journey to risk detection now."

"We'd best hump it, then," Ezra returned. "It's six, maybe seven miles to the place I've got in mind, and all open country in between."

"Take us there, Ezra," the Captain ordered. Twisting in his saddle to face the prisoners, he added, "We must hurry now. Any one of you attempting to slow down the procession will be dealt with in a most severe manner." He lifted an arm, as if he rode at the head of a troop of Dragoons rather than a ragtag bunch of half-frozen captives, then brought it forward and down. "Ho," he called, and Clay felt the tug of his collar as the prisoners moved out.

Clay was second in line on the long, heavy chain that connected the seven blacks. Plato led, and the young, hotheaded Sammy Lee walked behind Clay. Although Clay had been with the captives for some days now, he still knew very little about them. Sammy Lee was a Canadian by birth, a tall, handsome man in his late twenties who had come to Kansas to see for himself the injustices facing the Negro in the United

90

States and its territories. Behind Sammy Lee came James and Missy Parker, and their fourteen-year-old son, Nate. The Parkers had been homesteading up on the Soldier River when the Captain's men raided their sod home the week before. James and Missy had been born into slavery in Kentucky, but granted their freedom when their old master died. They'd lived in Ohio for a spell, where Nate was born, and had only recently migrated to Kansas Territory.

The girl whom Ezra and Jake had brought back with Clay was Jenny. No one save perhaps Missy Parker knew her last name, or much else about her. Plato informed Clay that Ezra had been on a scout when he'd come upon her pushing a wheelbarrow along the military road to Fort Riley. She had been heading west alone, he said, and as far as anyone knew she might have intended to walk all the way to California with her wooden-wheeled contraption loaded with some personal possessions and camping gear. Ezra followed her far enough to be reasonably certain she didn't live nearby or belong to any larger party. Then he rode out of a gully just as she was struggling through it and dropped a lasso over her shoulders. He'd dumped the wheelbarrow farther down the gully where it wouldn't be found, and brought the girl back to be fitted for a collar.

Jenny's escape and subsequent recapture by Ezra and Jake had been the result of some of Hog Waller's foolishness, according to Jake Jacobs, who related the story to Clay while he was gathering firewood under the younger man's charge.

"Ol' Hog was looking for some lovin', and tried to slip Jenny off her chain while the rest of us was sleepin'," Jake said, clearly troubled by the story. "But little Jenny, slip of a girl that she is, was too much woman for ol' Hog. She planted a toe in Hog's balls, then sloped. She must've been foggin' it, too, because it took me'n Ezra all day to catch up. Not that I would've minded if she'd got away."

Clay paused in his work to give Jake a calculating look. "That's odd sentiment for a slaver," he observed.

Jake stiffened. "Don't you go callin' me that." He paused, then blushed. "You just mind your chores there. Get along with 'em now."

"I was just wondering how you came to be riding with this bunch," Clay said, stooping for another piece of wood. He was hoping to lure Jake into a conversation so that he might learn more about Carry and what lay ahead, but Jake had turned reticent after that, and refused to be drawn out.

If the incident between Hog and Jenny bothered Jake, it was even more apparent that it had affected the girl deeply. Jenny remained withdrawn and jumpy. She never looked up when any of the whites were nearby, and remained distant even with the black men, although from time to time she revealed a spark of fondness for the boy, Nate.

It was a hard hour's trek to the grove of trees Ezra had picked out for them. The Captain's face turned grim as the sun started its slow climb into an overcast sky, but brightened noticeably when they came in sight of the woods. "I remember this place," he remarked to the group at large. "We camped here two summers ago, Ezra, on our way to Nebraska. Is there still a spring near its center?"

"There is," Ezra replied. "And a little glade below it where we can graze the horses in seclusion. The Neosho River's about two miles east, that line of trees yonder."

"Yes, I see it." Carry nodded in satisfaction. "Excellent! Excellent! Lead on then."

Ezra guided them into the woods, calling a halt at the edge of a grassy clearing. A spring seeped out of the ground nearby, and Clay sank to his ankles in the soft loam. At Plato's command, the seven blacks hiked to the far side of the clearing, and flopped in exhaustion in the tall, wet grass, while the Captain issued instructions to the whites regarding the setup of the day's camp.

Using his hat as a pillow, Clay lay back and shut his eyes. Plato huddled down beside him, speaking softly.

"You been wonderin', ain't cha?" Plato asked. "You been thinkin' 'bout that little ol' throat knife you got 'round your neck, and wonderin' if ol' Plato forgot it. But he ain't. No sir, he ain't forgot one bit."

Keeping his gaze on the dingy, slow-moving clouds, Clay said, "I'm not going to let them take me into the Nations, dad. Not without a fight." Clay's voice turned hoarse as he went on. "I'm not going back to hang because of Moses Gray, and I'm sure as hell not going to pick cotton for some lily-white, soft-palmed sonofa—"

Plato's hand came to rest lightly on Clay's chest, silencing him. "Shoot, son, I knows that. I reckon we all knows that. But you got to listen to ol' Plato now. You got to hear 'im real good, 'cause we is only gonna get us this one chance.

"The Cap'n is gonna send a couple of

these white boys out pretty soon to make sure they ain't no farms or settlements sprung up since he was last here. That's gonna leave only a handful in camp, and it's your mornin' to chop wood. *Today be the day, Clay Little Bull.*" Plato's hand pressed heavily against Clay's chest. "Son, we ain't never talked 'bout this, but I got to know. You ever kill a man afore?"

Clay paused, then shook his head. "No."

"Think you can, you gets the chance?"

Clay looked at Plato, and the old man read the answer in his eyes. "What's your plan?" Clay asked.

"Ain't got me no plan, young'un, 'ceptin' be ready when the time comes. We ain't gonna get us no sure-shot 'tunity here. That we is gonna have to make ourselves."

Clay nodded. Sammy Lee had leaned close to eavesdrop. "Today?" he asked.

"You just be ready, if so," Plato replied huskily. "You just make sure all that hard talk you been dishin' out ain't just talk."

"You just give me an opening," Sammy Lee vowed.

The Captain eventually chose Jake and Hog to reconnoiter the surrounding countryside. "There weren't any farms or settlements nearby when I was last here," he told them. "But a lot can happen in two years.

Jake, check out the Neosho. If any farmers have moved into the area, that's where they've settled. Hog, scout to the south of us, at least five miles."

"Sure," Jake replied. He and Hog mounted their horses and quickly rode out of sight.

"Seth," the Captain continued. "You will man the first watch. If memory serves me correctly, there's an oak tree near the lower side of this grove that should be easy to climb. Get up as high as you can. I'll send someone to relieve you at noon."

Nodding, Seth grabbed his carbine and hurried off. Only the Captain and Ezra remained now. The two men approached the prisoners, conferring quietly. They stopped in front of Clay, and Ezra reached down to pull his hat off. "Look at them eyes," Ezra said. "Can't be too many colored boys running around with green'uns like that."

Clay watched both men expectantly, wondering why the Captain had picked today, of all days, to finally approach him.

"You say he admitted it, as well?" the Captain asked.

"Uh huh, as much as. Said he was Choctaw, anyway."

Captain Carry chuckled. "Well, a name

96

hardly matters at this point. He's black, and he's ours." To Clay, he added, "I'm sure the others have filled you in on what to expect. Most of them have been in bondage at some point in their lives, before running away."

"Like I done tolt you, Cap'n, sir," Plato said. "My master give me my freedom. Your man, Ezra here, he seed the papers Marse George give me to make me free."

"I didn't see nothing, old man," Ezra growled, giving Plato a halfhearted kick with the side of his boot.

"And I was born a free man," Sammy Lee said hotly, straining against his collar. "In Canada."

"You should have stayed there," the Captain said mildly, then turned back to Clay. "According to Moses Gray, you were born a slave, is that correct?"

"I was born a Choctaw," Clay answered.

The Captain's lips curved into a sneer. "Then perhaps you'd be interested in seeing a broadsheet I have with your description on it." He pulled a sheet of paper from a coat pocket and unfolded it. "Do you read?"

Staring numbly at the coarsely woven flier, Clay slowly nodded. Without warning, Ezra stepped forward and slammed his fist into Clay's face. Clay flew backward with a startled cry, yanking Plato, Sammy Lee, and the boy, Nate, with him on the chain. The next thing he knew he was lying on his back, staring up at the gray clouds. He felt Plato's hands on his shoulder, pulling him upright. When he was sitting again, Plato leaned close and hissed, "You don't read! Damnit, Clay, you *don't* read!"

The Captain's face was splotched with color, his fists clenched. "I will not tolerate a liar, boy!" he thundered. "And so help me God, I'll peel the flesh from your cowardly back with a whip if you ever do it again!"

Clay cupped the side of his face with his hand. His ears rang and his eyes teared. A thin stream of blood trickled down his chin from where he'd bitten the inside of his mouth. Plato's voice was still at his ear, the words pushing urgently through a thick mire of pain. "Niggers don't read, son. You got to 'member that. Niggers don't read."

"I . . . read . . ." Clay grated hollowly. *"God-damnit, I read —"*

Plato's fingers dug into Clay's shoulder like the dull tines of an antler. "No, son, not no more you don't. Please, listen to ol' Plato."

Clay curled forward, drawing his knees up to his chest. Hidden, he let his right hand creep inside his coat, the fingers spidering

98

across his chest without conscious thought until they'd slipped inside his leather shirt to caress the buckskin sheath that held his throat knife. He was aware of Carry moving away, and of Ezra stepping into his place. He saw Ezra's muddy boots, his trousers wet to the knee from rainwater that had sluiced off the hem of his poncho. Clay wanted to lunge upward and slide his hands under Ezra's shaggy beard until he could press his thumbs into the slaver's windpipe and choke the life from him.

But he couldn't. Not with the iron collar locked around his neck, or the anchors that were Plato and Sammy Lee and the others, who would never be able to react fast enough. Clay pulled his hand away from the knife, let it drop to his lap.

"Do you want to read it?" Ezra asked coldly.

His jaws clenched in rage and humiliation, Clay slowly shook his head. "Can't . . . can't . . . read."

Laughing softly, Ezra stepped away. Captain Carry took his place, his voice calm now, almost light. "That's better," he said, as if truly pleased by Clay's progress, as a man might with a dog that had finally grasped the concept of *heel*. "Now then," the Captain went on in a brisk, businesslike manner, "what this broadsheet offers is a reward for your return to the Choctaw Indian Nation. It was issued by the Choctaw Council, and recognizes the Negro known as Clay Little Bull to be the property of one Moses Gray, who foreclosed on the Little Bull farm last spring, all implements, household furnishings and livestock — that's you, by the way — included. It contains a physical description that's quite accurate." He lowered the broadsheet. "But you'll be happy to know that's of no consequence anymore. You won't be returning to Red Creek."

Clay looked up, meeting Carry's eyes questioningly.

"No. Moses Gray promised you to us. We were to purchase you, of course, but that was before you ran away to Kansas. You're ours now." Carry folded the broadsheet and returned it to his pocket. "We're going to free you of your bonds for a while. You'll care for the horses first, then collect firewood and tidy up the camp. Ezra will watch you. If you do your chores correctly, you'll be rewarded with a piece of meat in your boiled corn tonight. If not, you'll get nothing. That's simple, isn't it?"

Clay nodded.

Smiling broadly, Carry stepped back to

allow Ezra room. The bearded scout bent forward, slipping a key into the lock on Clay's collar. Clay felt the tumblers snap open as the key turned, felt the collar sag, then fall apart. Grabbing Clay by the lapels of his mackinaw, Ezra hauled him to his feet. As the two men came nose to nose, Ezra's expression changed. A look of surprise crossed his face, and his eyes widened. He grunted and sucked in his gut, then grunted again. As if from a long way off, Clay heard the Captain ask what was wrong. Then Ezra was falling, the throat knife lodged firmly in his ribs. Clay snatched Ezra's pistol from its holster as the body fell away. Turning it on Carry, he thumbed back the hammer and pulled the trigger. The Captain stumbled backward as if trying to escape the gunsmoke that mushroomed from the pistol's muzzle. Clay fired again and watched the Captain fall, sprawling on his back in the rain-soaked grass. His hat bounced off his head, and his dark, stern eyes softened in death.

A stunned silence gripped the huddled prisoners. Clay stared down in disbelief. Ezra was curled in a fetal position at his feet. Blood stained the staghorn grip of the throat knife, dripping into the grass below. Clay held Ezra's English-made Kerr revolver in his left hand, powder smoke dribbling from the muzzle. The pistol felt strangely heavy, awkward and unnatural. He kept staring at it, trying to piece together in his mind the last few seconds — what had happened, and how.

Then he turned away as if in a daze, the pistol sagging. He was aware of Plato and Sammy Lee scrambling for the key still clutched in Ezra's hand, of Missy and Jenny standing together wide-eyed. He thought he should go to them, reassure them that everything was all right, but something was nagging at the back of his mind.

Seth!

Clay whirled, shifting the side-hammer revolver smoothly to his right hand, where it would be easier to cock, and thumbed back the hammer. Seth stood at the far side of the clearing, shouldering his carbine. "Don't!" Clay called sharply.

Seth pulled the carbine's hammer back to full cock, but Clay fired before he could squeeze the trigger. The revolver bucked in Clay's hand, but the distance was too great for decent accuracy, and the .45 bullet smacked into the trees to Seth's left.

Seth's aim wasn't any better. Fear lay stark as a naked corpse across the white man's face; Clay could see his hands shaking even from here. Seth's shot went high, whistling past at least a foot above Clay's head. Throwing the single-shot carbine away, Seth clawed for his pistol. Clay's heart was pounding loudly as he dropped to one knee, gripping the unfamiliar revolver tightly in both hands. Forcing himself to remain calm, he took careful aim and squeezed off his shot. On the far side of the clearing Seth cried out as the bullet slammed into his thigh. He spun and almost fell.

Almost.

Seth fired again, his bullet ripping through the thick grass at Clay's knee. Clay thumbed back the hammer and pulled the trigger, but this time there was no buck and thunder, no cloud of gray-white smoke. The Kerr's firing pin dropped with a sterile snap, the cylinder empty.

A look of surprise crossed Seth's face. With his still-loaded revolver thrust before him, he hobbled across the clearing. When he was about a dozen paces away, he stopped and brought his revolver in line with Clay's forehead. For a moment, neither man moved. Then a pistol roared, and Seth jerked and staggered. His face went slack, and the revolver slipped from his fingers into the grass. A moment later, Seth fell on top of it.

"Sweet Jesus," Clay breathed, glancing to where Plato stood with one of the Captain's engraved, ivory-handled Colt Navies trembling in his gnarled fists. The old man's eyes were wide, his expression one of sickness and dread. He looked at Clay and his jaw moved, forcing the words from his throat. "I . . . I ain't never killed a man afore, either," he said in a wavering voice. "Ain't . . . ain't never much wanted to . . . not even after all this."

Clay nodded. He understood. He felt sick himself, sick and wrung out.

"What are you talking about?" Sammy Lee asked incredulously. He yanked the revolver from Plato's hand and ran over to where Seth lay on his back. Pointing the pistol at the white man's body, he quickly emptied the remaining rounds into the corpse. Looking up, he shouted, "Do you think he would have hesitated to do the same to either of you? Do you think for one minute that any of these animals would have even considered the moral dilemma of killing a Negro? What's wrong with you?" He looked around the clearing, but no one answered him.

"Sammy," Plato said finally. "Put the pistol down, son."

Sammy Lee's voice softened. "No. Don't

you see? That's what's wrong with the Negro race. We've put the gun down too many times."

"Sammy," Plato said gently. "It ain't gonna work that way, son. It just ain't. Not now, not ever. It'll only makes things worse for others."

"Worse?" Sammy Lee shook his head in disbelief. "What can be worse than this?" There were tears in his eyes as he swept his hand over the clearing. He lifted the ivory-handled Colt and shook it at Plato. "We were dead, old man. *This* gave us life! This is what broke the chains of slavery from our necks and set us free! Not words, not reason! *This!*"

Plato looked helplessly at Clay. "You tell him," he said huskily. "You tell him what he sayin' be wrong. He thinks I'm an old man what don't know nothin', but you know I'm right. You tell Sammy Lee what happens to a black man what take up the gun."

But Clay refused. "We've got to get out of here," he said shakily. "There's two left, Jake and Hog, and they probably heard our shots. They won't come busting in here like this one." He nodded toward Seth. "Chances are they'll go for help." He looked at Plato, then James and Missy and Nate. "There's going to be a heap of law after us pretty soon. We've got to clear out of here while we can."

Clay's words seemed to break the spell that had immobilized them. In a panic, they rushed toward the horses. Clay went to the pinto and stroked the rangy gelding's neck to calm him, then moved back to the first packhorse. Ezra had pulled the charge from his rifle before shoving it inside the oilcloth cover of the mustang's pack. Working quickly, Clay loosened a corner of the canvas and dug out his shooting bag and powder horn, slipping them over his shoulder. Then he yanked the long, heavy-barreled rifle free and let it slide down through his fingers, stripping off the elkhide cover and tossing it over his shoulder. It didn't take long to run a dry patch down the bore, then measure out a full charge of double-F gunpowder and dump it down the barrel. Plucking a patch greased with bear's oil and a knuckle-sized .53 caliber round ball from his shooting bag, he thumbed the patch-cradled ball into the muzzle and punched it home with his ramrod. After capping the nipple, Clay took a deep breath. He felt better now, with the rifle loaded and in his hands.

Plato came over as Clay was sliding the rifle through a leather loop fastened to his saddlehorn. He had picked up Ezra's Kerr revolver from where Clay had dropped it, and stripped the gunbelt from the dead man's body. "Here," Plato said, thrusting the rig toward Clay. "Best you take this now."

"I ain't much on pistols, dad." He nodded to the rifle. "That's more my style."

"I reckon things has changed," the old man countered gently. "It might be time you started carryin' a pistol."

Clay was silent a moment, then grudgingly accepted the gunbelt. "Maybe you're right," he said, buckling it around his waist. In addition to the slim, flapless California holster, the belt held a pouch carrying paper cartridges, a brass capper and tin of extra caps, a double-cavity bullet mold, and a container of grease. Clay fingered a cartridge from the pouch, studied the revolver for a moment, then slowly reloaded all five chambers; when he finished, he lowered the hammer between two of the loaded chambers, where it would ride somewhat precariously, but without sitting on a live round.

The pistol sat high on Clay's strong side, back near his kidneys. On his left hip was a knife sheath of tooled, russet-colored leather. He pulled the blade from its scabbard. It was a coffin-handled bowie with a polished, eight-inch blade and bone grips, a much better weapon than the stone-worn Green River he'd carried before. He slid the blade back into its sheath. "Best find yourself a horse, dad. We've got to hightail it out of here right now."

While Clay checked the packs on his mustangs and Plato and the others readied their horses, Sammy Lee rifled the pockets of the dead men. He came over as Clay finished snugging down his last diamond hitch, carrying Clay's throat knife and a wad of greenbacks in an outstretched hand. "Here, no sense letting good money rot. Take some."

Clay looked at the script Sammy Lee offered, then gingerly plucked the knife from his hand without touching the cash.

"Don't you want the money?" Sammy Lee asked angrily.

"I reckon not," Clay answered. "You keep it. Or give it to the others."

Sammy Lee's face was tight with frustration. "They didn't want it either. Said it was blood money."

"Maybe they're right." Clay squatted and wiped the gore off the throat knife with wet grass, then dried it and returned it to its sheath under his shirt.

"No, they aren't," Sammy Lee said.

"They're just ignorant, letting superstition rule them. For some reason I'd thought you'd be more intelligent than that."

"I guess you were wrong," Clay replied blandly.

Sammy Lee's fingers closed over the greenbacks, and he shoved them into his pocket. "Suit yourself."

Plato, James, and Missy came over, their faces worried. "Has either of you seed little Jenny?" Plato asked.

Clay looked around the clearing. Nate was holding the horses nearby. Ezra, the Captain, and Seth were where they had fallen. But Jenny was nowhere in sight, and thinking back, Clay couldn't remember seeing her at all after Plato had removed the collars from their necks.

"That girl done lit out for the north," Missy said with conviction. "She be on her way to freedom, while the rest o' us lollygag 'round here waitin' for Jake and that Hog to gets back."

"Perhaps she's hiding," Sammy Lee suggested.

"We all came together," Plato said, clearly frightened for the girl. "We got to all go back together, too."

"Whoa, dad," Clay said. "I'm heading —"

"We *gots* to stick together," Plato interrupted sharply. He leaned close, his eyes pleading. "Don't you see, son, that it be the onliest way for us now?"

Clay shook his head. "I'm heading north, either to Westport or Leavenworth. I can't —"

"We're *all* headin' north," Plato exclaimed. "But we got to go together. We got to *stick* together, like we was glued. Mayhaps someday it'll not be that way, but right now it is, and it's the onliest chance colored folk like us has got anymore."

Sammy Lee snorted. "If you think time's going to change anything, you're a bigger fool than I took you for." He looked at the others. "He's right about staying together, though. We have to unite, but we have to do it from a position of strength. Otherwise, we're all doomed."

Missy shook her head impatiently. "You all sit here and talk 'bout it all you want. Me 'n James 'n Nate, we's goin'."

"What 'bout Jenny?" Plato reminded her.

"I done tolt you, that girl is makin' tracks, same as we should be doin'."

"We got to search these woods first," Plato said, eyeing the wall of trees that surrounded the clearing as if it might hide something more than a hungry snippet of a girl. "She might be hidin'. We can't 'bandon her."

"Well, me 'n James 'n Nate, we's goin'," Missy repeated. "We see Jenny, we'll tell her you fools is still back here lookin' for her. I wouldn't count on her comin' back to fetch you, though. That gal has done learned how to take ker of herself."

"Damnit," Clay said in exasperation. He swung astride the pinto's back. "Come on," he said to Plato. "I'll make a pass through the trees on my way out, but if I don't find her, I won't wait."

Although Plato looked as if he wanted to argue, Clay didn't give him a chance. He reined into the trees, the packhorses following the pinto out of habit.

Clay kept his rifle across his saddlebows, watching for Jake and Hog as much as for the girl. He kept remembering how easily he'd stumbled into the trap set for him by Ezra and Jake. Although he swore he'd never let it happen again, he was all too aware of his vulnerability. Even now, with Ezra's revolver around his waist and the rifle held before him, he knew in his gut that it could happen all over again if he wasn't careful.

Clay heard Plato and James and Sammy Lee calling Jenny's name, assuring her it was all right, and that she could come out of hiding. But as the pinto broke free of the trees and the empty prairie opened before him, he became convinced Missy was right. Jenny had fled as soon as the collar had been released from her neck, and there was no telling in which direction she might have gone. Clay studied the broad, rolling expanse of prairie before him longingly. Wet grass glistened in the washed-out light of the new day, and dark clouds mantled the landscape, threatening more rain. That was good. A heavy downpour would help mask their escape, washing away the tracks of their flight.

There was movement to Clay's right. James and Missy appeared, riding double on Seth's mount. Behind them came Nate, riding one of the Captain's packhorses bareback. They stopped at the edge of the trees as Clay had, looking out across the empty, rolling hills. James and Missy looked at Clay. No one spoke or made any gesture, but it was as if some silent communication passed between them. As one, they drove their heels against their mounts' ribs. The horses bolted forward in surprise. With a startled, "Hey!" Nate pounded after his parents.

They rode north at a run, but also at a

slight dogleg that took them away from each other. Clay angled west, away from the more populated country along the Missouri and Kansas border, while James and Missy and Nate canted off to the right. The wind picked up as Clay gave the pinto its head, and the first slashing drops of rain began to fall. Narrowing his eyes against it, he raced into the storm.

SEVEN

Tyler Calhoun awoke the next morning to a major storm kicking around in the pit of his stomach and the yawning muzzle of a big bore rifle looking ready to swallow the tip of his nose. Although his stomach was a matter of some concern, it was the rifle that caught his attention. Ty's gaze traveled up the long, octagon barrel to rest on the face of the Leavenworth City Sheriff, Bob Ripley. Ripley stood framed by the gray sky with the grim look of a man who was about to do something he didn't really relish, but with a no-nonsense glint in his eyes that affirmed his determination not to back away from it. He wore a derby hat against the pattering rain and a heavy wool coat with a fur collar as defense from the icy wind blowing in off the prairie. When he was sure Ty was awake, he stepped back and gave the rifle's muzzle a couple of quick, upward jerks.

"On your feet, Calhoun," the sheriff said sternly. "Come on now, wake up!"

Ty rubbed his eyes as he tried to pull his scattered thoughts together. He only vaguely recalled coming back to the stable behind Becker and Miles store last night, after a heavy meal at the Mandan Cafe. With all the beer he'd drunk at the Tiger's Eye and the meal afterward, he'd felt as wrung out as a damp rag, and hadn't attempted to find Matt and Keith, or check on Virgil. At the stable, he'd rolled his bedroll out in a pile of clean straw, undressed, then crawled into his blankets.

"Goddamnit, Calhoun, I'm a busy man. Get up."

Ty pushed his blankets back and carefully sat up. His head pounded dully, and his stomach lurched with the force of a Lake Erie breaker. He stifled a belch, then made a face at the sour taste it left on his tongue.

"A man who can't handle a hangover's got no business drinking, is my opinion," the sheriff stated. He took his finger away from the trigger long enough to peel back the lapel of his coat, revealing a nickel-plated badge pinned to his vest. "Name's Bob Ripley, in case you don't know. I'm the constable here in Leavenworth."

"I know who you are," Ty replied in a

scratchy voice. He climbed to his feet, ignoring the cut of the wind through his long-handles. But when he bent to pick up his trousers, the contents of his stomach shifted dangerously. Stifling a groan, he sank back to his pile of straw. "Constable, maybe you'd better go ahead and shoot me, because I don't think I can make it right now, and I know you don't like to wait."

Ripley swore and lowered his rifle. "Come on, Calhoun. I ain't gonna dress you, for Christ's sake."

Ty waited until the pounding in his head had quieted to a distant roar, then cautiously started to pull on his clothes. He felt a little better by the time he finished, but knew he'd need several more hours sleep and a light breakfast before he felt human again. He got to his feet and pulled on his hat and fringed buckskin jacket. Ripley eased back a couple of paces, lifting his rifle as a precaution. Outside, Ty saw Matt and Keith standing next to the corral gate. A deputy stood with them, holding a scatter-gun.

Wiping his gummy lips with the sleeve of his jacket, Ty said, "What's this about, Sheriff?"

"Suppose you tell me," Ripley replied slyly.

"I don't have any idea."

Ripley grunted, then motioned toward the gate with his rifle. "Let's take a little walk down to the jail. Maybe you'll figure it out by the time we get there."

Ripley's expression was serious as the two men left the stable. Ty exchanged a puzzled glance with Matt and Keith, but Ripley quickly smothered any attempt at conversation. "Keep your mouths shut until I tell you to open them," he ordered. Pointing toward the center of town with his chin, he added, "Come on. You know the way."

Ty tugged his hat down firmly against the gusty wind as the little party made its way up the street. The sun had yet to make its appearance, but its pearly light pervaded the town. Despite the early hour, there were quite a few people already up and about — merchants getting ready for another day, clerks and laborers hurrying to their jobs. Several stopped to watch the sheriff file past with his hungover company, calling out questions that Ripley stoically ignored.

The Leavenworth City Jail was a two-storied red brick structure with iron bars set into cement-framed windows. Ripley led them up the steps to the front door and inside as if escorting them to a gallows. Shutting the door, Ripley turned to a set of stairs and hollered, "Moss! Get down here. I've got some customers for you."

The thump of boots trodding bare wooden planks preceded the appearance of a skinny, stoop-shouldered man at the top of the stairs.

"Separate cells," Ripley instructed the jailer. "I don't want them talking until I've had a chance to question them individually."

"Wait a minute," Matt protested. "You're locking us up? You can't do that."

Ripley lifted his rifle, and the deputy his shotgun. The old jailer, Moss, chuckled smugly.

"You and your brother get on up there," Ripley told Matt. "Calhoun, you stay with me. I'll talk to you first."

"Come on," Moss ordered. Soberly, Matt and Keith followed the jailer, the deputy with his scattergun bringing up the rear.

"This way," Ripley said brusquely. He walked through a door at the rear of the big front room and led Ty down a dark hallway to a small porch at the rear of the jail. The porch overlooked the Missouri, at the bottom of a long, grassy slope. A number of steamboats were tied up at the levee downstream, with black smoke pouring from the stacks of a small packet as it prepared to get

118

under way. Ty breathed deeply of the damp, chilly air. He felt better after his walk from the stable, but was still shaky.

"Figured we'd talk out here," Ripley said with feigned amiability. "You still look a little peaked. Maybe some more fresh air will help."

"I'm obliged for your concern," Ty replied dryly.

Ripley smiled and pulled a cigar from an inside breast pocket. "If you talk now, without my having to pry it out of you, it'll go easier," he promised, striking a stubby lucifer against the brick wall of the jail and lighting his cigar. He carried the rifle in the crook of his left arm now, the barrel sloped innocently toward the floor.

"I don't have any idea what you want me to talk about," Ty said.

"You've got an education, don't you?"

"Some. Why?"

"It's just something I noticed. I try to pay attention to details like that, little clues about the men I'm dealing with."

"You don't think I'm guilty, do you?"

"Of what?"

"Whatever this is all about."

Ripley shrugged. "What I think doesn't matter. Tell me about last night, after you left the Tiger's Eye."

"I had some supper, then I went back to the stable and went to sleep."

"Anyone who could vouch for that?"

"The waiter at the Mandan Cafe, the night watchman at Becker and Miles." Ty hesitated. "Where's Virgil? Is that what this is about?"

"Virgil Nash is upstairs," Ripley answered bluntly. "Suspicion of murder."

"Murder!" Ty echoed. "Who?"

"Francis Duck."

"Duck? I don't believe it."

"Do you deny he had an altercation with Duck last night?"

"No, but . . ." Ty stopped, suddenly comprehending the sheriff's vague line of questioning. "You don't have any witnesses, do you?"

"I didn't say that."

"Sure you did. That's why you want to know where I was, why you're asking me about Virgil's run-in with Duck." Ty's hopes rose a notch. "Virgil Nash was nearly passed out when I left him in the alley beside the Tiger's Eye. He wasn't in any shape to go looking for trouble."

Ripley took the cigar from his mouth. "You're saying you left Nash in the alley beside the Tiger's Eye, drunk but still conscious?"

"That's right."

"What time?"

"Hell, I don't know. Somewhere between eight and nine o'clock, I'd guess."

"Francis Duck was found in that alley early this morning," Ripley said softly. "He was stabbed in the heart. Your friend, Nash, was found less than ten feet away, sleeping off his drunk with Duck's bloody knife in his hand."

"Jesus," Ty whispered.

"Yeah," Ripley said. He took a puff off his cigar, thinking, then said, "I'm going to lock you up, Calhoun. I gotta talk to your friends. I gotta check times with the people at the Mandan Cafe, and the night watchman at Becker and Miles. I gotta round up customers from the Tiger's Eye that might've seen something." He made a face. "Hell, I've got so many things to check out I probably won't eat breakfast until midnight."

"I didn't do it, Sheriff. I don't think Virgil did, either."

Frowning, Ripley said, "I hope you're right, because as far as I know a white man ain't never been hung in this territory for killing an Indian, and I'm damned if I want to be the first to have to do it."

EIGHT

Clay kept the pinto at a hard gallop until almost noon. The packhorses were strung out for more than a quarter of a mile behind him but still coming on, keeping the pinto in sight. As the pale orb of the sun neared its apex, Clay finally slowed to a jog, then a walk. The pinto was breathing heavily by then, and the Indian ponies, when they caught up, were flecked with a yellowish lather. Clay kept glancing over his shoulder for signs of pursuit, but the land appeared empty, and gradually his panic began to subside.

Still, he kept the horses moving along at a good clip, letting the miles fall swiftly behind him. He camped that night on an open plain, wrapped tightly in his robes with his rifle beside him and Ezra's Kerr revolver tucked under his mackinaw. But he couldn't sleep. Every time he started to doze off, he was roughly awakened by the sound of gunfire echoing in his dreams, the images of falling bodies imprinted against the dark screen of his eyelids.

Around midnight he got up and pushed on. He spooked a deer feeding at the mouth of a shallow draw early the next morning, and remembered that he hadn't eaten anything in almost thirty-six hours. Although hungry, he let the deer go, unwilling to invest the time it would take to stalk it. He rested the horses at noon, but pushed on soon afterward. It was just before nightfall when he came in sight of the trees where Ezra and Jake had waylaid him.

He hauled up half a mile away to study the woods. The little grove appeared as it had before, empty and forlorn. The stream still ran full tilt, its silt-gray waters slapping almost playfully at the tops of the banks. Clay waited curiously for some kind of emotion — anger or sadness or fear — but felt nothing. It was just another tiny island of trees, one of millions that fringed the great, tail-grass prairies of the West.

After a couple of minutes he rode on down and watered the horses. Although wary, he was no more cautious than usual. When he came to the spot where Ezra and Jake had ambushed him, he discovered that all traces of the encounter had been washed away by the rain. Not even the brambles where Jake had lain hidden displayed a torn piece of wool or raveled thread. On the far bank, the little clearing where Clay had contemplated spending the night beckoned as invitingly as before.

He splashed the pinto across the stream and dismounted. Although still edgy, the need to keep moving, to keep looking over his shoulder for pursuit, had lessened. He was tired and hungry, and for the first time in forty-eight hours he was able to look forward to a meal and a decent night's sleep.

He pulled the packs off the Indian ponies first, then hobbled them and turned them loose to graze. Then he unsaddled the pinto and picketed it close by. It took less than half an hour to set up his tent and rig the packs of furs and robes on top of the sawbucks, off the damp ground; it took even less time to bust up enough firewood to last the night.

With those basic needs taken care of, Clay took his rifle and eased into the woods. He moved stealthily, his eyes alert but his mind only half on the task at hand. His thoughts kept running back to Jake and Hog, wondering what mettle they were made of, and how they would react when they returned to the bloody clearing and discovered the slain bodies of the Captain and Ezra and Seth. Would they follow, determined to recapture as many of the escaped Negroes as possible? Or without the Captain's formidable will to sustain them, would they flee like thieves?

Clay had feared at first that they might recruit help from some nearby settlement, but as the panic of his initial flight calmed he'd decided that was unlikely. Catching runaway slaves was a dirty but legitimate business, but kidnapping free men and women and transporting them back into slavery was illegal. Clay doubted if either Jake or Hog wanted to risk complications by announcing their involvement. Still, no matter how unlawful the enterprise might have been to begin with, white men had been killed in the process of escaping it, and Clay knew that would change everything if they were ever recaptured.

He jerked to a stop, his gaze drawn to the base of a hickory about forty yards away. A cottontail had hopped out from behind its trunk and paused to nibble at a stem of grass. Slowly, Clay brought the rifle to his shoulder, sighted carefully on the rabbit's small, rounded head, and gently squeezed the trigger. The big-bore caplock belched thunder, and through the billowing cloud of powder smoke Clay saw the decapitated rabbit flip backward. He lowered his rifle while that odd mix of success and failure for a killing shot flowed through him. He looked to the sky and offered a silent prayer to the Everywhere Spirit, a wordless offering of gratitude for the meal It had provided, and regret for his need to take a life to preserve his own. Then he walked over and picked up the rabbit by its hind feet. He would take it back to his camp to gut and skin, and maybe drop a few morsels into the flames of his fire as thanks for the Spirit's assistance.

It surprised him a little, this sudden compulsion to follow a native ritual he had seen others perform, but had never practiced himself. Although Simon had revered nature as most outdoorsmen did, he had early on given up his ancestral gods. Growing up under the old Choctaw's tutelage, Clay had naturally developed similar attitudes, opinions that had been reinforced during his stay among the more primitive Wichitas. Yet here he was, praying to Man Above like any copper-skinned savage, prepared to sacrifice raw meat to spirits he wasn't even sure he believed in.

It was all too much to think about, as tired as he was. Returning to camp, Clay quickly prepared the rabbit for the spit. He tossed the entrails and skin into the brush, but saved the heart and liver, washing them in the stream as carefully as he did the carcass. With the rabbit skewered on a slim green limb over the fire, he went through his gear until he found his pipe and tobacco. He smoked quietly while waiting for the meat to cook, and although ravenous, ate only half of the rabbit, setting the rest aside for breakfast.

For a long time then, he just sat cross-legged before the fire, regarding the smoky embers in silence. It was dark by the time the last flame died. Weariness had settled into every fiber of Clay's body. His eyes felt gritty and dry, his mind numb. Finally he stirred, leaning forward to blow on the coals until they had flared up to a bright, pulsating red. With thumb and forefinger, he picked up the cottontail's heart and liver and dropped them in the coals. Gray smoke curled up from the tiny organs, buffeted by imperceptible currents of air. Self-consciously, Clay cupped his hands into the smoke and lifted them skyward, opening his palms to the heavens as he recited a prayer only half-remembered from his years among the Kiowas. Afterward, he sat staring upward through the latticework of bare branches at patches of starlight filtering through the thinning cloud cover. A feeling of contentment enveloped him, a sense that his decision with the rabbit's organs had been the right one. Dragging his rifle after him, he crawled into the tent and dropped onto his robes, falling instantly asleep.

The sound of crackling flames and the odor of sizzling bacon brought Clay awake the next morning. Lifting his face from the shaggy depths of the buffalo robe, he stared out the open rear of the tent at a wall of brush and timber. He remained that way for several seconds, frozen by the incongruity of sounds from outside the tent. For a moment a blind panic seized him, and his grip tightened on his rifle. He heard the murmur of familiar voices, followed by the *ping* of a steel utensil banged gently against the rim of a cast-iron skillet. Rolling over on his elbow, Clay peered out the front of the tent at the grinning black face of Plato, sitting on the far side of a leaping fire.

"I golly, I think ol' Clay be waitin' up, Sammy Lee," Plato announced cheerfully. "Reckon we ain't gonna have to eat this good fatback alone, after all."

A pair of long, skinny legs strode into view, then jackknifed into a squat to frame Sammy Lee's face and torso in the tent's

128

triangular opening. He studied Clay for a moment, then guffawed. "I don't think he's the plainsman you thought he was, old man."

"Shoot, even a plainsman's got to sleep sometime. Ain't that right, Clay?"

Clay slid out of the tent and stood up. Ezra's big sorrel and Captain Carry's high-blooded dun were picketed close to the pinto. Clay gave the spotted gelding a sour look of disapproval for not warning him of intruders.

"Now, I reckon that horse of yours mighta nickered, was we strangers," Plato said as if reading Clay's thoughts. "But we ain't, so you can't rightly fault him."

"How'd you find me?" Clay asked gruffly.

"Weren't easy, and that be a fact," Plato conceded. "Tell you the truth, we mostly just let our horses have their heads, and they brung us here. 'Course, we recognized that flashy horse of yours right off, didn't we, Sammy Lee?"

"If we were white men, we'd have had you in chains before you quit snoring," Sammy Lee said.

"I reckon not," Clay replied evenly. He glanced overhead. The clouds appeared to have broken up for good; the morning sky was a pale, metallic blue, as clean as a fresh-scrubbed plate.

"Things be lookin' up, don't you think?" Plato asked in a tone that suggested his own uncertainty.

Sammy Lee grunted in discontent. "Is that the way you see things, too?" he asked Clay. "Chains are off, everything's fine?"

"It helps," Clay answered calmly. He hunkered down beside the fire, eyeing the bacon Plato tended. "That looks mighty good, dad. Did you find it in Carry's packs?"

"Uh huh. Got some 'taters and onjuns too, you be interested."

"I'm interested," Clay said. He looked for the remains of the rabbit he'd left beside the fire last night, but it was gone. He didn't ask who'd eaten it. It hardly seemed to matter now. Sniffing the frying meat, he smiled in anticipation. "It must be true that Negroes make the best cooks," he said.

Plato gave him a quick, disappointed look. "What makes you talk foolishness like that?"

Clay shrugged. "Just talk," he said. "I didn't mean anything by it."

"You ain't Injun, you know?" Plato said as he slid the bacon around in the skillet with a long, wooden-handled fork. "I done figured that out. Negro is what you be, Mr. Little Bull. Don't matter none what name you take, you be black as molasses. Same as me, same as Sammy Lee."

In a quiet voice, Clay said, "I'd never considered myself that way, at least not until recently. I don't know if I believe it, though."

Sammy Lee grunted. "Well, you're young," he said. "The world will give you plenty of opportunities to reconsider." He had been nervously pacing the edge of the clearing, but only now did Clay notice the Captain's twin, ivory-handled Navy Colts strapped around his waist, the belt pulled up to the last notch. Sammy Lee was eyeing the surrounding woods suspiciously, and his long, delicate fingers kept touching the revolvers, as if for reassurance.

"Now, don't go upsettin' a man afore his breakfast, Sammy Lee," Plato chided. "Mayhaps that be the way things is where Clay be from."

"Bullshit," Sammy Lee said, then stalked into the woods.

Plato sighed, watching him go. "That there young feller is gonna cause a lot of grief for someone," he predicted sadly. "He be too mad. Wears it bad, too."

"Maybe he's got a point about carrying guns, though."

Plato's expression changed, the wrinkles in his cheeks deepening into tight, twisting fissures. "Guns ain't no answer. Not the way Sammy Lee wants to use 'em."

"So we just turn our backs to the likes of Captain Carry?"

"Didn't say that. But what's gonna work more is if we sticks together. We can't go runnin' off our own way, like we *did,* like James and Missy and that boy, Nate. They be all alone out there now, and Jenny, too. Ain't none of 'em gonna stand a snowball's chance on a hot griddle if a man like Carry comes on 'em again. We got to band together. Black folks is already doin' it, here'n about, makin' they own towns, stayin' close to one 'nother. That be the road we got to take, Clay. What they call *unity.* Same as those Northern folks be talkin' 'bout — the Union. We got to unionize."

Clay laughed. "We made a hell of a union, all right, marching along on chains behind that silver-haired son of a bitch like a string of jackasses."

"They always gonna be sons'bitches in this ol' world, Clay. You'd best figure on that right off. But you noticed we ain't marchin' behind him no more. We be free, and goin' home."

"But we had to leave a heap of dead white men behind to do it, too," Clay reminded him.

"I know, son, I know. And I ain't sayin' we shouldn't arm ourselves to do it again, comes to it. But that ain't what Sammy Lee's talkin' 'bout. No sir, he be talkin' war. Black folks ain't gonna win that kind of war."

Clay made a flat, cutting motion with his hand, signaling an end to the conversation. He stood abruptly, feeling an unreasonable resentment toward Plato's convictions. He was sure of only one thing anymore, and that was that he would never again give up his guns without a fight — not to anyone, white, black or red. "I'm going to saddle up," he said curtly. "If you and Sammy Lee intend to ride with me, you'd best be ready."

Plato smiled. "You'll be takin' time for a bite of this here side meat and 'taters, won't you?"

"Potatoes," Clay snapped. "They ain't 'taters, goddamnit, they're potatoes."

The old man's eyes widened. "My, oh, my," he said softly. "All right, Clay. Potatoes, then."

"Aw, hell, call 'em what you want. It doesn't matter —"

A gunshot rang out from the woods to the north, in the direction Sammy Lee had taken, and Clay jumped as if stung. Plato surged to his feet as a second shot followed.

Then four more came in rapid succession. Clay swore and grabbed his rifle, bag, and horn. Plato snatched up a shotgun, and the two men took off in the direction of the fading reports. "Easy, now," Plato cautioned. "Don't go rushin' —"

Clay slammed to a stop, cocking the big sidehammer of his rifle. "See anything?" he asked.

"Nope, nary a thing," Plato returned, his voice dropped to a whisper.

Clay studied the ground in front of him. Sammy Lee's trail was clearly defined across the soggy forest floor — a dark, serpentine trace winding through the damp undergrowth.

"Awful quiet, ain't it?" Plato observed uneasily.

Clay was thinking the same thing. His gaze swept the thick woods before him. "Maybe he saw a deer," he speculated. "Or a bear."

"Mebbeso a bear saw him first," Plato replied dryly.

"You see his trail there?" Clay asked, nodding to the ruffled path before them. When Plato nodded, Clay said, "You follow that. Take your time and keep your eyes out front. I'm going to angle off to the right a bit and flank you."

Plato nodded tautly. "You have a care, Clay. Sammy Lee ain't no kind of woods-man. Likely he'd take a shot at either one of us, was we to come on him sudden like."

"I'll watch for him," Clay promised. "Let's go."

They started off through the trees, Clay moving obliquely away from the older man. It wasn't a huge woods, no more than twenty or thirty acres, all told, but it was big enough to hide several men if they wanted to remain hidden.

It was Clay who spotted Sammy Lee first. He stopped, sliding his finger inside the iron trigger guard of his rifle. Sammy Lee lay in a heap on a little flat close to the stream. His gum poncho, taken from Carry's packs, covered him like a funeral shroud. Clay licked his lips, his gaze darting among the dark tree trunks and thickly clustered patches of brambles and alders. Nothing moved. Not even a leaf fluttered alone on a branch. Taking a long breath, he started down the gentle slope to where Sammy Lee lay. Plato arrived a moment later, easing onto the little flat with his shotgun cocked.

"That be far enough!"

Clay flinched. Looking carefully to his right, he saw what he had missed before, and almost laughed.

135

"Lord A'Mighty, girl," Plato hollered, his eyes saucered wide and white-rimmed when he spotted Jenny hunkered back in the hollow of a tree less than a dozen feet away. "Child, we searched high 'n low for you back yonder. What you doin' here?"

Jenny pushed back against the tree, raising her right hand, a palm-sized oval stone clenched in her fingers. "You just stay put," she warned. "You come any closer and I'll pop you like I done this'un."

"Jenny girl, we ain't gonna hurt you. It's me, ol' Plato, and Clay. We be your friends, child."

"Ain't nobody my friend, I'll tell you that. This wild man," she indicated Sammy Lee with a nod of her head, "tried to shoot me. That what kind of friends you be?"

Plato looked confused. "Sammy Lee tried to shoot you? Why?"

"He didn't say why. He just saw me and started shootin', so I whacked him with a rock."

Suddenly, Clay did laugh, lowering the hammer of his rifle to the half-cock safety position.

"You think that's funny, Mister?"

"Yeah," Clay said, still chuckling at the image of how it must have happened. "What did you do, scare him?"

"I reckon I might've. His first shot nearly took his own foot off."

"Lordy," Plato murmured, shaking his head. "That there be just what I mean," he said to Clay. "Boy like that ain't got no business thinkin' he's gonna start a war with anyone. Like to've shot his own foot off. My, oh, my, I can just see that."

"Well, I don't intend to shoot you," Clay said to Jenny. "Although I wouldn't shoot myself in the foot if I did."

"I believe that," Jenny said, sliding partway out of the rotting bole. "That was as pretty a shot as I ever seen last night, taking that bunny's head off like you done."

Surprised, Clay said, "You saw that?"

"Sure did. Weren't no more'n a soft whistle away. I'd a said something, only you was lookin' mighty queersome yourself right then, lookin' up at the sky and mumblin' hoodoo. What was that, anyway? Injun or African?"

"Indian," Clay replied, embarrassed. He was aware of Plato's searching look, but ignored it. Nodding toward Sammy Lee, he said, "Let's see if we can wake him up. Otherwise we'll have to carry him back to camp." He leaned his rifle against a forked sapling and knelt at the unconscious man's side.

"You better take them pistols away first," Jenny warned, shrinking back into the tree's hollow.

Plato set his shotgun aside and squatted opposite Clay. Flipping aside the poncho's hem, he pulled the loaded revolver from its holster. As a precaution he also picked up the empty pistol, then held both weapons out to the girl, waiting without comment until she scooted out of her hiding place and took them.

There was a knot the size of a robin's egg at the top of Sammy Lee's forehead, but no blood, nor sign of serious injury. Clay gently slapped Sammy Lee's cheeks until he groaned and squeezed his eyes shut even tighter than before. Smiling, Clay said to Plato, "You got any magic for a headache, dad? I've got a feeling he's going to need it."

"I got a cure for a headache," Jenny said starchily; she'd backed out of the way after accepting the handguns from Plato, and held one in each white-knuckled fist, her head held up defiantly. "It's called common sense. That way you don't go gettin' no rock busted upside your head."

"Jenny, Jenny," Plato murmured in wonderment. "How in the world did you get this far, girl?"

138

"I run," she said flatly. "You took that collar off'n my neck and I lit outta there like my britches was smokin'. I didn't need no horse. Them things is too darn slow."

"Maybe she's got something there, dad," Clay said.

"Not for my old bones, she don't," Plato replied, although Clay noticed he was smiling. Rising stiffly, Plato walked over to the shotgun, but paused before reaching for it. Glancing at Jenny, he said, "I'm gonna be pickin' up this here scattergun now. You ain't gonna whack me for it, are you?"

Sammy Lee moaned, his head rolling to one side, his fingers crabbing upward to gently investigate the top of his forehead. "Ohhhh," he lowed. "My head . . ."

Jenny huffed. "He be lucky I didn't take the fool thing off, the way this'un did that rabbit last night." She gave Clay a quick, furtive glance, then looked at Plato. "Well," she said tentatively. "I reckon I oughter be goin'."

"You ain't goin' nowhere," Plato replied firmly. "You come on back to camp. I got some bacon just 'bout ready, and some . . ." he gave Clay a sly look, "some *potatoes* that oughta be 'bout prime for eatin'."

Jenny looked pointedly at Clay. "It's his camp," she said. "He ain't tolt I was welcome there."

"You can come if you want," Clay said gruffly.

"That don't sound invitin'," Jenny replied stiffly. "I don't need no charity. I can make out just fine by my lonesome, I have to." When Plato chuckled, she gave him a scathing look. "Goes for you, too," she added. "I been on my own a good long time now. I don't need —"

"Jenny girl, come back to camp. We all need us a little food in our bellies, and a little time to just sit and think. I reckon we all feel a mite ragged 'round the edges. Come to think on it, I got some coffee, too. Might be a fine idea to brew us up a batch, give us some time to chew over what we oughta do next."

Clay looked up warily. "There's nothing to chew over, dad. Soon as breakfast is finished, I'm riding out."

Plato held out his hand, and after a moment's hesitation Jenny switched both revolvers to one side and took it. Plato winked at Clay. "You get Sammy Lee on his feet," he said. "Me and Jenny'll get that coffee boilin'. Time 'nough then to talk 'bout ridin'."

Sammy Lee didn't open his eyes until the sounds of Plato and Jenny's departure through the fallen leaves had faded. Then he looked at Clay, his face drawn with pain, the anger replaced by an expression of contrition. "It was the girl, wasn't it? She's the one who struck me?"

Clay nodded.

Sighing, Sammy Lee said, "I thought it was Jake Jacobs. I swear I looked right at her and saw Jake."

"It happens," Clay said.

"You think I'm a damn fool, don't you?"

"No, I don't," Clay admitted heavily. He lowered his hand, and Sammy Lee took it. Hauling him to his feet, Clay added, "To tell you the truth, when I woke up this morning and heard you and Plato talking outside my tent, I damn near panicked. I thought it was the Captain again. I reckon we're all a little jumpy yet."

Sammy Lee held onto Clay until his balance returned. "What now?" he asked.

Smiling wryly, Clay said, "Why, I reckon we'll head on back to camp and have some breakfast. You'll be eating crow, while I have the 'taters."

NINE

The jailer, Moss, appeared at Tyler Calhoun's iron-slatted door just before noon on his second day of incarceration. As the old man fumbled a ring of keys from the hook on his belt, Ty lifted his head from the skinny mattress where he had been lying.

"Sheriff wants to see you," Moss announced through the bars. He inserted a key in the lock and gave it a familiar twist. Ty swung his feet off the narrow cot and quickly pulled on his boots. Moss opened the heavy door and stepped back, closing his hand warningly over a short, leather-bound blackjack he carried on his belt. "Come on," he groused. "You ain't forgot the way."

Taking his jacket and hat, Ty stepped out of the cell and headed for the stairs leading down to the first floor. They entered the long hallway that led to the rear of the building. At Moss' command, they came to a halt outside a closed door. Moss rapped the frame with his 'jack, and a voice called for them to enter. Ty stepped into a small office, and Moss shut the door behind him.

Sheriff Bob Ripley sat across the room with his elbows propped on a cluttered desk, his head balanced low between a pair of beefy shoulders. He looked tired. His eyes were cradled by dark, puffy bags, and his normally slick-combed hair was disheveled.

"You look like hell," Ty observed mildly.

"Sit down, Calhoun."

Ty went to a cane-woven ladderback chair in front of Ripley's desk and sat, draping his coat and hat over his lap. "Did you find out who killed Francis Duck?"

Ripley's eyes narrowed. "You're sure it wasn't your pard, are you?"

"Pretty sure, yeah."

Ripley grunted. "Pretty sure?"

Ty shrugged. The window behind the sheriff was open, allowing a cool, damp breeze to waft inside, fragrant with the aromas of a frontier community after a long rainy spell — a mixture of prairie grasses and stove smoke, churned mud and manure, vegetable carts and dying flower gardens. A mule brayed in the distance; somewhere closer, children laughed.

Ripley leaned back in his chair. "I'm go-

143

ing to let you go," he stated without preamble. "Your story checks out." He pushed a sheet of paper and a pencil across the desk. "Sign that. It states that your stay in the Leavenworth City Jail was pleasant, and that you suffered no undue losses or damages."

"What about Virgil?"

"Your pards have already been released, including Nash."

For a moment Ty didn't move. Then he slowly reached for the paper and pencil. Ripley watched him sign the sheet, then took it from him and slid it inside the top drawer of his desk without looking at it.

Ty started to rise, then settled back in his chair. "What's going on, Sheriff? Why did you let Virgil go if you're convinced he killed Francis Duck?"

"I wanted to see if he'd run," Ripley answered bluntly. "He did. I set him free last night, and he was gone by morning. Lobenstein said he cashed in his share of the draft you boys had for the hides and meat you brought in, and hightailed it out of here right after dawn this morning."

Ty sat too stunned to speak. Ripley waited a moment, then laughed without humor. "You still feelin' pretty sure?"

"I don't guess I know what to think. I wish I could've talked to him."

"I let him go last night because I figured he'd run. I kept you overnight because I knew you'd try to talk him out of it. The Burdettes don't give a damn, but you do, whether you want to or not."

"Running doesn't prove his guilt," Ty said without conviction.

Ripley leaned back in his chair, rubbing his hands over his face. "No, it doesn't. Not legally, anyway. But I'll tell you something, even though it's none of your business. This whole deal stinks to high heaven. Duck was killed with a single thrust of a knife, presumably his own. And he was killed from behind. Maybe Nash did it, maybe he didn't. I don't know. But the way that redskin was killed, a stab straight to the heart, it would've taken a pretty steady hand or a hell of a lot of luck, and I ain't sure Nash had either one that night. Furthermore, Duck left the Tiger's Eye in the company of two Negroes of questionable character, and I mean damn questionable character. You understand? Now they've also disappeared. Something smells, all right. I just ain't got the time to sort it out."

"Because Francis Duck was an Indian?"

"Because Francis Duck was a trouble-maker," Ripley countered sharply, "and because he was up to no good or he

145

wouldn't have been hanging around with the likes of Buford Hart and Ross Lake. And because I know, I *know,* that son of a bitch Duck is the bastard who burned my house down last year. I don't give a damn how many witnesses he had, he was behind it, somehow."

Ty nodded, finally understanding.

Ripley poked a finger at Ty, the color in his face deepening. "Now, I'm going to tell you something else, Calhoun, which I doubt you'll like any more than what I already told you, which I can see by your expression that you don't. I don't much care about you or Nash or the Burdettes. I don't care about Francis Duck, either. Under different circumstances I might have pursued this case differently, but I didn't, and I'll tell you why. It's too damn complicated. There's an Indian involved, so the army's going to want to nose around, and maybe the Indian Affairs people, and they're going to want me to locate Hart and Lake and bring them in for questioning, and run down Nash, and God knows what else. And I'm not going to do it. It's as simple as that. But the army might, or the Indian Affairs folks. And if they do, with the evidence I've collected against Nash and the way he ran, then your partner's going to stand trial for murder, and the fires of hell won't stop that. If he's found guilty he'll probably go to a federal penitentiary. He wouldn't hang, no matter what I told him last night. Not even the army would swing a white man for killing an Indian. But he could easy serve some time behind bars."

Ty glanced out the window at the pale morning sky, scudded with white, fast-moving clouds. He had been watching those same clouds upstairs a few minutes earlier, from his cell. Finally, he said, "You're wrong about one thing, Sheriff. I don't care. Seems like I've been dragging Virgil's ass out of trouble since we were kids, but I'm not going to do it anymore."

A smile tugged at the corners of Ripley's mouth. "That's the first sensible thing I've heard out of you yet, Calhoun. Steer clear of that one. He's trouble. One other thing. I don't know where Nash went, but the Burdettes are going home. They've already booked passage on the *Alice McQueen.* You ought to do the same. You're too damn bright to hunt buffalo the rest of your life."

"I reckon I'll hang around awhile," Ty replied. He stood and exited the room, leaving the building through the back door, where he paused on the porch overlooking the Missouri. He breathed deeply of the

147

clean air, untainted by the sour stench of the jail. The feel of autumn hung heavy on the wind, and it brought a hesitant smile to Ty's face. Fall had always been his favorite time of the year, those cool, mellow days before the driving winds of winter whipped down from the north — like a final, festive reprieve, a reminder, perhaps, that life was good overall, and that a man had best remember that if he wanted to survive the rocky times.

It was mid-afternoon when Ty paused in front of a white picket fence fronting a two-story clapboard house on the main road south out of town. A neatly painted sign hung from a post in the front yard: *Mother Tucker's — Room and Board — Fifty Cents.* Green shutters framed the windows, and rose bushes climbed a trellis over the gate. Ty studied the scene with faint amusement. Mother Tucker's carefully tended boarding house seemed as out of place along the muddy streets of Leavenworth as a Cheyenne tipi would in Toledo, yet its attraction was obvious. For men like Matt and Keith, such a place would be a magnet, a distorted memory of home.

Ty ran his hand across the back of his neck. Since his release from jail that morning, he'd had a shave and a bath and his hair cut, although he'd kept his hair long in back. He felt freshly peeled and five pounds lighter, and couldn't help a wry grin. His clothes were new and stiff — bibless over-alls, a blue cotton shirt with white bone but-tons, and a black silk bandanna; even his hat was new — a wide-brimmed model with a flat, dented crown and a small pencil curl at the brim. He'd tried to replace his boots, too, but couldn't find anything that fit his feet better than the ones he wore now. He had brogans in his pack back at the wagons, and resolved to dig them out tonight to wear while he had these resoled.

Heading for the gate leading to Mother Tucker's, Ty saw Keith sitting in a rocker within the depths of the front porch. He had a thick, leather-bound Bible open on his lap, with his head bent intently forward. A forefinger traced the print across the page, like a hound's nose on the scent of a rabbit. He didn't look up until Ty pushed the gate open on squeaky hinges.

"Ty!" Keith exclaimed, then jumped to his feet and hurried down the steps. "By golly, I didn't expect to see you for a while. The way Ripley was talking yesterday, I thought he was going to hold you for several more days, at least." They shook hands, then

Keith's expression changed. "Did you hear about Virgil?"

"Ripley told me he ran. He also said you and Matt were pulling out."

Keith shrugged. "Yeah. Matt bought the tickets yesterday. But shoot, it's time. We've been out here for two years now. I've had my fill." He gave Ty a funny, woebegone look. "I guess Wade kind of . . . changed things."

"I reckon he did," Ty agreed quietly.

The two men took seats on the top step of the porch. "Matt and I settled up with Lobenstein this morning," Keith told him. "After expenses, your share came out to a little over nine hundred dollars. Lobenstein is holding it for you."

Ty whistled softly, impressed. There would come a time, he foresaw, when he wouldn't have to go into debt every year to put an outfit together.

"We thought Wade's portion ought to go to Virgil," Keith went on. "But under the circumstances, we decided to take it back to his family."

"That's probably best," Ty agreed.

Keith was quiet a moment, thinking, then shook his head. "Virgil was always the wild one. It's sure going to be a hard blow for his folks, isn't it? Losing Wade like that, then

150

thinking their other son might be a fugitive."

Keith was right about that, Ty thought. The Nashes had lived next door to his own parents in Toledo for almost thirty years, long before any of the children had come along. They had shared holidays, and often went together on picnics and swimming excursions along the Lake Erie shore. Virgil, being the eldest, had been something of a leader among the five youths. It was he who had introduced them to the masculine vices of smoking and chewing tobacco, of spitting and fighting and cursing, who had shared his expertise with marbles and mumble-typeg, and later, with girls. But Virgil had changed in his late teens. He became sullen and hard to get along with, shunning the company of old friends in favor of new ones made along the Lake Erie waterfront, where hard-bitten longshoremen sought their entertainment in cheap dives. He took to billiards and card playing, and began carrying a .40 caliber pepperbox pistol in the pocket of his jacket. Although Ty still saw him fairly often, the two had spent little time in each other's company until Ty asked him to come with them to Kansas.

He remembered that day well, even though it had been something over two years ago now. . . .

He had discovered Virgil sitting behind his father's small stable with a half-empty quart canning jar of corn liquor nestled in the brown grass at his side. A purple bruise shone from the puffy flesh beneath Virgil's left eye, and his lower lip was swollen to twice its normal size. Dried blood formed a thin, broken line down his chin, and spotted his shirt front. Ty jerked to a stop when he saw him, almost dropping his pipe and tobacco.

"What happened to you?" Ty exclaimed.

"Keep your mouth shut, asshole, or I'll give the same thing to you," Virgil snarled in response.

Ty ignored the threat. He sloped down at Virgil's side and put his back against the warm stable wall. "I was looking for you earlier," he said. "You didn't show up for work today, and Pa's fit to be tied."

Ty's father ran a rope factory down by the wharves, supplying sturdy hawsers and smaller lines for the lake traffic, as well as local farmers; both boys worked there full-time now that they were out of school.

"Is that old tightwad worried I'm going to cost him a nickel?"

"Come on, Virg, you know he's not like that. You've been missing more work than you've shown up for the last couple of weeks. What's going on?"

"Just never you mind."

"Pa said that if I saw you, I was to tell you to show up tomorrow or he'd have to fire you."

"Let him fire me," Virgil replied, but something in his voice betrayed him.

Slowly, giving himself time to think, Ty began to fill his pipe. He smoked only sporadically, and then was careful not to let his parents see him. Although at eighteen, he felt himself old enough to take on a few vices, he was still leery of his mother's disapproval. He lit the pipe with flint and steel and a piece of charred cloth, pinching out the char afterward to use again.

"You're going to start a fire someday," Virgil said, watching Ty snap the lid closed on his brass char container. "That stuff can smolder for hours."

Ty took the pipe from his mouth and jetted a stream of smoke toward the sky. "If matches weren't so expensive I'd use those."

Virgil tipped his head back, closing his eyes. "Matches are a rich man's folly. You and I aren't cut out for such a life."

"What's going on, Virg?" Ty repeated quietly, keeping his eyes on the woods behind the family pasture.

"If I tell you, you've got to promise not to tell your old man. Or mine. You don't tell anyone, hear?"

"I hear."

Virgil's stoic expression suddenly crumbled, and he squeezed his eyes shut. "God A'Mighty, Tyler, I'm in it now. Up to my neck. I owe money to some people down at the Schooner, and they're threatening to break my legs if I don't hand it over by the end of the week."

"The Schooner!" Ty's face registered shock. The Bloody Schooner was one of the roughest taverns in Toledo, or so he'd always heard; it catered to sailors off the lakes, and scallywags who prowled the dank alleyways and darkened streets of the waterfront at night. Rumor had it that the waters off the Toledo docks were littered with the weighted-down corpses of victims slipped out the back door of the Schooner. Having seen some of the clientele who frequented the tavern, Ty was inclined to believe it. "What the hell were you doing in the Schooner?"

"Playing cards," Virgil replied in a deflated voice. "I don't know what happened. I was winning at first, then I started to lose. A pal . . ." He paused, then shook his head. "No, not a pal. Just someone I met and thought was a friend. Anyway, he loaned me some money —"

"How much?"

"It doesn't matter," Virgil replied irritably. "Damnit, Ty, listen. I'm in trouble. This guy's wanting his money, and I don't have it. He . . . he wants me to steal it from your father."

"From Pa?" Ty's eyes widened. "Lord, Virgil, you can't steal it from Pa."

"I know that. But what am I going to do? I've got to come up with two hundred dollars by the —"

"Two hundred dollars!"

Virgil nodded morosely. "I know, goddamnit. I was drunk, Ty, pure and simple. Just a damn fool."

Ty whistled softly. And then, as if out of the blue, Kansas came to his mind. "Why don't we go out West and hunt buffalo?" he proposed offhandedly.

"Hell, why don't we go to Europe and dine with a king?"

"Matt and I have been talking about it all winter," Ty said. "Wade wants to go, too."

A glimmer of interest appeared in Virgil's eyes. "When are you leaving?"

"Well . . ." Ty ran the clay stem of his pipe across his lower lip. "We haven't really decided yet. Mostly we've just talked about it."

Virgil snorted. "You three have been talking about hunting buffalo ever since your old man let you have that squirrel rifle. If you're ever going to do it, you'd better get started. Another year here and you'll be so tied down to your old man's business you won't ever escape it."

Ty nodded glumly. The same thought had occurred to him. It seemed that every day he was becoming more and more immersed in the family business — not just walking the long lines anymore, but being handed larger responsibilities associated with the running of a manufacturing firm. His father had mentioned only last Sunday that he was thinking of promoting Ty to a clerking position within the small office complex itself, a move intended to aid his son's understanding of the firm's overall structure. It was going to be easy to slip into the role his father wanted for him, almost as easy as falling asleep at the end of a hard day's work, with nothing to look forward to but a long, dreamless sleep — until that time came when he would pass the business on to his own son.

"Tyler Calhoun, rope master," Virgil said derisively.

"Go to hell," Ty replied. "I ain't the one about to get my legs busted."

Virgil looked startled at first. Then he jumped to his feet, curling his arms and fists into a classic boxer's pose. "Get up, asshole. I'm gonna pound you into the dirt for that."

"Aw, shut up, Virgil. I didn't mean anything by it."

"Come on. On your feet."

But Ty refused. He said, "Sit down, Virg. I'm not afraid of you anymore." And he wasn't, either. It surprised him some. For the first time he realized how much his friendship with Virgil had been based half in fear, and half in pride that he was important enough to tag along with an older boy. Only now he realized it had always been Virgil who, unable to make friends among those his own age, had sought out the companionship of his younger brother and his friends. Ty shook his head, smiling to himself. "Maybe I ought to go to Kansas. It might be fun to make it on my own for a while."

Confused, Virgil lowered his arms.

Ty felt a growing excitement at the prospect. "Matt will come. Keith, too. And Wade. That makes four of us. Five, if you're in. Our parents won't try too hard to stop us if we all go together."

Sneering, Virgil said, "Is Tyler worried about his mama?"

Laughing, Ty replied, "Not nearly as much as you are about your buddies down at the Schooner."

Virgil's shoulders sagged and his face went slack, making him look more like a boy of twelve than a man of twenty-two. Finally he said, "I guess you're right. Maybe I ought to go to Kansas and start over."

It hadn't been quite that simple, of course, but three months later the five of them had set out, taking the Wabash and Erie Canal as far as Illinois, where they bought tickets for a train to St. Louis. From there they had ascended the Missouri by steamboat to Leavenworth, where they'd disembarked.

Or perhaps embarked would have been a better description — setting out upon a grassy sea, a grand adventure. It had been a fine two years, too, until Wade was killed on the banks of the Saline River. After that, it all started to unravel, their friendships seeming to disintegrate before their eyes, and none of them much wanting to patch it up.

In a way, Ty was glad Matt and Keith were going home. It would make starting over on his own just that much easier.

"Well, well, look who's slipped his noose."

158

Ty looked up. Matt Burdette stood in the dappled shade of the trellis, dressed in a dark suit with a string tie over his linen shirt. A bowler hat sat on his head, and his hair, Ty noticed, was cut short, as it had been before they left Ohio. The transformation was so complete, so unexpected, that for a moment Ty didn't know what to say.

"Ripley let him go," Keith explained.

"So I heard," Matt replied, pushing the gate open and coming inside. He stopped several feet away, but there was no welcome in his stance, no offer of a handshake. "Ripley tell you about Virgil?" he asked.

"Yeah."

"Well, that's Virg to the core, I guess," Matt said. He climbed the steps, going wide around Ty, as if to avoid even a chance brushing of sleeves. Pausing at the front door, he added, "I bought two tickets for the *Alice McQueen.* She leaves Friday morning at ten. Keith and I will be on it, but there's room for you if you want to come."

"I think I'll stay."

Matt nodded. "I thought as much. I made arrangements for us to meet at Lobenstein's Friday morning at eight. We'll settle up then, and you can either buy out Keith and me, or we'll sell our share to Lobenstein. Lobenstein said he'd have the paperwork ready, whichever way we decide to go." He opened the door without waiting for a reply, and disappeared inside.

Keith seemed embarrassed by his older brother's brusqueness. "He doesn't mean to be that way, Ty. You know he and Wade were good friends."

"Yeah. We all were, once." Ty stood and put on his hat.

"Where are you staying? Mother Tucker's got a spare bed, if you're interested."

"I think I'll bunk down at Becker and Miles," Ty replied. "I'll want to start shoeing the oxen as soon as Flannigan can get started."

"You're going back out again so soon?"

"Thought I might." He stepped onto the gravel path, nodded once, and said, "I'll see you Friday."

TEN

It was still dark when Wolf Tail threw his robe back and sat up. A cold, high plains wind, birthed in the snowy mountain ranges to the west, flowed over his lean, supple body. Gooseflesh pimpled the sun-burnished skin of his arms and thighs, and his tiny nipples puckered in the chill air. He rose to stand amid his rumpled bed of buffalo robes, naked save for his moccasins, and lifted his arms to the sighing currents, breathing deep of the clean, sweet air tinged with just a hint of distant pine. Soon, he knew, the knifing winds of winter would replace these more congenial zephyrs; ice and snow and bitter cold would savage the land. But in this ebbing Moon of Leaves Falling, the young Pawnee could still luxuriate in the cool breeze that bathed his body, could drink thirstily of the powerful elixir that was autumn.

Though the season was fading, the same

could not be said of Wolf Tail. Ten plus ten plus two summers had he seen upon these wild and glorious plains. Good summers they had been, too, times of plenty, of food and friends and swift horses, of young, sloe-eyed women, and widows who had already experienced the joys of lovemaking and hungered for more, once their time of grief was finished. And perhaps most important to a young, brash warrior of Wolf Tail's character was the strength of his people's enemies — the Sioux, Arapaho, Cheyenne, Comanche, and Kiowa — whose lands bordered those claimed by the Pawnee. For how else was a Nation to measure its greatness if not by the brawn of its enemies?

Wolf Tail knew that many of the elders disagreed with this ancient philosophy, pointing out in their maddeningly patient way that there had been a time when the Pawnees did not worry so much about the future of their Nation *as* a nation. The elders of the tribe, this segment of Skidi Pawnees sometimes referred to as Wolf People, spoke almost wistfully of a time before the growing tide of whites had appeared from the east. A time when their most pressing concerns had been for the migrations of the buffalo, their crops of *maize* and squash, the appeasements of their spiritual allies, and warfare with their neighbors.

But all that had changed with the coming of the white man, an event presaged long before the arrival of the first bearded pale-skin by guns, kettles, beads, steel-bladed knives, and tomahawks — artifacts of a tribe whose medicine was far more powerful than anything the Wolf People had ever encountered — trickling into their lands for a generation before actual contact.

The Pawnees had awaited the appearance of the white man with a mixture of anticipation and dread — anxious to receive for themselves what at first only their enemies possessed, yet equally fearful that whatever forces guided this alien race might ultimately destroy their own, as the heel of a man's moccasin could crush an ant without ever knowing of its murder.

Their apprehensions had been unfounded, however. For more than one hundred and fifty summers the white traders had come to their villages to barter wealth beyond measure for the robes and furs that the Mother, Earth, provided her children without charge. There had been many changes in that time. The language of the white-eyes had switched from French to Spanish to English, and occasionally back again. Their flags had changed color and design often, as had their dress, while their methods of doing business had evolved in both good and bad directions. Yet the tide had continued, the old ones were quick to point out, the numbers of white men coming onto the central plains growing steadily, the pace of that growth increasing rapidly just within the last generation. Soon, they predicted, the white man would devour their land as they had already devoured the lands of the eastern tribes, and expect the proud Wolf People to huddle like frightened rats on tiny reservations, while their more aggressive neighbors to the north, west, and south continued to raid freely.

The thought of such an ignominious downfall was almost too much for the younger members of the tribe to even imagine. In their minds, the lands along the lower Platte, Republican, and Loup Rivers had always belonged to the Pawnees, just as they had always been infested with the hair-faces. But there was nothing to fear in that. The white-eyes were strong, true, but no more so than the Comanches or Sioux. Their words were strange, the rituals of their holy men baffling, but were these things to strike terror in the heart of a warrior?

Wolf Tail had grown up listening to the

words of the white men — traders, missionaries, agents — but he did not believe in those words. It was better, he had decided long ago, to trade with the white men, and try to get along with them. But it would not be wise to trust them, for in trust lay the Pawnees' vulnerability.

A soft chuckle sounded from the darkness nearby. "My brother must be eager to follow the warrior's path, that he would arise so early," someone said in a voice still husky with sleep.

Smiling, Wolf Tail lowered his arms. "And can you say you are not also eager for this day, my friend?"

A nearby lump of buffalo robes stirred languidly. Then the face of Hides in the Grass poked out of the furry warmth like a turtle from its shell to greet the cold morning air. "It is true," Wolf Tail's oldest friend agreed. "I had a hard time falling asleep last night, thinking of what we begin today."

"Aieee," Wolf Tail said softly, in respect of those who still sought the luxury of sleep. "Today it is good to be a warrior of the Pawnee."

"Every day it is good to be a warrior of the Pawnee," Hides in the Grass asserted, throwing his robes back. "But today, when a man prepares for the war trail, it is especially good."

The two men dressed quickly. It took only moments to retighten the thongs on their moccasins and secure their belts around their waists before slipping on their breechcloths. Wolf Tail found his knife within the folds of his robe and slid the painted rawhide sheath into his belt above his naked left hip, then picked up a small leather pouch. He and Hides in the Grass started down the slope toward the river bottom, where a herd of several hundred horses and mules dozed and grazed along the near bank of the South Fork of the Republican.

At this point near its source, the moody river Wolf Tail knew so well along its lower reaches was hardly more than a trickle — twisted black ribbons of shallow water wending their many paths over a broad, sandy bed. Here, on these high, cactus-studded plains many days travel west of the Pawnees' traditional homelands, where the determined buffalo hunters had been forced to venture in search of the elusive herds; here, where the Cheyenne dwelled, and the Arapaho and Sioux hunted, here, the Pawnee had come to make the meat that they would turn into jerky and pemmican to see them through the arctic moons to come, to take the robes and hides that would clothe and shelter them, and bring them wealth from the white traders.

And here, as well, where Wolf Tail, Hides in the Grass, and a dozen other young braves would leave the larger hunting party to make one last raid against their enemies before the blustery winds of winter forced them inside their humped-earth lodges until the spring grasses once more reached for a warming sun. They would leave from this place, it was decided, so that the white missionaries and traders and Indian agents would not hear of their plans, and rush like small children to tattle to the Great White Father in the East, thus jeopardizing the annuities the Father sent them so that they would remain at peace.

Wolf Tail and Hides in the Grass skirted the pony herd to drop to a narrow shelf along the river. Already in the east the first gray streaks of dawn were fracturing the night's delicate grip, and there was much to be done yet if they wanted to be gone before the camp fully awoke.

At the river they found several others already at their ablutions — shifting, nebulous forms dotting the riverbed like flickering shadows against the pale sand. Veering upstream, Wolf Tail jumped a narrow channel to a hummock where the twisted white branch of dead ash jutted from the head of the shoal. Kneeling in the damp sand, he took a small round mirror from his pouch and propped it on the limb so that its surface caught the faint reflection of the dawn. From the same pouch he removed his paints, razor, and grease, laying them out in an orderly fashion at his side. He shaved first, using the pearl-handled straight-edge he'd traded from the whites. More by feel than sight, he wet the stubble on his head with handfuls of icy water, then ran the six-inch steel blade cautiously over his scalp, careful not to dip into his grease-stiffened roach — a heavy, three-inch wide strip of hair that ran from his forehead to the base of his neck, where a short braid wrapped in otter's fur brushed his shoulders. When he'd finished shaving, he dipped a fingerful of bear grease out of a container carved from the base of an elk's antler and applied it to his roach. Wolf Tail was proud of his hair, and wanted all who saw it to envy its dark, raven-like sheen; especially his enemies, who he knew would appreciate its uniqueness, and take extra risks to add it to their scalp poles. That was why he pampered it so, decorating it with small beads and owl feathers, why he kept the elk-antler tube of grease with him, even on raids. His hair was a means of taunting those he fought, a trophy to be flaunted in their faces but never surrendered.

By the time Wolf Tail was ready to apply his paint, the light had grown enough that he could see himself clearly in the mirror. He was meticulous with his paints, knowing that the proper applications were in large part what kept him out of harm's way during battle. He had paid a medicine man three good mules to help him interpret the best and most powerful designs — black across his lower face to represent death; red over his forehead and freshly shaved pate, in honor of the blood he would let; and yellow in a horizontal band that ran from ear to ear across the bridge of his nose and encompassed both eyes, the color of the sun that guided him through the darkest nights, the brightest days.

He added blue from a powder base mixed with water that he had purchased from a trader — the color being hard to find in a natural state, save from the guano of certain species of geese — to his torso in small, thumb-sized circles. On his legs he traced zigzag patterns of yellow to give him the speed of lightning, and around each ankle he added a band of red, further representation of the blood and gore he intended to spill.

When he was done, Wolf Tail rocked back on his heels and washed his hands in the stream. Picking up the mirror, he examined himself critically for flaws. Only when he was satisfied that everything was correct did he repack his paints and razor. Dipping another glop of grease from the elkhorn tube, he carefully smeared it over his body between the paint until his flesh seemed to glisten in the new morning light. Then he packed the elkhorn away, washing his hands a final time by using sand to scour the grease.

Standing, he discovered Hides in the Grass and three or four others waiting for him on the bank. Behind them, the Pawnee hunting camp was coming to life. A few fires already dotted the broad plain, and some of the women were drifting toward the pony herd to catch their pack animals, eager to return to the safety of their palisaded village, to see old friends and loved ones again, and to rejoice in a successful hunt. But as much as anything, Wolf Tail knew, they were keen to leave this land of the Cheyennes behind them, for they had been lucky this year, and able to claim the meat they needed without loss of life.

"Are you pretty enough, Wolf Tail?" Hides in the Grass asked glibly. "Or should we wait until Sun has shown himself, so that you can admire yourself in full light?"

Assuming a fierce scowl, Wolf Tail scampered up the bank. Tugging on one of Hides in the Grass' long braids, he asked, "And you, Hides in the Grass, are you warm enough under all that hair?"

Hides in the Grass laughed. "Yes," he replied simply, and the others laughed with him. Of the raiding party — fourteen strong in all — only Wolf Tail, Short Bird, Catches His Horse, and Heavy Badger sported the roached hairstyle normally associated with Pawnee fashion. "Come," Hides in the Grass added. "Soon the hunters will be up, and I do not wish to listen to their twittering about our late start."

A figure approached from the camp. Wolf Tail smiled warmly when he recognized his younger brother, Running Horse. Running Horse stopped a short distance away, and Wolf Tail went to meet him. As he drew close, Running Horse held out a bow made of sturdy *bois d'arc,* wrapped tightly in the cured skin of a rattlesnake, the diamond pattern of the scales aligned perfectly along the flat face; with it came a quiver made from a panther's skin, filled with some two dozen iron-tipped arrows. Running Horse handed these weapons to his brother reverently, but his dark eyes shone with excitement. Wolf Tail accepted the bow and quiver with a dignity honoring Running Horse's pride in his oldest brother. He knew Running Horse wished to accompany the warriors on this foray against the Kiowas and Comanches, but at ten summers, he was still too young, especially for a horse-stealing raid that custom decreed must be started afoot.

"Soon," Wolf Tail promised, in answer to the longing he saw in Running Horse's eyes, even as he accepted the steel-headed tomahawk and long coil of rawhide rope his brother held out to him.

"Soon," Running Horse echoed as Wolf Tail slid the 'hawk's handle through his belt at the small of his back, then draped the *reata* over his right shoulder.

Next Wolf Tail received his fusil, the smooth-bore flintlock trade gun he cherished because he had taken it from the hands of a dead Lakota warrior, along with his first scalp. He slipped the powder horn and shooting bag over his left shoulder, opposite the *reata*. In addition to the paraphernalia needed to fire his trade gun, the bag contained an extra pair of moccasins, flint and steel and tow, and a small bundle of jerky. It would be all he would take with him on this long journey south, all he would need if his medicine was good. He slipped his pouch of paints, mirror, and razor into the oversized bag so that he might touch up the designs before battle, then placed a hand on Running Horse's shoulder. "Go on," he said. "There is much to be done before the others are safely returned to their homes. Your young eyes will be needed."

Running Horse made a face, knowing Wolf Tail only sought to appease him, but then turned and headed for camp. Wolf Tail looked at the others; one by one, they nodded. Biting back a smile of anticipation, Wolf Tail started across the flat plain east of the pony herd. He was soon joined by the others, appearing silently from the shrinking shadows until all fourteen warriors had come together in a long, sinuous line. Wolf Tail led, and as the last man joined the column, he lifted his pace to a jog, an easy, mile-eating gait he knew he could maintain all day if he had to.

Back at the Pawnee camp, Running Horse watched the warriors disappear into an arroyo, dreaming of the day when he would lead his own raiding party.

■ ■ ■ ■

On the fourth day after leaving the corpse-strewn clearing in the valley of the Neosho, Clay halted his party at the edge of the Santa Fe Trail. Bracing both hands on top his saddlehorn, he leaned forward to ease his weight from the saddle, studying the broad expanse of rutted tracks and dried dung that cut diagonally across their route. A small woods grew just off the Trail, half embracing a spring-fed pond, the ground around it worn to hardpan and spotted like an appaloosa's rump with the black ashes of old campfires. Although the place was obviously a favorite camping stop for travelers, there was no sign that anyone had used it recently.

Plato, Jenny, and Sammy Lee drifted up around him, staring silently at the well-marked road. They looked exhausted, Clay thought, wrung out by hard miles and an unrelenting fear that had dogged them ever since leaving the Neosho. But Clay suspected the road to Santa Fe would change that. It did for him. Here was something tangible, a clearly defined objective attained after days of flight across an open and immutable landscape, proof at last that they had indeed been making progress, putting the past behind them.

"My, oh, my," Plato exhaled, sliding awkwardly to the ground. "These ol' hips of mine be mighty glad to see this. We'll take us a rest here."

Sammy Lee dismounted and began to loosen the cinch on his saddle. Jenny was already ranging into the trees, looking for firewood. Although there were still a couple of hours of daylight left, it was plain they all expected to stop there, within sight of the Trail. Arching to chase a kink from his lower back, Plato said, "By the sweet Almighty, that be a purty sight." Smiling over his shoulder at the others, he added, "Take us to Mexico, that road will."

"That road'll take us any damn place we please," Sammy Lee declared.

But Plato's face had sobered when he saw Clay still astride his pinto. "You gonna get down, son?" he asked. "I reckon we earned us a spell of relaxin'."

Sammy Lee pulled the saddle off his horse and dumped it in a drift of leaves at the base of a tree. His brows furrowed, watching Clay. "There's no point in going on today. We can camp here where there's wood and water, and decide tonight what we want to do tomorrow."

175

"I reckon not," Clay said, his gaze lingering on the road.

Plato came back to stand beside the pinto, putting his hand on the gelding's shoulder. "This here be a white man's world, son, this here Kansas. It ain't no place to try to make it on your lonesome. Only way folks like us is gonna survive is if we stick together. Surely you done seen that with the Captain and them. Only reason we be free today is 'cause we stuck together. It just saddens my ol' heart that James and Missy and Nate ain't with us."

"There's wisdom in your words, dad, and I won't argue it. But I have to follow my own trail."

"What trail be that, son?"

Clay was silent for a moment, thinking. It occurred to him that in the months since Simon's death he had been little more than a feather hounded by wayward winds, blown this way and that by the fancy of others. His brief stint in bondage had opened his eyes, had made him realize just how much he'd lost sight of his own strengths and abilities. Straightening in his saddle, he said, "To tell you the truth, I'm not quite sure, but I reckon I'll know it when I see it."

Plato moved his hand to Clay's knee, squeezing gently. "We need you here, Clay, amongst us. You need us, too, though you can't see that just yet. But we need you real bad, son." He glanced at Sammy Lee, standing above his saddle, and Jenny beside him, clutching an armload of deadwood. "It ain't fair I got to say this th'out talkin' it over with ever'one first, but we got to go to Mexico. It was where I was headin' when Carry's men snared me. Bunch of folks gettin' together up in a town they call Omaha, figurin' on goin' to Mexico together, where it be warmer than that north country. Black folks is already there, they say. Now we all got to go, get shet of this country. We can be free in Mexico, and forgit 'bout what happened back there on that ol' Neosho."

"We wouldn't be any freer in Mexico than we are right here," Sammy Lee said. He put his hand on one of the ivory-handled Colts holstered at his waist. "Freedom isn't won by flight, old man."

Plato looked fearfully at Clay. "See what I mean? What's gonna happen if we don't all stick together? We got to find our place in that there Mexican desert, just like ol' Moses done in the Bible. Don't matter if it takes us forty years to do it, either. Them that comes behind will enjoy the freedom we found for them. Be a warm freedom, too. Help a man's hips."

"It'll get even hotter when some Mexican comes along to take it away," Sammy Lee interjected harshly.

Clay looked at Jenny. "What about you?"

"I'm goin' to Cherry Creek," she said adamantly. "I got plans of my own."

Dropping his gaze to Plato, Clay said, "It looks like you're bucking a stacked deck."

Plato let his hand fall from Clay's knee. Sadness wrenched Clay's heart, but he hardened himself against it. He had his own future to explore. Gathering the pinto's reins, he said, "Watch your backtrail, dad, and good luck to you. Damnit," he twisted in the saddle to take in Sammy Lee and Jenny, "good luck to all of you."

No one spoke as Clay rode away, the packhorses breaking away to follow on their own accord. When he reached the Santa Fe Trail, he tightened his jaw determinedly and kicked the pinto into a trot.

It was after dark when Clay hauled up on the outskirts of Leavenworth City. He felt vaguely intimidated by the sprawling field of lights spread out before him. When he'd asked a Shawnee farmer near the headwaters of the Wakarusa where he might find the best prices for his robes and furs, the Indian had convinced him Leavenworth was the place to go. "It's smaller than Westport or Topeka," the Shawnee said, "but there's a man there named Lobenstein who'll treat you fairly."

That had been early yesterday, the morning after leaving Plato, Jenny, and Sammy Lee beside the Trail. Since then Clay hadn't had any trouble finding people to help him sort out a route to Leavenworth. He hadn't realized how many roads there were in eastern Kansas, though; even the Santa Fe Trail had several feeder pikes running into it from different cities. Plus there was the Oregon Trail and the military road to Fort Riley, which some people were already calling the Smoky Hill Trail, not to mention the numerous rutted lanes that led to small farms, trading posts, and isolated settlements. Although in many ways it reminded him of the roads and trails back in the Nations, it would have been a difficult maze to work out if there hadn't been so many farms along the way where he could stop and ask directions.

Clay's biggest surprise as he wound his way through the increasingly wooded hills toward Leavenworth was the number of Indians he kept running into. It seemed as if three out of every four farms he approached were owned by a member of some tribe, relocated from one of the eastern states. Besides Shawnees, he met Delawares, Potowatomies, Kickapoos, Iowas, and even a couple of old-timers from the Sac and Fox Confederation, who regaled him with stories of the hell they'd raised over in Illinois during the Black Hawk War in the thirties, where they'd had a pretty good time of it, they agreed, until the long knives finally whipped their butts and sent them out here to live.

Everyone Clay talked to was open and friendly, and warmed up even more when they learned he'd grown up in the Choctaw Nation and considered himself a member of that tribe. But many of them seemed confused about his intentions. Several asked if he was on a mission for his master; others wondered if he intended to purchase his freedom with the robes and furs he carried on his pack animals. Although the issue of slavery in Kansas was a familiar topic everywhere he went, few of the people he talked to thought the anti-slavery vote stood much of a chance. Kansas was a free state for the time, one old Kickapoo told him, but it wouldn't stay that way very long. And a Sac cautioned him away from Leavenworth altogether.

"There are a lot of pro-slavery people

around Leavenworth right now," the Indian stated gravely. "Border trash from Missouri and farther south, mostly, who want to see the vote go in support of slavery. If I were you, I'd go to Topeka. A lot of anti-slavery people live in Topeka."

"I've heard of a tanner in Leavenworth called Lobenstein," Clay replied. "They say he gives the best prices in Kansas for robes and furs."

"I have also heard of this man, Lobenstein," the Sac acknowledged. "They say he is fair, though shrewd. But you'd better be careful. The Border Ruffians around Leavenworth want to see slavery legalized in the territory. They don't care how much money this man Lobenstein gives for a buffalo robe."

Clay tried to dismiss the Sac's warning by telling himself he was a free man, and that he could by damn come and go as he pleased, but as he drew closer to the Missouri border he finally had to acknowledge that Captain Carry and his band of thieves had seriously shaken that conviction.

Coming north out of the Nations, Clay hadn't given much thought to what he would do after selling his pelts, other than try to find a place for himself among the white-eyes. But now, with the warnings of

Plato and the Sac echoing in his mind, and the feel of Captain Carry's iron collar still imprinted on the flesh of his neck, he began to question the wisdom of that plan.

As he rode slowly eastward, Clay's thoughts kept returning to the Kiowas, and his attempt earlier that year to go back to them. Although he hadn't forgotten the monotony of his summer among the Wichita, he couldn't help believing that life with one of the wilder tribes might prove more stimulating, and in some ways at least, safer. But would the Kiowa accept him? Would they remember Night's Son, the child who had been abducted by the Osage so many years before? Would they believe him when he told them he had returned out of his love for the People? Or would they think him a spy for one of the eastern tribes, or even the long knives?

The prospects looked gloomy all the way around until Clay finally decided he had little choice but to go on, and then decide after selling his robes and pelts what he wanted to do.

He was close enough to town by the time darkness fell that he decided to go on in and take his chances. It wasn't difficult to find the commercial district. A long stretch of brick buildings, many of them two and three stories tall, guided him toward the river. He wound his pack string through the muddy streets until he came to a livery sitting on the shallow bluff above the Missouri River. Although the doors ware closed, there was a lantern glowing from an iron hook over the side door. Clay swung in at a hitch rail and stepped down. A knock brought the nightwatchman grumbling to the door, but he hauled up sharply when he saw Clay, a scowl drawing his features taut.

"Costs money to stable your horses here, boy," the watchman said. He was a slightly built gnome of a man, with pieces of straw caught in the sparse fringe of silver hair that flanked his bald pate. His eyes were puffy from sleep, his clothes rumpled.

Heat flushed Clay's face, but he kept his voice calm. "How much?"

"Two bits a head. A nickel more if you want 'em grained."

"Open the doors," Clay said flatly. "And I'll want fresh straw in the stalls, too."

The watchman hesitated, but then stepped back and closed the side door. A moment later one of the larger double doors swung outward, and Clay led his horses inside. The watchman pulled the lantern off the outside hook and brought it into the entryway.

"Down at the far end and on the left," the

watchman muttered after pocketing Clay's money. "You can have the last three stalls, though I reckon you'll have to double up with a couple of your ponies." He set the lantern on a nail keg and disappeared into a modified stall next to the side door, where a cot and a leather-bound trunk resided, and clothes hung from nails driven into the walls.

Clay led his horses to the rear of the barn. The stalls were large enough to accommodate two animals, and already bedded with bright yellow straw. He stripped the saddles and packs from the horses and doubled all four into two stalls, then lugged his gear and the bundles of robes and furs into the third stall, where he loosened his bedroll from the back of his saddle and spread it out on the straw. He returned the lantern to its outside hook, then pulled the big door shut and latched it. As he made his way back through the darkness to the last stall, the watchman hollered, "I don't abide snorers."

"Good for you," Clay called back. He took off his hat and moccasins and gunbelt and placed them next to his bed. The mackinaw he hung on the end of the stall; although it hadn't rained in several days, the heavy garment was still damp. Then he crawled into his robe and pulled it up to his chin. He lay that way for a long time, staring into the inky shadows of the rafters while his thoughts wandered back over the past few weeks. A hard, cold lump formed slowly in his throat, until finally he rolled onto his side and pulled the robe over his ears. "Welcome to the land of the white-eyes," he murmured to himself, just before falling asleep.

ELEVEN

In Red Creek, Choctaw Nation, the mantel clock in Moses Gray's parlor began to chime the hour. At its first strike, Moses' head popped up, a wild, feral expression distorting his features until he remembered where he was — who he was.

With recall there came a low, pitiful moan, and he slumped back in his leather-upholstered chair, letting his head fall against the padded headrest. Listening to the melodious tolling from the next room, he counted an even dozen strokes to mark the witching hour of midnight. Then his gaze dropped to the broad, empty expanse of mahogany desktop in front of him, and a wave of revulsion surged through him like a jolt of cheap river whiskey. How many times, he wondered, had he sat at this very spot and listened to the parlor clock strike midnight? How many gallons of lamp oil had he burned in pursuit of a few more acres to add to his already vast holdings, a few more head of cattle or horses or mules to enlarge his far-flung herds, a few more dollars to swell his Fort Smith bank account? How many hours had he spent at this very desk, erecting an ever-thickening barrier between Moses Gray the entrepreneur, and the sickly, half-starved youth called Gray Boy, who had nearly perished along the Trail of Tears?

In days past, the dark surface of Moses' desk had been cluttered with dispatches, ledgers, quotes, and bills of lading — business communications from as far away as Memphis and New Orleans, and as near as Jack's Fork and Fort Gibson. Those days were gone now, their paper remains swept in an unorganized pile into the desk drawer beside his left knee by the shriveled limb that had once been his right arm.

Lifting the warped appendage from his lap, Moses exposed it to the flickering lamplight with much the same repugnance he might have bestowed on a dead rat found bloated behind the kitchen stove. The sniper's bullet had taken him in the elbow, shattering the joint and wreaking havoc with the nerves and tendons that once controlled his wrist and fingers.

After the shooting, Moses had been taken

to Fort Smith, Arkansas, in a spring wagon rigged with a feather mattress, but by the time he arrived there wasn't much a frontier sawbones could do. The doctor had urged amputation, but Moses refused. In a delirium of pain, fever and morphine, he had been unwilling to accept the full extent of the damage, and so, cursing the doctor as an Indian hater and a charlatan, he'd returned to the Choctaw Nation in the same spring wagon that had delivered him to Fort Smith.

In an ever-deepening, drug-enhanced fog, Moses had retreated to his house in Red Creek. From there he'd sent word throughout the Nations that he would pay one thousand dollars in gold to anyone who could reduce the pain in his right arm, and return it to normal function. The promise of such wealth had quickly flushed out just about every quack and faith healer within a two hundred mile radius, but neither rattlesnake venom tea nor goat dung and honey poultices had been of any help. As the summer waned, Moses began to turn away those who came to his door promising relief, but his arm continued to wither, a grotesque reminder of the price some men paid for success.

Moses returned the deformity to the

shadows of his lap. A half-empty bottle of Kentucky bourbon sat on the desk in front of him, and with his left hand he awkwardly thumbed the cork from its mouth and let it bounce to the floor. With a trembling hand, he filled the shot glass, sneering at the liquor splashed across the desk's surface. Before the shooting, he would have considered such an accident unpardonable, but now it elicited only a sardonic dismissal. Bringing the bourbon to his lips, he downed it in two fiery swallows.

Enjoying the harsh burn of too much bourbon drunk too fast, Moses tipped his head back and closed his eyes. He knew he should go to bed, try to catch a few hours sleep before dawn awakened the noisy rooster his wife, Sally, kept in the coop behind the house. He needed to ride down to the plantation to see how the harvest was progressing, a task he had been putting off for several weeks now. In theory, Moses had twenty fieldhands shucking over two hundred and fifty acres of corn. In reality, the whole operation was in the hands of an overseer with a confirmed fondness for Red Deer Carter's smuggled whiskey, so there was no telling what might actually be happening.

In past years the harvest had kept Moses

as restless as a catamount on a short leash. He'd stayed at the plantation day and night until the last boll of cotton had been baled, the last ear of corn gleaned, the last sheaf of tobacco hung to dry in the open-sided sheds behind the cattle barn. He'd kept his blood bay thoroughbred lathered as he spurred from field to field, haranguing the slaves to work harder and be less wasteful, pushing his overseer to get more out of the lazy, black-skinned bastards.

And at night, in the two-story log plantation house, he had been unmerciful in his couplings with one or more of the four Negresses he kept there, away from the mournful eyes of his wife.

During the harvest, driving the men like dogs and treating the women even worse, Moses Gray had been able to achieve an almost maniacal sense of euphoria; his every whim was catered to without question, its speedy completion guaranteed by the black coil of bullwhip strapped to his gunbelt.

On Red Creek Plantation, Moses Gray was god, and woe be to the man or beast who invoked his wrath.

Or so it had been until the cultivating season last spring, when a petulant little Indian-raised Negro named Clay Little Bull had fired a bullet through the downstairs bedroom window of the plantation house, where Moses had been bedding one of his wenches.

Moses stiffened now, as the memory resurfaced, his face screwing into a mask of outrage, his right arm flinching unconsciously at the shoulder. He'd never questioned that the sniper was Clay, even though a lot of people did; the theft of property from the Little Bull farm had been too damning to rattle Moses' conviction of Clay's guilt. As the summer advanced, so did his thoughts of revenge — or justice, as he preferred to call it.

At first Moses hadn't been particular about its execution, and had even written a business associate in Tennessee who dealt in slaves and livestock to offer him the unbroken Negro at a reasonable price. But after several weeks of morphine and bourbon, Moses had capriciously changed his mind. He put out the word that he wanted Clay Little Bull for himself, and that he was willing to pay five hundred dollars to any man, woman, or child instrumental in bringing the renegade African in.

When Moses learned that Clay had gone west to trade with the wild tribes, he'd feared he would never see him again, and his mood had deteriorated badly. But just

191

as the tobacco harvest was beginning in earnest, word arrived that Little Bull had been spotted in the Cross Timbers, traveling east with several packhorses in tow. Moses' determination to see justice served had been swiftly reignited, but before he could even gather a decent posse, someone had tipped Clay off to the danger awaiting him in Red Creek, causing the wily fugitive to flee before Moses' men could reach him.

Moses kept his posse together for a month, sending it out in fragmented groups to comb the surrounding hills, but nothing was ever found, not even a pony track. Some folks said Clay went to Kansas, others that he'd gone south into Texas. He was seen by a paid informant crossing a ferry into Arkansas, then spotted the next day reentering the Cross Timbers on his way back west. It seemed the only thing everyone did agree on was that hell would freeze over before Clay Little Bull's shadow ever darkened the Choctaw Nation again.

Moses Gray had been infuriated when he finally accepted Clay's escape. In a rage, he'd gunned down his five best coon hounds. Then he'd stumbled into the house he kept in Red Creek and locked himself in the study with a pistol and a bottle of bourbon, and not even Sally had dared enter its shadowy interior during those first tempestuous hours.

Awakening near noon the next day, hungover and gaggy, Moses had immediately ordered the dismissal of his posse. As an afterthought, he penned a letter to his old friend, John Bear, on the Choctaw Council, asking that the Red Creek deputies Weed Jackson and Lyn Broken Horn be released from duty for incompetence. Then he'd swept the stacks of paperwork on his desk into the drawer beside his knee, announcing in a childish display of temper his intention to focus all of his energy on Clay's capture.

Since then, Moses had simmered in the juices of indecision. He rarely ventured out of his study, and only left the house to visit the honeysuckle-covered privy out back, and that only after dark, so frightened was he of being seen by others — judged by them, laughed at by them.

The great Moses Gray, they snickered in his mind. *Cut down like a bear from a tree by a half-wild savage.*

The voices haunted Moses Gray's dreams nightly, and often made him cringe during the day. In some dim recess of his mind, he knew that things were getting out of hand. His consumption of bourbon and morphine was on the rise, and thoughts of revenge dominated his thoughts. But the ever-increasing pain in his right arm refused to allow him the luxury of ignoring what had been so brutally taken away, both physically and in the quality of his status in the tribe. The people of the Choctaw Nation had to be taught that no one crossed Moses Gray without suffering appropriate consequences. He had lived his life by that code; he wouldn't abandon it now.

Awkwardly, he poured another shot of bourbon. He could accept that the law had failed him, as had the Council and the men he'd hired to bring in Little Bull. There were always other means of accomplishing a goal once a person set his mind to it, though, and the more Moses considered the task at hand, the more convinced he became that Jacques Peliter was the man to accomplish it. If anyone could ferret out Little Bull's trail, no matter in which direction it might lead or how cold it had become, if anyone could penetrate either the white man's bricked and cobbled world or the harsh environs of the western Indians, it would be that stone-hearted French Canadian with the cold, gray killer's eyes.

Pulling open a desk drawer, Moses extracted a sheet of good linen stationery, a bell-shaped bottle of ink, and a mechanical pen. Cursing his clumsiness, he began to scrawl out a letter of hire with his left hand. He'd barely finished the salutation when a chill passed down his spine, and his heart beat a little quicker. Looking up, his red-rimmed eyes widened when he saw Sally standing at the open door of his study, an enigmatic half smile on her lips.

"Let him go," she said in Choctaw. "Let him live out his life in peace."

Staring into the emotionless pits of his wife's dark eyes, Moses unconsciously licked his lips. "Someone has to pay," he replied raspily.

"Someone has already paid," Sally reminded him, the words soft as a summer's breeze, cold as the bottom of a grave.

She moved away from the door without the slightest sound, and for a long time afterward Moses listened for the creak of steps that would mark her passage upstairs to her own private bedroom. He never heard the steps, nor the sound of a door opening or closing, but after a while the chill passed and he knew she had either left — or had never been there at all.

Christian Lobenstein's private office was a small, chilly compartment just off the main counting room. It had pale green walls and a high, whitewashed ceiling. The floor was bare, tracked with dried mud, the windows streaked and dirty, the sashes littered with dead flies and a mesh of snowy cobwebs. A sturdy but undecorative desk faced the door. A small, potbellied stove occupied one of the inner walls; a row of wooden file cabinets lined another. A floor safe stood in one corner on steel rollers, a European hunting scene painted on its closed door.

In addition to these sparse and neglected furnishings, someone had added a trio of chairs arranged in a shallow curve in front of Lobenstein's desk, with an ashstand and spittoon nearby for smokers or spitters.

Tyler Calhoun sat in the chair closest to the window. The Burdettes occupied the other two chairs, and behind the broad desk Christian Lobenstein absently drummed his fingers.

Although he was still relatively young, the hide dealer's thick hair and dense beard were already showing a few iron-gray splinters. His face was broad and firm, the flesh radiating outward from his deep-set eyes fractured by crow's-feet. He was heavyset and somber — given to bouts of depression that sometimes lasted for months — but he had been an old friend of Ty's father, the two men having met years before in the gold fields of California. He had proved to be a good friend to Ty, too, and had helped finance their first season's expedition to the buffalo ranges. Given their history, it seemed only natural that, with the partnership drawing to a close, they should return once more to Lobenstein's office.

The meeting had been strained but cordial. Matt retained his air of indifference, while Keith mostly just sat and looked morose, only occasionally adding comment to something his brother or Ty said. The dickering had been brief, and to Ty's surprise, more than fair. The two brothers had sat up late the previous evening hammering out the terms they would seek. Despite Matt's aloofness, the deal he outlined that morning was almost more than Ty was willing to accept. Stiff-lipped, he had argued that he wasn't a charity case, that his credit was good with both Lobenstein and the company of Becker and Miles; what he couldn't raise in cash, he could easily fill out with a note of credit from one or the other of those firms.

But Matt was adamant. With the funds the five partners had accumulated over the past two years, they had been able to pay off all of their debts and still have a little cash left over, not to mention the partnership's property — including two wagons, eight yoke of oxen, three saddle horses, basic camp items, and some specialty gear such as cases of skinning knives, farrier tools, a foot-trundled grinding stone, and a six man wall tent they seldom used but kept just in case. What was left, financially, was marginal, but still more than any of them would have made back in Toledo.

"The venture paid for itself," Matt declared as the final figures were tallied. "I'm satisfied."

Lobenstein's gaze narrowed. "You are sure of this, Matthew? A much better price you could get for the Hamilton and Finn wagon, from the Santa Fe traders."

"Sure, if I wanted to wait around until next spring."

"Not so," Lobenstein argued. "For this price a buyer I am sure could be found within a matter of days. The money could be forwarded —"

But Matt cut him off. "No. Keith and I have already made up our minds."

"I don't like this," Ty said. "This isn't fair to either of you."

"Consider it an investment," Matt replied, "Say one percent of the profits, and you pay us off when you can."

Ty shook his head. "That's too much of a

risk. You know what it's like out there. I could go broke with just one bad season."

Matt laughed — his first in quite a while, Ty thought. "I don't anticipate you'll go broke," he said. "In fact, I have a hunch you'll do all right. You were made for this land in a way none of the rest of us ever were, Ty. You'll make it, and in the process you might just make us a little profit some day. And if not . . ." He shrugged dismissingly.

"A good deal for you, Tyler," Lobenstein put in softly.

For a moment Ty didn't know what to say. He had thought everything between them had withered with Wade's death, but now he understood that a few strong ties remained. Behind his desk, Lobenstein was smiling broadly, tears at the corners of his eyes.

In the end, Ty purchased the Burdettes' share of the outfit — the oxen and horses, wagons, camp gear, and what supplies they had brought back with them from their last trip to the prairies — for just under eighteen hundred dollars. He had to borrow some of the funds from Lobenstein to pay them off, but outfitting on credit was such a common means of business on the plains that neither Ty nor Lobenstein hesitated.

After signing the necessary paperwork, they shook hands all around. Ty offered to buy Matt and Keith a drink, but Matt declined for both of them. The *Alice McQueen* was scheduled to leave in less than half an hour, and he wanted to be on board before the first whistle blew.

"Good luck," Matt said to Ty. They shook again, and this time Matt's grip was like a vise around his old friend's hand. "Take care of yourself," he added.

Tears blurred Ty's vision as Matt turned away. He shook hands with Keith and nodded, afraid just then to try to speak. When the door shut behind the Burdettes, he took a ragged breath and walked to the window overlooking the hideyard so the tanner wouldn't see his face.

"The old country, I remember leaving her," Lobenstein said gently. "My mama and papa — all my family I said goodbye to. A hard business, that was." He walked over to the potbellied stove and lightly patted the sides of a coffeepot sitting on top. "Good," he murmured. "It is still warm, the coffee." He filled a pair of thick china mugs, then motioned to a chair. Ty sank into it, letting his muscles go slack. He accepted the mug Lobenstein offered him and sipped noisily. The hide dealer backed up to his desk, leaning against it and studying Ty. "Now we talk a little, eh?" he said. "Them Cheyenne, your scalp they going to lift, you know?"

"Not if I can get 'em to trade, instead."

"Four or five white men they might trade with," Lobenstein predicted solemnly. "One man, two, they just scalp, then take your trade goods."

Irritably, Ty said, "Those are the chances. We've done some trading in the past. It'll get better."

"Their language you do not even know. Only Oscar Garrett knows a little of the hand talk, but Oscar, he is not so reliable anymore. Four years I have been in Leavenworth now, Tyler, and never have I known Oscar Garrett to be reliable."

Oscar Garrett was one of the men they'd hired last year as a skinner and camp tender. He was an older man with stooped shoulders, baggy eyes, and a fondness for booze that was wrecking his body. But he had spent most of his life on the frontier, first as a bullwhacker on the Santa Fe Trail, then as a hunter and guide for some of the bigger outfits hauling freight in and out of Mexico. He spoke Spanish tolerably well and could get along in sign language, the universal language of the Plains Indians. But Loben-

201

stein made a valid point. Garrett had grown cranky as his body started to fail him, and frequently blamed others for mistakes that were clearly his own. He was surly, resistant to authority, temperamental, and dangerous. As a hired man, Oscar Garrett often teetered on that fine line between being a liability or an asset, almost but not quite more trouble than he was worth.

"Tyler, I do not think it would be wise to go out alone, or even with Oscar Garrett," Lobenstein continued. "Find for yourself another partner, someone a little older, with experience. And skinners, to work the hides. Six or eight men you should have. Ten would be better."

Ty laughed. "I'll be lucky to afford one man to skin for me, and a good partner isn't easy to find." He didn't add that he was feeling a certain amount of excitement at the prospect of being on his own for the first time in his life, and that although a partner made sense in a lot of ways, he wasn't going to hook up with some sorejointed old mountain man just to have an extra hand along. If he went with anyone, he decided, it would be with someone closer to his own age, an equal who didn't think his every word was law, the way Oscar Garrett usually did.

Lobenstein sighed. "So now the young bucks do not listen to the wiser stags, eh? Well, you will learn, if your scalp does not go to some Indian."

Ty shrugged and sipped his coffee. It was strong as nails and about as bitter, but it was warm, and it took the edge off the chill in the room. "We'll see," was his only reply.

"And of Virgil?" Lobenstein inquired. "Wade's share we sent to his papa and his mama in Toledo, but Virgil, a one-fifth share he still owns, no?"

Ty's grip tightened around his coffee mug. "I reckon he does, if he wants to claim it."

"You watch out for that one, Tyler," Lobenstein advised. "Matthew and I, we talked of Virgil earlier this week. Neither of us trusts that one so much, you know?"

"I know, but Virgil isn't here right now, and I don't look for him to show up again."

They talked of inconsequential things for a while. Lobenstein told Ty of his years in the old country, working at his father's tannery, and of coming to America and prospecting for gold in California, before settling in Leavenworth.

"It is a good land, this Kansas," Lobenstein said. "A man can do well here with a little hard work. You have pluck, Tyler. You did not go running back home when things turned hard for you. That is a good sign, I think."

"It *is* a good land," Ty agreed, his eyes brightening with enthusiasm. "You've been out there, you've seen what it's like. It's virgin country, and largely unexplored. All I'd ever heard about the West since I was a kid was what a wonderful country the Rocky Mountains were, about all the fortunes that were made and lost out there in the beaver trade, all the adventure. I doubt if there's a pass in those mountains that hasn't been trapped a hundred times over. And all the big fur companies had to do was cross the Great American Desert to get there." He laughed at the irony of it. "But they were wrong when they dismissed the plains. They've spent the last forty years following the Platte, the Missouri, the Santa Fe Trail, but there probably aren't a dozen white men who've been where I have been these last couple of years." Ty stood, setting his cup on the hide dealer's desk so he could pace back and forth across the room. "I've seen herds of buffalo so big you couldn't ride through them in a week, wolves as thick as lice, and skunk and 'coon and beaver to fill a thousand traps. More furs, hides and meat than a man could shoot or trap in a lifetime, and it's hardly been touched."

"Some of the old-timers you talk about, they would not so much agree," Lobenstein pointed out. "The forts they have, all up and down the Missouri, and along the Front Range, too."

"There aren't any forts where I'm going," Ty replied.

"And where is that?"

"Out along the upper reaches of the Smoky Hill and Republican rivers."

Lobenstein's eyes widened. "So far out again! But why, Tyler? Surely there are hides and meat closer?"

Ty stopped pacing, a strange look coming over his face. "Why, the same reason you and Pa went to California, I guess."

Lobenstein nodded, a smile twitching his thick beard. "*Ach,* a young man's fancy, eh? The next hill he always has to see over, the next river where the hunting is a little better. All right, then. But you think about that partner thing, Tyler. That Smoky Hill country is a damn rough land. Not just the Cheyennes you got to watch for out there, but the Pawnees, the Kiowas, the Comanches, maybe even a few Arapahos and Sioux. All bad Indians, ready to lift your scalp from your head in a minute."

"I'll look around," Ty promised. He lifted his jacket from the back of the chair and set

205

his hat on his head. "Thanks for the coffee, Mr. Lobenstein, and the advice. I'll keep it in mind."

"Come," Lobenstein said, pushing away from his desk. "We will walk together to the front door."

They left the small, chilly office to pass through the counting room, where half a dozen clerks toiled over various ledgers and bills of order. Entering the main trading room, they discovered Lobenstein's chief clerk, Enoch Harker, standing red-faced behind the counter. A second man stood opposite him, a Negro in a buckskin shirt, muddy pants, and a battered felt hat from which long, loose black ringlets fell to his shoulders. A pack of wolf pelts was cut open on the floor at his feet, a couple of the hides already draped across the counter.

"Mr. Lobenstein, sir," Harker said in a pleading voice. "Would you please come over here and talk to this buck? He's wanting three dollars apiece for these pelts."

"They're Indian-tanned," the black man explained, lifting a corner of a hide and running his thumb over the glossy, silver-hued hair. "No nicks, no cuts. You won't find any better."

Lobenstein hesitated, then said to Ty, "Business calls, my young friend. But if I do not see you before, then in the spring, eh?"

"In the spring," Ty promised, shaking the hide dealer's hand.

"Good luck to you, Tyler Calhoun," Lobenstein called as Ty started for the door. "Good luck and good fortune."

Ty waved and smiled, but at the door he paused to watch as Lobenstein joined his chief clerk behind the counter. Ty eyed the black man speculatively. In his two years on the frontier he had never seen a Negro dressed as this one was. It was plain that the moccasins, the shirt, even the bedraggled feather in his hatband, were of Indian origin.

Lobenstein picked up one of the wolf pelts and ran his fingers through the thick hair.

"There's been water damage," Harker claimed, pointing to a dangling leg.

"It's just wet," the black man retorted. "It isn't ruined."

"No," Lobenstein agreed, lifting the skin to his nose and sniffing for rot. "No permanent damage do I see here, that's true." He glanced at the stack of pelts on the floor. "Another one you will give me to look at."

Ty twisted the knob and pulled the door open. Behind him, Lobenstein was asking the black man where he had gotten so many wolf pelts, and as Ty stepped outside, he heard the man reply, "Iron Hand's village of Wichitas, down on the Washita."

Outside, Ty paused to contemplate the shaggy pinto and trio of packhorses lined up at the rail. Stepping down into the drying mud of the street, he lifted a corner of oilcloth from one of the mustangs to reveal a beautifully tanned buffalo robe beneath it. Running his fingers through the thick shoulder hair, Ty whistled in appreciation; it was as fine a robe as any he had ever seen, and far better than any he'd ever traded for. He dropped the oilcloth back in place and started across the street, the black man's words hanging in his mind:

Iron Hand's village of Wichitas, down on the Washita.

Twelve

Rain Dancing On Water quickened her stride as she left the last small cluster of tipis behind. In the deepening twilight away from the village, she felt safe enough for the first time that evening to allow a smile to brush her full lips.

I go with Satank, to hunt buffalo.

Even now, her husband's words thrilled her.

Yellow Bear had made his announcement during the evening meal. He would accompany the large hunting party that Satank was organizing to explore the valleys under the caprock rim of the *llano estacado,* far to the southwest, where the village shamans had assured them they would find the herds they sought. As was the custom of the People, whom the white-eyes called *Kiowa,* during the Moon When the Leaves Turned Yellow, many of the village's women and children would follow the hunters. And if the People's medicine were good and Man Above was pleased with His children, they would return sometime during the following moon with their travois sagging under the weight of meat to supplement the poor hunting that traditionally plagued them through the long months of winter, and with hides that would be cured into leather and rawhide and robes.

But it wasn't the promise of plentiful food, or the riches that the robes and leather would buy from the Comanchero traders, that excited Rain Dancing. It was Yellow Bear's decision that he would take with him only his first two wives, Spotted Bird and Thunder Woman. Although Rain Dancing On Water had kept her countenance prudently neutral as Yellow Bear outlined his plans for the coming hunt, her heart had sung with joy.

Rain Dancing was well aware that Yellow Bear was dissatisfied with her as a wife. Daily, his tongue grew sharper, like the sting of a lead-tipped quirt, and his expression when he looked at her seldom revealed anything more than a smoldering contempt. He found fault in almost everything she did now — the wood she collected with the other women for their evening fire was always too long or too short or too green;

the hides of the deer and antelope he brought her were cured too poorly to trade; she spilled too much of the water she hauled up from the river in the pitch-lined canvas bucket he had brought back from a raid against the *tejanos,* the Texans; the bedrolls weren't rolled tightly enough, or placed far enough back in the lodge to allow sufficient room during the day. Something, always something. And soon now, he would start to question her long, nightly walks in the woods along the Prairie Dog River, strolls she told the others gave her a chance to think and grieve, while they laughed and told stories around the fire.

Yellow Bear had readily accepted her purported need for solitude at first. Perhaps he'd even welcomed her absences. But lately she'd noticed that his eyes lingered on her for long minutes as she slipped into her blanket coat. Perhaps, Rain Dancing mused, Yellow Bear still remembered the accusations her first husband had leveled against her last spring. Perhaps he also wondered why the Kiowa-Apache warrior, Goes Along, still remained in their village, rather than return to his own people to the southwest.

Perhaps. But Rain Dancing had ceased to care. She was only a fourth wife now, little more than a drudge in the lodge of Yellow Bear, and by his own admission more of a burden than a welcome addition to his home.

That home was crowded now, with Spotted Bird, who was Yellow Bear's sits-beside-him wife — his first wife — and their two children, plus Thunder Woman and Running Fawn, who along with Rain Dancing had come to Yellow Bear's lodge after their first husband had been killed by *tejanos* the previous spring. Seven people occupying a single, smoky-brown twelve-hide lodge.

Rain Dancing On Water hated it all. She couldn't move without bumping into someone, and the other women's incessant chattering reminded her of magpies on a killing field. Sometimes she thought she would go crazy if she didn't escape soon, and the promises of Spotted Bird and Thunder Woman — that the hides Yellow Bear brought back from the fall hunt would be made into a second lodge for Running Fawn, Rain Dancing, and the children, appeased her not at all. There might have been a time when she would have been content as the fourth wife of a warrior of Yellow Bear's standing, but not anymore.

Rain Dancing paused atop a bank overlooking a thicket of plums, long since harvested by the women of the village. A cool breeze swept down out of the north, fluttering her shortened hair — hair she herself had cut in mourning for her first husband. Rain Dancing shivered involuntarily. Although it was considered ill-mannered to speak the name of one who had passed over the Hanging Road to the Other Side, she was uneasy with even the thought of him, as if his presence in her life were not yet finished.

If that were so, then Rain Dancing suspected she knew the reason her first husband's spirit lingered close to the village. But she had ceased to care about that, too.

Idly, she ran a finger up the sleeve of her blanket coat to trace the healing scars on her lower arms, the wounds still puckered and pinkish where she had hacked at the flesh with her knife. She remembered all too well the day of the war party's return. The younger men, those with only a few such raids behind them, had driven a herd of stolen horses and long-eared mules numbering well over ten times ten fingers. Many of the beasts had been laden with booty plundered from the squat adobe homes of the Mexican and *tejano* villages the warriors had raided along the river the white-eyes called the Rio Grande. There had been captives, as well. Three young Mexican girls had been brought back as slaves, plus one man — a youthful, blue-eyed *Creole* whom the warriors had quickly staked out naked and spread-eagled to the ground, then promptly forgotten.

There was much to celebrate in the war party's return, but even more to lament. Five brave warriors had been killed in that distant land, among them the husband of the sisters, Thunder Woman, Running Fawn, and Rain Dancing On Water.

Rain Dancing had gone through the rituals of mourning alongside her sisters. She had cut off her hair in huge, jagged handfuls and thrown them on the ground. She had hacked at her arms with a knife until they shone with blood. She had wailed and keened, and gone without food. And, along with the others who had lost a loved one, she had extracted some small measure of release through the torture of the *Creole*. They had stripped away his flesh in tiny pieces and fed them to the dogs, so that he might watch as his own meat was devoured. They had split and mutilated his tongue until it flapped grotesquely, and smashed his teeth to bloody, nerve-exposed stumps. They had chopped off his fingers and thrown them in the fire, then dumped the cherry-red coals over his stomach, or pinched them between his toes. They had seared his eyes with a red-hot poker, and carefully popped his eardrums with bone awls. And when, after three suns, he was finally dead, they had taken his scalp and burned it, and cut off his penis and testicles and crammed them into his mouth. Then they'd dragged the body onto the plains downwind of the village and left it for the coyotes and vultures to feed on.

Rain Dancing had enjoyed the torture. Through it, she had been able to vent some of her own frustration. But she hadn't been able to share the grief her sisters felt over the death of their first husband. She had cut her hair, but not as short as theirs. She had sliced the flesh of her arms with a knife, but the gashes weren't as long nor nearly as deep. And when Thunder Woman, and then Running Fawn, had severed the ends of their pinky fingers at the first joint with a butcher knife to show the true measure of their pain, Rain Dancing had pretended not to see, and wailed all the louder so that no one would suspect her lack of anguish.

Standing above the plum thicket in the early darkness, Rain Dancing's face turned hard as stone. She had escaped one bad marriage only to land squarely in another that was just as bad, if not worse for on his deathbed, her first husband had asked his friend, Yellow Bear, to take his wives and make them his own. It was a vow Yellow Bear was determined to carry out, but he had not forgotten his friend's feelings toward his third wife, Rain Dancing. He had not failed to remember the rage that had consumed his boyhood chum upon finding her with the Kiowa-Apache, Goes Along, in the bushes along the Prairie Dog River. Her first husband's humiliation had not yet been avenged when the two men took to the warrior's trail. Now it appeared that Yellow Bear had resolved to finish the task himself, and in the process, perhaps, assuage some of his own feelings of anger and loss.

The clatter of a dry, falling leaf interrupted Rain Dancing's thoughts, and her expression softened with sudden anticipation. Throwing a hurried glance over her shoulder and seeing no one nearby, she raced down the gentle incline and into the thorny plum thicket. She followed a familiar path through the moonlit shadows until she came to a tiny clearing cushioned with tall grass. There she stopped, her gaze darting. In the center of the clearing a soft, thickly furred buffalo robe was spread over the grass hair-side up, but there was no other sign of human presence. Laughing softly, Rain Dancing ran to the robe and threw aside her blanket coat; without pause, she quickly pulled loose the leather thongs at her shoulders, letting the buckskin dress fall free, pooling at her ankles.

She stood motionless then, naked save for her moccasins, the dusky moonlight bathing her taut, walnut-hued body with silver highlights. The cool breeze touched her breasts, hardening her nipples. Like a creature of the night, sensual and earthy, she waited, growing moist and more ready at every rapid beat of her heart. She heard the whispery slide of moccasins coming up behind her, but didn't turn. Instead she arched her spine, thrusting her buttocks back expectantly. She felt his penis first, the turgid organ sliding like velvet over her loins. Long, cool fingers came to rest lightly on her ribs, then slid around and up to cup her aching breasts. His body came fully against hers, and she felt the slow, liquid sinking of her stomach, the quick, uninhibited surrender of all that she was and all that she hoped to be.

Rain Dancing and Goes Along sank to the buffalo robe, merging slowly and completely, two becoming one in their need, and all else vanishing.

■ ■ ■

Clay Little Bull halted his horse at the head of a long alleyway running between a network of pole corrals, and folded his arms over his saddlehorn. A frown knitted his brow as he eyed the shack at the far end of the alley — a squat, weathered structure of warped planks, with a crooked window flanking an equally out-of-kilter door, and a rusting stovepipe slanting from the north wall, held in place by strands of twisted wire.

The shack stood in sharp contrast to the carefully painted sign that hung from the cross beam at the head of the alley, proclaiming in bold blue lettering: *Bramberg's Stockyards,* and below that, *Horses, Mules, Cattle, Oxen, Hogs, Goats;* and still lower, *We Buy & Sell.* Hugh Bramberg's name was printed at the lower left-hand corner; *Est. 1856* was on the right. For the illiterate, the artist had sketched a draft horse on either side of the main title, the way a tinsmith might add a drawing of a candle lantern to his sign, or a saloon would prominently display an image of a foaming mug of beer.

Most of the pens were empty this late in the year. Clay saw a dozen or so Guernsey heifers in one corner of the complex, a mix of horses and mules in another corral, and could hear the plaintive bleating of a goat from one of the smaller pens out back. Several loafers cluttered the front yard of Bramberg's office, enjoying the early afternoon sunshine. From their dress, Clay pegged them as local farmers. Two of them were playing checkers on a board balanced on top of a wooden keg; the others sat or stood or squatted where they could keep an eye on the game while they talked. Even from the alley's entrance, Clay could see the blue haze of pipe smoke that hung over them in the still air.

He straightened and gathered the pinto's reins. Based on what he'd heard in Leavenworth, he figured he was up against an even more formidable foe in Hugh Bramberg than he had been with Christian Lobenstein, and that damn old tight-fisted Dutchman had been nearly the death of him, squeezing every nickel twice before letting it drop into Clay's outstretched palm. Still, he'd done all right with his furs and robes, garnering even a little more than he'd hoped for, although he'd had to work hard for it. Now he wanted to sell his Indian ponies, and everyone he talked to said Bramberg was probably the only dealer around who'd buy livestock this late in the year.

Clay nudged the pinto with his heels, leading the mustangs down the alley. One of the checker players looked up as he drew near, then leaned toward the door and spoke inside. Seconds later a stockily built man in bibbed overalls and a wool shirt appeared at the shack's entrance. Shoving his hands behind the faded denim bib of his overalls, the heavyset man leaned a shoulder into the jamb and waited until Clay halted his horses in the middle of the yard.

"Howdy," Bramberg said without enthusiasm.

Clay nodded an equally disinterested greeting and wrapped the lead rope around his saddlehorn. He started to dismount, but Bramberg stopped him before his leg could pass over the cantle.

"No need gettin' off. I ain't in the market."

Clay's face hardened as he resettled in the saddle. "You ain't in the market for what?"

Bramberg smirked.

Stifling his ire, Clay said, "Folks in town told me you might be interested in buying some horses."

"Folks in town is always sendin' people out here with stray stock. I expect that's what you got there, ain't it? Strays?"

"I traded these ponies from the Wichita."

One of the checkers players guffawed.

Bramberg smiled cockily. "Which means you ain't got no bill of sale for 'em."

Clay shook his head. "No, I don't."

Scratching his stubbled chin reflectively, Bramberg moseyed into the yard. "I don't generally buy a hoss without a bill of sale," he informed Clay pointedly. "For all I know these animals could'a been stolt. They's been a lot of thievery out on the reserves, and the redskins are screamin' bloody hell about it. Not that I blame 'em. I'd scream, too. Difference is, after I was done screamin', I'd do something about it."

Clay remained silent while Bramberg rattled on. The husky trader wandered over to where he could examine all three pack-horses without appearing overly curious. "These ponies ain't even shod," he said after a bit, lacing his voice with sarcasm. "Hell, they'd probably break their fool necks the first time someone slapped shoes on 'em."

Clay dismounted without speaking and went back to loosen the lead rope of the last horse in line. He led it over to Bramberg, halting it broadside. "It's a good horse," Clay said. "It was raised on the plains and used by women to pack in meat or carry their belongings when they moved camp. It's pulled a travois and is used to the smell of blood. It's broke to the saddle and

221

can be mounted from either side. It stands hobbled, but won't tangle itself in a picket rope, either, if that's what you want to use. It'd be just the animal for somebody looking for a hunting horse."

Bramberg grunted irritably. "Ain't nobody in these parts lookin' for huntin' hosses, boy. What they's needin' is workin' stock, something that'll pull a plow all day and not gaunt up and die on 'em."

"The talk in town is that gold was discovered on Cherry Creek, out in western Kansas. Men will be wanting a horse that can take them there, and the best animal for that will be an Indian pony, not some clumsy plow horse that'll gaunt up and die without a bucket of oats every morning and evening."

Bramberg's eyes narrowed. "I know my business, boy. A pony like this ain't gonna bring more'n a couple bucks come spring. Hardly worth the expense to feed it through the winter. And as far as gold in Kansas, I'll believe that when I by God see it blowin' in the dust."

"Was I buying," Clay replied tautly. "You'd tell me this horse was worth a hundred dollars, for the very same reasons I just mentioned."

Bramberg stiffened at Clay's response, and

was on the verge of answering when the clop of hooves from the alley diverted his attention. They both turned to observe a lean young man on a bay riding toward them, leading a pair of saddle horses behind him. Bramberg squared his shoulders and gave Clay a searing glance. " 'Scuse me, boy. I got a customer to 'tend to."

Clay bit back his anger as the stock dealer walked away. It had been like this ever since his arrival in Leavenworth. After selling his robes and furs to Lobenstein, he'd gone into a nearby saloon to have a beer, but the barkeep had glared at him until, his face suffusing with heat, Clay realized there was a separate section for Negroes at the back of the room. Taken off guard, he'd quietly retreated to a rickety table at the rear of the building, where he'd waited with growing anger for the barkeep to bring him his drink. Sitting stiffly in a broken chair held together with wire and cheap hide glue, Clay couldn't help noticing how much dirtier this tiny, segregated portion of the saloon was compared to the larger white section. When his drink came, Clay paid for it without comment, but then could only stare at the chipped, greasy stein. Finally he'd walked out past the mugging faces of the saloon's white patrons, leaving his beer untouched.

Nearly the same thing had happened later that afternoon when he'd gone into a barber shop for a shave, haircut, and bath. The barber had looked momentarily stunned as Clay strode in and took a seat to await his turn in the shop's single chair; then his face darkened, and he'd loudly ordered Clay out of the business. They didn't serve coloreds there, the barber had stuttered in indignation; Clay would have to go to shantytown if he wanted a shave.

Stung and humiliated, his jaw aching from clenching his teeth so hard, Clay had gone off in search of shantytown, locating it downriver from the main business district and hard on the Missouri's right bank. There were a few small businesses — Abner Bell's Hotel and Saloon being the largest — and a barber shop. Although the inhabitants were mostly black, Clay spotted a few Indians and Mexicans, and even some ragged-looking white-eyes along its muddy streets. In shantytown, Clay at last found a smidgen of acceptance, although he noticed he was still regarded as something of an oddity for his dress and weapons.

As a whole, his first day in Leavenworth had been an eye-opening and altogether unpleasant experience. Now it looked as if it were going to happen all over again.

"Howdy," Bramberg called cheerfully to the white man riding into the yard.

The horseman drew up several yards away, nodding to Clay first, then to Bramberg. He wore new-looking work clothes, but had on the broad-brimmed hat and long hair of a plainsman. His fringed buckskin jacket had seen hard use; its sleeves and hem had been scraped with soapstone, but the leather still showed the dark stains of blood and dirt, the grease of countless meals cooked over smoky fires. A hunter, Clay figured. Although he looked vaguely familiar, Clay couldn't place him right off.

"I've got a couple of horses I wanted to sell," the rider announced. "The name's Tyler Calhoun." He swung down and shook Bramberg's hand. Clay remembered him then — the young man coming out of Lobenstein's inner office the day Clay sold his robes and furs.

"Always in the market for good hosses," Bramberg replied with a friendliness Clay knew was meant to nettle him. "Bring 'em around here and let me take a look at 'em."

Ty's gaze flitted uncertainly to Clay. "You were dealing with him, weren't you? Go ahead, I can wait."

"Nonsense! I ain't makin' a white man

wait on no darky. Let's see your hosses."

Ty glanced at Clay, then Bramberg, and his friendliness disappeared. Turning back to Clay, he said, "Were you finished?"

"I reckon I am," Clay replied, the words strained. He led the Indian pony back into line, hitching its lead rope to the empty pack saddle of the animal in front of it. His anger raged like a wildfire in his gut, but he kept it under control by concentrating on the knot, on straightening the ponies out one behind the other. When he finished, he climbed into the pinto's saddle and gathered his reins.

As if on impulse, Ty said, "Where are you from?"

Clay's returning stare was flat and cold. "That's a mite personal, ain't it?"

"Yeah, I reckon it is," Ty admitted. "I saw you at Lobenstein's the other day. I thought I heard you say you'd been out trading with the wild tribes."

Bramberg laughed. "Nigras ain't hunters or traders, Calhoun. They're runners. This boy probably cabbaged these ponies outta some Delaware's back pasture."

Clay's jaw tightened until his teeth grated in his ears. He wanted to put his hand on the bowie sheathed at his waist, to slide the long, polished blade free and watch Bramberg's eyes widen in fear, but he didn't. He was achingly aware of the loafers standing in front of the ramshackle office, watching the proceedings with broad grins on their slack, dirty faces. At least two of them carried their pistols openly, and there was no mistaking the outline of a cut-down revolver in one of Bramberg's baggy hip pockets. Clay started to rein away, but Ty's voice caused him to pause. "If you're heading back to town, I'll ride with you."

Frowning, Bramberg said, "I thought you wanted to sell them hosses."

"Not to you," Ty replied bluntly. Mounting, he guided his big bay gelding over to Clay's side. Speaking loudly enough for the burly livestock trader to overhear, he added, "I was thinking of riding up to the post sutler's at Fort Leavenworth. He'll buy good horses sometimes. You'd be welcome to come along if you wanted to."

Clay only thought about it for a couple of seconds, then he nodded. The anger he felt toward Bramberg and his band of grinning fools still swirled hotly inside of him, but it had been tempered somewhat by this stranger with the quirky sense of honor. "Sounds like a good idea," he acknowledged with more calmness than he felt. He gigged the pinto toward the alley, and Ty fell in beside him. Bramberg's voice followed them out of the yard.

"Don't come back, Calhoun. I won't abide a nigger lover. Won't deal with 'em, by God."

Clay and Ty kept riding, and at the road that led north out of town, toward the fort, they kicked their mounts into an easy lope.

The Fort Leavenworth sutler gave Clay twenty dollars apiece for his mustangs and the packsaddles. It wasn't a great deal, but it was fair, considering the season, and Clay was satisfied. The sutler had also heard rumors of gold in western Kansas, where the territorial border butted up hard against the Rocky Mountains. "If it's true," he confided, "I'll make a right smart profit off these animals. But if it isn't, I won't even get my money out of them. Not after haying them all winter."

"I heard the rumors in Lawrence, coming in," Ty said. "The whole town was fired up about it."

"It's a gamble, all right. Word comes out of those mountains every few years about how somebody's found a bucket of nuggets, but it never pans out. Still, I figure it will one of these days. It just stands to reason that if they found gold in California, they'll find it somewhere else, too."

Ty sold his extra horses for a slightly higher price, they being American mounts, bigger and better blooded. Afterward, the two of them went into the sutler's store and bought a couple of beers and some cigars, which they took to a nearby table. They sat and smoked and sipped leisurely at their drinks, talking amiably enough, but with a certain guarded caution, each man feeling the other out. Ty told Clay about his recently dissolved partnership, and his plans to go back out again within the week. He was aiming for the Smoky Hill country, he said, where he had a hunter's ranch out beyond the settlement of Salina; he had wintered there the year before, and thought it would make a good base camp for the coming season, as well. "That's why I asked if I'd heard you correctly the other day," he added. "I've been thinking of taking on a partner, someone familiar with the plains and experienced in trading." But he stopped short of making an offer.

Clay, in turn, related bits and pieces of his own story, focusing mostly on his foray among the Wichitas. About the rest, he avoided more than he revealed. "I grew up a Choctaw in that Nation, but decided to move on," he said vaguely. "I've traded before, but the Washita is as far west as I've ever been." Clay also stopped short of proposing a partnership. So far, at least, he liked what he'd seen of Tyler Calhoun, but he'd barely arrived in Leavenworth, and he wanted to take a few days to see the elephant.

They had another beer, then went outside. The sun was just sliding below the horizon, the shadows behind the solid stone buildings of the fort growing long and cold and sharply drawn in the crisp autumn light. Ty buttoned his jacket, and Clay put on his mackinaw. They mounted and rode south, silent now as each man followed his own line of thoughts, struggling with his own uncertain future. They didn't speak again until they reached the outskirts of Leavenworth City.

"Well, my outfit's parked at Becker and Miles store," Ty said hesitantly.

Clay nodded. "I've got a room in shantytown, above Abner Bell's Saloon." He offered a wry grin. "It ain't fancy, but the lice aren't troublesome and the roof doesn't leak. Of course, it hasn't rained yet."

Ty laughed. "Sounds better than a pile of straw, for a fact."

They shook hands, and Ty added, "I'll be putting out in another three or four days. If

I don't see you before, take care of yourself."

"I will," Clay said. He held the pinto back a few minutes, watching Ty ride away. He had just about given up on white men over the past few days. For the first time since arriving in Leavenworth, he wondered if he hadn't been a little premature.

THIRTEEN

"Honey, you look as down in the mouth as a frog with its hinder stickin' out be'twix a snake's lips."

The words startled Clay, and he jerked his head up. What he saw made him sit straighter, smiling self-consciously. "I was just thinking," he said.

"Well, I got the cure for that," the woman assured him. " 'Course, you gotta ask me to sit down first."

Clumsily, Clay moved his hat off the only other chair at the table, then courteously rose, though bumping the edge of the table with his hip in the process and nearly spilling his beer.

"Well, I'll be," the woman said, feigning surprise. "A gentleman, besides." She slid into the empty chair at his side, a wavy-haired mulatto whom Clay had seen occasionally since taking up residence in an upstairs room. She was an attractive woman, young and plump and butter-toothed, dressed in a cheap gingham dress that had been altered in imitation of an outfit more befitting an uptown prostitute — a scooped neckline to show off her ample cleavage, sleeves shortened to just below her shoulder, the hem raised above her knees. She patted the seat of Clay's chair. "Sit down, honey. My name's Dee Dee. What's your'n?"

"Clay" he replied, sitting. "Clay Little Bull."

"Well, how-do, Mr. Clay Little Bull," Dee Dee said, affecting a shy but fetching grin. "That's an odd name . . . Little Bull?"

"It's Choctaw," Clay told her pridefully. Somewhere in the back of his mind a voice shouted for him to shut up and quit acting like a rube, but then his gaze fell to the shadowy vee between her breasts and the voice suffered a quick death.

Dee Dee laughed and scooted closer, so close Clay could smell the whiskey-tinged rush of her breath, could feel the warmth that radiated from her bosom, the pressure of her knee against his. "Well, Mr. Clay Little Bull," Dee Dee said. "I got me a policy. Never argue with a man who might buy me a drink. I got you pegged right? You fixin' to buy me a drink?"

"Right as rain," Clay said. He turned to

233

signal the ebony-skinned bartender, only to discover him already approaching with a pair of shot glasses and a bottle. The bartender placed one glass in front of Dee Dee, then gave Clay a questioning appraisal.

"Best fill him a glass, too, Abner," Dee Dee said brightly. "You want some whiskey, don't cha, honey? Beer is for wimpy white folks."

Before Clay could form a reply, Bell was tipping a label-less brown bottle over the glass at Clay's elbow. "This one's on the house," he said.

"Drink up," Dee Dee urged, giving Clay a nudge with her shoulder. "I don't like to drink with a sober man. He ain't gener'ly any fun."

Clay laughed and reached for the glass. "I don't think . . ." he started to say, then lost his train of thought.

Both Dee Dee and Abner Bell laughed, and after a moment's confusion, Clay joined them. He glanced at the wag-on-the-wall — the caseless gears and springs of a working clock — hanging between the rows of whiskey bottles and fired clay jugs behind the bar. It was a quarter of eleven. As best he could remember, he had been here about five hours now. He'd played some monte with a couple of black stevedores when he'd first arrived, but quit after losing five dol-lars. Then he'd gone to stand at the bar, telling himself he should probably get something to eat before settling down to any serious drinking, but somehow he'd never gotten around to it. He wasn't sure when he'd moved back here to sit alone at a table, or how many beers he'd had since then, but it must have been a few. He hadn't realized how drunk he was until he started talking to Dee Dee.

They had three or four more whiskeys apiece, and by midnight she was leaning so heavily against his shoulder that his arm was starting to go to sleep. When he reluctantly tried to pull it away to flex some circulation back into it, Dee Dee got a wicked look on her face and told him she knew a place where his hand would be far more comfort-able. Taking it in both of her own, she lifted it to the warm canyon between her breasts, pushing his tingling fingers down until all but his thumb had disappeared between the yielding mounds of flesh.

Clay caught his breath, staring dumbly at his hand cradled by Dee Dee's smooth brown breasts. For the first time he noticed how the rigid tips of her nipples showed clearly through the thin fabric of her dress, the way the material lay so revealingly over her hips and thighs. It came to him with a jolt that underneath the flimsy gingham Dee Dee was as naked as the day she was born, and the discovery ignited a lust in his belly that was like the bursting of flames. He took a long, shuddering breath, and looked into her eyes.

Dee Dee's expression hardened almost imperceptibly. "I ain't free, you know," she told him with mock ferocity. "A gal's gotta look out for herself, and I ain't reduced myself to takin' in laundry or wipin' no white kid's ass. You understand?"

Clay nodded; he had understood from the very beginning. "No, a body like yours ain't made for washing clothes or nannying." Stroking the satiny underside of one soft breast with his fingers, he smiled lewdly. "Well, maybe nannying, but only for those of us who can truly appreciate the art."

Roaring laughter, Dee Dee plucked his hand from her bosom and let it drop. "Now, ain't you the funny one," she declared. "Well, you just come 'long with me, Mr. Little Bull. I got some tricks I bet them Choctaw gals don't know nuthin' about. Keep your pecker in your pants while I go fetch my coat."

Clay rose carefully and pulled on his hat, watching the quick swing of Dee Dee's hips as she hurried across the room. She grabbed a man's heavy coat from a nail on the wall behind the bar and slid into it, making a face at Clay as she did. In one of the corners of his mind he was able to marvel at how effortlessly she seemed to move after downing at least as many whiskeys as he had, but then that thought slipped away as he negotiated a path through the tables to her side. Linking an arm through his, she guided him to the back door.

A blast of cold wind swept over them as they exited the saloon, shocking Clay with its strength. He had grown warm with all he had drunk that night, but the dark breezes blowing in off the prairies quickly cooled his sweaty brow.

"Damn," Dee Dee said with what might have been real concern, "Ol' Man Winter's breathin' down our necks, Mr. Little Bull. I shorely hope you know how to keep a gal warm, a night like this."

Clay didn't respond. As they plunged into the shadows behind the saloon he felt a sudden wariness struggling through the layers of alcoholic haze. Dee Dee was hurrying him along with the breeze, both of her arms locked around his right one, her hip tight against the Kerr revolver holstered at his waist. Instinctively, Clay pulled back, attempting to free his imprisoned arm.

Dee Dee gave him a funny look. "What's the matter, honey, you ain't gonna puke, are you?" Her voice turned abruptly hard with the fear that he might. "You do, you better not splatter my new coat. I'll be damned if I'm gonna have some drunk nigger ruin what I had to hump my hinder off for."

"I ain't no drunk nigger," Clay lashed out, jerking on his arm.

Dee Dee's tone turned quickly sweet once more. "Choctaw, I mean. Oh, Clay, don't get mad. It's just that I only got this here coat, and it's about the warmest thing I ever owned." Her grip tightened on his arm. "Come on, honey. My legs is freezin'."

Clay tried to reel in his whirling senses. Dee Dee was pulling him toward the river again, the lights of shantytown disappearing behind them. They came to a narrow path along the river and turned onto it, heading downstream. He was fuzzily aware of a hodgepodge collection of dark shacks on his right, mostly hidden behind a border of thick brambles. Although no lights showed from the scattered buildings, Clay had a strong sense of people dwelling there — living and working and loving, and now, at this late hour, sleeping. He thought he could hear the murmur of voices, the soft mewling of an infant, but couldn't be sure with the wind rattling the branches of the blackberry bushes at his side.

"Wh . . . where we going?" he asked, balking as the trail wound deeper into the thicket.

"We goin' to my place, honey," Dee Dee cooed.

Clay was aware of her face peering up at him in the filtered moonlight coming through the trees. She looked scared, he thought, her eyes wide and panicky. It was enough to awaken in him a sixth sense, a feeling of something being wrong that had struggled for his attention ever since leaving Abner Bell's saloon. Gooseflesh rippled his arms, and his scalp crawled.

"Wassa matter, honey?" Dee Dee asked. "You ain't changin' your mind, are you?"

"I . . ." The words trailed off. Brambles at the edge of the thicket rustled too loudly to be caused by the wind. Clay tried to face them, but Dee Dee clung to his arm, tugging urgently. "Come on, honey, it ain't far now."

"Lemme go, goddamnit," Clay cried as the rustling grew louder. Struggling to look over his shoulder, he caught a fleeting glimpse of a darting shadow. Cursing, he pushed away from Dee Dee's clutching arms and grabbed for his knife.

"Clay, no!" Dee Dee screamed.

He whipped the bowie free with a cold, leathery snick. A shadow leaped forward. Clay ducked and heard the passage of something heavy and wooden part the air above his head. He thrust with his knife but missed, and the shadow retreated.

Dee Dee screamed again. Clay whirled in a crouch, slashing waist-high. The tip of his knife caught briefly at something that gave with a ragged, tearing sound; there was a raspy cry of pain and fear, then the second shadow slid away. Before Clay could turn back, a stunning blow slammed into the side of his head. An explosion of light and agony filled him, wiping away his senses like a wet rag over a slate board. He fell hard, rolling to the edge of the path where he lay helpless, his brain wobbling between consciousness and a welcoming black void.

Consciousness won, but it was a hard-fought victory. Sound returned first. From a long way off he could hear Dee Dee sobbing; closer, a string of curses. Hands grabbed him. Blunt, jabbing fingers explored his pockets. He tried to voice a protest, to lift his arm to ward off his attackers, but nothing worked right.

He must have passed out then, because the next thing he saw was Dee Dee kneeling over him, whispering, "Clay, oh, Clay. Why'd you have to fight 'em? Why couldn't you just come along quiet, like any other dumb, drunk nigger?"

He reached out to try to touch her cheek, but she slapped his groping hand away. "You damn fool," she snarled. "Now you done ruined ever'thing."

Coming awake the second time was like floating upward out of a pool of warm water into the biting maw of a blue norther. Clay shivered violently from the cold. A throbbing pain coursed through his body, keeping time to the cadence of his heart. He heard the wind moaning in the brambles, the lapping of waves against the Missouri's shore. Forcing his eyes open, he discovered a mantle of stars overhead, and through the branches of the blackberry bushes, the oblong globe of a waning moon. Cautiously, he lifted a hand to his head. The left side of his face felt hot and swollen, the flesh around the eye so tight he was only able to squint past the bruised flesh.

Suppressing a groan, Clay rolled onto his side, then pushed to his hands and knees. He felt the revolver holstered at his waist slide down his belt to hang under his belly, and for the first time remembered the Kerr. He couldn't help a lopsided smile when he considered the difference the pistol would have made compared to his knife, but he wasn't used to carrying one, and in the heat of battle he'd forgotten it completely.

Almost as an afterthought, he moved his hand under the mackinaw, but wasn't surprised to find his poke missing, and with it the money he'd gotten for his packhorses.

Crawling over to where his knife lay in the middle of the path, he resheathed it, then carefully got to his feet. He was alone, but that didn't surprise him either. Slowly, he made his way back up the path to Abner Bell's Hotel and Saloon. The cold wind and the pain in his face washed away the last tendrils of drunkenness, so that by the time he reached the saloon he felt sick but sober.

The saloon was closed for the night, the lower windows dark, the back door locked. Clay stood for a moment with his hands on the frame, until a slow anger took him and gave him strength. He put his shoulder to the door and pushed, and when it didn't give, he pushed harder, his anger growing. There was a *pop* from within, then the protesting grate of screws ripped slowly from wood. The door swung open. Stepping into the dark interior of the saloon, Clay shut the door and palmed his pistol. The big main room reeked with the odors of stale beer and raw whiskey, of vomit and tobacco spit and cheap cigars; underfoot, the sticky, caking sawdust shoveled over the floor clung to the soles of his moccasins. The stench made his stomach lurch dangerously, and he made his way to the stairs, climbing swiftly to the cleaner air of the second floor.

His moccasins made no more than a whisper as he cat-footed down the uncarpeted hallway. The door to his room stood slightly ajar, allowing a shaft of lamplight to spill into the hall. Clay's heart beat rapidly as he curled his thumb over the Kerr's sidehammer. Quietly, he edged one eye past the jamb until he could peer inside.

Clay had expected to find his assailants from the riverside path, or perhaps Dee Dee. But it was Abner Bell who stood at the side of the narrow iron bed rifling the contents of Clay's saddlebags. Cautiously, Clay placed his left hand against the door and pushed inward. The warped pine lumber swung back only an inch before one rusty hinge started to squeak. Bell looked up, startled, but before he could react Clay stepped into the room with his pistol leveled.

"Don't you so much as twitch," Clay growled. "Not one muscle."

"Clay!" Bell gulped. "I . . . I . . ." He left the rest unspoken.

Clay elbowed the door shut, then eared the Kerr's hammer all the way back. "It ain't there," he told the shaken bar owner. "Now back away from the bed."

"Jesus, Clay, I'd heard you were hurt. I was looking for some bandages —"

"Shut up," Clay said sharply.

Abner Bell licked nervously at his lips. "You're making a mistake, Clay. Dee Dee came back and said you'd been jumped. I was just —"

"I told you to shut up, Bell. If I were you, I'd do it. Right now you ain't gut-shot, but you're liable to end up that way."

Bell nodded and clamped his mouth shut. Clay walked over and yanked a pocket pistol from a shoulder rig under the bartender's coat and tossed it behind a chest of drawers. Then, with the Kerr's muzzle, he motioned toward the wall. Bell put his back against it without protest.

"Who was it?" Clay asked quietly. "Who jumped me?"

"I don't know."

Clay let the Kerr ease forward a couple of inches.

"Listen, Clay, it was just business," Abner Bell blurted suddenly. "But I didn't get a thing out of it, not a dime. Look, I ain't no angel, all right? I'm admitting that right up front. A couple of hard cases came up to me'n Dee Dee earlier tonight with a little proposition, who am I to turn 'em down? But I haven't seen 'em since, or Dee Dee either. I don't know what happened out there, and I don't want to know. As far as I'm concerned it was a bad deal, and I'm willin' to let it drop. But if you kill me, the law's gonna —"

"I doubt it," Clay said, interrupting.

"Huh?"

"I said, I doubt if the law would care if I killed you, at least not so long as you didn't bleed over any of the white part of town."

"Jesus, Clay," Abner Bell breathed.

"Those hard cases you mentioned lifted close to sixty dollars off me tonight. I want it back."

"I don't know where they went, I swear to God on that. I don't even know their names."

"It doesn't have to be the same sixty dollars," Clay replied.

Bell caught on immediately, and his voice

rose. "You're gonna rob me? That ain't fair."

Clay laughed humorlessly. "I knew thieves down in the Nations who felt the same way. Just no sense of ownership. I walk in here and catch you with your hands buried to the elbow in my stuff, and you want to squawk about what's fair when I demand my money back?"

"But it ain't your money," Bell protested. "It's my money."

Clay smiled thinly. "Not anymore, it isn't." He moved around the side of the bed, and with one hand began to repack his saddlebags, buckling the flaps when he finished. His rifle stood in the corner in its elkhide case, the powder horn and shooting bag on the floor beside it, as if someone had made a hurried search of the bag before moving on to more likely hiding places. Clay slid the straps of the bag and horn over his shoulder, then cradled his saddlebags, bedroll, and rifle in his left arm. The money Bell was looking for, the two hundred and twenty dollars he'd gotten from Lobenstein for his robes and furs, was rolled up in the tip of the elkhide guncase, but Clay didn't tell him that. Letting the muzzle of the Kerr dip, then come back into line, Clay said, "Time to pay up, Abner."

"I . . . I got some cash in my belt."

"Lay it out here."

Bell fumbled under the hem of his vest, then tossed a money belt onto the bed. Keeping a close watch on the bartender, Clay flipped the belt over like he would a dead snake, then unbuttoned the leather flap and scattered a stack of bills across the threadbare quilt. Bell's eyes widened in fright. "I got more'n a hundred dollars there. You ain't takin' it all, are you?"

"Just the sixty dollars you owe me, plus fifteen more for the bruise under my eye." Clay shoved the money into the pocket of his mackinaw. "Although I ought to take it all, just to teach you a lesson."

"Hell, Clay, folks have been trying to teach me a lesson since the day I started talkin'. I reckon the best lesson you could teach me was the Lord's own forgivness, and leave that fifteen dollars behind. That don't look like fifteen dollars worth of bruise, anyway."

Clay backed toward the door. "It's finished now, Bell, understand? Let it drop, because if you don't, if you try to follow me or have me followed or cause me trouble in any way, I'll come back here and put a bullet through your belly."

Abner Bell's head bobbed quickly. "That's fair," he said.

Clay reached behind him and yanked the

door open, then stepped through it. He backed down the hall until he came to the head of the stairs, then turned and plunged downward. At the bottom he spun again, backing rapidly to the outside door, but Bell didn't show himself. Breathing a sigh of relief, Clay holstered the Kerr and slipped outside.

He spent the night in the livery where he'd stabled the pinto his first night in town. Early the next day he hiked to Becker and Miles Mercantile. Tyler Calhoun was in the corral behind the store, smearing salve over a patch of raw flesh on an ox's hip. He looked up when Clay draped his arms over the top rail; an expression of concern crossed his face first, then he grinned and held up the can of salve. "Want some?"

Clay laughed. "Do I look that rough?" he asked.

"I'd say you not only saw the elephant, but the damn thing must've kicked you in the face."

"Feels that way," Clay admitted dryly.

Ty walked over, wiping his hands on a rag. "You change your mind about putting out for the buffalo ranges?"

"It's something to talk about."

Ty was quiet a moment, considering

Clay's response. Then he nodded. "Had your breakfast yet?" he asked.

They went to the Mandan Cafe, and although the waiter gave Clay a dubious look, he took their orders without comment. Ty seemed uncomfortable after he'd left. "Is that the way it's been for you?" he asked Clay.

"Pretty much. Folks warned me there were a lot of proslavery people around Leavenworth. I guess I just didn't fully understand what that meant."

"Well, you don't look like an Indian," Ty allowed. "But it's still a shame. Leavenworth is a good city, with high potential, but it's got its hackles up over the free-soilers now. If Congress would just settle the slavery issue once and for all, things could get back to normal. As it stands, it's tearing the whole territory apart, like brothers fighting over the same woman. Do you know what the papers back East call us? Bleeding Kansas. They aren't too far from wrong, either."

Would it be that simple, Clay wanted to ask, *that a single legislative decision could rid the territory of hate and prejudice?* He didn't pursue the question, though. There were other things on his mind. "You said you were looking for a partner."

Ty nodded. "I'm looking for someone experienced in trading with the wild tribes, someone who can show me the ropes. I've got a man who's treated with them some, but he's old and cantankerous, and not much help."

"I wouldn't make much of a partner. I've only got about three hundred dollars. That freighter must've set you back that much."

"Three hundred dollars would help, although to tell you the truth, I'm not overly concerned about financial equality right now. I'm pretty well outfitted as it stands, but I do need someone I can depend on. The man I mentioned, Oscar Garrett, is a good skinner, but he's not someone I'd want to count on."

"And you figure I am?"

"There's never any way of knowing something like that until the fat's in the fire, but you seem all right, and you have experience." His fingers drummed the tabletop. "Clay, every cent I have is tied up in those wagons and oxen and supplies. I can't lose sight of that, or give up my authority to make the final decisions. So as far as a partnership goes, I was thinking I'd only cut you in for a percentage of the profits the first year, say twenty percent, but with the option of buying deeper into the outfit next season, if you're interested."

Clay nodded thoughtfully. Ty's proposal seemed fair, considering the imbalance of investment. But it was no more than that, since if something did go wrong they would both end up flat busted. "Where would I stand with the hired men?" he asked. "I'd need to know how much say I've got over them."

"No one has much say over Oscar Garrett, but you'd have as much as me, for whatever that's worth. I hope to pick up another skinner or two before we set out, but if I can't, we'll have to make do with just the three of us. Oscar won't like it, but hell, Oscar doesn't like much of anything anymore. I won't lie to you, Clay, he'll be a handful — especially considering the color of your skin — but he'll either come around or we'll let him go."

"That the way you plan to work it? Your partner comes first?"

"Yeah, that's the way I plan to work it."

Clay considered Ty's words, and decided he liked them. "All right," he said, reaching across the table to shake Ty's hand. "You've got yourself a partner."

Ty smiled broadly. "Well, I'll be damned," he exclaimed. "It looks like the firm of

Calhoun and Little Bull is in business and bound for the buffalo ranges!"

FOURTEEN

It was mid-afternoon when Ty swung down off his big bay in front of Becker and Miles store and looped the reins through the ring of an iron hitching post. Inside, he found Silas Becker standing behind the counter in a clerk's apron, his bald head shining in the light of a single overhead lamp, his wire-framed glasses perched delicately on the end of his nose. He looked up as Ty entered, and a puzzled expression crossed his face.

"Back so soon?" Becker asked.

Ty stopped abruptly. "Why wouldn't I be?"

"Because Oscar Garrett said it would be tomorrow before you got your permits straightened out at the fort."

Ty felt the muscles across the back of his head draw tight. Glancing down the narrow aisle to the door that led to the warehouse out back, he asked, "Where is he?"

"Said that since you weren't coming back

today, you'd load up tomorrow."

"You haven't even started!"

"Not without a representative from your outfit to sign the invoice. You know how we operate, Ty. No one wants you getting out there in the middle of nowhere and discovering something essential missing."

"Yeah, I know," Ty said shortly. "Which way did he go?"

Pursing his lips in disapproval, Becker said, "North. He didn't say where, but you can guess as well as I can."

"Is everything ready out back?"

"Yes. I had a couple of my men back your wagons up to the loading dock to be ready first thing in the morning, but we can start right now if you want to."

"Not yet," Ty growled, pivoting on his heels. "I'll be back in a bit."

Becker glanced at the clock on the wall behind him. "Don't be too long. The men'll want to go home at six."

Goddamnit, he should've known better than to trust Garrett, Ty thought as he made his way to the nearest saloon. Lobenstein had warned him about the old drunkard, but he'd been in such a hurry to get back to the buffalo ranges, to put the stink of the city behind him for another season, that he'd hired Garrett anyway. Not that he probably wouldn't have had to eventually — with winter looming so close, most of the men he'd approached for the job had shied away as if he had the pox. But Garrett could still prove to be a costly mistake somewhere down the trail.

Clay had spent the day helping Jimmy Flannigan shoe the last of the oxen at the Hamilton and Finn Wagon Works, while Ty rode up to Fort Leavenworth to renew his licenses to hunt and trade in Indian lands. Oscar had been sleeping off a last spree before putting out, but Ty had awakened him with the instructions that if he hadn't returned by noon — he was wanting to poke around some of the smaller settlements on the way back to try to locate another hand or two — then Garrett was to get the wagons loaded with the aid of some of Becker's men. Ty had expected his supplies to be strapped in place by the time he returned, the manifest signed, the oxen fed and watered, and Oscar and Clay waiting for him at the corrals.

Now this, and Garrett not on the payroll two days.

Ty tried the Missouri House first, pausing just inside the door to survey the line of drinkers at the bar. He gave the stairs leading to the cribs upstairs a glance, then dismissed them. Oscar Garrett's love was for the bottle; Ty couldn't picture him spending money on a whore, no matter how long it might be before he saw his next one. He made a quick circuit just for the hell of it, checking the nooks and crannies around the room, then returned to the boardwalk and made his way to the next saloon.

The day was nearing its end when he came to the Red Dog Tavern, on the riverfront. He cursed himself for not thinking of the cheaper dives first, where a barfly like Oscar might feel more at home than in the better establishments higher up the bluff. Ty pushed through the door and stopped. There was a keg-and-plank bar running down one side of the room, and a trio of tables and mismatched chairs spaced along the uneven floor in front of it. Tin candle lanterns threw off a dim, smoky light. The whiskey, Ty knew, would be half raw in a place like this, with a bite like that of a surly dog, but the cost would be easy on a man's wallet.

There was a moderate crowd — mostly loafers and rivermen — with a sprinkling of soldiers, their sharp blue uniforms standing out amid the duller clothing of the civilians. Even in the poor light, Oscar Garrett was easy to spot. He lay slumped and spraddle-legged at the back of the room, propped against the rear wall.

Ty's anger had cooled since leaving Becker and Miles, so that by the time he found the old plainsman passed out on the Red Dog's floor, he felt more pity than irritation. He crossed the room to stand silently above the reeking alcoholic, seeing him not as he was now — thin-limbed and frail, his jowls slack, stubbled with iron-gray whiskers, his lank hair lying in greasy strings around his face — but as he must have been as a younger man, strong and virile and quick as a badger, standing tall for all his shortness, and afraid of nothing. Softly, his lips barely moving, Ty murmured, "Hell, old-timer, maybe you've earned it."

He stooped and gathered the elderly man in his arms, slinging him almost tenderly over his shoulder. He felt a pang of sorrow to realize how light and fragile Oscar's body felt; the legs hooked behind Ty's arm seemed like little more than twigs. Tucking Oscar's shapeless, sweaty hat under his belt, Ty made his way to the door, ignoring the laughter and jibes that followed him outside. There was a group of loafers standing in front of the saloon when he exited. One of them grinned hugely at the sight of Ty's cargo, and opened his mouth to comment.

"Don't," Ty threatened mildly, staring into the man's eyes. The loafer looked momentarily puzzled, then he frowned and started to speak again. Oscar was draped over Ty's right shoulder, occupying his right arm, but his left was free; he jabbed it hard into the loafer's face before he could utter a word. The loafer stumbled backward with a startled squawk. His heels slipped over the edge of the boardwalk and he hung there for a moment, his arms windmilling wildly as he continued to tip toward the street; then his balance deserted him altogether, and he flopped backward into the thick mire. Laughter erupted from the other loafers as Ty turned away. Stone-faced, half angered once more by the embarrassment Oscar had caused him, he started back up the hill toward the main part of town.

He carried Oscar to an open-faced shed behind Becker and Miles and laid him out on a pile of clean straw. "There," he grunted. "I hope you puke your guts out in the morning." He stared down at the leathery plainsman for a couple of minutes, then went to his own bedroll and pulled out a heavy wool blanket. Kneeling at the old man's side, he gently rolled him into it. "You damn fool," Ty muttered under his breath, and wondered briefly whether he was speaking to Garrett or himself.

Standing, Ty glanced at the empty wagons backed up against Becker and Miles loading dock, the warehouse doors pulled firmly shut. One of the oxen was missing, so Ty reckoned Clay was still helping Flannigan with the shoeing. He started for the store, but stopped when he spotted a kid standing at the gate, a pair of dirty gray sacks sitting in the dirt at his feet. Frowning impatiently, Ty called, "You want something?"

"Are you Tyler Calhoun?"

"Who wants to know?"

"My name is Jonas Sands. If you're Mr. Calhoun, I'd like to have a word with you."

Ty hesitated, then shrugged. "Come on in, then."

Jonas climbed through the rails and walked across the corral. He was short and blond and blue-eyed, with a freckled, button nose and the concave belly of a man who'd missed more than a few meals of late. His trousers were muddy, his cheeks shaded by exhaustion.

"What can I do for you?" Ty asked.

"I'm looking for a job. Mr. Becker said you might be hiring."

"I might," Ty admitted cautiously. "What can you do?"

"I can work. I'm a good worker."

"I haven't seen you around town before, have I?"

Jonas shook his head.

On a hunch, Ty asked, "You a runaway?"

The kid eyed him suspiciously. "I can do a man's work for as long as it lasts, then ask for more."

"Fair enough," Ty conceded, smiling. "How old are you?"

"Old enough, I guess."

"How old?"

"Seventeen," Jonas said.

"Yeah," Ty replied dryly, mentally subtracting two years. "Where are you from?"

"Chicago," Jonas replied after a pause.

"Family there?"

"No."

"Do you know what I do?"

"You're a plainsman," Jonas answered. "You wander the plains hunting, or trading with Indians. That's what I want to be — a plainsman."

"Have you got a rifle?"

"No."

"A good knife?"

"Uh uh."

"Ever skin an animal?"

"I've plucked chickens."

"Ain't no chickens where I'm going," Ty said sternly. "It's wolf and buffalo country

260

mostly, though there's plenty of elk and deer and antelope. And grizzly bears that'll chew your head off for a snack." His voice roughened. "There's Indians, too. My last partner was killed by Cheyennes, out on the Saline River. I'll be hunting that same general area again this year." He shook his head, thinking of Wade. "Naw, go on home, boy. It takes more savvy than you've got to spend a season out there."

Jonas' eyes narrowed. "Where do I get that?" he demanded. "I mean, where do you buy savvy? Is there a store around here that sells it?"

"You've got a sharp tongue for someone looking for hire," Ty observed.

"I need a job," Jonas replied.

Ty didn't answer right away. He stared at the kid a long time, waiting for him to look down or away. When he didn't after several minutes, Ty grunted. "You're wanting to go real bad, aren't you?"

"I aim to be a plainsman," Jonas replied evenly. "The quicker I pick up that savvy you mentioned, the quicker I'll become one."

From the depths of the open-faced shed, Oscar Garrett groaned and broke wind.

Ty turned his gaze to the wagons at Becker and Miles' loading dock. It was obvious the kid had lied to him on a number of points, yet he'd seemed painfully honest about the rest. And did his past really matter? The frontier was full of runaways and orphans, many no older than Jonas, and not a few who were a lot younger. Ty scratched uncertainly at his jaw, then swung back to face the youth. "It ain't no picnic where we're going," he barked. "If you work for me you'll work your butt off, all day and all night when need be, and it'll need be more than you'll want. You'll do what you're told without sass or whining, and you'll do it quick and you'll do it right. There ain't no walking off this job, boy, not unless you intend to hoof it all the way back by yourself, which ain't likely because you wouldn't make it. You'd freeze or starve, or some Pawnee buck would take your hair and ears and maybe your fingers, if he had a notion to let his squaw make him a finger bone belt for dress up. You'll sweat when it's snowing and peg hides in the dark and scratch lice on your own time, by God. You'll take care of the stock like they were babies, because they cost me forty dollars a head and you won't cost me anything until I get back, and that's only if you or I or both of us *get* back, and then only if it's a profitable season. The pay's twenty-five dollars a month and all the hump meat you can stomach." Ty shut up then, glaring at the kid, wanting to slap the grin off his face. He didn't though. He just shook his head, remembering the way he'd felt himself, the first time he'd put out for the buffalo ranges. "Boy," he said finally, "you're in it with both feet now, I hope you realize that."

"Sure, that's what I came out here for."

"Come on then, goddamnit. We've got wagons to load."

They shoed the roan last. Clay led the heavy horned ox out of the corral behind Becker and Miles with a length of trace chain through the ring in the cow's nose, and took her down the street to the Hamilton and Finn Wagon Works. The farrier's shop was located in a lean-to off the south side of the big barn where Samuel Finn oversaw the construction of his wagons.

The blacksmith was a big, blocky Irishman named Jimmy Flannigan. He shook his head in good-humored reproach when he saw Clay leading the ox across the street. Tossing aside a piece of scrap iron he had been inspecting, he moved to the shop's entrance and crossed his arms over his chest. "I had not seen that ol' bunch quitter the old man sold to Ty last spring. I thought maybe he'd gotten rid of it."

Clay put his hand on the ox's shoulder, bringing it to a halt. "Bunch-quitter?"

"Aye. The old man was fit to be tied when he owned 'er," Jimmy confided with a chuckle. "Was ready to shoot 'er more'n once, he was."

"What old man?"

"Old man Hamilton, senior partner in the firm, and Samuel's daddy-in-law, to boot. Hamilton bought the ox off a wagon master just in from Santa Fe the autumn before — ye know we keep a few head handy to move the wagons around the yard, or in and out of the shop — but yon cow was born with an eye for travel, she were. It could never be turned loose to graze, then caught up again when it was needed, like the rest of 'em. So the old man sold it to Ty. Any other hunter would've shot it by now, but it does not surprise me that he didn't."

"How's that?" Clay asked.

"Ty's different, man. Ain't ye noticed?"

"Yeah, maybe I have," Clay replied uncertainly.

"Well, let's be about it," Jimmy said. He went to his forge and began pumping on the buffalo hide bellows. Soon the charcoal in his waist-high brick firepot glowed a deep red.

Clay led the roan cow to the ox sling — four stout posts set in the ground to the side of the shop door — and looped the trace chain over a spike driven into a fifth post. With the cow secured between the posts, he moved back along the hard-muscled body to where two massive leather straps lay on the ground beneath her, fastened to a stout crossbar on the off side. Clay pulled the front strap up under the roan's rib cage, just behind her front legs, then loosened a rope wrapped around an iron bar bolted to the outside of the near post; the rope freed an oaken block and tackle on the crossbeam overhead, which he hooked to an iron ring sewn into the strap under the cow's ribs. Wrapping the heavy rope back around the iron bar, he repeated the procedure with the rear strap and a second block and tackle. By the time he finished, Jimmy had returned with his far-rier's tools in a wooden toolbox. Setting the box to one side, Jimmy came over to examine the roan's left foreleg, its cloven hoof coated with mud.

" 'Tis not too bad," Jimmy observed, fingering away the worst of the muck. "This one won't be takin' long, I'm thinkin'."

Clay unwrapped the tackle on the forward cinch and pulled the leather strap tight against the ox's ribs. Together then, he and Jimmy hauled down on the block and tackle. The cow grunted and swung her head in alarm as the leather cinch bit into her flesh. The two men strained on the rope until the ox's front hooves barely brushed the hard ground. Then they tied off the tackle and stepped back.

"Whew," Jimmy breathed. "She be a heavy brute, for sure."

"It ain't that she's any heavier than the others," Clay said, puffing. "It's just that she's the eighth one we've done today."

"It makes a difference," Jimmy agreed solemnly. They moved to the rear strap then, and took a firm grip on the rope. When they were finished the ox stood lightly on the ground, a startled expression marking its broad, bovine face.

Unlike a horse or a mule, which could stand freely on three legs, oxen required additional support while being shod. Jimmy's ox sling offered a buttress of sorts, thus saving the farrier from having the cow lean into him; it also helped control the more unruly beasts by taking away the leverage they needed to fight the shoeing process.

Despite the cool temperatures, both men were sweating by the time they finished. But Jimmy was in a hurry now, with the day nearly gone. He took only a quick swig of water from a tin cup sitting beside the door, then bent to his task. He splashed water over the hooves first, washing away the mud, then pried off the old shoes — two to a hoof, like a pair of apostrophe marks hammered out of iron. He clipped the hooves with heavy trimmers, then shaped them with a rasp. Finally he fitted the new shoes, still warm from the forge, hammering out the final shape on a two hundred pound anvil with a steel-headed mallet.

It was killing work, but Jimmy had been taught the trade by his father, who had learned it from *his* father, who'd shod oxen in Ireland long before his son came to America. The burly farrier was a professional, and he made quick work of the chore. Less than an hour after hoisting the roan into the heavy leather sling, they were loosening the tackle and lowering her back to the ground. The cow tossed her head and bellowed, stepping out gingerly on her new shoes as Clay led her to a nearby corral and wrapped the chain around a rail.

Jimmy ducked into the shop, reappearing a moment later with a couple of bottles of beer clenched in one large, work-scarred fist. He handed a bottle to Clay, then opened the second for himself, pulling the sealed cork with his teeth and spitting it aside.

"Well, a good day's work, wouldn't ye say?"

"Middling," Clay agreed, wiping the perspiration from his face with a sleeve before the wind chilled him. He took a long pull on his beer, letting the dark malt slide soothingly over his parched throat. Dusk was creeping like a thief along the deserted alleyways, and the nip that had hovered over town all day began to deepen as the sun retreated. The two men drank in silence, listening to the chorus of hammers coming from the wagon works next door as an iron rim was fitted to a wooden wheel. While that final chore was being completed, other laborers shuttered windows and prepared to close up shop. Clay leaned with his back to the wall, the sole of one foot resting on the building's limestone foundation, the bottom of his bottle propped atop that knee. Weariness claimed his body, but it was a good kind of tired, a satisfying ache born from a solid day's work — his first as a partner with Ty. In all, with Ty's help the first day and Clay's today, Jimmy Flannigan had shod sixteen oxen and three horses — Ty's bay, Clay's pinto, and a dappled gray Ty had kept as an extra mount.

Clay finished his beer and set the bottle aside. "Thanks, Jimmy."

"Sure," the blacksmith replied absently. He was staring intently across the street, where a bull-like figure was approaching the farrier's shop.

"What is it?" Clay asked.

"The local law," Jimmy answered, stifling a belch. "Bob Ripley."

Clay felt the easy contentment of a hard day's work and a cold beer dissolve instantly. He remained where he was as the lawman paused at the edge of the yard to stomp the worst of the mud off his boots. A scowl creased the sheriff's face as he gave Jimmy a brief nod, then shifted his attention to Clay.

"Your name Little Bull?" Ripley asked gruffly. When Clay nodded, the sheriff's scowl deepened. "Come with me," he ordered bluntly.

Ripley headed for the alley beside the farrier's shop without looking back. Clay glanced once at Jimmy, then shrugged his shoulders and followed.

Ripley waited in the middle of the Hamilton and Finn wagon lot, using a big freighter with a cracked axle as a windbreak. He had a cigar clenched between his teeth, and was cupping his hands around a sputtering lucifer as he tried to light it. He looked up as Clay approached, but continued to puff on his cigar until it was fired to his satisfaction. Tossing the match aside, he said, "Where you from, Little Bull?"

Clay hesitated. "What's this about?"

"You let me ask the questions, boy."

Clay's face grew warm, and his fingers tightened into a fist. Seeing his reaction, Ripley jerked the cigar from his mouth and pointed it at Clay like a pistol. "You listen up, bub, I don't hold for bullshit from Africans, be they free or otherwise. Now you talk straight, or I'll run your black ass to jail so fast folks will think it's a cyclone coming down the street."

"I ain't an African, Sheriff. I'm Choctaw."

A frosty smile flickered across Ripley's face. "So you know who I am, huh? Well, that's good, that's real good. I like that." He put the cigar back in his mouth, working it to one side. "So you're Choctaw, huh? Then you must've come straight north on your way to Leavenworth. But not by the military road, right? Not through Fort Scott. Up along the Neosho, maybe?"

Clay's throat went dry, and a shoulder twitched. Again, Ripley noted the slight reaction.

"What's the matter, boy? Something I say sit wrong?"

Forcing himself to remain calm, Clay replied, "I just ain't a Negro, Sheriff, that's all. I'm Choctaw, but I've been trading with the Wichitas. Ask Lobenstein."

Ripley took in Clay's moccasins and the fringed buckskin shirt. "Well, you don't look like a Leavenworth darky, I'll grant you that." Then his voice hardened. "Were you down on the Neosho a couple of weeks ago?"

"No, I came up the Santa Fe Trail."

"You got people who can vouch for that?"

"A few." Keeping his voice even, Clay reeled off as many names and locations as he could remember, hoping Ripley wouldn't notice how abruptly his descriptions ended barely seventy miles out. "What happened on the Neosho?" he asked when he'd finished, wanting to draw the sheriff's attention away from his painfully short list of witnesses.

"A bunch of white men were killed by runaways," Ripley answered brusquely. "The law's gonna run 'em down, then hang 'em. What do you have to say about that?"

Clay shrugged. "Good luck, I guess."

"You're a lying sonofabitch, aren't you?" Ripley said. He stared at Clay's face, the puffy flesh and partially closed eye. "What happened?"

271

"I was kicked by an ox."

Ripley grunted. "Good for the ox, I say." Then without another word, he stalked off.

Clay remained standing rigidly beside the big Hamilton and Finn wagon, watching until the sheriff was out of sight. Then, with a visibly trembling hand, he reached out to grasp the six-inch-wide iron rim of the freighter's front wheel. His head swam as the memory of Captain Carry's iron collar exploded in his mind. After a couple of minutes he was able to let go of the wheel, and walked back to where the roan ox waited in front of the blacksmith shop.

Jimmy came to the door when he saw Clay. "Ye all right, lad?"

"Yeah, I'm fine."

"The bastard rough ye up, did he?"

Clay shook his head. "No, I'm all right. Just not partial to the law, I guess."

"Then ye be a smart man, I'm thinkin', for the law in these parts is hard on the Negro. I've seen it meself, and ye've seen worse, no doubt. Ye be doin' the right thing, Clay, heading west. Ye'll be a free man out there. Freer than ye'll ever be around here."

"That's possible," Clay agreed, but he wasn't thinking of the buffalo ranges, or of Iron Hand's village. He was thinking of the Kiowa, and a boy who used to be called

Night's Son.

He loosened the roan's chain and pulled the ox around. "Thanks, Jimmy. You're a good man."

"Aw, be off with yeself. But do it soon, Clay. Leavenworth is no place for a dark-skinned man. Not in these bleedin', bloody years, it ain't."

FIFTEEN

A hand gripped Jonas Sands' shoulder, dragging him from his slumber. He slapped at it grumpily, mumbling to be left alone. Then the fingers tightened, pinching into the flesh at the base of his neck, and a voice commanded, "Come on, Sands, get up."

Jonas came awake with a start, peering owl-eyed over the top of his blankets. In the east, framed by the darkened hoop of the wagon cover, the sky was pitch black, studded with starlight. At his side, Tyler Calhoun gave him another shake.

"You awake?" Ty demanded.

"Uh huh."

Laughing, Ty said, "You don't sound like it." He slapped Jonas' leg with the back of his hand. "Come on, it's time to roll."

Jonas threw back his blankets and sat up while Ty crawled to the rear of the prairie schooner and disappeared over the tailgate. He shivered in the pre-dawn cold until he remembered his coat . . . and hat . . . and boots . . . and a smile crept across his face as he felt for his new clothing. He pulled on his boots first, then the broad-brimmed hat. Standing, he shook out first one leg, then the other of his stiff, new trousers. Then he tucked in his shirt and slipped into his canvas jacket. Dropping to his knees, he fumbled in the dark until he located the items he wanted most. Rising once more, his head bowed under the rounded canvas, he buckled the gunbelt around his waist, tugging at the holster and knife sheath until they rode where he wanted them. For a moment then he just stood there, feeling the pull of the weapons and the weight of the hat. His grin widened embarrassingly, but he couldn't help it. He wanted to whoop for joy, but knew that such a display of enthusiasm would be inappropriate. Yet the grin remained as he dropped to the ground and hurried after Ty. . . .

It had been well after midnight before they finished loading the wagons. Silas Becker had let his hired men go home before Ty returned with Oscar, although the store-keeper and his son had stayed behind to help. In the light of a pair of lanterns, Ty and Becker stood on the loading dock and checked off the various sacks, crates, and boxes as they were wheeled from the store-room by Becker's son, Rufus, and set where Jonas and Clay could reach them and stack them in the wagons. Jonas had been keenly aware of both Ty and Clay watching him closely as the evening lengthened, and he was proud afterward that they had only corrected his choice of placement twice — the first time when he stacked a twenty-five pound keg of gunpowder next to the side-board, where it would be more exposed to the weather and river crossings, and the second when he began to bury a case of rifle caps on the floorboards beneath too much weight.

Jonas had been nearly awestruck when he entered the big Hamilton and Finn freighter, with its six-foot wheels and side-boards that topped out close to ten feet above the ground. For the life of him, he couldn't figure out what Ty wanted to take with them that would require so much space. Standing on the thick planks of the floor inside the empty wagon box, it had seemed as if they could carry enough mer-chandise to supply an entire city. Yet as the hours passed, both the freighter and the prairie schooner had been filled. Jonas could hardly believe all the stuff they took. There was plenty for themselves — powder and lead and caps, cases of skinning knives, a fifty-pound foot-trundled grindstone, sacks of flour, beans, potatoes, dried fruits, turnips, sugar, coffee and tea, a five-gallon jug of whiskey, plus sidepork and cases of airtights filled with peaches, sardines, and tomatoes. They took jars of pickling seed for the tongues they intended to cure and haul back to market, hundred-pound burlap sacks of coarse salt for the hides and meat, and sugar for the hams and hump meat that would be smoked. Most of the larger items — two fifty-gallon cast-iron kettles, an array of smaller pots, a weather-faded wall tent with collapsible poles, blankets, sleeping robes, and oilcloth tarps — were already on board but had to be rearranged to fit around the new stuff coming on.

They had taken on trade goods for the Indians, as well — cases of red-and-green-handled butcher knives, two dozen smooth-bored flintlock trade guns in pinewood cases, more powder and lead, and gunflints instead of caps. There were cases of pocket mirrors and combs and beads and bolts of cloth. They took two hundred pounds of tobacco in twisted, five pound carrots, and five hundred pounds of brown sugar in two-pound cones, plus two fifty gallon kegs of molasses and enough coffee to float a good-sized keelboat. They took sheets of tin and copper that could be fashioned into jewelry or arrowheads, plus boxes of those items already made. Other crates carried earrings, tomahawks, and trade swords. Most of the trade goods would be stored through the winter months, while they hunted for meat, hides, tongues, and tallow, according to Ty. In the spring, when the tribes began to stir and the meat became increasingly poor, they would try to locate an Indian village and trade for winter robes.

When they had their own stuff loaded, Ty and Becker had examined the space left over, haggling quietly between themselves. Then Becker turned to his son and said, "Bring out that order for Dooley."

Stuffing his copy of the invoice into a buckskin pouch at his waist, Ty had come into the wagon. "We're gonna haul some freight for a guy named Sam Dooley, out past Salina," he explained. "It'll make for a heavier load and slower travel, but it'll cut some of our expenses."

Jonas nodded as if he understood, while Rufus Becker wheeled the first sacks of pinto beans out of the warehouse and slid them off an iron-wheeled dolly at the edge of the dock.

As cold as it was — they could see their

breath in the lantern light — Jonas had been sweating by the time they finished. Rufus brought out the last of Dooley's order, then wheeled his dolly inside and closed the warehouse door. After stacking the last few items in the schooner, Jonas dropped to the loading dock beside Clay and arched his back against the knotted muscles in his lower back. After Silas Becker disappeared through a side door, Ty had approached Jonas with a grudging look of respect. "You did all right, boy. Are you tired?"

"Nope."

Ty grinned knowingly. "Close to four tons of merchandise between those two wagons, and you're not even tired?" He looked at Clay and winked. "Looks like we've hired a worker."

"Or a liar," Clay replied with a smile.

"Well, I am feeling kind of sore," Jonas admitted. What he didn't say was that he had probably done more work tonight than he'd done in his entire life back home in Boston, and that every muscle was screaming in agony. But he was still afraid they might fire him, or refuse to let him accompany them onto the prairie, if they knew how inexperienced he really was.

"We'll leave the wagons here," Ty said to Clay. "Becker's night watchman will keep an eye on them for us. I'll meet you in the Missouri House in a couple of minutes and buy you a beer."

"All right," Clay said, shrugging into his mackinaw.

Ty jumped down off the loading dock, calling over his shoulder to Jonas, "Come on. We ain't quite finished yet."

Jonas' shoulders sagged at the thought of more work, but he followed without complaint. They walked around to the front of the store, and Ty knocked loudly at the glass. Inside, Becker and his son were conferring over a stack of paperwork. They looked up at Ty's knock, then Rufus came around the counter to pull the bolt on the door. Ty pushed inside with Jonas at his heels.

"Problem?" Rufus asked.

"No," Ty replied. "Just need a few things I didn't have on my original list." He jerked a thumb at Jonas. "Outfit him, will you? A pair of boots and some extra trousers and shirts and such. Get him a good coat, too, and maybe a lighter jacket, and several pairs of gloves. And something that'll shed rain — like a rubber poncho. He'll need a revolver and a knife and some kind of rifle; they don't have to be new, but they need to be in good order. Put it on my tab, and I'll take it out of his wages come spring." He looked at Jonas. "That fair?"

"I can pay," Jonas said. "I don't need credit."

Ty's eyes narrowed suspiciously, taking in Jonas' ragged, dirty clothes. Then he shrugged and said, "Suit yourself." Glancing at Rufus, he added, "Get him a new hat, too, something that'll keep the sun off his neck. Make sure he gets everything he needs, and if he can't pay for it all, put the rest on my bill."

"Sure," Rufus said. "I'll fix him up right."

"We'll be at the Missouri House," Ty told Jonas. "Just down the street. Come over when you're finished here, and we'll have supper."

For close to an hour then, Rufus had led Jonas up and down the long, canyon-like aisles of the store, lighting their way with a wide-based tin lamp. Jonas got a pair of boots to replace his brogans first, settling on sturdy, low-heeled mule-ears that came to mid-shin. Next he had purchased three pairs of heavy duty canvas trousers, two in a natural duck color of light tan, and the third in the new indigo blue that was just starting to make its way onto the plains. The pants were stiff and scratchy, but Rufus assured him they would loosen up in time, becoming as comfortable as an old wool robe on a winter's night.

He bought four shirts in various colors — simple, three-button, cotton pullover types — two pair of two-piece woolens, twelve pairs of socks, a black neck rag, a set of webbed canvas braces, or suspenders, and a sturdy vest.

Finally Rufus led him to the hats, and Jonas' eyes grew wide. Becker and Miles offered a large selection, everything from towering stovepipes to the broad-brimmed plainsman styles worn by Ty and Clay. Jonas settled on a plainsman model, with a sugar-loaf crown and a four-inch brim, black in color. It was one of the cheaper varieties, blocked in rabbit's fur rather than beaver, and Rufus warned him that it wouldn't hold its shape long in wet weather or with hard use, but that was all right with Jonas. He would shape it to suit himself, and make it his own.

He chose a knee-length greatcoat for the coldest months, made of heavy wool and with a cape to shed rain, and a lighter, wool-lined canvas jacket for in-between. He bought several pairs of leather gloves, with gauntlets to protect his wrists, and four heavy wool blankets and an oiled tarp for a groundcloth. Next he added a plate, fork, spoon, and tin cup.

Then Rufus took him to the counter, moving around to the opposite side to reveal in the flickering lamplight a rack filled with rifles, muskets, and shotguns. Jonas' heart beat a little faster at the thought of actually owning one of those long, elegant weapons.

Rufus eyed the rack speculatively for a moment, then chose a heavy-barreled half-stock and set it on the counter. "A Hawken," he announced authoritatively. "There isn't a better rifle on the plains today."

Jonas carefully hefted it, astonished by its weight, disappointed in its simplicity. It was a caplock, with a small iron patchbox inlaid into the stock on the right side, a beaver-tail cheek piece on the left.

"A muzzle-loader," Jonas said in a lukewarm tone.

Rufus smiled. "It's what ninety percent of the hunters carry." He touched the browned octagon barrel with the tip of his index finger. "Fifty-two caliber, thirty-six inch barrel, a full inch across the flats. Plus an adjustable rear sight notched for one hundred, one hundred and fifty, and two hundred yards. Aren't a lot of those out there yet. It'll give you better accuracy for long-range shooting."

But Jonas had been unimpressed. "I was

thinking of a breechloader," he confided, laying the Hawken back on the counter. "Maybe a Sharps."

"If you've got the money, a Sharps is a good choice," Rufus acknowledged. He took a carbine off the rack and placed it next to the muzzle-loader. He grinned at Jonas' expression as the younger man eyed the two weapons side-by-side. "Kind of stubby-looking compared to the Hawken, ain't it?"

"Kind of," Jonas agreed, picking it up. It was light, too.

"Fifty-four caliber," Rufus explained. "It shoots a linen cartridge that we sell here by the box, or you can buy the tools and cloth and make your own. It's a little more trouble than a front-stuffer, but it shoots faster. As long as you have the cartridges, anyway."

Jonas shouldered the carbine, sighting on a storefront lamp across the street. The carbine came up smoothly, tucking into his shoulder as if it were custom-made. He ran his thumb over the bulky sidelock and slanting breech, then lowered the hinged trigger guard to open the chamber.

"On second thought, a Sharps might be just the ticket for you," Rufus said. "It seems a better fit than the Hawken."

Jonas lowered the weapon. "How much?"

he asked.

In the end, with a reloading outfit and enough powder, lead, and caps for three hundred rounds, he had to shell out fifty-seven dollars. The price, nearly twice what the Hawken would have cost similarly outfitted, stunned him. He eyed the pile of clothing lying nearby, yet to be tallied, and began to worry that he might not have enough to pay for it after all. But Rufus hadn't been finished with him yet. Ty had left instructions that Jonas be outfitted with a good revolver and a knife, as well, so Rufus returned the Hawken to its rack, then reached under the counter and started bringing out handguns.

Jonas knew even less about revolvers than he did rifles, but it didn't take him long to find one that fit his smaller hand, a Colt Model 1849, in .31 caliber, sometimes called a Pocket Pistol because of its shorter barrel. Rufus tossed a plain, reddish-brown holster and belt on the counter beside it and put the rest away. Jonas started to feel overwhelmed when Rufus brought out a selection of large-bladed hunting knives.

"You'll use Ty's Green Rivers for your everyday work," Rufus told him. "But a man ain't really a man unless he's got a personal knife."

In the end, Jonas had chosen a hand-forged knife in a common bowie design, with polished horn grips, stubby iron guards, and a ten-inch blade. Rufus added a plain, brass-tacked leather sheath without comment.

"That pretty well rounds it out, I think," Rufus said. "I'll pick out some tools you'll need to work on everything in the field — screwdrivers, cleaning jags and the like. Plus the odds and ends a man ought to carry with him anytime he goes into the woods — flint and steel in case your matches get wet, a whetstone, those kinds of things. Meanwhile, there's a dressing room in the back. You can change there, if you want to, while I add up the total."

Wordlessly, Jonas scooped up what he would need and started down an aisle. "Here," Rufus called, stopping him. He lit a second lamp with a wax taper. "You'll need some light. And these." He shoved the revolver, knife, and carbine across the counter.

His arms full and the lamp clutched tightly in one hand, Jonas had stumbled back to the dressing room. When he came out twenty minutes later and stood in front of the wavy, floor-length mirror, he could barely believe the transformation. Gone was the runaway youth. In his stead there stood a bona fide frontiersman, a man sure enough, save for the broad, silly grin plastered across his face.

Rufus chuckled, coming up behind him. "Man, I wish I were you," he said.

"Me? Why?"

"Going out to the plains to hunt buffalo and fight Indians. The only Indians I'll ever see are the tame ones that come into the store to trade."

Turning back to the mirror, Jonas had tipped his hat back an inch or so and decided he could work on reducing the size of his grin later.

Ty and Clay waited for Jonas at the Missouri House, sipping beers while they went over the last-minute details of the coming season. Ty tried to think of anything he might have overlooked, but came up dry. His thoughts kept shifting to the future, all the things that could go wrong down the line, and how he might avoid them, or handle them if they did, until he finally had to give up. A man didn't control the weather, or the notions of the Plains tribes. He didn't have much to say about rattlesnakes or ornery buffalo or hidden prairie dog holes, either, any one of which could cripple or kill a careless ox, horse, or man. Nor could he could foresee every bog or bed of quicksand in every river crossing, or second-guess when the metal in a rifle might weaken and blow up. And if he tried, he'd either drive himself crazy or become so overwhelmed he wouldn't go out in the first place.

Lost in his own thoughts, Ty didn't notice Clay's quietness for a while. Clearing his throat, he said, "You haven't had much to say tonight."

Clay stirred, then shrugged. "I'm just thinking," he replied.

"Anything in particular?"

After a pause, he said, "Extra men. I thought maybe I'd ride ahead and try to hire a couple of skinners in Topeka."

"That's an idea," Ty admitted, but he couldn't help noticing how Clay avoided his eyes or — now that he thought about it — how tense he had seemed all evening. Thinking back, Ty realized he had been that way ever since returning from Flannigan's.

Leaning back in his chair, Clay rubbed wearily at the back of his neck. "Yeah, figured I'd leave tonight. I could wait for you in Topeka, or somewhere down the trail."

"What's going on, Clay?"

Clay looked up, an expression flashing across his face that warned Ty to back off, to mind his own business. "You said you wanted a couple more men. You changed your mind?"

"No, I just figured we'd look around when we got there."

"It takes time to look around," Clay answered. "Be quicker if one of us went ahead. That way, the whole outfit wouldn't have to stop."

Ty shrugged. He knew there was more eating at Clay than a desire to hire extra men, but he couldn't make a man talk if he didn't want to. And it made sense to have one of them ride ahead to line up a couple of skinners. "Do it," he said finally. "Check around Lawrence first, but if you can't find anyone there, try Topeka. We'll be along in a couple of days."

Clay nodded with what might have been relief. "Sure. I'll see you somewhere down the road." He pushed his chair back and stood up, grabbing his hat off the table. But before he could turn away, Ty stopped him.

"Clay, you know you're part of this outfit now. We stick together, on the range or in town. If you've got trouble, if the Border Ruffians are making threats —"

"I'm just itchy to get started," Clay said,

interrupting. "I came to see the elephant, and like you said, the damn thing kicked me in the face. I think I'll feel more at home out there." He nodded toward the back wall, to the west.

"All right. You're leaving now?"

"As soon as I can saddle my horse." He paused, then nodded. "Keep your nose to the wind, pard."

"You, too, Clay." He watched him walk out the door, puzzled by his behavior.

The bartender appeared at Ty's side, picking up the nearly-full stein Clay had left behind. "I'll just take this out back and dump it," he said confidentially. "Then wash it good."

"No, leave it," Ty said, stiffening.

"Leave it?"

"It's paid for. I'll drink it when I finish this." He tapped the side of his own mug with a finger.

The barkeep's face reddened. "Mister, a nigger just drank outta this mug. You gonna tell me you aim to drink from the same glass as an African?"

Ty's gaze turned hard as flint. "That's right," he replied coldly. "You got something to say about it?"

Setting the stein back on the table, the bartender said, "Suit yourself," with undisguised loathing.

"One more thing," Ty said. "He's Choctaw."

"A nigger's a nigger, far as I'm concerned," the barkeep snarled. "Makes no difference to me what variety he is."

"It does to him," Ty answered softly. "And all of a sudden, it does to me, too."

Jonas arrived ten minutes later, carrying a bulging burlap sack filled with his possibles. A fleeting smile crossed Ty's face when he spotted the pistol on Jonas' hip, the Sharps carbine cradled in his left arm. "Looks like ol' Rufus spared no expense," he remarked as Jonas clumped to the table in his new mule ears.

The kitchen had long since closed, but Ty had talked a waiter into leaving some cold roast beef, bread, and a jar of huckleberry jam on the table. Jonas dug in wordlessly, but Ty only picked at his food. When they finished, Ty placed a dollar on the table and the two men walked back to the corral behind Becker and Miles. Ty had hoped to catch some sleep before putting out, but by the time they returned it was nearly two o'clock. Oscar was still passed out in the shed, his snores rattling the shingles. Ty led Jonas into the corral with a lantern and introduced him to the animals, pointing out the roan ox in particular. "That's Brownie," he said. "Make sure there's a trace chain in her nose ring, and that she's hobbled good anytime you turn her loose. She's a bunch-quitter, and if you don't watch her close she'll be halfway to the Missouri River the minute you turn your back on her."

They led the oxen out of the muddy corral one by one, and tied them to fenceposts. Ty showed Jonas how to curry their coats, paying special attention to their necks and shoulders, where the heavy yokes would ride. He showed him how to inspect the animals for bots or wounds, how to check their hooves to make sure the shoes were tight, and clean out the muck from between their cloven hooves to prevent rot or disease. While Jonas worked on the oxen, Ty led his big bay gelding and the dappled gray out of a smaller corral and did the same for them. When they were done, Jonas crawled inside the prairie schooner with his bedroll, but Ty was too keyed up to sleep. He wandered over to the loading dock where he could stand out of the wind, and lit his pipe. He told himself he ought to at least lie down and rest, but knew it wouldn't do any good. He had never been his own boss before, at least not in the sense that he was now, and as the hour of departure neared, every decision he made seemed bigger and more important.

He hadn't planned to start until the first blush of dawn colored the sky, but after an hour the waiting got to be too much. Putting away his pipe, Ty went to wake his men.

Jonas wasn't much trouble, but Oscar might as well have been drugged, so deep was his sleep. In the end, Ty had to flop him into the prairie schooner with Jonas' help, wrapping him in a buffalo robe to keep him from freezing.

"He'll be all right when he sobers up," Ty assured the younger man, "but you'll have to handle one of the teams by yourself. Can you do it?"

Although Jonas looked surprised by the question, he nodded gamely.

They hitched up the Hamilton and Finn first, backing the wheelers into place and easing the heavy poplar yokes over their necks, locking the bows with wooden pins, then securing with clevises the long, heavy logging chains that ran from iron ring to iron ring in the center of each yoke. When they were finished they had five yokes — ten paired head — standing compliantly in place. The wheelers were closest to the wagon, then the pointers, the first and second swing teams, and finally the leaders in the forward position. They didn't use swing teams on the prairie schooner, since they only needed three yokes for the lighter wagon. The last thing Ty did was lead his horse and the dappled gray behind the freighter and tie them to the tailgate.

With the wagons ready to roll, Ty walked up the alley between the store and the corrals to check the street. Everything seemed quiet. There were still a few horses standing at the hitching rails in front of one of the saloons to the north, but no other freight outfit in sight. Returning to the wagons, he pulled a long-handled bullwhacker's whip from its socket on the near side of the prairie schooner and handed it to Jonas.

"I'll take the lead with the larger wagon," Ty said. "You bring up the rear. More than likely your team will just naturally follow along. All you have to do is make sure they keep up and don't wander off the road. Think you're up to that?"

"I'll do it," Jonas said, nodding.

"Just remember that *'gee'* means right, *'haw'* means left, *'whoa'* stops 'em, and *'get up'* sets everything to rolling." Ty grinned. "You'll do fine. Like I said, they'll probably just follow the freighter, like they've been doing the past two years."

Jonas pulled the collar of his canvas jacket tighter around his neck. "Don't worry about me," he said. "I'll be right behind you."

"Then let's roll." Ty walked over to the Hamilton and Finn and drew his own whip from its socket. He glanced back once. Jonas was watching him expectantly, his long whip held high, his stiff-brimmed hat pulled low over his forehead. Turning back to his team, Ty whistled sharply and barked, "Get up! You, Brownie, Janey, *get!*" He swung the six-foot shaft of his whip over his head once, then let go of the braided leather lash, the poppers cracking sharp as a gunshot above the heads of the leaders. The oxen leaned forward, easing their weight familiarly into the yokes, pulling the chains taut. The big freighter creaked as its weight shifted; the left front wheel slid around, then rolled forward. Ty cracked his whip once more, shouting, *"Hup!"* to let the cattle know he meant business.

He took the team into the street, shouted, *"Gee,"* once, and lined them out to the south. He kept looking back as they made their way down the broad thoroughfare, but the schooner seemed to be rolling smoothly.

They made four miles by dawn, when Ty guided the Hamilton and Finn off the road and into an empty freighter's camp. The sun was just starting its climb over the thickly wooded hills behind them, its light glittering off the frost-glazed fields. He and Jonas unhitched the teams and turned them loose to graze. Then, while Jonas went off in search of firewood, Ty climbed aboard the prairie schooner to rouse Oscar Garrett. Poking his head over the tailgate, he wrinkled his nose in revulsion. "Goddamnit, old man, you messed yourself, didn't you?"

A low groan rose from the wagon's interior. Clambering inside, Ty grabbed a handful of Garrett's robe and gave it a sharp tug. A thin, liver-spotted hand slithered out from under the buffalo covering and slapped feebly at the air. "Go 'way," Oscar moaned in a reedy, whiskey-husked voice. "Damnit, leave me be. I'm dyin'."

"You ain't dying, unless you're suffocating from your own stink," Ty growled. He flipped back a corner of the robe, revealing Oscar's hollow, ashen face. "Sweet Jesus," Ty said, covering his nose with his hand. "You've puked all over yourself. I'll bet you pissed your pants, too."

Oscar's head rolled loosely. His closed eyelids fluttered, then opened. Squinting upward, his gaze roamed the hooped canvas until it came to rest on Ty. "Tyler?" he croaked. "Lord help me, boy, is that you?"

"Come on, old man, get up and clean yourself off. Let's get some breakfast down your gullet, too. I need you to handle one of the teams."

Oscar shook his head, groaning softly. "Best you go on without me, Ty. I don't think I'm gonna make it."

Ty laughed harshly. "We've already started, you worthless drunk. We left last night."

Oscar closed his eyes, and his claw-like hand fell atop his robe. "You goddamn traitor," he rasped softly.

"Come on, we've got a full day ahead of us." Ty leaned back, watching until he was sure the old man was awake, then climbed out of the wagon and went around to the grub box, bolted to the side of the wagon. He removed a slab of bacon, some potatoes, a spider — a cast-iron skillet with four six-inch legs and a two-foot handle — and a two-gallon coffeepot with a sack of roasted beans and a tiny hand grinder stored inside. He took it all to a nearby firepit that still had an armful of kindling at its side, and used a flint and steel to strike a fire.

Although it took a while, Oscar eventually crawled out of the wagon, dragging his soiled robe with him and dumping it on the ground. He stood by the tailgate for several minutes, hanging onto it as if afraid he'd keel over if he let go.

Ignoring him, Ty sliced strips of bacon into the spider. In time, Oscar came over and sank cross-legged to the ground beside the fire, resting his elbows on his knees and cupping his forehead in his hands. "Damnit, Tyler, you should've left me in . . . well, wherever the hell it was we were at. Leavenworth, weren't it?"

"Go scrub yourself off," Ty said without looking up. "There's no point in the rest of us losing our appetites because of the way you smell."

Oscar raised his head, a trace of independence flaring in his watery blue eyes. "We'll both be stinkin' a hell of a lot worse'n this, once we start skinnin' buff."

"Maybe, but we ain't skinning anything yet. Go on now. There's a clean shirt in your warbag."

"I ain't no snot-nosed brat," Oscar retorted sullenly. "I won't put up with you treatin' me like one, either."

Ty let the old man's reply slide, and kept his attention focused on breakfast. There had been times in the past when the old plainsman had seemed on the verge of challenging one or the other of the five partners, only to back off when they all stuck together.

But Ty was on his own now, and he was curious to see how Oscar would react with just him calling the shots. His gut feeling was that sooner or later he'd have to set Garrett in place, either that or suffer intolerably down the road.

Jonas came out of the trees with an armload of wood that he dumped beside the fire with a clatter, then stepped back to stare at the older man. Oscar's brows furrowed as he squinted up at Jonas, then looked woefully at Ty. "Tell me you didn't hire this pup for the winter, Tyler. Tell me this is just some pissant stray you picked up and are gonna kick loose at the next settlement."

"Oscar, this is Jonas Sands. He'll do the dog work around camp, and maybe help with the skinning and hides. Jonas, this is Oscar Garrett. When he sobers up, you watch him close and listen to what he says. Oscar was tramping these plains long before either one of us were born."

"Pleased to meet you, sir," Jonas said, extending a hand.

Oscar glowered a moment, then leaned forward. *"Boo!"* he said loudly, and Jonas flinched and jerked his hand back.

"Oh, God," Oscar groaned, wagging his head sadly. "Weren't it bad enough you tied yourself up with a worthless old sot like me and that goddamn bunch-quitter?" His gaze roamed out toward the feeding oxen. "She still with us, ol' Brownie, or did you finally smarten up and shoot the bitch?"

Ty followed the direction of Oscar's gaze. Even with the chain fastened to her nose ring and the hobbles on her forelegs, the roan ox was edging towards the woods and escape. "Keep an eye on her," he told Jonas. Looking at Oscar, he added, "Jonas is a good hand. He brought that wagon here all the way from Leavenworth."

"While I was passed out drunk in back, is that what you're sayin'?"

"More or less. Loosen your rein, Oscar. Jonas is green, but he'll learn."

"Was a time I'd've throwed a runt like that back 'til it was done suckin', Ty."

"Yeah, but that was before you crawled inside a bottle, wasn't it?" Ty answered cruelly.

Oscar looked away, blinking back sudden tears of shame. "By God, you're gonna be a hardass, ain't cha? I seed ol' Matt'n Keith 'fore they took off for their mama's lap. They said you'd changed. Well, go ahead and have your say, but we'll see who holds his ground, it comes time to get a skin off'n a buffler 'fore she freezes up." He glared at Jonas. "You might be green as spring grass

300

now, sonny, but that green'll wear off mighty quick where we're goin'."

"I'll do my share," Jonas replied defensively.

"You will, by God. I'll see to that."

Ty tossed a final piece of bacon in the skillet and stood up, wiping his knife clean on a rag. "Jonas, go fetch some more wood. Head Brownie off while you're at it. Oscar, go clean the puke off your chin before you start preaching to anyone." When neither man moved immediately, he roared, "I said *git!* Goddamnit, I ain't standing here listening to you two bicker like an old married couple!"

Jonas scurried off, but Oscar remained where he was, staring at Ty with a strangely serene expression. "Knowed a man what barked his orders like that once't. Back in '46, it were. We was haulin' freight for Kearney's Army of the West, durin' the Mexican conflict. Boys put up with it damn near to El Paso, then they took him out in the desert and shot him in the balls. Coon never did see ol' Paso town."

Ty's voice hardened. "Oscar, if you ever threaten me again, I'll kick your ass all the way back to Leavenworth. Now go clean up. And clean off that buffalo robe, too. I don't want it stinking up the wagon."

Oscar creaked slowly to his feet, paused as if he wanted to say more, then slashed the air with his hand in a dismissing gesture. "The hell with you, Tyler Calhoun," he snarled, then stepped around the fire and made his way to a stream that flanked the road.

Ty sighed and hunkered down beside the fire. He fed it a few of the larger pieces of the wood that Jonas had brought in, poking them absently into the crackling flames. Then he picked up a potato and started to cube it.

Sixteen

They moved out again as soon as breakfast was finished. Oscar bullwhacked the Hamilton and Finn while Jonas brought up the rear with the prairie schooner. Ty saddled his bay while the two hired men yoked their teams, and as soon as the wagons were moving he rode on ahead, needing some time to himself.

The road was dry and relatively smooth after the long rainy spell, the oxen fresh after their grain-fed rest. They made good time, traveling almost due west now, and leaving the more timbered land behind as the sun sank toward the horizon.

They camped that night beside a sparsely wooded stream, where they had to use old, dried ox dung to fuel their fire. Oscar ate sparingly, barely nibbling on a biscuit and some sidepork, and limiting himself to a single cup of coffee. When he finished, he went to bed without a word, and within minutes his raucous snoring ripped the night air. While Jonas took the dirty dishes down to the stream to wash, Ty brought out his pipe and tobacco, but didn't light it. He was tired after the last thirty-six hours of pushing, but it was a pleasant kind of tired, and he knew he would sleep well that night.

After storing the clean dishes in the grub box, Jonas came over to squat on the balls of his feet at the fire. He'd taken off his jacket while washing dishes, and his sleeves were soaked to the elbow, the front of his shirt splashed wet. Holding his reddened hands close to the flames, he rubbed them briskly together, without comment or complaint, and Ty nodded his approval.

"I noticed that shooter of yours isn't capped," Ty said casually.

Jonas looked up and shrugged, his eyes baggy from fatigue. "I've been wanting to load it, I just haven't had time."

Thinking back, Ty could see where he hadn't. He'd put the kid to work almost from the moment he approached him in Becker and Miles' corral the day before, and only given him an hour or so to sleep in that time. Jonas looked exhausted, barely able to keep his balance above the fire. But they were on the trail now, and couldn't afford the luxury of carelessness. Not out here, where it could cost a man his life.

"Go get your stuff," Ty said. "I'll show you how to load that pistol, if you don't already know. Bring your carbine, too."

Jonas hung by the fire for a moment, then rose and trudged to the wagon. He returned a few minutes later with a shooting bag and a can of triple-F gunpowder. Sitting cross-legged on the ground, he opened the bag's flap.

"Rufus Becker said this was everything I'd need," Jonas remarked as he started bringing the bag's contents into the light. There was a brass powder flask with a pre-measured spout; a flat, round brass capper; a little leather sack filled with .320 balls; a tin container of hard lubricant. He also had a kit for cleaning, and some tools to work on the revolver in the field.

Ty had him scrub the bore and chambers with a light cotton rag, then snap a cap over each nipple to dry what oil the rag failed to reach. He showed him how to pour powder into each tiny chamber, followed by the ball, then how to seat it with the loading lever hinged under the barrel, before coating the mouth of each chamber with a thin layer of lubricant to prevent cross-firing. Under Ty's instructions, Jonas loaded all five chambers, but only capped four; keeping the fifth nipple free as a place to rest the hammer kept them from having to rely on the less dependable notches cut into the cylinder between each chamber. Lastly, Ty had him use a smidgen of grease to seal each cap.

"It'll keep one chamber from igniting two or three others," Ty explained, "and maybe blowing your hand off in the process. Plus it'll help keep your powder dry in wet weather."

Jonas' eyes sparkled as he held the loaded revolver up to the firelight.

"It ain't a big gun," Ty commented, "but then, I've never seen a shooter who could hit anything over thirty or forty yards away with a revolver, anyway, and this'll do for close-up work. Just don't try to shoot a buffalo with it. You'll only make it mad.

"We'll shoot it tomorrow during the noon break, then I'll show you how to clean it. You'll spend more time cleaning the damn thing than you will firing it — every day or so in wet weather — but the extra work will pay off the first time you need it."

Jonas slipped the Colt into its holster. "You and Oscar carry your pistols on your left hips with the butts facing forward, but Clay carries his on his right hip, with the butt facing back."

"This one's yours," Ty said. "Carry it

however it's comfortable for you." He picked up the Sharps, running his hand along the polished walnut stock, then up the round, blued barrel to the humped, brass-bladed front sight. He nodded in appreciation. "You made a good choice here, Jonas. The Sharps is building a hell of a reputation on the plains. I kind of wish I had one, instead of my Hawken."

Jonas' gaze dropped to the muzzle-loader Ty had kept with him ever since leaving Leavenworth, across his saddlebows during the day, and leaning against his saddle here at the fire now. "Have you killed a lot of buffalo with that?" he asked.

"A few," Ty said softly. "I'll let you try it when we get where we're going, see how it compares to your Sharps."

"Where's that?" Jonas asked. "How far west, I mean, to where we're going?"

"A ways yet," Ty admitted, putting the route together in his mind. "I'd guess two hundred miles, maybe more."

Jonas whistled softly.

"A long way," Ty agreed. He handed the carbine to Jonas. "Here, clean the bore like you did your side-shooter. Load it, but don't cap it. Do you know how?"

Jonas nodded. "Rufus showed me."

"Do it, then. I'll check the stock, make

307

sure Brownie hasn't thrown her hobbles. When I get back we'll split the night watch between us."

"Watch?" An odd look crossed Jonas' face. "Indians?"

"I'd be more concerned about Border Ruffians around here, looking to raise hell with anyone who doesn't share their views about slavery." He grinned. "You said yesterday you were looking for prairie savvy. What did I tell you?"

"You said I was in it with both feet, but you didn't mention how deep it was."

"It's deep, Jonas. It's way over both our heads. But that doesn't mean we have to go under, not if we're careful, and watch the other man's back as well as our own. Savvy?"

Jonas nodded soberly. "Yeah, I savvy."

They passed through Lawrence late the next afternoon, crossing the Kaw River on a rope ferry, but they didn't stop. Another two days saw them through Topeka. Here, Ty called a halt in a grove of trees just outside of town. "Stay with the wagons," he told Oscar and Jonas. "I'll be back in an hour."

He rode back to town, but there was no sign of Clay, nor anyone who remembered seeing him. Ty returned to the wagons feeling torn and worried, but had no choice but to push on. Although it seemed unlikely, he knew he had to consider the possibility that Clay had decided he didn't want a partnership in a buffalo hunting outfit after all, and had gone off on his own hook.

Oscar sulked when Ty gave the order to move out, but kept his opinions to himself. Ty knew he was angry at being told to stay behind, and that he'd probably had his heart set on a drink. Jonas was quiet, too, but Ty could tell the younger man's mood was affected more by Clay's absence than any urge to visit Topeka.

They camped that night near the head of a grassy draw on the road to Fort Riley. Ty located a grove of half-grown black walnut trees surrounding a spring, with a little flat just below it, and waved the wagons in. He made a quick circuit around the trees while the wagons struggled up the draw and found no sign of a nearby dwelling.

Oscar was steaming when Ty returned. He'd parked the freighter at the edge of the flat, and had apparently been waiting in a tiff beside his wheelers ever since. As soon as Ty dismounted, Oscar threw his whip to the ground and stomped over.

"You know what the damn fool did, don't cha?" Oscar demanded as Ty flipped the near stirrup over the saddle's seat. "He started unhitchin' his teams 'fore settin' his brakes and chockin' the wheels. He thinks this flat is *flat,* but by damn, Ty, it ain't. That wagon would've rolled right back into the draw if I hadn't been here to set things straight. Would'a busted 'er up good, too. Might'a ruined it! Then where would you'da been? Just one wagon, and that that goddamn heavy sonofabitchin' freighter, which is about as worthless for huntin' as this kid is for bullwhackin'."

"Then it's a good thing you were here, isn't it?" Ty said. He worked a finger into the knotted latigo and gave it a couple of tugs.

Oscar's face darkened. "Damnit, Tyler, that whelp ain't got no more business out here than I do sittin' in a fancy parlor in St. Louie. The little shit ain't been *tried.* He's too fresh off the tit for what we got in mind."

It took all of Ty's resolve to calmly continue unsaddling his horse. Sliding an arm under the hulk's frame, he pulled it off the gelding's back and dropped it in the grass. "Why don't you go unhitch, maybe help Jonas with his team while you're at it?"

"Screw him," Oscar snapped. "Onliest way that peckerwood's gonna learn is to do it hisself."

310

Ty blinked rapidly. "Oscar, that's my wagon you're talking about, and my team. Show him what to do, but let him do it. He's quick, he'll figure it out with a little help."

Grumbling under his breath, Oscar went to unhitch his oxen. Ty took a deep, shaky breath, turning just as Jonas showed up from the direction of the prairie schooner, looking as crestfallen as a jilted beau. "Jesus Christ," Ty said jarringly. "Just let it drop, Jonas. You ain't the first man to forget to set a brake or chock a wheel, and you won't be the last, so just shut up about it."

Jonas' head rocked back in surprise. Then his lower lip started to tremble and he turned quickly away, hurrying past the wagons and back down the draw.

"Goddamn," Ty said to himself. "Just god-damnit it all to hell, anyway."

They ate their supper in silence. Oscar simmered in a rage that was no doubt fueled by the ill effects of his long drunk back in Leavenworth, and Jonas just picked at his food, staring at his plate in exhaustion. There were blisters on the younger man's palms from handling the heavy whip, and he'd been limping all day, walking bow-legged to take as much weight as he could off the bottoms of his feet. A couple of days rest would probably help them both, Ty thought, and he briefly considered doing it while he went back in search of Clay, then decided against it. In part, he was half afraid to leave the two men alone for any length of time. He knew Oscar was a dangerous man, a savage by most standards. Some of the stories he'd told them last season — of casual killings, brutal rapes, and indiscriminate theft — had left Ty nearly numb. Oscar Garrett had been raised in a world so completely different from his own, and probably Jonas', that it was doubtful either of them would ever understand the vicious paradigms that guided the older man. In many ways, men like Oscar reminded Ty of feral dogs — friendly enough until one of them became sick or injured, then a whole pack would turn on the hurt beast, tearing its flanks, ripping the flesh from its haunches, devouring it with no more hesitation than it would a rabbit. *No,* Ty mused, *a kid like Jonas wouldn't last long at all against a man like Oscar Garrett.*

From somewhere above the walnut grove, a horse snuffled. Oscar swore and dropped his plate. "Injuns, goddamnit!" he hissed, reaching for his rifle.

"Hold on," Ty ordered, pressing his hand

lightly against Oscar's arm. "Both of you stay put." He stood and wrapped his fingers around the butt of his pistol.

It wasn't quite full dark yet, but it was close, and Ty had to strain to make out anything in the shadows of the black walnuts. It was a splash of white that caught his attention first, then the soft thud of a horse approaching at a walk. The horse stopped at the edge of the trees, and a voice called out, "Hello the camp."

"This is Tyler Calhoun's outfit, bound for the buffalo ranges," Ty answered. "Come on in, if you're of a notion."

"What the hell's goin' on here?" Oscar mumbled from his seat next to the fire. "Do you know this jasper, Ty?"

"I might." Ty watched until the horseman came into the light, then smiled and let his hand fall away from his Colt. "Damn, Clay, I was beginning to think you'd run out on us."

Clay dismounted, his expression subdued. Oscar stood, clearly confused. "Who the hell is this?" he demanded of Ty. "Is this who you was lookin' for back in Topekee?"

"This is my partner," Ty explained, "Clay Little Bull."

"Partner!" Oscar looked dumbfounded.

Ty nodded, not at all surprised by Garrett's forgetfulness. "Yeah, my partner, Oscar, and your new boss. You met him in Leavenworth, the day you were supposed to help load the wagons."

"I don't remember meetin' no nigra in Leavenworth," Oscar replied. He let his rifle slide through his hands until the steel buttplate bounced off the hard prairie sod between his feet. "Your partner, huh? Well I'll be go to hell."

Clay dropped the pinto's reins and walked over to the fire, sliding his knife from its scabbard. "You will," he promised, placing the tip of the blade against Oscar's breast, "the next time you call me a nigger."

As soon as they had the wagons back on the Fort Riley road the next morning, Clay and Ty jogged their horses ahead a couple of hundred yards, where they could speak without being overheard. It was still early, the air cool and the breeze just starting to stir. Although the sun wasn't yet up, Clay could tell it was going to be a beautiful day, the sky high and wide, already shading into a deep, rich blue.

The two men rode side-by-side without speaking for maybe a mile before Clay finally broke the silence. "I reckon I owe you an apology. I won't let it happen again."

"Don't worry about it."

"I ain't dumb, Ty," Clay said stubbornly. "I know you stopped in Topeka and asked around, so you know I wasn't there."

Ty looked off into the distance. "I heard about the slavers they found down on the Neosho. Is that what this is about?"

Clay was silent a moment, debating how much he wanted to reveal, how far he could trust this white-eye. In the end, all he said was, "I heard about that, too. I guess Kansas ain't the haven for a black man I thought it would be."

"What about a Choctaw?"

"Choctaw," Clay answered bitterly. "Yeah, I'll be sure to bring that up the day some white mob puts a noose around my neck."

Ty gave him a searching look. "I ain't puttin' a noose around your neck, Clay. Slavers are a low lot, and if you had a hand in that affair, then I'd say you did Kansas a favor. And if you didn't, I could still understand why you'd be nervous about it. The damn militias are always looking for someone to string up."

"Gets so a man doesn't know what to do," Clay admitted after a long pause. "Like pulling my knife on Garrett last night. They'd have hung me for that in Leavenworth." He looked at Ty, his expression pained. "I don't know if I could've done it there. I'm not sure I would've had the courage."

"Fear isn't anything to be ashamed of. You ought to know that. And there's some who would say you were smart not to pull a knife on a white man anywhere, these days. Pride's a good thing to have, but it ain't necessarily worth dying for."

"They don't want just your freedom, Ty, those proslavers," Clay said softly. "They want your soul, too. They want to yank it right out of you and crush it in their fists like it was a clod of dirt."

"Some do, but not everyone. Topeka has a large anti-slavery population. There's plenty of people in Leavenworth who would like to see Kansas become a free state, for that matter."

"Well, you could've fooled me," Clay said dryly.

Ty smiled sympathetically. "It'll be better out on the short grass, you'll see."

Clay didn't respond. He felt off-balance, caught between the man he had once thought himself and the person he somehow seemed to have become since Simon's death.

For a long time then, there was no sound save the clopping of their horses' hooves and the chirping of birds in the tall prairie grasses along the road. After a spell, bringing his thoughts back to the present, Clay said, "Just the same, I'm obliged for your understanding about my not showing up in Topeka."

"Forget it," Ty said.

Clay let it drop, but he knew he wouldn't forget it. He had a lot to sort out, about himself and where he fit in this strange new country, and about the white-eyes, too — men like Ty and Jimmy Flannigan, and even Jonas. They didn't fit the neat little cubbyholes Simon and Plato and Sammy Lee had assigned them. Like himself, they were outsiders . . . square pegs. But they were good men, too, and that counted for a lot, and made the rest so damn puzzling.

SEVENTEEN

Cornelius Rothchild was late. The sun was two hours gone now, the narrow lane he followed lit by only a dusting of scudded starlight that made the chore of negotiating the twisting road tunneling through the forest northwest of Leavenworth all the more difficult. Despite the poor light, Cornelius kept the long-legged sorrel mare he'd rented from the livery moving at a brisk pace, the well-sprung surrey bouncing in a lively manner over the jagged ruts that threaded the little used back road. The truth was, Cornelius Rothchild was afraid of the dark, and had he not been forced to wait back at the rundown farm of the Delaware Indian, Louis Apple Tree, he would have been home hours ago.

Last spring, Apple Tree had borrowed two hundred and eighty dollars from the bank where Cornelius worked. He'd wanted to pay off a debt incurred at a horse race up in

Nebraska Territory the previous fall, that debt having accrued enough interest over the preceding winter that the men Apple Tree owed were threatening to burn down his house, and maybe break his legs while they were there. So Louis had come to Cornelius to borrow the money, signing over a herd of ten Jersey milk cows as collateral.

Although Cornelius knew Apple Tree was a poor risk, he had been quick to see a potential for gain, so he'd approved the loan, then sat back to see what would develop.

Predictably, the cows had soon disappeared. Louis claimed they were stolen, but Cornelius had his own opinion, having firsthand information that Apple Tree was back to his old gambling habits in Nebraska. Now the bank wanted its money returned — three hundred and twenty dollars, counting the interest.

It was late afternoon when Louis finally showed up at the family farm, swaying slightly from too much bootjack cider. When informed of the purpose of Cornelius' visit, the Indian had sneeringly informed him he didn't owe him anything, and that if the bank wanted its money, it should try to recover the Jerseys that had been rustled off his property earlier that summer.

"It's them thieves that owe you now," Louis slurred as he handed his portly, stoic wife a string of headless squirrels, then sank into a hand-made chair of wrist-sized limbs and rawhide.

Louis' reply was the kind of remark Cornelius lived for. He reached inside the breast pocket of his plaid suit coat and tossed a yellow envelope onto the rough-hewn kitchen table.

"What's that?" Louis asked suspiciously.

Indians, Cornelius had learned in his years as a frontier banker and occasional independent speculator in land and other properties, had developed a healthy distrust of the talking leaves of the white men, even though many of them could read as well as any Caucasian, thanks to the missionary schools that dotted the reservations.

"It's a foreclosure deed on your house and land," Cornelius told him. "As stated on the last page of your loan application, Clause Twelve, if for any reason you are unable to make restitution of the monies borrowed from the bank, the bank has the right to recoup said monies in any reasonable fashion. In this instance, since the total accumulation of your liquid assets comes to less than the three hundred and twenty dollars owed us, the bank has decided to foreclose on your farm."

Louis scowled. "You saying you're gonna take our place? Is that what all that fancy talk means?"

Cornelius smiled broadly. "In a nutshell, yes. Of course, we don't intend to act upon our rights immediately. We want you to have time to talk to your agent here on the reserve. Perhaps he could offer some advice, or help you procure the money to pay off your debt."

"That Quaker bastard," Louis snarled. "He'd like to see me lose everything. He's been riding my ass like a jockey ever since he got here."

"Yes, so I've heard. He thinks you spend too much time drinking illegal whiskey and gambling away whatever money you make on horse races and cockfights."

"I'll tell you the same thing I told Agent Duff, and that's that you can both skate to hell in the next ice storm. I don't need a bunch of white men coming in here tellin' me I need to plant more corn or put a better roof on my cabin."

Cornelius shrugged nonchalantly. "It's entirely up to you, my friend, but remember, it was *you* who borrowed two hundred and eighty dollars from my bank last spring, and we want our money back. I might also add that after January first, the interest will jump another twenty dollars."

"Get outta my house!" Louis yelled. He struggled to his feet and stumbled to the butcher block, where he shoved his silent wife aside and grabbed the massive butcher knife she'd been using on the squirrels. He waved the bloody blade dangerously close to his own ear, but any further threats were severed by the sight of the pocket revolver Cornelius had produced from a shoulder holster.

"I will not be intimidated," Cornelius staunchly informed the abruptly frozen Delaware. "We acted in good faith when we loaned you that money, and have every right to demand its return."

Louis let the heavy knife sag. "All right," he growled. "How much time have I got?"

"We'll begin foreclosure after January fifteenth."

"Christ, I can't raise three hundred and twenty dollars by the middle of January. Gimme longer. Let me get a buffalo hunt organized. A bunch of us'll go out and get some winter robes. My ol' woman'll tan 'em in the spring, and I'll take 'em to Lobenstein. How's that sound?"

"I'm sorry, but we can't wait that long." Cornelius rose, keeping his pistol handy just in case. Jutting his chin toward the envelope on the table, he added, "It's all there, Louis. Copies of everything. Take it to Agent Duff and see if he'll help you."

Apple Tree's face twisted in anger. "You're a bastard, Rothchild, just like Duff, both of you thinkin' you can lord it over me like I was trash. But you ain't takin' this place. The damn white man owes me this much, for what they took from my people."

"Perhaps, but I'm not the one who's foreclosing on your property. The bank is, and it has the authority to back it up, if need be. You might want to think of your wife and children for a change."

"You think about 'em," Louis snapped like a quirt-stung hound. "I got a shitpot full of money to think about."

Cornelius nodded, satisfied. He slid his revolver back into its holster and moved to the door. "That sounds like a wise decision," he said. "Much better than having me blow your head off." Then he stepped outside, into the gathering dusk, and climbed into his rented surrey.

It had gone pretty well, Cornelius mused as he wheeled the lightweight vehicle down the lopsided lane and onto the narrow trace of the wagon road that would take him back to Leavenworth. He was always a little disappointed when a debtor took the news of an impending foreclosure with the inanimate aplomb of a dullard. It was more fun when they showed some spunk, especially at the end, when he whipped out his pistol and cocked it in their faces. It was priceless, the expressions they manifested at the realization that Cornelius Rothchild was no mere pasty-faced banker grown fat on other men's hard luck, that he was, in fact, a man of considerable crust.

Louis Apple Tree's reaction had been truly delightful. Partially drunk, surly, dirty, and sneeringly arrogant, he had been a classic example of the kind of man Cornelius liked most to cut down a few notches. The only impediment to a perfect ending had been the man's tardiness in returning home from his squirrel hunt.

While there was light, Cornelius kept the sorrel at a reckless; mile-eating trot, slowing only when the fire went out of the sky and the trees closed in overhead. Even then, he didn't spare the whip any. In time it became a sort of contest between him and the sorrel, a means of venting his frustration at the Delaware for causing him to be so late. He kept popping the mare's hips with his whip, then sawing back hard on the lines when she attempted to break into a faster gait.

The horse was reacting nastily, tossing her head, attempting to take the light snaffle bit in her teeth and run. A couple of times Cornelius thought she might have kicked back at him with a rear hoof, although it was hard to tell in the dark, what with the rough condition of the road and all. He popped her a good one with his whip both times, however, just in case, and gradually his fear of the night began to disappear beneath a shroud of anger at the mare's resistance.

So caught up was he in his battle with the sorrel that he failed to notice the three horsemen sitting their mounts across the road in front of him, bathed in a ghostly column of starlight breaking through the clouds. It wasn't until the sorrel threw up her head and came to a sudden, surrey-skewing stop that Cornelius spotted the masked riders blocking his path. Instinctively, his hand darted inside his jacket for the revolver, but even as he drew it, one of the horsemen spurred his mount forward and slashed the back of Cornelius' hand with a riding crop.

Cornelius hollered loudly, as much in surprise as pain, and the stubby-barreled revolver spun out of his fingers and disappeared in the grass bordering the road. A second rider jogged his horse forward and jerked the sorrel's lines from Cornelius' opposite hand. The third man palmed an engraved, ivory-handled Colt, one of a pair holstered at his waist, and pointed it at Cornelius' chest.

"Robbery!" Cornelius cried. "By the heavens, this won't be tolerated —"

"Shut up, Rothchild," the man who'd quirted him commanded. He tipped his hat back, revealing a broad, chocolate-hued forehead, thin, almost womanly brows, and deep-set eyes the color of charcoal. With an abrupt motion, he jerked the bandanna off the lower portion of his face.

"Hart!" Cornelius exclaimed. He sank back in the surrey's patent leather seat, rubbing unconsciously at the stinging flesh of his right hand. He glanced at the man holding the sorrel's bit and recognized him by his shape — Ross Lake. The third man was a stranger, tall and slim to the point of appearing frail, but without any sign of a tremor in the gleaming blued barrel of the revolver aimed at Cornelius' heart.

"We've been waiting for you," Buford Hart said in his deep, hammer-on-wood voice. Before Cornelius could reply, Ross piped up from beside the sorrel's head.

"Gawd A'Mighty, Rothchild, what have you been doing to this horse? It's lathered up like you've run it all the way from Apple Tree's."

"H-how do you know of my business at Louis Apple Tree's?" Cornelius sputtered indignantly.

With a creak of saddle leather, Buford cocked his head to one side and spat past his boot. "God's honest truth, Rothchild, I don't give a rat's ass what you've been up to out at Louis' place. What I want to know is, where the hell's the money you promised me'n Ross?"

Cornelius licked nervously at his lips. His glance darted skeptically to the third man, then flitted away. "That business proposition didn't pan out due to the premature demise of the subject."

"What you mean," Buford returned scathingly, "is that you're trying to wheedle out of our deal because some dumb-as-shit white man got blamed for killing Francis Duck."

"For Christ's sake, Hart, keep your voice down," Cornelius snapped.

"Rothchild," Buford said calmly, "you owe us a hundred dollars for knifing that bastard. You got that kind of money on you tonight?"

"Of course not," Cornelius replied. "Are you telling me it wasn't the hunter, Virgil Nash, who killed Francis Duck?"

"What do you think?" Ross answered, as if talking to a half-wit.

"I read the papers," Cornelius challenged, still speaking to Hart. "They stated —"

"I know what they said," Buford interrupted.

"Then you must realize that any monies owed you were invalidated when Duck was killed by another individual."

Buford's brows furrowed down until his eyes were nearly eclipsed. "Listen, you fat, greasy toad, you found the papers you wanted in the tree behind your house, didn't you?"

Reluctantly, Cornelius nodded. Here was an element he'd momentarily forgotten.

"How the hell do you think they got there, dumbshit?"

"I . . . I assumed you took advantage of the situation, that you knew he'd been knifed and . . . possibly . . . well . . . took advantage of the situation . . . when he was knifed —" Cornelius' voice faltered.

Deliberately, Buford freed a single button on his long wool coat and brushed it back. From a simple black holster, he drew an old Colt's Third Model Dragoon and leveled it on the center of Cornelius' forehead.

Swallowing audibly, Cornelius said, "If you shoot me now, Hart, you'll never see your money."

Ross laughed; even Buford smiled. "Oh, we'll get our money, Rothchild. You didn't think Francis Duck had the balls to break into your house and steal those papers to begin with, did you?"

"I . . ." Cornelius' breath was coming rapidly now, his pulse pounding in his ears. "If not him . . . who?"

"Me," Hart answered, smiling. "Kind of ironic, ain't it? The Indian hires me'n Ross to break into your house and steal them papers that tells the world you cheated him outta half the property Leavenworth is sitting on today, then you hire us to steal 'em back, and kill Duck once and for all. It would've been a pretty funny joke, something me'n Ross might've laughed over for a long time . . . if you hadn't tried to cheat us." He thumbed the Dragoon's hammer back.

"My God, if you shoot me —"

"We already know where you hide your cash," Hart reminded him.

"Listen," Cornelius pleaded. "I . . . I can't die. I . . . I'm not ready yet. I've got things . . . listen, you know Carpenter's wife, the one who wears perfume? I've been seeing her while her husband's at work. She hasn't given in yet, but I was hoping —"

Ross hooted loudly. "By damn, listen to that, Buf! Ol' Corny's been trying to dip his wick in a married woman's pot!" He started to laugh, releasing the sorrel's line as he bent forward.

Hart looked away, shaking his head. "That's the most pitiful excuse for living I've ever heard, Rothchild. I've got half a notion to plug you just for telling me about it."

For a moment, Cornelius thought he saw his chance, but the third man, the one who had remained silent the whole time, spotted it at the same instant and coolly cocked his ivory-handled revolver. Cornelius lowered his buggy whip, his hands shaking violently.

"You should've gone ahead and tried it," Buford said sadly. "Hell, who knows, you might've made it."

Sweat bathed Cornelius' face, dripping from his pudgy chin to soak his shirtfront. "Listen, Hart, I don't keep my money in that box behind the armoire anymore. I . . . I have a new place, one you might not find. But you're right, of course. A deal is a deal, and it was foolish of me to assume someone else killed Francis Duck without checking it out further, especially in lieu of the papers that showed up in the fork of my china-berry tree, right where you said you'd leave them. For that, you both deserve a bonus, say an extra hundred dollars apiece. How does that sound?"

"It ain't enough," Ross said. He reached out to grip the sorrel's headstall; when he spoke again, every trace of humor had vanished from his voice. "I say this is where we give Sammy Lee his chance, Buf. All I've heard from him is a bunch of rot about how us niggers gotta take what's rightfully ours. I figure this is as good a time as any to see if he's got what it takes."

Cornelius glanced wildly at the man holding the ivory-handled Colt. Sammy Lee's gaze drifted questioningly to Hart. "How about it?" Sammy Lee asked. "You want me to kill him?"

"You sure you can?" Hart asked with a trace of taunting. "Saying you've snapped a cap on a white man and actually doing it —"

The night was suddenly shattered by the blast of Sammy Lee's pistol. Cornelius saw the eruption of orange muzzle flash a split second before the slug tore into his chest, slamming him back against the surrey's shiny leather seat with enough force to make the whole rig rock like a baby's cradle. He lay there a moment, his muscles rigid in shock, while a giant hand seemed to wiggle inside the hole Sammy Lee's bullet had ripped in his flesh and grab his heart. As the invisible hand started to squeeze, he heard Ross Lake's distant whoop of surprise, and from even farther away, a muted, "God*damn*!" Then a light flashed above him, brighter than even the morning sun. With tears of relief spilling down his cheeks, Cornelius Rothchild reached for it.

It was raining in Springfield — a cold autumn deluge that rattled windows and sluiced off the tin and tar-paper roofs in gushing torrents, turning wood dark and the streets to mud.

Jake Jacobs paused on the boardwalk outside the flophouse where he had a bunk in an open upstairs room shared with a dozen other men, and buttoned what buttons remained on his claw-tailed black coat. Thrusting mittenless hands into the shabby coat's deep pockets, he tilted his face to the drifting mist that blew in under the veranda. The wet, feathery touch of the rain made him smile. Despite the inclement weather, empty pockets, and the nagging hunger in his belly, Jake Jacobs was a happy man. For openers, he had a meal waiting for him at the Boar's Head Restaurant, and he already knew what he wanted — buffalo ham baked with lemon slices, stewed turnips, corn-bread, and sweet potato pie. It made his mouth water just to think about it, and what leftovers there were he would take back with him to the flophouse for tomorrow's break-fast — unless Anna invited him to spend the night with her in her room above the restaurant, which in Jake's opinion would make the day just about perfect.

Anna waitressed at the Boar's Head. She was a grass widow ten years his senior, but she'd taken a shine to him the first time he'd walked into the restaurant looking for a handout. It was Anna who had convinced Samuel Caruthers, the Boar's Head propri-etor, to let Jake take the old man's team and wagon and fetch a load of coal the day before, paying him off with Sunday dinner today. That was no guarantee she'd allow Jake to slip under the quilts with her tonight, of course, for she was a fickle woman and given to bouts of depression. But she had done it before, despite old man Caruthers' views on loose morals.

So Jake had food enough and more for today, and maybe work tomorrow cutting firewood for the charcoal mill north of town — nigger work, sure, but money enough in it to pay his twenty-five cents a night at the flophouse and enough left over to buy some hard rolls and cheese.

It wasn't much of a life, Jake supposed, but he'd made do with less. And it was a hell of a lot more than he'd expected to have a few weeks ago, coming into the clearing where Captain Carry had elected to camp and finding everyone dead and the clearing empty save for the chains that had been left to rust in the wet grass.

Jake recalled that day vividly, especially the fear. For all he'd known, the niggers were lying in wait for him even then. Maybe they'd surrounded the clearing and were just waiting for him to get off his horse to make a steadier target for their guns. If that was the case, then they'd been sorely disappointed, for Jake had seen all he wanted to see in a glance. He'd whipped his horse around and high tailed it out of there as if the hounds of hell were after him — and for all he knew, they were.

He'd kept on running, too, not stopping until he reached Joplin, Missouri, and then only staying long enough to catch an uneasy night's sleep and buy a little food and some grain for his horse. He'd pushed on through the mountains of southern Missouri as far as Springfield, where his horse finally gave out, keeling over on the outskirts of town and dying without a sound. With ten-dollars in his pocket and over a hundred miles between him and the bloody clearing along the Neosho where the killings had taken place, Jake began to breathe a little easier. The money didn't last long, but that was all right. There were plenty of odd jobs around, and he was young and didn't need much. For the time being, it was enough that the flophouse where he bunked was warm, and that he had a good, if somewhat shabby, coat, and a hat to shed the rain. While it was true his boots leaked and his socks had holes in them, those were only minor inconveniences, to Jake's way of thinking. Something would come along to turn his luck around. Something always did, one way or the other.

An oxcart came down the muddy street. Jake smiled as it drew even, and tipped his hat to the old black man driving it. The man gave him a funny look and a polite nod and hurried on, and Jake stepped out into the full fall of rain. Although it was too early for dinner, he had nothing else to do and nowhere to go, so he figured he might as well drop by the Boar's Head and flirt a little with Anna, if she'd let him.

Lordy, but she was fickle.

He hadn't gone a dozen paces when he became aware of a group of horsemen rid-

335

ing in from the south. He stopped and gave them the once-over. There were five of them, all riding good mounts. Through the veil of rain, with their collars turned up and their broad-brimmed hats pulled low, there was something vaguely sinister in their appearance. A biblical quote came to him, one he had heard in the Catholic Home for Boys, in Cincinnati.

The Horsemen of the Apocalypse.

Odd, that such a thought would come to him now. He actually remembered very little from his years in the orphanage. He had no idea who'd read him the quote, or if he even recalled it correctly. But the words came to him now, watching these five men, and an involuntary shudder coursed down his spine. He spun on his rundown heels and went on, telling himself that strangers were hardly a novelty to Springfield, nor any business of his when they did show up.

He cut through an alley that would take him to River Street, and the Boar's Head on the north side of town, out near the charcoal mill with its smoking kilns. Although the cold rain quickly penetrated his worn-out clothing, Jake couldn't help but appreciate this kind of weather, especially on a Sunday. It kept people indoors, and brought an unusual tranquility to the normally bustling burg.

He exited the alley and turned north, whistling as he stepped onto the boardwalk, out of the mud. He was still a couple of blocks from the restaurant when he became aware of the five horsemen turning out of the alley behind him. He stopped, and the song he'd been whistling shriveled up and died. He'd sold his saddle and rifle soon after arriving in town, but his pistol was a solid weight against his hip. He poked a finger through the hole in the bottom of his coat pocket and felt the scuffed leather of his holster. The pistol was a Navy model .36, with five beans in the wheel. More than enough, he told himself, then laughed and started walking again.

Jake, you are still edgy about those niggers, he said to himself. *Ain't nobody in Springfield knows you were in Kansas, or that you were running with Captain Carry.*

The Captain's body, and those of Seth and Ezra, had been discovered by a party of woodchoppers a couple of weeks ago, and emotions were running pretty high in southwest Missouri. Black folks were keeping to their quarters, and a lot of whites were talking about how maybe it was time to teach the local nigger population a lesson in obedience, lest they develop any wayward notions of their own. Half of the population, it seemed, was scared cockeyed another Nat Turner was on the loose, ready to lead a fresh revolt.

Jake shied away from such stormy conversations whenever possible, reasoning that as long as he kept mum, no one would find out about his involvement in the Neosho Massacre, as some of the more radical whites were calling it.

He forced himself to start whistling again, an upbeat little tune with no name that he knew of, nor lyrics, just a song he'd picked up in a saloon somewhere that had stuck in his mind. The horsemen drew closer, but Jake kept his back to them. They were just a bunch of strangers, he reassured himself, probably looking for shelter from the rain, or maybe some food. If they asked, he'd tell them about the Boar's Head, and maybe old man Caruthers would take it kindly the next time Jake came around looking for a bite to eat with no money in his pockets to pay for it. And maybe, if the old man balked at Jake's request, he'd just remind him with something like: "You remember them five riders came through town last November? Remember who sent 'em here?"

And old man Caruthers would say . . .

"Jacobs? Jake Jacobs?"

Jake stopped, his stomach giving a little lurch as he turned to face the five horsemen fanned out in the street beside him. He was kind of surprised that none of them had drawn a weapon.

"Who's asking?" Jake asked with more bravado than he felt.

"Are you Jacobs?" the man in the center of the group snapped.

Jake swallowed hard and nodded. Staring at the speaker was like looking at a ghost, and it made him tremble inside.

"Hello, Jake," the man at the far end of the line said. "Remember me?"

"Hog? Lordy, Hog, is that you?"

"Did ya think I'd forget?" Hog Waller asked caustically.

"Shut up, Mr. Waller," the rider in the center said, just like the Captain used to. Only the Captain had always called him *Hog*, instead of *Mr. Waller*. The man nudged his horse forward a couple of feet, and Jake felt his knees turn wobbly. Staring into the man's eyes was like looking into the Captain's, except this man was older and somewhat leaner, his beard a darker shade of gray. "Do you know who I am, Mr. Jacobs?"

"I reckon you'd be Douglas Carry, the Captain's brother."

"*Colonel* Carry," the gray-bearded man

replied, as if correcting a child's mispronunciation. He leaned forward, his dark eyes boring into Jake. "I want a good look at you, Jacobs," the Colonel said. "I want to remember forever the face of the coward who abandoned my brother to those murderous heathens on the Neosho, then hid himself away from his duty."

Jake's eyes widened. "Colonel, them niggers was armed to the teeth. Me'n Hog was out scoutin', and by the time I got back it was just plain too late."

"You were working for my brother, who was working for me," Colonel Carry reminded him sharply. "I take it personally that you failed in your duty, both to protect your commander in the field, and the failure to complete a task assigned to you." Carry straightened, squaring his shoulders under the steady patter of rain. "Are you a stupid man, Mr. Jacobs?"

"No, sir, I don't believe I am."

"Then perhaps you could explain to me why a man who accepts the appellation of 'Hog' without insult managed to make his way to my door with the news that my brother and two trustworthy confederates had been savagely murdered by a band of renegade Negroes, yet I find you, with no small amount of effort, wandering the

340

streets of Springfield, Missouri, as if you hadn't a care in the world. Does that strike you as odd, Mr. Jacobs?"

"Aw, hell, Colonel," Jake said, spreading his arms wide. "I didn't know what to do. Them Africans was caught illegal as hell, and we all knew it. I couldn't go to the law —"

"Not the law, Mr Jacobs!" the Colonel thundered. *"My door! Do you understand? My door, with the information that my only brother was dead!"*

Jake took a step backward, as if he could lighten the impact of the Colonel's wrath with distance. He kept expecting Carry to pull his pistol and shoot him, or, more likely, have one of his men do it. Jake didn't know much about the lives of rich men, but he did know they generally hired out their dirty work to others, having made more than a few bucks that way himself. But apparently the Colonel had other plans.

"Get your horse, Mr. Jacobs. You will be coming with us."

"With you? Where?"

A look of deep disgust crossed the Colonel's face. "We are going after the animals who murdered my brother. You will accompany us to assist Mr. Waller in identifying the culprits. I warn you now, Mr. Jacobs, that I intend to have the head of every man, woman, and child who participated in that brutal spree."

"Sweet Jesus," Jake breathed. Then a thought popped into his head, and he grasped desperately for it. "Colonel, I can't go with you," he blurted. "My horse died. I don't even have a saddle anymore."

The Colonel's look of disgust deepened. A trickle of sweat wormed through Jake's hair behind his right ear and ran down under the collar of his shirt. Finally, the Colonel blew out a long breath. "Mr. Quint."

"Yes, sir," one of the horsemen replied.

"Purchase a suitable mount for Mr. Jacobs, will you? And a saddle, too." He looked at Jake. "Where is your outfit, your bedroll and rifle? Or have you lost those, as well?"

"No, sir, I didn't. Well, I sold my rifle, but my bedroll's over at the Higgins Hotel."

The Colonel looked at the man next to him.

"A flophouse," the man explained.

"Of course. All right then. Mr. Quint, meet us at the Higgins Hotel inside of thirty minutes."

"Yes, sir," Quint replied, wheeling his mount away as if finding a livery open on a

Sunday and buying a horse was the easiest task in the world.

"Mr. Jacobs, as of this moment you are in my employ. I will not insult the dignity of the good men you'll be accompanying by referring to you as their associate. Along with Mr. Waller, you will fetch wood and water, and tend to whatever mundane chores I or my men assign you. Your key purpose in being brought along is to assist in the identification of my brother's killers. Is that understood?"

Jake nodded. With a man like the Colonel calling the shots, he figured that was about the best he could do. But he was going to miss that Sunday dinner at the Boar's Head, and Anna's playfulness, if she'd been in a playful mood. He'd always said nothing stayed the same for long, and that sooner or later a man's luck always changed. The damn trouble was, a fellow could never know whether it was going to change for the better, or the worse.

EIGHTEEN

It was a long haul from Leavenworth to Salina, but not especially difficult. They followed the military road to Fort Riley, with established camps and ferries or bridges across the streams that couldn't be easily forded. From Fort Riley westward, the trail became a little more arduous, but it was still well-marked. With the heavy wagons and the plodding gait of the oxen, it took them two weeks — a trip Clay knew he could have made in four days by horseback — but the wagons were vital to the success of the expedition, the big Hamilton and Finn alone capable of carrying five thousand pounds of meat, tallow and hides, compared to the two hundred pounds or so a man might lash to the back of a packhorse. Tyler Calhoun was out to make a profit on the buffalo ranges, and by damn, so was Clay Little Bull.

At Salina the road veered south toward

Fort Larned and the Santa Fe Trail. It was there that Ty led them away from the beaten path, striking out across the dry, rolling plains in a westerly direction. Three days later they halted atop a bluff overlooking the valley of the Smoky Hill River, with Sam Dooley's trading post laid out below them.

Dooley had chosen his spot for a post wisely, Clay decided after studying the layout for several minutes. Although there was a good-sized grove of cottonwood trees growing at the mouth of a side canyon to the north, Dooley had constructed his post of non-flammable adobe, raising it well away from the trees and bluffs, where a disgruntled sniper might take refuge. The building itself was L-shaped, with the lower portion having a flat sod roof, a porch, and two glass-paned windows fronting the yard and overlooking the river; the longer portion of the building was squat and windowless, with a crude dirt loading dock built up in front of a wide door. A lean-to was built off the back wall of the warehouse, enclosed by a small pole corral. From his vantage point on the bluff, Clay could just make out the tops of the hoops of a prairie schooner parked on the far side of the building, the canvas stripped off and stowed away for the winter.

The post was set back about a hundred yards from the Smoky Hill, with a broad meadow in between grazing a dozen brindled oxen on its rich grass. A smaller stream snaked out of the trees to the north and curved past the building on the near side, furnishing water for the corral.

The rattling of the wagons grew louder, then stopped. A moment later, Oscar Garrett slouched forward with his long-staffed whip balanced over one shoulder. "Dooley's?" he asked gruffly.

"I reckon," Ty replied, reining closer.

Oscar grunted his approval, eyeing the distant post. "Coon knows him a thing or two 'bout Injun country, I'd say. He could've picked a hell of a lot worse place to dig in."

Jonas drove his wagon alongside the freighter and called, *"Whoa,"* tapping the near leader's shoulder with the tip of his whip.

Oscar mocked a shudder. "That kid's got a voice like a screech owl sitting outside a feller's window at night," he grumbled.

"When was the last time you slept indoors, Oscar?" Ty asked, needling the older man.

"By God, it don't matter when it was. I give it up 'cause of screech owls. Now by damn if we ain't packin' one along like a canary in a cage."

Clay looked back to where Jonas was setting the schooner's brake, oblivious to Oscar's sarcasm. It was just as well, he thought. Oscar still hadn't accepted the kid, and Jonas' just-starting-to-deepen, oft-cracking voice was only one of several traits that seemed to rile the older man.

Gathering his reins, Ty said, "You going to need any help on the brakes?"

Oscar gave the trail down from the bluff a contemptuous glance, then spat. "Naw, I could handle this itty-bitty hill blindfolded. You might stick close to the kid, though. I ain't keen on the idea of him losin' his team and rear-endin' me."

"Move 'em out, then," Ty said. "Clay, hang back with Jonas, will you? I'll ride on down and see if anyone's home." He gigged the bay with his heels, moving out at a fast walk.

Oscar returned to his wagon, ignoring Jonas completely as the two passed. Coming up beside the pinto, Jonas gawked, then blurted, "Trees!"

"What's the matter?" Clay asked, laughing. "Did you think we'd left them behind for good?"

"Yeah," Jonas admitted. "I haven't seen anything bigger than a prickly pear cactus since we left Salina."

"You two gonna stand there jabberin' all day, or are you gonna get outta my way?" Oscar hollered.

Clay chuckled as he reined the pinto aside. Oscar set his team in motion with a yell and a curse. Jonas watched somberly as the older man "Hupped" his oxen over the edge of the bluff and started down the steep incline. Oscar stayed close to his wheelers all the way, where he could keep a hand on the brake line. When he was about halfway down, where the trail started to level out, Clay said, "Think you can handle that, Jonas?"

"It doesn't look any steeper than some of the riverbanks we've crossed, just a little longer, is all." He sounded game for it, but Clay couldn't help noticing the tautness of his mouth, and the whitened knuckles that gripped the shaft of his whip.

"Stay beside your wheelers," Clay instructed. "Keep the brakes firm, but not so tight they start smoking. This isn't the place to burn out a pad." Jonas took a deep breath, then went back to bring up his wagon.

Despite Ty's worries, the boy did fine, making the bottom of the grade without a hitch. Jogging his horse alongside, Clay said,

"Good job, pard."

Jonas flashed him a look of gratitude, but kept his attention on the oxen, his face still pallid from the descent. Smiling, Clay galloped on to the post.

Oscar was just pulling into the yard when Clay rode up. He swung wide around the freighter and stepped down beside Ty's bay, wrapping the pinto's reins around the railing.

After the bright sunlight of mid-morning, it took a while for Clay's eyes to adjust to the dimness inside. When they did, he discovered a room not unlike most of the trading posts he'd encountered over the years. A solid counter of planed ash split the room lengthwise. On the customer's side was a stove and woodbox filled with buffalo chips and cottonwood kindling; a brass spittoon peeked from behind one squat, cast-iron leg like a miniature sun. There were a couple of tables with chairs, and benches along the wall with wooden pegs driven into the adobe bricks above them where a man could hang his coat or bullwhip. The floor was hardpacked dirt, though level enough, and the windows offered a watery view of the meadow.

Behind the counter, beyond the reach of pilfering fingers, were shelves stacked high with bolts of cloth and heavy wool blankets, kettles and pots and wooden buckets, boxes containing everything from buttons to pins to paper cartridges. There were kegs of molasses, sacks of sugar, and five and ten-pound pigs of lead for molding into bullets — plus half a hundred others items a man might need or want, some displayed to catch the eye, like a train of tiny, cardboard-backed mirrors pinned to a strip of cloth that an Indian might want to weave into the mane of his favorite pony. Other items were stacked so deep and tightly together it was probable Dooley himself didn't know exactly what was there.

The place was deserted except for Ty and a lone individual behind the counter, a man of medium height and stocky build, with an unruly mop of curly black hair. He wore work clothes that had seen hard use, and toted a heavy pistol in a belt holster. A double-barreled shotgun leaned against the counter at his elbow, the twin muzzles peeping over the top like the deadly eyes of a rattlesnake. He lifted his shaggy brows as Clay walked in, and gave Ty a questioning glance.

"Sam, meet my new partner, Clay Little Bull. Clay, this is Sam Dooley."

"A partner, ye say?" Dooley replied,

sounding surprised. "And what o' Matt 'n Keith? Are they nae with ye no more?"

"They went back to Toledo."

"But ye decided tae stay? Good lad, Tyler. 'Tis men such as yeself that'll settle Kansas. Settle the damned slavery question, too, I might add." Leaning across the counter, Dooley grasped Clay's hand, pumping it heartily. " 'Tis good to meet ye, Mr. Little Bull. A black man'll find hisself a safe haven here, I'll guarantee it."

"Little Bull," Clay replied emphatically, annoyed by Dooley's automatic assumption of race. "It's Choctaw."

"From yon Nations, are ye? A long way from ye stompin' grounds, I'd say."

"Not nearly as far as you, judging by your accent," Clay retorted.

Dooley laughed good-naturedly. "True enough, me friend, true enough. I was born in bonny auld Scotland many a year ago, but Kansas be me home now, and proud I am tae be here." He eyed Clay speculatively. "So, ye be partnerin' with Tyler Calhoun, eh? He's a good mon, from what 'is skinners tell me, but liable tae work ye tail off, comes the huntin'."

"Clay's done his share of hunting," Ty put in. "Trading, too."

"Well, ye'll nae be huntin' alone this year,

351

'tis certain. A couple o' outfits have built ranches south o' Salina this past summer, along the Fort Larned Road, and a mon named Kirkwood has a place up north, on a tributary o' the Saline. Not tae mention the free roamers, such as Virgil."

"Virgil?" Ty echoed in a mildly strangled voice.

"Aye. Did ye nae know ye auld partner was already ahead of ye?"

"No, I didn't. I haven't seen Virg in weeks. To tell you the truth, I half figured he'd gone home, too."

"Not unless they've moved the town lock, stock'n barrel aboot a day's ride west o' here. Ye auld ranch, I hear. Has 'isself a small wagon and a team o' mules, plus a man tae skin what he shoots, but he's built nae cabin that I know of."

Ty looked puzzled. "What do you mean?"

"Ye've nae heard, then? The Cheyennes burned ye out last summer, mon, after ye left the Smoky Hill and took ye outfit north tae the Saline."

Ty sighed. "No, I hadn't heard about that, either."

"Aye, they did. Virg and 'is partner was gonna build 'em a dugout, last they was in."

"Just the two of them?"

Dooley nodded gravely. "A pair of damn

fools, if ye ask me. And Virgil losin' 'is brother not three months ago." He clucked his tongue like a disapproving parent.

Ty gave Clay an apologetic glance. On the long ride out, both men had opened up a little about their pasts, and Clay knew Virgil Nash still owned a share of the outfit that he could claim if he desired. But Ty seemed unperturbed. Shrugging his shoulders, he said, "Well, Virg is a problem I hadn't counted on, but we'll have to wait to see how much trouble he'll try to stir up."

"He's a trouble maker, is what he is," Dooley maintained, giving Ty a knowing look. "I do nae mean to bad-mouth the mon, him losin' 'is brother and all, and ye know I liked Wade well enough, but that Virgil be a different sort, Ty. And he's got whiskey this year, more than the government allows for personal use. Two thirty-gallon barrels o' the stuff that I saw, and nae way o' knowing if I saw it all. T'will be like throwing coal oil ontae a prairie fire if the Cheyennes ever find it. And find it they will, they ever run across the mon's tracks. They be a primitive lot, those Injuns, and ha'thens all, but nae stupid. Not by a long chalk are they stupid."

"How he'd get so much whiskey past the troops at Fort Riley?" Clay asked, remembering how the soldiers there had gone through their wagons with a fine-toothed comb, looking for contraband.

"Well, 'tis a good question, that, and one I asked 'im meself, for 'tis nae as easy tae slip around a fort as some might think. But ye know Virgil." He glanced at Ty as if for confirmation. "He tolt me tae mind me trap or he'd 'ave me liver for breakfast. I think he meant it, tae. The mon's half crazy anymore."

"Yeah, that'd be Virgil," Ty agreed.

The door swung open, allowing a shaft of sunlight to blanket a portion of the floor. Oscar and Jonas came in together, and Oscar made a beeline for the counter, several feet down from Clay and Ty and Sam Dooley. Leaning into the counter, he let his gaze rake the shelves against the rear wall. "You got any whiskey in this place?" he called without preamble.

Dooley seemed embarrassed by the question, and gave Ty a shy look. "Speakin' o' the devil's elixir, was we?"

Clay understood. If liquor was illegal in Indian territory, it was also an important and accepted part of the trade, and a man didn't go far without keeping a few gallons on hand for thirsty customers. Especially those who ran the trading posts. What mattered, Clay figured, was how he used it.

"I might 'ave a drop or two o' the stuff, was ye interested," Dooley admitted.

"A drop or two ain't gonna cut the mustard," Oscar returned. "I got me a mouthful of trail dust to wash out. I was hopin' for a bottle."

Dooley moved down the counter to stand opposite the lanky plainsman. "I'm nae a whiskey peddler," he said sternly, "but I do keep a wee jug o' the stuff in the back room for me own use, when I feel the sniffles comin' on. I'll sell ye a cup o' that if ye want it bad enough, but I'll nae sell ye a bottle."

Oscar's eyes narrowed in suspicion. "What's 'bad enough' mean?"

"Four bits."

"Four bits! I kin buy a whole damn bottle for four bits in Leavenworth."

"Yes, ye can," Dooley replied evenly, then waited for Oscar to make up his mind.

"That's robbery," Oscar declared after a long pause.

"Ye know the army's stance toward liquor, mon. We was just talkin' o' it, me'n Ty'n Clay. 'Tis a rare commodity indeed, and comes dear when ye can find it. If ye want a cup, it'll cost ye four bits."

"It'd better not be rotgut," Oscar grumbled indignantly, reaching for the buckskin poke he carried in a pouch on his belt.

"Likely it is, but 'tis the best ye'll find this side of Salina."

Muttering, Oscar tossed a fifty-cent piece onto the counter. Dooley scooped it up and dropped it in his pocket. He disappeared into the back room, returning a few minutes later with a tin cup filled almost to the brim. The distrust in Oscar's eyes quickly vanished as Dooley set the cup before him. He wrapped both hands around the dented mug and brought it almost lovingly to his lips, like a child might lift a puppy whose forehead he was about to kiss. Oscar's Adam's apple bobbed three times before he lowered the cup and smacked his lips. "By God, that's good," he said hoarsely, flashing a smile far more rare than frontier whiskey. "Mister, this is prime likker, as good as any I drank in Leavenworth."

"Let me know if ye want any more," Dooley replied. Glancing at Jonas, standing against the far wall with his hat in his hands, he added, "How about ye, son? Would ye care for a cup?"

Jonas shook his head. "No, thanks."

Oscar snorted. "The kid don't drink, trader man. He don't whore or smoke or chew or even pull his pud, either."

"I just don't feel like wasting my money

on vice," Jonas replied stiffly.

Shaking his head, Oscar said, "That kid is so dumb he'd suck a skunk's ass if you tolt him it was a honeycomb."

"Damnit!" Jonas shouted, his voice booming in the closed confines of the room. Then he slapped his hat hard against the wall, raising a cloud of dust from the adobe bricks, before plunging through the door and back outside.

"Well, I'll be go to hell," Oscar said in genuine surprise, staring at the open door. He looked at Ty. "Did you see that? I ain't sure, but I might'a just caught a glimpse of backbone there."

"You might be surprised what you'll find, you keep pushing him like you have," Ty said.

"Naw. The kid ain't got what it takes, Calhoun. He growed up pampered, and it takes the hair of the bear to make it out here. That runt ain't got it."

Dooley brought out beers for himself and Ty and Clay, and for the next hour or so they spoke of what was new up and down the trail. Ty told Dooley of the growing animosity over slavery, the burnings, shootings, and lynchings by quasi-military groups plaguing both sides of the Kansas-Missouri border, and of the increasing interest in

Leavenworth of the rumors of gold in the western part of the territory. There was talk, Ty confided, of the freighting firm of Majors, Russell, and Wadell establishing a new road and stage line along the Smoky Hill River the following summer — information that brought a gleam to Dooley's jaded eyes.

The trader, in turn, passed along what he knew of the plains — gossip about the new hunters moving into the area, and word that the Cheyennes were growing restless again. The Pawnees had been sighted as far south and west as the South Fork of the Republican, hunting buffalo; most of them had gone back to their dirt lodges along the Elk River in Nebraska, Dooley acknowledged, but the word along the moccasin telegraph was that a bunch of young bucks had split off after the winter's supply of meat and robes had been taken, and gone south into Comanche and Kiowa territory on a horse-stealing foray. The Cheyennes, he added, were watching sharp for the Pawnees, hoping to add a few new scalps to their ponies' bridles.

"It's a wonder they ain't burned you out," Oscar commented.

"Well, I'm nae alone here," Dooley answered. "I've a couple o' hired men along the Smoky Hill now, cuttin' hay for the winter, and a hunter out lookin' for meat.

'Tis four o' us, and enough, I figure. Besides, I'm nae out tae fight the Cheyenne, nor take their land or buffalo. I'm a trader, and they know it."

"I didn't see any lodges outside," Clay mentioned. "I would've thought there'd be a few loafers around."

"Not yet," Dooley admitted. "I'm still new tae the country, but it'll happen eventually, I'm thinkin'. Red Elk brought 'is village here for a spell just a few weeks ago, and word will spread from that. But I do nae look tae be doin' any heavy tradin' until green-up time next year, when the winter robes start tricklin' in."

"I've met Red Elk," Ty said. "I kind of liked him."

"Well and sure, he's a good mon, Ty, but do nae forget he's got a few years on 'im, and the wisdom what comes with it. 'Tis the hotheads ye'll need tae be concernin' yeself with. I had a bit o' trouble with some o' 'em meself, wantin' liquor. Red Elk kept the' lid on the kettle that time, I'll say that for 'im, but I doubt the auld bugger would interfere was some warrior wantin' tae lift the top knot of a hunter. They're nae takin' kindly tae the buffalo men, they ain't, now."

"It's come to that, then?" Ty asked with regret.

"Aye, I'm afeared so. Red and white don't mix as easily out here as it once did."

"We'll watch ourselves," Ty said, "but I'm wanting to do a little trading next spring myself, if I get the chance."

"Well, they be aboot, and that's the truth. Ye'll likely get ye chance, they don't come at ye shootin' first."

Ty put both hands against the counter and pushed away from it. "Those are the odds, I guess. We've got some supplies for you from Becker and Miles. What say we get 'em unloaded? I want to make a few more miles before sunset." He looked at Oscar. "Or before our chief bullwhacker gets too drunk to stand on his feet."

Oscar gave him a petulant glare. "I reckon I'll get that team where you want it, drunk or sober."

Dooley laughed. "He'll be sober, I'm thinkin', by the time he helps sweat me supplies off ye wagons. Come on, then, let's be aboot it. We'll unload first, then I'll fix ye a bite tae eat, before ye be off."

NINETEEN

Sloping back against a fallen log, Jonas Sands took a deep breath of the crisp, wintry air as he dragged his shirt sleeve across his sweating forehead. His back ached, and his hands felt like balls of fire inside his gloves. Even his feet hurt, a remnant, he supposed, of the long days bullwhacking the prairie schooner across eastern Kansas.

He rolled his shoulders to work out some of the kinks that had nestled along his spine, then stripped off his gloves and plopped them on top of the log. From the upper end of the grove of cottonwoods, he could hear the steady ring of axes where Ty and Oscar still labored.

After almost three weeks on the trail, Jonas had looked forward to reaching their destination and setting up camp like true hunters of the prairies, but this wasn't what he had in mind at all. In fact, except for that night in Becker and Miles, when he'd fitted himself out like a proper frontiersman, nothing in Kansas had been as he'd expected. Reality had provided a harsh awakening from the childhood fantasies Jonas had so carefully nurtured. In nearly a month of traversing the borderlands, he had yet to spy a prancing steed or herd of stampeding bison, and the only noble red men he'd seen so far had, almost to a man, been wearing bibless overalls and work shirts. Jonas had come West seeking glory and adventure, but there was no glory in Kansas that he had found, and if this was adventure, then he'd already experienced his fill of it on a bucksaw behind his father's house in Boston.

Sensing movement behind him, Jonas turned to find Clay Little Bull striding up from the creek with a tin kettle of water. Leaning against the log beside him, Clay handed him the pail. "Have a drink," he offered.

Jonas accepted the kettle gratefully. In the past few weeks he had grown to like Clay, even more than Ty, who had grown somewhat distant as the little party struggled westward. At night around the fire, after the chores were finished, it was Clay who most often talked to Jonas, or somehow pulled him into the conversation. If not for Clay,

Jonas had the uneasy notion that he would have felt completely isolated out here.

"Looks like you've been hard at it," Clay said, eyeing the nearby stack of firewood approvingly.

"I didn't think anything could be more boring than following those oxen across the prairies, but this is close," Jonas replied.

"You'll feel differently when there's a foot of snow on the ground. Wood'll burn hotter than chips, and last longer, too. The old-timers say wet chips makes the poorest kind of wood, and I agree, although I've used it when I had to."

There was wood aplenty here, Jonas thought. It was an attractive site that Ty had chosen. They all agreed on that. Even Jonas, who knew little of such matters, had to admit that the sheltered valley in the forks of the Smoky Hill and a stream coming in from the north that they'd dubbed Tornado Creek, looked good. There was plenty of grass for the livestock along the Smoky Hill, and cold, fresh water on two sides. A line of broken, chalk-colored bluffs to the north and west helped deflect the sweeping, high-plains winds that never seemed to stop blowing.

But best of all were the trees. Jonas guessed there must have been seven or eight acres of cottonwood bordering the west bank of Tornado Creek, with a broken patch straight through the middle where a twister had torn loose trees as big around as the barrel of an ox, splintering them into tiny pieces.

They had pulled down the scorched remains of Ty's old cabin close to the forks on their first day here, leaving only the mud and stone chimney the Cheyennes hadn't bothered to topple. With dead timber snaked down from the cottonwood grove by oxen, they had rebuilt the cabin in just under two hard days, roofing it with stout limbs and bark shingles they then covered with a six-inch layer of sod. The finished product was a sorry affair, in Jonas' opinion, scarcely fifteen feet square, with a low entrance in the east wall and holes cut in the chinking to serve as windows. There was no door yet, nor shutters for the uneven, oblong windows, and at night the wind barely paused as it whistled through the cracks and crannies. The others seemed unaffected by such rudimentary lodgings, but for Jonas, the crude shack served as a reminder of the comforts he'd left behind, the doubts that had dogged him ever since leaving home.

"When are we going to put up a door and

windows?" he asked suddenly.

"Soon, probably. We'll use a flint hide for the door, and gut for the windows."

Jonas gave Clay a skeptical look. "Gut? You mean intestines?"

"Uh huh. It'll let some light in, but keep the wind out. It's cheaper than glass, which we don't have anyway, and a whole lot more practical."

"Won't it stink?"

Clay laughed. "Oscar'd ride your ass 'til spring if he heard you ask a question like that."

Jonas made a face. "He probably will anyway. Besides, the way he smells, I doubt if he'd notice a new odor."

"You know, it isn't any of my business, but the sooner you have it out with Garrett, the sooner you two'll get along."

"You mean fight him? He'd cut me in two with that big knife of his."

"You're carrying a knife, too," Clay pointed out.

Icy fingers of fear strummed Jonas' spine, and tears sprang to the corners of his eyes. He kept his face averted so that Clay wouldn't see them.

"Hell, Garrett's mostly talk, anyway," Clay went on. "I doubt if he'd pull his knife unless you pulled yours first. That's something

365

you ought to remember, Jonas. Keep your pistol and knife sheathed unless you're sure you want to use them, and chances are the other guy will, too."

"He's bigger than I am, Clay," Jonas said softly. "And he's meaner."

"Yeah, he is both of those, all right. But ol' Oscar's kind of like the weather, Jonas. Sooner or later, you're going to have to deal with him."

"He'll beat the tar out of me."

"Likely he will. But you don't necessarily have to best him to make him back off. Just show him you won't put up with his crap anymore. He'll pull in his horns. If he doesn't, then Ty or I will have a talk with him."

"You pulled your knife," Jonas said, his tone still subdued. "There west of Topeka, when he called you . . . that word."

Clay sighed. "Yeah, but I've been down that pike before, Jonas. I've gotten my nose bloodied more than once. It's part of being a man."

"Not in Boston, it isn't."

"Well, you know what I'd say to that. So the sooner you get it over with, the sooner your life will improve. Take my word on it, pard. There's only one way to deal with a man like Garrett. Unless you want to back-shoot him, though I don't figure you for that type." Picking up the kettle, Clay added, "I'm going back to work, because the sooner we finish *this,* the sooner we start hunting."

Jonas watched Clay walk off, threading his way through the broken timber with the confident stride of a full-fledged man. Swallowing back the lump that had formed in his throat, Jonas pulled on his gloves and hefted his ax. Facing the log, he lifted the ax high, then brought it down with a savage force. The bit cut deep into the long dead wood; bark and chips flew, and a dry *thunk* echoed off the bluffs. He swung again, then again, faster now, the steel head of the ax blurring as fresh tears streaked his cheeks.

TWENTY

The Pawnee raiding party split up at the Arkansas River. Heavy Badger, who had always been something of a rival to Wolf Tail, took half of the braves with him and disappeared into the broken sand hills south of the river, while Wolf Tail, Hides in the Grass, and five others turned downstream toward the land of the Kiowas.

Heavy Badger's intent was to penetrate the Comanche heartland. It was common knowledge that the Southern Snake People owned the finest horses on the plains, he said, and just as well known that, behind only the fierce Pawnees, the Comanches were the mightiest warriors to tread the Earth. Surely, Heavy Badger claimed, even the smallest child could see that to steal horses from such a formidable foe would require far more stealth and courage than a similar feat against a lesser tribe.

Wolf Tail had been unimpressed by Heavy

Badger's words. The Kiowas, Wolf Tail argued the night before the party's separation, had been allied with the Comanches for as long as he could remember, and possessed horses every bit the equal of Comanche mounts, and every bit as difficult to steal. Besides, the Kiowas were closer, and known to winter along the Arkansas. This late in the season, it would be wiser to strike the Kiowas than to risk wandering aimlessly across the open plains to the south in hopes of stumbling upon a Comanche encampment.

No one was surprised when Heavy Badger dismissed Wolf Tail's logic. Were the Pawnees any more afraid of a few snowflakes than they were of the Comanches? he'd demanded. And who among them really believed a Kiowa pony was the equal of one bred by the Southern Snakes?

These arguments seemed pointless to Wolf Tail, who considered them fodder for long winter evenings around a blazing fire, and not something to debate in a land surrounded by their enemies. Besides, fewer horse thieves meant more horses to share between them. Wolf Tail was glad Heavy Badger had taken the more foolish warriors with him. Let them come limping home empty-handed next winter, he decided, their feet half-frozen in worn-out moccasins, their noses blistered from wind and cold, to admire the sturdy Kiowa ponies he and the others would have long since returned with.

Wolf Tail led his small party eastward at a jog. A cool breeze moved with the river, soughing among the arching branches of cottonwood and box elder overhead. It had been many days now since they'd left the Pawnee hunting camp on the South Fork of the Republican, but they had yet to find anything more promising than a few faded pony tracks in the drying mud along the Arkansas. Although Wolf Tail was impatient to meet his enemies, he had to acknowledge that it was probably a good thing they hadn't encountered them yet. Laden as the Pawnee buffalo hunters were with meat and hides, he knew they wouldn't be able to travel very fast; in all likelihood they still hadn't reached the humped-earth lodges along the Elk River that were their homes, in what the white men called Nebraska Territory. Had Wolf Tail and his band come upon an enemy village too soon, they might have invited a closer scrutiny of the Republican's South Fork area that would have resulted in the discovery of the homeward bound hunters and their women and children. No, Wolf Tail thought, it would be far more prudent to strike an enemy here, within this nebulous borderland along the Arkansas shared by the Comanche, Cheyenne, and Kiowa.

When the cottonwoods and box elders began to thin out, Wolf Tail called a halt. From the skimpy shelter of a chokecherry bush already stripped of its fruit, he studied both banks of the river. On his left the water's gurgling current tugged at the rushes lining its muddy shore. On the north bank, and about eighty rods downstream, a black and white plover browsed a spit of sand for a midday meal. Closer, blue dragonflies fluttered at the edge of the marshy grass, and gnats swarmed in shifting black veils. Although it was as tranquil a scene as any Wolf Tail had ever encountered, he trusted his instincts too much to ignore the uneasiness that had come over him as soon as they stopped. He glanced at the chokecherry bush at his side, the branches plucked so clean that not even a cluster of rotting, crow-pecked berries remained. Suddenly, prickly fingers of warning shot up and down his spine.

Hides in the Grass came over, puffing lightly after their long run. "Where are they, my brother? Surely the Kiowas have not fled upon hearing of our coming."

Wolf Tail smiled thinly at his friend's ill attempt at humor, but never let his gaze wander from the view before him — the flats along the river, the broken hills to the south. "I doubt it," he replied. "Our enemies are strong, but they are not always wise."

"Then we will use their foolishness to our advantage," Hides in the Grass boasted.

"Be quiet," Wolf Tail breathed.

"What is it?" Hides in the Grass asked after a moment, clearly puzzled. "I see nothing."

"Then you are blind," Short Bird said abruptly. "There, coming out of that draw."

Wolf Tail eased down in the tall grass with the others, his gaze fixed on the distant horsemen who had just emerged from the sandy walls of an arroyo a hundred rods away.

"Kiowas," Short Bird announced. "Probably a war party."

Wolf Tail wasn't so sure. He watched the riders as they guided their ponies onto the flat, fanning out as they neared the river. There were four of them, and although it was hard to tell from behind his screen of grass, they looked like old men — their hair graying, their shoulders stooped.

"This is not a war party," Hides in the Grass said.

"Then raiders," Short Bird charged, "such as ourselves."

"Perhaps," Wolf Tail murmured. "But I think these warriors are too old for such games."

"*Aieee*," Hides in the Grass agreed softly. "My brother is right. These men are old. See the way they sit their ponies? It is plain their joints are sore with an old man's stiffness."

"They are still our enemy," Short Bird grumbled. "Will we sit here and let them pass unchallenged?"

"No," Wolf Tail replied. "But neither will we rush out like small children greeting their father's return. Have patience, my friend. First we will see if any others come after them. Then we will see in which direction these old ones ride."

The Kiowas stopped their ponies about halfway across the flat and calmly scrutinized the rushes along the river. Now and then one of them glanced toward the trees where the Pawnees remained as motionless as stumps in the tall, bearded grass, or behind them, at the sand hills. Wolf Tail couldn't help but admire their caution. These old men had seen many summers, but despite any infirmities that might inhabit their bodies or dull their senses, he knew they would not be easily fooled.

"They are not hunters," Broken Bow pointed out. "There are no packhorses."

"Perhaps they are out for a ride before Morning Star seals the land with His icy breath," Hides in the Grass suggested.

"Quiet," Wolf Tail hissed, lowering himself deeper into the grass. "They come." Moving carefully, so as to not disturb the vegetation around him, he primed his fusil. He knew they were in a poor position to surprise the Kiowas. Had the situation been different, he would have attempted a trap where the Pawnees could have fallen upon these aging warriors with their tomahawks and knives — slashing, hacking, taking strength in the bloodletting of their enemies — but it had been the Kiowas who had surprised *them,* and Wolf Tail knew they would have to remain where they were and hope for the best. With luck, they might kill all four men, and capture their ponies and arms. That would be good if it could be done, just not as much fun as a hand-to-hand encounter.

When the Kiowas were still fifty rods away, Wolf Tail eared back the fusil's big hammer, then ever so slowly brought the weapon's flat brass buttplate to his shoulder, sighting down the blued barrel to the tiny

374

brass bead that served as the front sight. Like a shotgun, the smooth-bored trade gun didn't have a rear sight; with a range of only twenty to thirty rods, it didn't really need one, especially not with a target the size of a man.

"I can see them," Hides in the Grass whispered.

Wolf Tail could see them, too, riding at an angle that would take them into the woods just to the Pawnee's left, between them and the river. Two of the Kiowas rode out front, several horse lengths apart and about half a dozen rods in advance of the last two. Wolf Tail knew they would be watching closely, searching for any sign of trouble. For the first time, it occurred to the young Pawnee that their imperfect position might have its advantages. The Kiowas' attention seemed to be focused on the thick growth of rushes along the riverbank, and only occasionally shifted into the thinly spaced trees, or toward the low hills to the south. The grass beneath the trees was littered with fallen limbs, splintered stumps, and scattered clumps of low brush. If the Kiowas saw any disturbance in the landscape at all, they must have assumed it was one of these.

Wolf Tail drew a bead on the lead rider, then let the fusil's muzzle glide back to cover the most distant horseman, a stout old man wearing a buffalo robe around his waist and a hat made from the pelt of a fox, with the face still intact, sitting above his forehead like an extra set of eyes.

"They are within range," Short Bird announced quietly.

Wolf Tail could hear the tautness in the warrior's voice. He felt it in himself, like the thrumming of a sinew string on a strong bow in the first heartbeats after an arrow's release. The dull thudding of the ponies' hooves could be felt through the soft sod; the blowing whicker of one of the horses as it lowered its head for a mouthful of grass carried clearly. Wolf Tail relished the sweet feel of expectation, savoring it as he did the first bite of raw liver, taken warm and bloody from the carcass of a just killed buffalo. But the anticipation was not to last. The lead warrior's mount suddenly lifted its head, nostrils extended to test the wind. Its rider hauled back on the single jawline rein and started to lift an arm in warning. It was a move never completed. From behind Wolf Tail came the deafening roar of half a dozen fusils, his own weapon adding to the din. Billowing clouds of powder smoke erupted from the grass like tiny thunderheads, momentarily obliterating Wolf Tail's view. He didn't wait for it to clear. Leaping to his feet, leaving the empty smoothbore in the grass, he sprinted forward, emerging from the roiling smoke like a painted demon waving a tomahawk.

All four of the Kiowas had been unhorsed by the Pawnees' volley, but only the nearest one lay unmoving. The other three were already struggling to their feet, stringing their bows. Wolf Tail dodged the first two braves and raced toward the man with the foxhide cap, knocked askew above his iron-gray braids. The old warrior had tossed aside his buffalo robe, revealing a paunchy stomach made slick and shiny on one side with blood. When he saw Wolf Tail coming toward him he dropped his bow and reached for his knife. Wolf Tail howled in delight as the old man turned toward him, his knife at the ready. But it wasn't much of a fight. Wolf Tail was too young, too swift. He easily dodged the old warrior's blade, then brought his tomahawk down in a streak of reflected sunlight. The steel-head hawk bit deep into the old man's skull, ruining his hat. The force of the blow jolted Wolf Tail all the way to his shoulder, and blood and brains spurted warm over his wrist.

The elderly Kiowa crumbled without a sound. Jerking the 'hawk free, Wolf Tail lifted the crimson-stained weapon above his head and shook it toward the east, where Sun rose each morning. *"Aieee!"* he shouted, feeling the hot pulse of victory coursing through his veins. *"Aieee! Aieee!"*

Then he turned and stalked back to where the others were already stripping the bodies of the dead Kiowas in preparation for mutilation. Hides in the Grass looked up, his grin fading when he saw the expression on his friend's face. Straightening from his grisly task, Hides in the Grass asked, "What is it, my brother?" His gaze darted toward the arroyo, where the four old ones had originally appeared. "Are there others?"

"Yes," Wolf Tail replied, turning until he could also view the distant draw. "The chokecherry bush where we hid was stripped by women to flavor their pemmican, and these old men were scouts. That means there is a village nearby, and that younger men are not there."

"Hunting?" Hides in the Grass mused.

"It does not matter," Wolf Tail replied. He smiled coldly. "It is only important that they are gone, and that the village — the ponies, the women, whatever we want — is now ours."

The showdown between Jonas and Oscar

didn't occur for another three days, and by that time the little hunter's ranch was pretty well in shape, as far as Clay was concerned. The cabin was finished, with a corral on the north side to hold their horses. A smoke-house had been framed from cottonwood poles they would wall and roof with green hides once the hunting started in earnest. Pickling vats they would line with hides had been dug for salting tongues, and wooden frames, a foot wide by a foot and a half long and six inches deep, had been rigged to block the tallow into bricks that Lobenstein would sell to candle factories. A small mountain range of firewood ran around the outside of the cabin where it would be easy to reach, and where it would add its own small measure of insulation until it was needed. All that remained to be done was to construct a south-facing lean-to in the corral to keep the horses out of the worst of the weather. Clay and Ty had talked of building a larger corral for the oxen, but decided against it. They would let the cattle graze loose most of the time, anyway. Except for Brownie, whom they kept hob-bled and chained, none of the animals were prone to wander. Although there was some concern about wolves, which would show up as soon as the buffalo did, Ty thought that as long as they kept the oxen close to the cabin at night, they would be all right. An added factor was that the buffalo were scarce along the Smoky Hill, and although both men were convinced the big herds would return, they also knew there was a chance they wouldn't, and that they might have to pull up stakes to go in search of them.

Clay and Ty were standing at a corner of the horse corral with their arms propped over the top rail, reviewing the next day's work, when Jonas and Oscar returned from the woods above the ranch. Even in the deepening dusk, Clay could see by the drawn expression on Jonas' face that the old man must have ridden him hard that day.

Ty also noticed it, for as the youth *hawed* his team toward a pile of poles already cut and trimmed for the lean-to, he said, "That son of a bitch, Garrett," in a low, angry voice.

"He goes for the weakest link in the chain, doesn't he?"

"He wasn't that bad last summer," Ty said, "but we had more men working for us then. Oscar buddied up with one of them, and they kept pretty much to themselves. He's different this year."

"He's a mean one, though," Clay replied. "Like a sow bear at weaning time. I've seen —" He shut up abruptly. At the woodpile, Oscar Garrett was reeling backward from an uppercut to the jaw. The old man's arms flailed wildly until his heel snagged a clump of grass and dumped him to his butt.

"What the —" Clay started, then burst into laughter.

"Hell," Ty finished weakly.

Still laughing, Clay said, "It was bound to happen." He grabbed his partner's arm as Ty started toward the ruckus. "Let 'em have at it."

"You don't know Oscar like I do," Ty said grimly. "He'll kill Jonas for that."

They moved closer just as Oscar regained his feet, then stooped to retrieve his hat. He clamped it on his head, his face a mask of rage.

"I'm gonna gut you, boy," Oscar snarled, his hand flashing to the heavy bowie at his waist. "I'm gonna cut you open like you was a dead buffler."

"No knives," Clay said sharply, in alarm.

Oscar jerked his head around, but so intense was the old man's anger that Clay wasn't even sure he'd heard.

Ty put his hand on his Colt. "You heard him," he barked. "Keep your knife sheathed."

Oscar's gaze slid from Clay to Ty, then back to Jonas. He shoved the well-worn sticker back in its scabbard. "It don't matter none to me, boy. I kin break your neck just as easy."

"You can try," Jonas said, his voice shaking badly.

"Sweet Jesus," Ty murmured.

"Easy," Clay breathed. "Let the kid have his chance."

"His chance for what? To have the shit beat out of him?"

"If that's what it takes."

"You ready, boy?" Oscar asked, then surged forward.

Jonas stood his ground, lashing out with a left that Oscar tried to duck but couldn't. The older man's head rocked back, and for a moment his wide open eyes showed only white. Clay thought he would surely go down, but he didn't. When he recovered his balance, he lunged toward the youth with a roar, his fist batting the air like a gnarled chunk of iron strapped to the end of a sturdy limb. Again, Jonas stood firm, swaying back to avoid the blow, then stepping in, lashing the older man's midsection with a pair of swift punches.

Oscar stumbled backward, arms folded

around his gaunt stomach. His face was mottled and he was puffing hard, but there was murder in his eyes now, and Jonas raised his fists warily. Oscar straightened slowly, then edged forward with a new respect for his opponent. Jonas stepped back. A flicker of doubt crossed the older man's face that was so out of character that Clay didn't even realize it was a ruse. As Jonas slid forward to deliver another string of punches, Oscar cocked a fist awkwardly above his shoulder. Taking quick advantage of the opening, Jonas darted in.

As far as Clay could tell, the boy never even saw the heavy-booted foot that slammed upward like a sledgehammer, smashing into his crotch. He squawked once, a kind of gasping, squeaking inhalation of breath, and as he started to fall, Oscar swung. The old man's knuckles connected solidly with Jonas' cheek, splitting the flesh over the bone like wet paper. While Jonas crumbled in a huddled mass of agony, Oscar drew his foot back to deliver a rib-crunching blow to the youth's side. Before he could complete the kick, though, Ty's revolver exploded, the slug tearing up a chunk of sod at the old man's feet, stopping him cold. Oscar looked at Ty as he might a stranger. Then, jerkily, he moved back several yards. Gasping harshly, he said, "So that's where your stick floats, is it, Ty-boy?"

"You've won," Ty answered tautly. "Now let it drop."

"I don't fight to win," Oscar snarled. "Git that through your skull. Git it through the kid's skull, too. He ever swings at me agin, I'll kill him."

"Lay off him, Oscar. He's a good worker —"

"You hear me!" the old man shrieked. *"I'll kill the little whelp, he ever crosses me agin!"* Spinning on the balls of his feet, Oscar started for the woods, a creature of the wilderness seeking solitude in darkness.

Clay ignored the old man's retreat. He knelt at Jonas' side and gently rolled him onto his back. Jonas' arms flopped limply, his eyes tightly closed.

"Damnit," Ty said, holstering his pistol as he came to stand above them. "I told you that old bastard would try to kill him."

"I reckon you did," Clay replied distantly. With the back of his hand, he gently patted Jonas' unbloodied cheek, but the young man refused to come around. "Help me get him into the cabin, will you?" Looking up, his eyes swimming in anger, he added, "I swear, Ty, if that old man's crippled this boy . . ."

"If he has, I'll help you hang him," Ty promised. They lifted Jonas to a sitting position, then slid their arms under his shoulders.

Before they could pull him to his feet, though, Clay spotted movement from the corner of his eye. Jumping free, he snaked the coffin-handled bowie from its scabbard. Near the cabin's door, a stranger studied them quizzically from the back of a long-legged black horse — a tall man dressed in tattered clothing, his hair long and greasy and unkempt, his beard tangled and short. Smoky blue eyes peered at them from beneath the drooping brim of a sugar loaf hat. "Looks like I missed a hell of a show," the stranger observed.

Ty lowered Jonas to the ground, then stood and put a hand casually on the butt of his revolver. "Hello, Virgil."

A mocking grin crossed the ragged man's face. "Hello, Ty. You been taking good care of my share of the outfit, have you?"

TWENTY-ONE

They stripped Jonas to his longhandles and wrapped him in a pair of soft-cured buffalo robes. While Clay kindled a fire to warm the cabin, Ty caught Virgil's attention and jerked his head toward the door. The two men walked outside and around the corner, out of the worst of the wind.

"I just came from Dooley's," Virgil explained. "He said you were back. I gotta admit I didn't expect you. I figured you'd hightail it back to Ohio with Matt and Keith." He laughed. "I sure as hell didn't think you'd pair up with a nigger."

"I'd watch that mouth, Virg. You let your tongue flap around too loose and Clay's liable to tie it in a knot."

"Screw him," Virgil said flatly, reaching inside a breast pocket for a cigar. He lit it with a match, cocking one eye to keep it on Ty. "You boys have done a fair job rebuilding this place. Does your darky know it's half mine?"

"Half?" Ty grinned thinly. "You've got a fifth share coming, and that's it. I bought out Matt and Keith, and we sent Wade's money home to your folks."

Virgil seemed to mull that over, then he shrugged. "That's fair, I reckon, but I'm low on powder and caps."

"If you're low on gunpowder and caps, you can have a fifth of what we've got, but no more. I'll not hamstring myself because you lit out of Leavenworth too fast to outfit yourself."

Taking the cigar from his mouth, Virgil gave Ty a gauging look. "You're mighty damn bossy for a partner."

"We're not partners," Ty replied. "I'm partnering with Clay. You're just a nuisance from the past."

"That's a hell of a thing to say," Virgil flared. "I remember when you were too chickenshit to come out here by yourself. You were beggin' me and Wade and the Burdettes to come with you."

"I seem to recall you had your own reasons for leaving Toledo."

Virgil's face darkened. "I'll go back some-day to settle that score. I ain't the green kid I was two years ago."

"Neither am I, Virg."

"No, likely you ain't. So maybe Wade's being butchered by those stinking savages did us both some good."

"Did you kill Francis Duck?"

Virgil looked momentarily confused. "Is that what you think? That I ran because I'm guilty?"

"That's what most people think."

"Well I'll be damned," Virgil said, then chuckled. "I'll tell you what, Ty, I don't much give a shit what most people think. I don't even give a shit what you think. But I guess I am curious. You figure I knifed that redskin, huh?"

"I don't know," Ty admitted. "That's why I'm asking."

"Hell, you ain't changed at all, have you?"

"Did you do it?"

Virgil took a drag on his cigar. As he did, the wind whipped unexpectedly around the cabin, and a shower of orange sparks and ash peppered the front of his coat. Facing the wind, Virgil jetted his smoke into it, as if he could force the prairie breeze to split around his will. Then he turned away, blinking against the smoke and ash that had blown back in his eyes. "Goddamnit!" he shouted. "It never stops blowing out here." His features changed then, a moody reflectiveness shading his eyes. "Yeah, I ran. I guess I panicked. But it was more than that. It was Wade, too, and the way he died. Hell, Ty, I kept seeing him in my dreams, all cut open like he wasn't even a human being, but just some partially butchered animal abandoned on the prairie. So I ran. I made it as far as Arrow Rock, Missouri, before I slowed down enough to think about it. I spent a week there. Then I met John Dunlap."

"Your skinner?"

"Uh huh, kind of a partner, too. He's had some experience with the Cheyenne, and hates 'em as much as I do. Anyway, we threw in together, and went to Westport to buy an outfit. Then we came out here. When we saw what the redskins did to the cabin, we moved on."

"Where?"

"Don't get your hopes up," Virgil replied, laughing. "We've just been wandering around, waiting for the buffalo to come back. Oh, we took some skins — elk and deer, mostly — but there's no money in that unless you tan 'em into buckskin, and that's too much work for a white man. We finally just pitched 'em and was headed for Salina when we passed through Dooley's and heard you were back. We decided to come this way instead. I left John along the trail, but he'll roll in sometime tomorrow."

"Then what?"

"Why, we're partners, ain't we, Ty? You and me and John and the nigger?" He smirked.

"Oscar Garrett called Clay a nigger once, but just once," Ty said mildly. "Clay nearly knifed him for it."

"Garrett! You hired that old drunk? Christ, are you loco?"

"He's a good skinner, and he knows the plains."

"He's more trouble than he's worth. Where is he?" Then Virgil laughed. "Naw, don't tell me. He's off pouting like some little kid who's had his feelin's hurt, ain't he? Is he the one who busted up the kid?"

Ty shrugged.

"That old bastard," Virgil said, shaking his head. "Well, I'll tell you what, Ty, since you can't afford to buy me out and I ain't looking for a letter of credit, I think I'll just throw in with you boys. Same deal as before — a fifth ownership in the outfit, and a fifth of the take at the end of the season." He paused, and a corner of his mouth twitched in a smile. "In case you're wondering, I've still got that contract Lobenstein helped us draw up, and there ain't a goddamn thing you can do about it."

"No, probably not," Ty agreed, "and I'll be damned if I'll ride all the way back to Leavenworth just to find out. But you listen, Virg, if you come in, you'll do your share and more. This is a hunter's ranch, I aim to make it pay."

"Just don't forget I'm a partner," Virgil replied evenly. "I won't take orders from an African, I don't care how good he is with a knife."

Rain Dancing On Water paused after exiting the lodge of her second husband, Yellow Bear. Out of habit, she glanced toward the shrinking evening light, the direction from which he and the other Kiowa hunters would appear. They had been gone for more than a moon now, the men, women, and older children who had accompanied the hunters toward the far-flung *llano estacado* in search of buffalo. Daily now, scouts from the village ranged westward in anticipation of their successful return.

That would be when the real work for the women would begin, Rain Dancing knew. The meat would have to be cut up and either dried into jerky, or dried and pounded to crumbs that would be mixed with suet and the dried berries and plums the women had collected over the summer to make pemmican. The hides would be scraped free of every particle of fat, then softened with a mixture of brain and ash to make fleecy robes that would offer a deep winter warmth, soft beds, or trade items for the wandering Comancheros. They would scrape away the hair on the poorer hides, then tan the hide into leather for clothing or lodge skins. There would be much to do in the shortening days before the icy breaths of Winter Man swept the plains, covering the grass with its first hard dusting of snow. But none of that mattered to Rain Dancing. Not anymore.

It was chilly and growing dark. Only a few women were still out and about, bringing in a last bucketful of water, or a final armload of firewood. None of them paid any attention to Rain Dancing when she lifted a painted rawhide parfleche containing some food and extra clothing from behind a stack of kindling next to the lodge's entrance. Turning her back on the dying light, she hurried toward the plum thicket where she and Goes Along had met so often in the past. This would be the last time she would have to sneak away like a common trollop. Tonight, finally, Goes Along had promised to meet her with horses, to take her far away to the land of his own people, the Kiowa-

Apaches.

Rain Dancing prayed that Yellow Bear would not come after them, that he would be glad to be rid of his fourth wife, whom he had never cared for and had only accepted out of obligation to her first husband after his death. Goes Along hadn't wanted to place that much trust to luck, though. It had been his idea to wait until winter seemed imminent before making their escape. Goes Along, Rain Dancing knew, was counting on bad weather to discourage Yellow Bear's pursuit.

For a long time Rain Dancing had feared that Goes Along would not take her with him when he left. He had hinted at it more than once during the past moon, and Rain Dancing had begun to fear that Goes Along had wanted her only for her body. But tonight, they would leave the village of northern Kiowas forever.

Rain Dancing halted at the edge of the plum thicket, where Goes Along was to meet her. She whistled softly, in imitation of a meadowlark, but there was no answering call, no movement among the shadows to betray his presence. Rain Dancing's spirits quickly sagged. Had she misjudged him, after all?

Then she heard movement, the thud of a

pony's hoof against the hard ground under the trees, the crackle of fallen leaves. With a smile, Rain Dancing ran down the incline into the deeper shadows. She hadn't gone more than a dozen paces before some nebulous hint of danger stopped her cold. Crouching, she peered ahead in the murky light. By turning her head slightly to one side and using her peripheral vision, she was able to make out a band of ponies near the creek, the dark silhouette of several men standing next to them.

Rain Dancing's heart thudded loudly in her chest. She knew that whoever lurked there beside the creek was not of her village. Cautiously, she inched closer to the plum thicket and its concealing shadows. As she did, she became aware of a peculiar odor, a rank mixture of bear grease and body sweat. Her muscles tensed as she dropped her parfleche and spun on the balls of her feet, but before she could flee a hand slid around her face, clamping tightly over her mouth. An arm encircled her waist, and she was yanked violently backward, her scream stopped before it could pass her lips. A raspy male voice chortled in her ear, followed by a hushed whisper in foreign words. Then a dark shape loomed before her. Rain Dancing's eyes widened above the hand pinching her mouth shut. A war club rose against the first stars appearing in the east, then fell with a distant thump against the side of her head.

A cold wind rattled the limbs overhead as the three horsemen made their lonely way through the woods. Sammy Lee glanced skyward as he guided his long-legged sorrel after his new partners. A thin wafer of moon glowed through clouds, but its light was illusive, more promise than reality.

Sammy Lee wasn't sure where they were anymore. Somewhere deep within the Potowatomie Reserve, he thought, but he'd lost all sense of direction soon after Buford Hart led them off the rutted road at sundown, at least six hours ago. For all Sammy Lee knew, they might be closing in on the Nebraska line. But he trusted Buford's sense of direction, if not his fealty.

It was a pretty sorry mess he'd gotten himself into, and not at all what he'd had in mind when he left Plato and Jenny along the Santa Fe Trail to follow Clay Little Bull to Leavenworth.

Sammy Lee had soon lost Clay's trail. Stopping at the first trading post he came to, he had been startled and a little worried to learn that no one had seen a black man riding a flashy pinto and leading a string of packhorses. His luck farther down the trail proved just as dismal. No one admitted to having seen Clay, and after a while, Sammy Lee quit asking.

He'd reached Leavenworth without trouble, but had no better luck finding Clay there than he'd had along the Trail. Not that he'd asked in every saloon or hide dealer's shop in town. Sammy Lee hadn't seen any point in wasting time in the white section of town, so after just a couple of inquiries he'd made his way to shantytown, and a place called Abner Bell's Saloon. The bartender gave Sammy Lee a chary eye when he asked about Clay, then shook his head and moved away.

It was in Abner Bell's saloon that Sammy Lee first ran into Buford Hart and Ross Lake. He'd taken an immediate liking to the pair. They were crude and rough-shod, but Sammy Lee admired the way they conducted themselves. They were men who went where they pleased, and carried their pistols as if they knew how to use them. Sammy Lee was also impressed by the fact that Hart and Lake spent as much time up in the main part of town as they did in the warrens along the river. It spoke highly of their determination not to be dismissed because of their color, he decided. As for himself, he had quickly discovered that carrying a brace of ivory-handled Colts did little to enhance his status when dealing with a stony eyed white man. As it turned out, a lot of men in Leavenworth carried pistols — none as fancy as the two Sammy Lee packed, but all of them just as efficient.

Sammy Lee had hoped things would change after hooking up with Hart and Lake. Certainly they shared his disdain for the white race, and especially the discrepancies in living styles between Negroes and Caucasians. The whites had too damn much money, Ross had said to Sammy Lee one chilly evening as the two sat beside the Missouri and shared a bottle of blackberry wine. That was the way he and Buford saw it, anyway, and that was why they lived the way they did. After that, the conversation drifted along more veiled lines, with Ross hinting at the splendid possibilities a man with the right grit might enjoy, and Sammy Lee trying to imply that he was that man, without really coming out and saying he wanted in. Finally, three-quarters of the way through the bottle, Sammy Lee told Ross about the white slavers he'd killed on the Neosho. Made reckless by drink, he'd exaggerated his part in the story by eliminating

Clay altogether, but he didn't regret it. Not after he saw the new look of respect that came into Ross' eyes.

"No shit?" Ross exclaimed. "You killed a bunch of white men and ain't been hanged for it?"

"Killed 'em all," Sammy Lee boasted drunkenly. "Ain't worried 'bout hangin', either. I got plenty of powder and lead left, some white-assed sonofabitch wants to give me sass."

Ross seemed to mull that over for a while. Then he whistled softly and nodded. "Now ain't that the goddamn truth of it?"

Two weeks later, they accosted the fat banker on a dark road somewhere in the northern portion of the Delaware Reserve, and Sammy Lee got his chance to prove his grit. It made him smile to remember the way Buford and Ross had nearly come unglued when he coolly shot the sweating white man square in the chest. Both of them had wanted to light out for the Indian Nations, but Sammy Lee talked them out of it. He'd almost gone to the Nations once before — in Captain Carry's chains; he had no intention of going there of his own free will.

The attitude of both men changed toward Sammy Lee after that. The law was looking for Rothchild's murderer among the Delawares, paying particular attention to Louis Apple Tree, the man Rothchild had threatened with foreclosure. That seemed to satisfy Buford and Ross, and they soon returned to business as usual. But it hadn't satisfied Sammy Lee. It had barely whetted his appetite.

Buford drew rein, and Ross and Sammy Lee drifted up beside him. "There she be," Buford announced in his raspy voice. He pointed through the trees to a squat log cabin, a picket shed thrown up to one side. Somewhere out of sight, a cow lowed.

"Where's he pasture his horses?" Ross asked.

"Down south a ways," Buford answered. "Got himself a jackleg fence thrown up across a little limestone side canyon, with the prettiest ponies this side of Kentucky locked inside."

"How many'd you say?"

"You've asked him that question a dozen times," Sammy Lee interjected. "Fourteen head, counting the thoroughbred."

"It's the thoroughbred we want, though," Buford insisted. "She's worth all the rest put together."

"But they all have thoroughbred blood in 'em, right?" Ross asked.

Sammy Lee gritted his teeth. He'd been with the two hardcases long enough now to know it was nervousness that made Ross so wordy. He'd seen the short-legged outlaw act this way before, and in a way, he figured it accounted for his own irritability. But damn if he wasn't getting tired of it. He wished Ross would just shut up, so they could get on with their job.

"Some of 'em," Buford replied to Ross' query. "Not all, but some of 'em."

"Well, hell," Ross said. "Let's go then."

"We'll work our way south along the trees," Buford said. "That ol' boy had him a couple of hounds, last time I was out this way. I don't want 'em catching wind of us."

"Come on, goddamnit," Sammy Lee growled. "You two chatter like a couple of old women."

Buford chuckled easily. "Hold your piss, Sammy, we're going." He reined his horse toward the edge of the trees.

Sammy Lee spurred after him, cutting ahead of Ross. He put his hand on the butt of his strong-side Colt, stroking the cool ivory. Coming out of the trees, they turned south, riding single file. The cabin was across the valley, perhaps a quarter of a mile away, its windows dark at this late hour. Sammy Lee could hear Ross muttering under his breath behind him, and knew it bothered the shorter man to bring up the rear. He jogged his sorrel up alongside Buford.

"What do you want?" Buford asked, eyeing him suspiciously.

"I want to know what we're doing out here, robbing Indians instead of white men."

"What are you talking about?"

"When I joined up I thought we were going to play hell with the pro-slavers and Border Ruffians, but except for that banker, all we've done is make life miserable for some redskins. We steal their horses and cattle, and half the time sell them to white men. Where's the good in that?"

"Where'd you get the notion we were going to play hell with Border Ruffians?"

"From you and Ross."

Buford laughed softly, in respect of the hounds across the valley. "Shit, that was just talk. We ain't messin' with white men, pro-slavers or not. We'd hang for sure; was we caught."

Sammy Lee felt his anger growing. "That's not what you said in Leavenworth."

"Whiskey talk," Buford replied dismissingly.

Sammy Lee's hand moved to the butt of his Colt. He didn't know why, although he was sure it wasn't to draw it. Maybe all he sought was the reassurance that came from brushing its ivory grips with his fingers, as he'd gotten into the habit of doing. But Buford was touchy on a job. He jerked his horse to a stop and pulled it around hard, and before Sammy Lee knew what was going on, he found himself staring down the barrel of Buford's Dragoon.

"Don't you ever touch them pretty pistols of yours like you was thinking of pulling one on me," Buford said tautly. "I'll screw this job right now by putting a bullet through your skinny black hide, and that's the God's honest truth."

Sammy Lee blinked rapidly. Ross crowded up behind him, sear ratching as he thumbed the hammer of his own pistol to full cock.

"What's up, Buf?"

"Nothing's up," Buford snapped. "Put that pistol away, before you shoot somebody."

"I saw you pull down on the kid," Ross said peevishly. "Hell, I was just trying to help."

"Well, you ain't, so put that pistol up."

There was silence for a moment, then Ross lowered his hammer. But Sammy Lee didn't look around. He couldn't take his eyes off the muzzle of Buford's pistol.

"You with us, Sammy, or against us?" Buford asked.

Sammy Lee didn't even have to think about that one. He knew that as soon as he voiced any intent to quit the gang, one or the other of them would pop a cap against him. Sammy Lee was angry, but he wasn't a fool. He said, "Hell, I'm with you, Buford, you know that. I was just wondering when we were going to rob some white folks."

"I'll tell you what, Sammy, you just save your wondering for when we get up to BlackBird this winter." He pulled his pistol away from Sammy Lee's face and holstered it. "Savvy?"

"Sure," Sammy Lee said, but his face was hot with humiliation. "Sure, Buf, that's fine."

"And don't call me Buf. You ain't known me long enough to call me that."

"All right." Sammy Lee clenched his fists until the knuckles ached, though he was careful to keep them away from his pistols. He knew he would never forget this night, just as he knew that sooner or later he would make Buford pay for it. Sooner or later, he swore, he would make them both pay.

TWENTY-TWO

Clay climbed the ridge on the east side of Tornado Creek and turned to face the wind. The sun had set some time ago, but it was a clear night, with a three-quarters moon shining over his right shoulder and the brittle splash of starshine frosting the black canopy of the sky. It always amazed him how well he could see after dark with just the light of the stars and the moon. It was a thing easily forgotten when a man spent too much time indoors after sunset, he thought.

He settled down in the tall grass atop the ridge and pulled the collar of his mackinaw up around his neck. It had become something of a habit with him this past week to come out here after supper and sit alone to think. It had turned hot and stuffy inside the cabin once they'd stretched elk gut over the windows and fashioned a crude door from the animal's hide. It had barely been big enough for four men and their supplies as it was. The addition of Virgil Nash and his skinner, plus their supplies, seemed to bulge the sturdy log walls to their limits.

It was odd, Clay thought, how the close confines of the cabin didn't seem to bother the others. It reminded him of the time he and Simon had made their only trip together to Fort Smith, Arkansas. Simon had insisted it was to have a competent gunsmith convert Clay's flintlock rifle to a caplock, but Clay knew now the old Choctaw had done it to expand Clay's education beyond the one-room mission schoolhouse in Red Creek, and the district's wooded boundaries. Even now, Clay could recall the feeling of awe he'd experienced at the size of the community; the houses had been packed so close together a man could scarcely breathe, a sensation made all the more real by the smoke of a thousand coal and wood fires that fogged the streets day and night.

Maybe there was something in the nature of the white-eyes that caused them to crave such intimacy, Clay mused. Yet when he tried to rationalize it by comparing it to the villages he'd known in the Choctaw Nation, or with the way the Wichitas and Kiowas lived, he was more amazed at the similarities than the contrasts. Scrape away the thin veneer of cultural differences, he realized,

and they were all pretty much the same —
living and loving and dying, happy and sad
by turn, eating and sleeping on a schedule
dictated by their environment. He remembered the way his scalp had crawled the day
Sheriff Ripley accosted him in the Hamilton and Finn Wagon Yard, and wondered
suddenly if a white man would have reacted
any differently.

So maybe it wasn't just the white-eyes
who sought comfort and security in numbers, he thought. Maybe it was a human
phenomenon, a world-wide thing. It still
raked at his nerves to share such a tiny cabin
with five other men, especially in the evening
when they were all crammed inside together.
Only the knowledge that Nash and Dunlap
were building a dugout on the east bank of
Tornado Creek for themselves kept Clay
from setting up his own camp among the
trees.

He studied the cabin. In the stinted
moonlight, the squat, flat-roofed structure
resembled nothing so much as a large stump
sitting back about twenty feet from the narrow banks of the creek; only the yellow bars
of firelight seeping from the cracks and
crevices like butter squeezed from a leaky
churn disturbed that image. Clay pictured
the men inside as they had been when he'd

left — Jonas sitting on his bedroll against the rear wall, looking better after the beating Oscar Garrett had given him last week, but still stiff in the hips and favoring his groin; Ty would be lounging between Jonas and Garrett as if by accident, a faraway look in his eyes as he mentally calculated the piddling number of hides and tongues they'd taken so far against the debt owed to Becker and Miles, and the wages that had yet to be paid. Virgil Nash and John Dunlap always sat nearest the door. Dunlap was a short, light-featured man with blond hair as fine as cured corn silk, but with the habit of looking anywhere except directly into the eyes of the person he was speaking to.

They would be talking buffalo, Clay knew. It was about all they spoke of anymore — buffalo, and when the big herds would return. The few hides they'd taken so far had come mostly from solitary old stubhorns they'd found scattered throughout the breaks along the Smoky Hill — animals too old or crippled or ornery to follow the seasonal migrations of the rest of the herd. The meat from the bulls was almost always too tough to cure for market, hard enough to stomach themselves. But hunting had given them something to do, and Lobenstein would take the hides, selling the leather to saddleries. Ty had taken the opportunity to show Jonas the ropes, as well — how to skin a big animal, and care for its hide afterward. But they weren't even making wages, and Clay knew the poor showing weighed heavily on Ty.

The cabin door opened, and Jonas slipped outside. Clay watched him limp away from the dwelling, then pause, his head swiveling as if searching for something. Clay gave a low whistle, and after a moment's hesitation, Jonas started toward him.

Clay slid his pipe from his hatband and filled it from a buckskin pouch while Jonas crossed the creek and climbed the ridge. Sinking into the grass at Clay's side, Jonas pulled his coat tight around his slim frame. Striking a piece of steel into his char, Clay said, "So, you get fed up with all the gobbling, too?"

"They're like a bunch of starlings sometimes," Jonas lamented. "And always the same thing . . . the biggest bull, the fastest cow."

"It does annoy a man after a while, and that's a fact." Clay draped the orange spark caught in the black char cloth over the bowl of his pipe, and inhaled deeply. When he had it fired to his satisfaction, he pinched out the char and put it away.

"Ty says you and I are to go out again tomorrow and do some hunting," Jonas said quietly.

"Sounds good."

"Yeah. It'll be nice to get away for a while."

"You don't sound too chipper, pard. Is ol' Oscar poking at you again?"

Jonas' low bark of laughter was bitter. "Nope. As far as he's concerned, I don't even exist. He won't even look at me anymore."

Clay smiled. "You took him down a notch or two last week, Jonas. I doubt if he knows quite how to treat you yet, but he sure as hell ought to have learned you won't take his guff anymore. That's something, I reckon."

"Maybe," Jonas acknowledged. "But Nash and Dunlap think I'm a fool, too."

Nash and Dunlap are cast from the same mold as Garrett," Clay replied. "Don't let them get under your skin."

"Is that all there is out here, Clay, people like that?"

"I'm out here. So's Ty."

"You're outnumbered," Jonas pointed out dryly.

"Naw, we're about even. There's you, remember? That makes it three to three."

"Sure," Jonas said without enthusiasm.

"It'll get better. Meanwhile, we'll see what we can scare up tomorrow. I've never known a man who didn't perk up with a good rifle in his hands."

Jonas didn't reply. He seemed to sink within himself, into his own thoughts, which was fine with Clay. He smoked quietly and admired the stars. A few thin clouds drifted overhead, but nothing large enough to hinder the light. His thoughts drifted for a while, until he became aware of a faint vibration in his buttocks. He shifted unconsciously, but the feeling persisted. Finally, Jonas lifted his head to look around. "Do you feel that?" he asked.

Clay put his hand on the ground, a look of excitement coming to his face. "I'll be damned," he whispered, then, more urgently, "Come on, Jonas!"

The two men surged to their feet and hurried down the ridge and across the creek. Clay grabbed his saddle and tack as he passed the lean-to, and slid between the poles of the corral. Tossing his catch rope to Jonas, he said, "Fetch me that dappled gray of Ty's over there."

While Jonas went to comply, Clay slapped his hulk onto the pinto's back and tightened the cinch. After bridling the pinto, he fashioned a crude hackamore from his catch rope for the gray, then led both horses out of the corral. "Take my horse," he said, handing the younger man his reins. "A saddle'll be easier on your balls than a horse's spine." Grabbing a handful of mane, he swung astride the gray.

Jonas clambered onto the pinto and they reined toward the Smoky Hill, crossing at a ford about half a mile upstream from the cabin. On the south bank, Clay guided his mount to a trail that wound up through the bluffs along the river. Twenty minutes later they hauled up on top, Clay's heart quickening at the view. To the south and west, as far as the eye could see in the pale moonlight, the broad, gently rolling plains were covered with a thick brown carpet of grazing buffalo. He heard Jonas gasp as he halted the pinto nearby, but didn't look around; he couldn't have torn his eyes from the sight before him if the horse he rode started to speak.

"There . . . there must be . . . millions," Jonas uttered softly. "Like fish in the ocean."

"Like the grass," Clay agreed, keeping a tight rein on the gray's hackamore to prevent it from bolting forward. Jonas was having an equally difficult time controlling the pinto. Both horses trembled visibly, their heads high and alert, nostrils flaring as they sucked in the pungent aroma of the herd. Clay breathed deeply of the scent, as well, the musky odor making him feel alive and eager, lighter in spirit than he'd felt in months.

The herd was moving slowly northward, toward the Smoky Hill. The animals' low, hog-like grunts filled the night air; dew claws clicked like wooden knitting needles, and knee joints popped and groaned as the ponderous beasts eased toward another bite of grass. Occasionally a cow coughed or snorted, or a calf bleated. A gnat hummed at Clay's ear. He slapped it away, but it was soon back, joined by two or three more. He laughed when he saw Jonas waving the pesky insects away from his own face.

"There it Is, Jonas. That's what driven Ty these past weeks, what brought us all out here to the edge of nowhere. By God, as far as the eye can see, and more behind those, I'd wager."

"There's so many. They'll drain the river."

Clay laughed in delight. "Naw, they won't drain it, but they'll sure as hell muddy it up. Look at the direction they're grazing in, north by a little west."

"At least that'll take them away from the ranch."

"Take 'em upriver, too. But they'll spread

out once they hit a good source of water. Upstream, downstream. They'll piss up the Smoky Hill until it runs green. We'll have to pull our water from the spring, for sure."

"I didn't know," Jonas said, shaking his head in disbelief. "I used to hear people talk about the millions of buffalo that roamed the western plains, but no one could comprehend this without seeing it for themselves."

"Well, you've seen it, pard, that's certain sure, and in another month you'll know more about buffalo than most of the population east of the Mississippi ever will."

"I think," Jonas said reverently, "that I already do."

By dawn the herd had them surrounded, grazing to within a hundred yards of the cabin. Standing on a wagon tongue, Ty stared upstream at the thousands of lumbering, hump-shouldered beasts in his view. It was a sight to stir the heart of any man who loved the wild lands as he did; yet there was within him an odd sense of melancholy, too. They were ready. They had done all they could to prepare. Now the killing would begin in earnest. But the coming slaughter created an incongruity of feelings he hadn't expected. He had to remind himself that this was a job — dirty, but legitimate — and no different than raising hogs or cattle for market, except that the hides paid a little better and the tallow burned cleaner.

He heard the clopping of hooves behind him and glanced over his shoulder as Virgil drew up beside the wagon.

"Goddamn, I wasn't sure how I'd feel about hunting again, but seein' all them hairy dollars out there, I'm as primed as a whore at sundown," Virgil announced.

"You're going out?"

"Hell, yeah, I'm goin' out. We can finish that damn dugout later. I aim to make some money today."

"Which way you headed?"

Virgil pointed upstream with his chin. "Straight ahead, Ty-boy. Gonna put a dent in that ol' herd, or bust my gun-barrel tryin'."

"Make sure you go far enough upstream. It'll stink to high heaven around here in another week, the way it is. No point in —"

"You just worry about filling your own wagons, hoss," Virgil interrupted. "I've been hunting as long as you have."

"Virg."

"Yeah?" He glanced down with a cocky expression.

"I want you to go at least two miles

upstream before you start shooting. If you don't, I'll kick the living shit out of you. Understand?"

Virgil's face darkened. "I wouldn't push my luck, Tyler, was I you."

"You ain't me, and I meant what I said. Two miles." For a moment, Ty thought Virgil might argue further. He wouldn't have put it past him to climb off his horse right there and fight. But instead, Virgil jerked his black gelding around, driving his spurs into the animal's ribs and riding off at a gallop. A couple of minutes later, John Dunlap rattled after him in a heavy farm wagon drawn by a four mule hitch.

"What was that about?" Clay asked, coming up with the pinto's reins in hand.

"Just planning the day's hunt," Ty replied drolly. He stepped off the freighter's tongue and loosened the reins to his bay.

Clay stared thoughtfully after Virgil's retreating form. "Who won?" he asked.

"I did, today." Ty glanced toward the meadow where Jonas and Oscar were yoking three spans of oxen to the prairie schooner. Flipping his stirrup over the saddle's seat to check the cinch, he said carefully, "Have you ever still-hunted?"

"Sure, for deer and such. But not out here in the open."

"Ride with me today. I want to show you a few tricks I've picked up."

Clay's brows furrowed. "I've hunted buffalo before, Ty. I know how it's done." He nodded toward the staking grounds, where nearly a score of bull hides were already pegged out to dry. "Half of those are mine, remember?"

"Sure, but you ran them, right?"

"I'm not a tail hunter," Clay replied stiffly.

"Come along today. If you don't like what you see, you can hunt your own way tomorrow."

Clay shrugged noncommittally, and Ty let it drop. He knew Clay was used to the chase, to plunging his mount in among the racing bison and firing from horseback at a dead run. He had tried it himself a time or two, and had never felt anything quite so exhilarating. But at the end of a day's hunt he would have harvested less than half a dozen animals over a distance of as much as five miles, and scattered the remainder of the herd to hell and gone. A man couldn't make any money that way, or kill enough to even keep a crew busy. Ty had discovered a more economical method of hunting buffalo, a means of dropping enough shaggies within such close proximity of each other that they could skin all day without having to move their wagon.

He retrieved his rifle, shooting bag, and powder horn from the rear of the freighter. "Have you ever had a stand?" he asked Clay.

"I don't even know what you're talking about."

"That's why I want you to come with me. I want to show you how I hunt, how a lot of men out here are starting to hunt, now that there's a steady market for meat and hides."

Although Clay looked doubtful, Ty knew his curiosity was piqued. Swinging into their saddles, the two men rode down to the Smoky Hill, their horses carving dark paths through the heavy frost along the river bottom. They crossed at the same ford Clay and Jonas had used the night before, and started up the trail to the high plains above. Glancing back as they neared the top, Ty saw Jonas leaving the ranch. Oscar wasn't in sight, but knowing the old man as he did, Ty figured he was inside the prairie schooner, wrapped in a cushioning robe to keep warm. He turned back to the trail, satisfied that Jonas would be able to follow them, and that if any trouble occurred, Oscar would be there to help him out of it.

At the top of the bluff, Ty pulled up sharply. "Good God," he exclaimed, taking in the far-flung herd that stretched from horizon to horizon on three sides.

"It's a sight, ain't it?" Clay remarked.

"I've never seen a herd this large, not in the two years I've been out here."

"Me, neither," Clay admitted, "though I've heard old-timers talk of it. I figured they were just stories until last night."

Ty's eyes suddenly twinkled. "Damn, Clay, I was worried the buffalo might not show up at all this season, but we couldn't shoot through this bunch in a hundred years."

"There's a lot of hides and meat out there."

"A lot of hard work, too. Come on." He reined east, away from the ranch, and Clay fell in beside him. They rode for a couple of miles at a slow walk. The buffalo were thick, but not packed together like sardines in an airtight. From a distance they looked like a solid mass, but up close Ty estimated less than half a dozen animals to an acre, spread out and feeding slowly as they made their way to the Smoky Hill, moving at less than half a mile per hour. As the horsemen passed by, the nearest buffalo often shied away a few paces, but then resumed their grazing as the hunters moved on.

Wolves slunk through the herd on every side, seeking out the weak, or young and unsuspecting. The buffalo ignored these predators as they did the ravens and crows that flocked overhead, or the cowbirds that rode their wooly spines to feed on lice, fleas, and ticks — a giant, slow-moving host to a dozen or more species that depended on the great herds for survival.

Once Ty and Clay were far enough away from the ranch, it didn't take long to find a bunch to their liking. They rode wide around a smaller herd within the herd until they were downwind of it, then dismounted and hobbled their horses in a sandy draw. Ty led the way on foot, his blanket-cased Hawken cradled in his left arm. When they were within eighty yards of the smaller herd, they crawled out of the draw and settled down side-by-side, cross-legged. Reaching inside his blanket case, Ty withdrew his rifle and a pair of hickory sticks about thirty-six inches long and half an inch in diameter, held together about six inches from the top with a rivet fashioned from a square nail, the lower legs tapered to blunt points. Laying his rifle aside for a moment, Ty spread the two legs and jabbed them into the hard prairie soil. "Cross-sticks," he explained to Clay. "I rest the barrel across the crotch, and it's like having a third arm."

"I'll be damned," Clay murmured.

"How many buffalo have you dropped in a run?"

"Three is the best I've ever managed, but I've seen others, Indians hunting with bows and arrows, kill up to a dozen, and in a shorter run, too."

Ty grinned as he pulled his rifle across his lap and thumbed a fresh cap over the nipple. "Every bunch has a leader," he remarked, cradling the Hawken's barrel in his cross-sticks.

Clay gave him a disgruntled look. "That tan cow, off to the left."

"Be my guess, too," Ty said. He snugged the iron buttplate into his shoulder and nestled his cheek against the polished walnut stock. Lowering his sights to a point just behind and slightly above the buffalo's elbow, he set the rear trigger, then rested the ball of his forefinger against the front trigger. He drew a deep breath, held it, then gently squeezed. The big .50 caliber rifle roared, belching a cloud of gray powder smoke.

Ty lifted his head. Through the roiling smoke he saw the cow lurch as if slammed in the ribs by a giant fist. She took a wobbly step forward, then dropped as if pole-axed. Save for a couple of animals standing close to her that started, the herd continued to graze as if nothing had happened. Ty pulled the rifle back and ran a damp patch through the bore, then calmly reloaded.

"They aren't running," Clay observed, his gaze darting from animal to animal.

"You said you've killed three in one run. I've dropped sixteen this way, all within a space of a hundred yards."

Clay nodded in understanding. It wasn't glorious, but it was efficient. "You've made your point," he said. "I'll have to whittle a pair of cross-sticks for myself."

"Try these," Ty offered, scooting aside.

With rifle in hand, Clay slid behind the hickory cross-sticks, resting the heavy octagon barrel of his long gun in the forks.

"Look at the way that cow with the gimpy hip is nosing the wind," Ty pointed out.

"I see her."

"She's got a whiff of blood. She'll get nervous and start off in a minute. Drop her next."

Clay nodded and took aim. Ty watched the quick, familiar way Clay handled his rifle, and fought off a grin. He had decided back in Leavenworth that Clay had the look of a hunter — that smooth, catlike graceful-ness, the easy self-reliance of a man intimate with his surroundings, and a sharp, critical eye that missed little of what went on around him. It appeared now that he had judged him correctly. It would be good to have a partner like Clay to fall back on if the need arose.

The crippled cow made her way to the fallen leader and lowered her head to hook the dead animal's flank, as if to force her back to her feet. But before her horn touched the leader's hide, Clay's rifle bellowed. The crippled cow took a startled step backward. She stood quietly for a moment, head lowered, her beard brushing the ground. Then a gush of blood spewed from her mouth and nostrils, and she collapsed in a heap.

Ty smiled. "A good shot, too," he murmured.

Clay looked at him. "What's that?"

"Nothing," Ty replied, still grinning. "Nothing at all." He thumbed a fresh cap over his reloaded Hawken and scooted behind the cross-sticks as Clay slid away. "Let's make some meat."

TWENTY-THREE

It was them, no doubt about that. Jake Jacobs would have given everything he owned right then, clean down to his socks, if it hadn't been, but there was no use denying it. Not with Hog Waller's high-pitched voice already yammering excitedly in the Colonel's ear.

"That will be enough, Mr. Waller," the Colonel rebuked sharply. Hog swayed back with a hurt expression. Colonel Douglas Carry turned his attention to Jake. "Do you concur, Mr. Jacobs?"

Jake glanced again at the family huddled outside the door of their dumpy sod house. Sunlight glinted off their ebony faces, spotlighting fear and uncertainty.

"Mr. Jacobs," the Colonel prodded. "Are these the Negroes known as James, Missy, and Nate Parker?"

Jake took a deep breath. "Well, it wasn't them, Colonel. Oh, they was there, all right, but they ain't the ones what killed your brother. I figure that had to be Clay or Sammy Lee. These folks . . ." he waved a hand vaguely toward the soddy, ". . . shucks, Colonel, they never give us no harm."

"But they were there?" the Colonel reiterated impatiently. "Participants by proximity. And they fled afterward, as criminals are wont to do, rather than turn themselves in to the law? Isn't that correct?"

Jake was having trouble breathing. "Lordy, Colonel," he said softly, "they was just caught up in it. Ezra and Seth brought 'em in, but they didn't give us no trouble the whole time, and I don't believe they lifted a gun that day. I just don't believe they would've done something like that."

"Lifted neither a gun nor a hand, Mr. Jacobs, a hand that might have prevented the senseless murder of my brother and his associates. Isn't that correct, as well? And isn't it also correct that once a Negro has tasted the sweet nectar of mischief, they are bound by their own rampant lusts to attempt it again?" The Colonel's voice rose; his cheeks, above the trimmed silver beard, glowed red, and his voice shook with the self-righteousness of a minister. "Isn't that right, Mr. Jacobs?" he roared.

Jake flinched, his eyes on the ground.

Shaking his head, he said, "No, sir, I don't believe it is. I think —"

"Then you are a fool, Mr. Jacobs, as I have long suspected. I shall ask you a final time, are these the Negroes who assisted in the murder of my brother and his men?"

Tears came to Jake's eyes. He forced himself to look up. James had apparently ordered his wife and son inside the soddy. He stood before its door alone, scared but determined. Jake finally nodded. "I don't believe they killed anyone, Colonel, but they was there."

"Their names?" Carry demanded in a stone-hard voice.

"James," Jake whispered. "James and Missy, and the boy's name is Nate."

The Colonel took a deep breath. "Very well. Mr. Hawkes." He turned to the lanky gunman sitting a well-put-together thoroughbred at his side. "You know what to do."

"Yes, sir," Bill Hawkes replied. He looked at the other two men, one of them his brother, Boyd, and a second man who went only by the name of Quint. "Let's go," Bill snapped, touching his mount's ribs with small-roweled spurs.

Jake sniffed as quietly as possible and rubbed a sleeve under his nose. He was glad the Colonel hadn't ordered him and Hog to accompany the three hired killers across the recently-plowed field that fronted the soddy. It would be hard enough to watch from afar. But Jake's hopes of remaining a distant witness were soon dashed. Bill, Boyd, and Quint spread out as they approached the soddy, stopping their mounts at the edge of the yard. Jake could tell by the movements of their heads that they were talking to James. The Colonel waited a few minutes more, then ordered Jake and Hog to follow him across the furrowed field.

The Colonel gigged his mount forward without waiting for a reply, and Hog fell in behind like a well-trained hound. After a moment's hesitation, Jake booted his own animal after them, hanging on tightly to the lead rope of a reluctant packhorse. At the soddy Jake veered off to the side, but Colonel Carry forced his mount between the horses of Bill and Boyd, wordlessly establishing his position. "Any trouble?" he inquired.

"Nary a minute's," Bill replied easily. At some point since crossing the plowed field, he had dug a plug of tobacco from his coat pocket and bitten off a chew. It bulged in his cheek now like a pus-filled boil. Leaning casually away from the Colonel, he squirted a gob of amber fluid past his boot, then straightened and wiped his mouth with a gloved hand. "Nigger claims he wasn't anywhere near the Neosho when the Captain was shot. Ain't that what you said, boy?"

But James had already recognized Jake and Hog, and a look of despair marked his face. "It wasn't me," he said desperately. "I was chained up when all the shootin' took place."

"If not you, then who?" the Colonel asked him.

James shook his head. "Don't know," he blurted. "Don't know nuthin' 'bout it. I was still in chains."

Bill's smile was thin and bleak. "Ain't that just like a nigger? Kills three men in cold blood, then forgets all about it before the season changes."

"Where are the others?" Colonel Carry asked bluntly. "Plato, Jenny, Sammy Lee, Clay?"

"Don't know nuthin' 'bout them folks," James replied evasively. "I been here tendin' my place the whole time."

"Why, that's a damn lie," Hog exclaimed.

"Mr. Waller," the Colonel admonished. "Control yourself."

"Colonel, that nigra was one of 'em. I'd

swear to that on a stack of Bibles."

"Of course he was," the Colonel answered calmly. "He is lying to save his neck, but we'll find them. Just as we found this one." He turned to the man beside him. "Mr. Hawkes?"

"Anytime you're ready, Colonel."

"Proceed."

Bill dismounted and walked back to the packhorse. He sneered at Jake as he passed. "What's the matter, Jacobs? You're looking a little green around the gills."

"There ain't no call for this," Jake managed, but Bill only laughed as he pulled a stout hemp rope from the pack.

At the soddy, James had backed up until he could reach behind him, fumbling along the wall until he found what he wanted. Lifting a broadax in both hands, he called, "You jus' put that there rope away, mister. Ain't nobody here causin' no trouble. You jus' leave us be now, you hear?"

Jake threw the Colonel a frantic look, but he could tell by the feverish gleam in the man's eyes that he had no intention of interfering. This was between the three man killers and James now. The Colonel had relegated himself to the role of a spectator.

Bill stood beside his horse, shaping a

noose. "Boyd," he said casually, "disarm him."

Boyd pulled his pistol and pointed it at James. "This the way you want it to end, boy? Drop that ax, or I'll shoot your hand off."

"No, sir, I ain't a gonna drop this here ax. You gonna have to come and take it 'way from me, you want —"

Boyd fired. His slug ripped into the flesh of James' forearm, shattering the bone. The black man cried out in pain and shock as he fell against the soddy's wall. A woman screamed from inside, then the door flew open and Missy rushed out. She screamed again when she saw James braced against the wall, his sleeve bright with blood. Grabbing a wooden-tined pitchfork, she rushed the three horsemen, but a second shot from Boyd's pistol cut her down before she'd covered a dozen paces.

"*Missy!*" James shouted hoarsely.

"*Ma!*" Nate's cry echoed from inside the soddy. He leaped from the darkened interior and ran toward his mother. Boyd's third shot took him in the knee, throwing him to the cold ground of the soddy's yard.

"For God's sake!" Jake screeched, looking wildly at the Colonel. "Stop this, man! They didn't kill your brother! They didn't have anything —"

"*Jacobs!*" the Colonel thundered, glaring at Jake with murder in his eyes. "Keep your mouth shut, you Missouri trash."

Chuckling, Bill advanced on James. Boyd and Quint dismounted, Quint having also drawn his pistol. James pushed away from the soddy's wall, the ax forgotten on the ground at his feet. Tears streamed down his dark cheeks as he stumbled toward his wife, sobbing her name. On the ground, Missy groaned and rolled to her side, revealing a bloody patch of material over her stomach. Her fingers glistened wetly as she tried to staunch the flow of blood.

"Shit," Hog muttered, subdued at last. "He gut-shot her."

"You, too, Mr. Waller," the Colonel warned. "Let these men work."

"Come here, boy," Bill said, staring at James, who had dropped to his knees beside Missy. He rolled her onto her back with his good arm, his face was twisted in anguish. "Baby," he said. "My sweet baby."

With an impatient curse, Bill walked over and dropped the finished noose around James' neck. It was only when he jerked it tight that James seemed to remember he wasn't alone. As Bill pulled on the rope, James began to struggle, clawing at the rough fibers with the fingers of his good hand. His breath came out in a ragged gurgle as Bill yanked him over backward, then dragged him to the soddy.

"Nooo!" Nate wailed, rolling on the ground with both hands wrapped around his broken knee. "Please, don't! *Please!*"

"Shut up," Boyd snarled, aiming a kick at the fallen youth. "You'll get your turn in a minute."

"This'll do," Bill announced, eyeing the sturdy ridgepole that extended from the center of the roof. "All we need is enough height to get his feet off the ground."

James was still struggling futilely at the rope, his shattered right arm flopping uselessly. Quint walked over to slam his pistol hard against the black man's head, causing him to sag.

"Easy," the Colonel cautioned. "I want him conscious when he hangs."

Bill tossed the coiled rope over the ridgepole. Boyd mounted his horse and took the loose end of the rope, giving it a hitch around his saddlehorn. He gave the Colonel an expectant glance, and at his nod, began backing his horse away from the soddy, though at an angle so that the rope wouldn't slide off the ridgepole. James' struggles became more violent as the noose drew taut. He kicked at the ground, then the soddy's wall, and ripped the swelling flesh of his neck with his left hand. Bill laughed and said, "Take him up a little more, brother."

"Damn, Bill, maybe that ridgepole ain't gonna be high enough," Boyd commented. "He's a tall one."

"It'll be high enough," Bill assured him. As he stepped back, Jake became aware of the erection that strained the front of Bill Hawkes' trousers like an oversized knuckle. With a sick, suffocating hollowness, he suddenly realized what killing meant to men like Bill and Boyd and Quint, that the pleasure they took from a job didn't necessarily come from the roll of cash they received for their deeds.

"How's that?" Boyd called.

"Good," Bill replied, gauging the gap between the black man's feet and the ground. He and Quint took the rope from Boyd's saddle and secured it to the jutting end of one of the soddy's eaves. Stepping back, Bill brushed his gloved hands together and looked at Carry. "That suit you, Colonel?"

Carry was watching James' diminishing struggles as if transfixed. Finally, the Colonel nodded and leaned back in his saddle. James' kicking had ceased; his left arm hung limp at his side, the nails bloody where he'd torn his own flesh.

"Yes." Carry spoke the single word in a rush. "Yes, that suits me perfectly." He continued to stare at James, his expression bright with excitement. Quint, meanwhile, went to the woman and knelt at her side. He let his hand hover over her mouth for a couple of minutes, then looked up with regret. "This one's dead, Colonel."

Disappointment replaced the pleasure of a moment before on the colonel's face. "Well, I suppose it's of little consequence, although I would have enjoyed seeing her hang beside her mate." He looked at Nate, sitting mutely on the ground between his parents, staring dully into the distance. "Get on with it," he ordered brusquely.

"Colonel," Bill said hesitantly. "We've only got four ropes. If we hang this kid, and leave 'em both to swing, that'll leave us with just two. We could buy some more, but . . ."

"No, no, our message here will be clear, and expenses are important. Boyd, since your pistol has already been fouled, would you kill the young one? Bill, you and Mr. Quint search the house. If you find anything that might have belonged to my brother, bring it to me. Otherwise, torch the place with their possessions inside."

"It ain't gonna burn, Colonel," Quint pointed out.

"Nevertheless, our message will still be clear to those who come later. Fire what you can, Mr. Quint. Nature will take care of the rest in time."

"Yes, sir."

Boyd reined over to Nate, pulling his pistol.

"Colonel," Jake whispered.

"Shut up, Mr. Jacobs," the Colonel replied distantly.

Jake was aware of Nate watching him with a curious detachment, as if death had already claimed what was important from him. Jake lowered his gaze, tears rolling down his cheeks, but he only flinched when Boyd's pistol cracked.

"Well, that's three of the murderers accounted for." The Colonel looked at Jake and smiled. "Only four more to find and execute, correct, Mr. Jacobs?"

"I . . . I reckon so . . . Colonel."

Sun was straight overhead when Wolf Tail took his new, Kiowa-tanned buffalo robe and fusil and clambered through the jumbled rocks to where Hides in the Grass lay between a pair of sandstone boulders, watching their backtrail. Dropping to his stomach to avoid outlining himself against the cold, gray sky, Wolf Tail wormed in beside his old friend. Silently, he scanned the broad, flat plain that separated the Pawnees' hideout from the distant, tree-lined channel of the Arkansas River.

"Nothing moves, my brother," Hides in the Grass murmured, handing Wolf Tail a tarnished brass telescope taken from the Kiowa.

Wolf Tail extended the scope without comment. He knew Hides in the Grass had already spotted every jack-rabbit and prairie dog on the flat. He had probably counted the saucer-shaped aeries of the turkey vultures that roosted in the cottonwoods along the river each spring, the huge nests looking tiny from here, but marking this well-known crossing of the Arkansas as they had for countless generations of war parties. Wolf Tail looked anyway, letting the scope swing unhurriedly back and forth across the empty flat, then readjusting it to focus on the sand hills beyond the river. As Hides in the Grass had stated, nothing moved. Not even a turkey vulture.

"Our enemies will not follow us here," Wolf Tail announced with more conviction than he felt. "We have stolen too many horses, and left them only a few broken down nags too crippled to keep up. They will be as helpless as the white-eyed dirt-diggers until their warriors return."

"Then where are the others?" Hides in the Grass queried softly.

Wolf Tail knew it worried his friend that the other members of the Pawnee raiding party hadn't shown up. This was the sixth sun since their raid on the Kiowa village, and the Pawnees had split up that first night to confuse any pursuit. It had been agreed that they would meet north of the Arkansas and east of the Kiowa village within four suns, so that they could return home together to share the triumphs of a successful raid — more than sixty horses stolen, seven scalps collected, including the four old men ambushed along the Arkansas, and the young Kiowa woman Wolf Tail had abducted beside the plum thicket outside the village.

But there were many crossings on the Arkansas, and in their haste to be off the young warriors had forgotten to specify the crossing where they would rendezvous. Perhaps the others had used a different ford, and were waiting even now for Wolf Tail, Hides in the Grass, and Short Bird to show up; or perhaps they had tired of waiting altogether, and already turned their stolen ponies homeward.

Wolf Tail slid the spyglass closed and handed it back to Hides in the Grass. "We have remained here long enough," he said. "They are probably on their way home now, as we should be." He glanced at the sky, studying the lowering clouds that had moved in only that morning, promising rain, if not sleet.

"What if they have run into trouble?" Hides in the Grass asked. "What if the Kiowa hunters returned sooner than we expected, and followed Broken Bow, Raven's Beak, Runs His Ponies Hard and Little White Man?"

Irritably, Wolf Tail replied, "We have many horses, and a woman to horn anytime we choose. We should be celebrating, not cowering here afraid to lift our heads above these rocks. Are we not Pawnee?"

Hides in the Grass was unmoved. "You are too impatient, my friend, too anxious to hear the women sing your praise upon our return."

"As we all should be," Wolf Tail countered. "It has been a good raid that has made us all rich."

Hides in the Grass chuckled. "Not rich, but richer, that is true. It is good to have some extra ponies. That will be a fine thing to point out this winter, when I court Blue Swan."

"Then let us leave this place. I do not wish to return to find the others already there, asking us if we got lost."

"No," Hides in the Grass replied calmly. "I will stay a while longer. If the others have run into an enemy war party, there could be wounded who would need our help."

Wolf Tail made an angry gesture. "Then you will remain here alone, Hides in the Grass. Short Bird and I will take our ponies and the woman and go."

"I have already spoken with Short Bird, and he also agrees that we should wait."

"Then you will both —" Wolf Tail froze. He sensed movement at his side, a subtle stirring, as if the land itself were shifting.

"It is only a rattlesnake," Hides in the Grass told him. "I saw it earlier, an old bull that has not yet found a den for its winter's sleep."

Wolf Tail pushed himself back until he could peer under the slanting boulder he had been lying beside. "You should have told me," he said in an accusatory tone. "It might have bitten me."

"It is too sluggish from the cold to think about biting anyone." He gave Wolf Tail a curious glance. "You are not thinking of making war on that rattlesnake, are you?"

Wolf Tail squinted into the darkness under the big rock. "I see him. There is a crevice, and he is at its rear."

"Yes. Are your ears filled with sand? I heard him there earlier."

Wolf Tail's countenance brightened as a new thought occurred to him. Pulling his fusil close, he whipped the ramrod from its thimbles beneath the barrel.

Hides in the Grass scowled. "I would not count on him being *too* old or cold-witted," he cautioned. "These rocks still hold plenty of Sun's warmth."

"I believe you," Wolf Tail replied. "But I have an idea. Come help me. It will be fun."

Hides in the Grass gave the Crossing Where the Vultures Roost in Spring a final glance, then slid back from the skyline. "What is this idea of yours that will be so much fun?"

Wolf Tail shoved his ramrod into the crevice, provoking an immediate whirring. "See, he is an old one. Listen to the power of those rattles. There must be ten buttons on his tail, at least."

"More than that, I would think," Hides in the Grass answered gloomily.

The ramrod jerked in Wolf Tail's hand as the snake struck, causing the young Pawnee to laugh delightedly. "See, an old warrior, like those Kiowas we killed on the Arkansas. But I have already struck coup against this one."

"I think maybe it is the old warrior who struck coup against you, my friend. Be careful, lest he break your ramrod, as well."

"You are a worrier, Hides in the Grass. Soon your hair will turn to the color of snow from so much thinking." Wolf Tail caught his lower lip between his teeth as he forced the brass tip of his ramrod under the snake's belly, then drew it toward him. "See, he is too cold to resist. He lets me drag him wherever I please, and does not strike a second time."

"Perhaps it is wisdom, rather than a cold wind, that stays this rattler's fangs," Hides in the Grass said gravely. "Watch yourself closely, brother, for no creature lives into old age by striking the wrong target twice."

Although Wolf Tail smiled condescendingly, he also heeded Hides in the Grass' advice, increasing his distance from the crevice's mouth even as he continued to work the snake toward him. "Be ready," he said to Hides in the Grass, pushing his fusil toward him. "When I pull him out, clamp the buttplate of my long gun behind his head."

"You do not intend to kill him, to eat his meat?"

"No, I have better use for this old warrior." He edged back another foot or so, said, *"Now!"* sharply, and gave the ramrod a quick jerk. The rattler, an eight-footer, flipped into the sunlight, its white belly flashing momentarily. Then it snapped into a tight coil of muscle, its huge, wedge-shaped head reared back threateningly, its buttons buzzing angrily. But before the snake could strike, Hides in the Grass slammed Wolf Tail's fusil down from the side, catching it behind the head and pinning it to the ground.

"Hah! You did it!" Wolf Tail cried happily.

A drop of sweat was already beading on the tip of Hides in the Grass' slim nose. "Yes, I did it. Now hurry with whatever game you wish to play. This old bull is a strong one."

Carefully, Wolf Tail reached behind the fusil to capture the snake's whirling tail. The rattler's whole body seemed to convulse as Wolf Tail's fingers closed around the cool, dry skin. Hides in the Grass grunted, then pressed down even harder on the fusil. "Hurry!" he snapped.

Wolf Tail pulled his knife, steadied the pale amber buttons with the ball of his thumb, and with one swift stroke cut the rattles free.

Once again the snake jerked violently. As it did, Wolf Tail and Hides in the Grass jumped back, scrambling out of the rattler's long reach. Staring at the snake's inward curving fangs, the needle-sharp tips glistening with secreted venom, Hides in the Grass's nostrils flared hotly. "All that for a set of buttons no different than the ones you have back at your father's lodge?"

Wolf Tail held the bloody string close to Hides in the Grass's ear and gave it a sudden shake, laughing when Hides in the Grass leaned away. "For the woman," Wolf Tail explained, slipping the rattles into his fire-making pouch. "We will have some fun tonight, scaring her with it."

"Wolf Tail, sometimes you are a leader who makes me proud to be your friend, but sometimes you are like a little boy who still enjoys shooting arrows at the dolls of the girls in our village."

"You will laugh just as much as I do when you see the look on her face," Wolf Tail promised. "Come, it is time we stopped squatting here like constipated vultures. Let us go home together."

But Hides in the Grass shook his head. "You go. Short Bird and I will stay a while longer, just to be sure."

Wolf Tail shrugged, then grinned. "Suit yourself, but I would find another place to keep watch from. That bull rattlesnake will not soon forget what was done to him here today."

Hides in the Grass turned his gaze morosely on the distant crossing. "I fear the Kiowas will feel the same way, my brother," he replied solemnly.

TWENTY-FOUR

They were pulling fresh hides off the prairie schooner and staking them out hair side up on the flat just south of the cabin when Clay spotted the Indians. He paused in his work long enough to glance at his rifle, leaning against the wagon's rear wheel, then started for the pegging ground with a rolled-up hide balanced over his shoulder. He caught Ty's eye as the two men passed, and nodded toward the bluff south of the river. "We've got company," he announced casually.

Ty glanced over his shoulder, and his face paled. "Damn," he said.

Jonas, coming up behind Clay with a seventy-pound hide clutched awkwardly in both arms, stopped dead in his tracks when he spotted the two distant figures. Within another minute Oscar and Virgil had joined them. John Dunlap remained on the wagon, where he had been dragging the hides they'd taken that day to the tailgate.

"Pawnees," Oscar stated offhandedly, then spat to the side. "Sorry bastards, they is."

"Are they dangerous?" Jonas asked.

"Not at six to two odds," Virgil answered stonily. Clay gave him a glance. Virgil stood with his weight on the balls of his feet, his eyes narrowed to slits.

"They're probably just passing through," Clay said, as much to Virgil as Jonas. "I doubt if they'll cause any trouble."

"Wouldn't bother me if they tried," Virgil replied.

Ty stepped away from the group and lifted his arm over his head, motioning the Indians in with broad gestures.

"What the hell you doin'?" Oscar asked, scowling. "Ain't we got enough lice in this camp from all these stinkin' hides?"

"Maybe they're scouts for a village," Ty answered, keeping his gaze on the Indians as they edged their ponies over the lip of the bluff. "Maybe they'll have robes to trade."

"Aw, hell," Oscar grumbled. "A Pawnee ain't got nuthin' worth tradin' that ain't been stolt first."

"I didn't haul all those trade goods out here to clutter up the cabin," Ty said. "Let's see what they've got."

"Likely all they's got is some white coon's

scalp," Oscar replied sourly.

Clay watched as the two Indians guided their ponies carefully down the trail toward the river, then shifted the bulky hide on his shoulder. "Come on," he said to Jonas. "We've got time to roll these out before they get here. We can stake 'em down later."

He eyed the pegging ground. They had about seventy-five hides already staked out to dry across the little flat, and a stack of forty or so cured skins that rose from the grass like a pint-size butte.

Clay flopped the hide he was carrying to the hard ground at the edge of the field and unrolled it flesh side up. If not for the Pawnees, he would have stretched and staked it to the ground through slits cut in the edge of the skin, generally about twenty wooden pegs to a hide, so that in a few days time it would dry flat and hard as a board. At that point Oscar would come out to turn them over and sprinkle a mixture of arsenic and water over the hair to keep out the hide bugs, although Clay reckoned poison wouldn't be needed much longer. The weather had changed a few days previous, the sky clouding over in earnest and the temperatures dropping sharply; the winds had picked up too, keening loudly enough at the eaves of the cabin at night to make sleep difficult. It had rained off and on, although never enough to keep them from hunting. Still, there seemed little doubt that the balmy days of Indian summer were behind them; the cold fogged their breath from morning to night now, and a rim of ice had formed along the shallow pools of Tornado Creek.

The Indians were fording the Smoky Hill by the time Clay and Jonas returned to the wagon. Ty met them there anxiously. "How should we handle this?" he asked Clay.

"No differently than we would any other rider coming into camp. Play it by ear, but be ready for anything."

"I left my rifle in the cabin," Ty added worriedly.

"I reckon that's as good a place for it as any," Clay responded. He glanced again at his own rifle, but left it where it was. Virgil and Oscar and John Dunlap had gathered near the cabin to watch the Indians' approach, all three of them fully armed.

As the Pawnees splashed up the near bank of the river, Clay was mildly surprised to discover that one of them was a woman. As they drew closer, he realized she was a captive. Her face was lumpy on one side, where she had been struck hard by a fist or club, and her long black hair was uncombed, ratted by the wind. Although she wore a blanket against the cold northern winds, from the looks of her hunched shoulders its protection must have been minimal.

The man was younger than Clay would have expected, dressed in leggings and breechcloth and a fringed war shirt under a knee-length blanket coat. A fresh, iron-gray scalplock dangled from the front ramrod thimble of a hard-used flintlock trade gun, and a bow and quiver of arrows were slanted across his back. His head was shaved in a fashion favored by some Pawnees, with a stiffly greased roach running from his forehead to the back of his neck; the shiny black hair was decorated with feathers and bits of trade doth, the scalp on either side painted a dull red. He rode a wiry dun, its muzzle flecked with gray whiskers.

They halted at the edge of the pegging grounds, the warrior's gaze taking in the hides staked out over a couple of acres, the crude cabin, and the men standing in front of it. A look of icy rage clouded the Indian's face, and Clay thought: *Here's trouble.*

The Pawnee kicked his horse forward. The woman followed without command, the automatic response of a slave. They threaded their ponies through the hides and pulled up again about ten yards away. Glaring at

Ty and Clay, the warrior began a rapid tirade in Pawnee, twice flinging a hand toward the hide grounds. Ty looked at Clay in embarrassment. "I don't remember the words," he said. "The sign language Oscar taught me last spring. I can't even remember how to say hello."

"I'll speak to him," Clay said. From the corner of his eye he could see Virgil and Oscar moving toward them, their expressions hard as granite.

"What the hell's he so ticked off about?" Virgil demanded.

"That's what I'm about to find out." Using his hands, but speaking English so that the others could follow, Clay said, "Welcome."

In sign, the Pawnee replied: *Who are you? What are you doing here?*

"We are hunters," Clay replied. "We have come here to make meat to take back to our villages in the east."

This is Pawnee land, the Indian stated bluntly. *You are not welcome here. Leave it, now.*

"What's he saying?" Ty asked.

Oscar guffawed. "The coon's tellin' us to get off'n his place, is what he's sayin'."

"Huh!" Virgil grunted. "That ain't likely."

"Ask him to get down," Ty said. "Tell him

449

we'll give him coffee. Tell him we have sugar, too."

"Don't tell 'im to get down," Oscar squawked, giving Ty a startled look. "Hell, boy, he ain't no scout for no village. Onliest thing this buck's got to trade is that there squaw, and she ain't no Pawnee, I kin tell you that right off. Kiowa, she is. Or Comanch. One or t'other."

Clay glanced sharply at the woman, at the cut of her clothes and the shape of her moccasins, at the flaking streak of Vermillion she'd used to highlight the part of her hair at some point before her capture. With a jolt, he realized the old man was right. She was Kiowa. The awareness created an odd sensation in him. At one time in his life this Pawnee would have been his enemy, he realized; now he tried to convince them both of his friendship, his desire to trade.

"See what he'd take for the woman," Virgil said with a taut smile. "See if he'd trade some beads for her."

"He won't trade her," Clay said.

"Try it anyway."

"Naw, the boy's right," Oscar said. "He wouldn't take no beads for her, that's certain sure. Maybe a rifle, 'stead of that old fuzee he's a totin', maybe that and the dapple that nobody rides."

450

"We aren't trading rifles for a woman," Ty put in quickly. "We aren't trading the gray for her, either. If anyone loses a horse, we'll need that animal."

But Virgil wouldn't let it go. "Ask him, see what he says."

"We don't need a woman," Ty said, staring hard at Virgil.

Oscar laughed. "Speak for yourself, sonny." He looked at Jonas with a sardonic grin. "How 'bout it, runt? Think you'd like to fork that Kiowa filly?"

Ty turned slowly to face the older man. "Go put some coffee on, Oscar."

"Wha— what?"

Speaking with deliberate precision, Ty said, "Go put some coffee on. We'll give this Pawnee some coffee, and maybe give his woman some trinkets."

Oscar's face reddened combatively. "Ain't you been listenin', boy? She's a slave, no better'n a dog. A man don't buy no trinkets for his dog."

"That's true," Clay said reluctantly. "Give him some coffee if you want, but anything you give the woman he'll just take for himself."

As if ignored too long, the Pawnee burst into an animated discourse, gesturing wildly with his arms. Clay followed as best he could, but caught only bits and pieces of the whole.

"What now?" Virgil asked, amused. "Is he wanting a deed to the place before we pull out?"

"Says our horses be eatin' Pawnee grass, too," Oscar translated. Chuckling, he added, "Seems we ain't doin' nuthin' to this whelp's likin'."

"What's his name?" Ty asked.

Clay made the motions, watching the Indian sign in return. Oscar cackled loudly when he finished, slapping his thigh with the flat of his hand. "Wolf Tail, boys. Coon says his name be Wolf Tail. Now ain't that a hoot?"

Abruptly, Wolf Tail swung his leg over his mount's withers and dropped to the ground. He stooped and tore up a handful of short, brown grass, lifting it over his head and shaking it angrily. Then he opened his fingers to let the wind carry the strands of grass away. With his hands, he began to speak rapidly:

Pawnee land. Pawnee grass. He flung an arm toward the distant horizon. *Everything from here to as far as a pony can run in ten sleeps, Pawnee land. The grass, the buffalo, the trees, the sky, the rain, all Pawnee. Like I* am *Pawnee. Like my horse is Pawnee. Every-thing.*"

"This buck has got hisself a one-track mind," Oscar said in a voice suddenly drained of humor.

"Tell him we've got coffee," Ty said. "Tell him we'll drink some coffee and talk."

"I don't think he wants coffee," Clay said.

Ty exhaled loudly. "All right, then we'll give him some to take along."

"Sonny, you've got a fixation on coffee like that buck does on us trespassin'." Oscar growled. "Get it through your thinker, all this redskin wants is your hair. Don't go givin' him no coffee."

"Maybe some coffee to take along would be a good idea," Clay said uncertainly. "He's too mad to think about trading now, but maybe he'd cool off if he thought about it." He looked at Oscar. "Go get a sack of coffee and a cone of brown sugar."

Oscar snorted. "Get 'em yourself, boy."

"Get the coffee," Ty said sharply.

"I'll fetch it," Dunlap called from the cabin, then disappeared inside. Clay glanced at the woman, staring dispassionately over their heads as if they weren't even there.

"She's a pretty one, ain't she?" Virgil said in a mocking tone. "Makes a man's head swim just to look at her."

453

Clay thought there was more truth to Virgil's words than he'd intended. Behind the dirt and grime, underneath the tangled hair and the bruised, swollen flesh, was the face of a beautiful woman. Clay had to fight the urge to rub his wrists, where Captain Carry's manacles had bit into his own flesh not that long ago. *I should do something about this,* he told himself. *I should stop this somehow.*

He remembered the slaves he'd known around Red Creek, and those he'd seen on his trip to Fort Smith, Arkansas, and felt the weight of helplessness.

What can I do? he asked himself then. *What could any man do, short of killing the Pawnee?*

He actually considered it for a moment. It would probably be easy to do, just pull his pistol and blaze away. The Pawnee was so close there wouldn't be any chance of missing. Just point and fire, and the woman was free. Yet even as he thought about it, he knew he couldn't. Not when he still periodically awoke in a cold sweat in the middle of the night, the faces of the Captain and Ezra and Seth swirling through his disintegrating dreams like ghosts. "Jesus," he murmured, rubbing a hand over his face. "Jesus H.

Christ." He took a deep breath, then looked at Ty.

"Are you all right?" Ty asked.

Clay nodded.

"Then tell him Dunlap's bringing coffee," Ty instructed.

"What about the woman?"

"She can have some, too."

"That's not what I mean," Clay said raggedly. "She's a captive, Ty, dragged away from her people against her will. What are we going do about that?"

Ty gave him a gauging look. "It's none of our affair, Clay."

"If not ours, then whose?" Clay insisted, angry at himself for pushing onto another what he didn't know how to correct himself.

"The army," Ty replied pragmatically. "We can report her capture to the commander at Fort Riley the next time we pass through."

"That'll be spring, at the earliest," Clay said doggedly. "What's going to happen to her in the meantime?"

"There's nothing we can do about her, Clay. It's none of our business."

Clay's jaws knotted in frustration, but he could tell by the smiles on the faces of Virgil and Oscar that he wouldn't be able to press it much further. Not without one or both of them jumping into the fray with their own lewd suggestions. Resolutely, Clay repeated Ty's offer of coffee. Wolf Tail snorted derisively. In sign, he replied that he didn't want their coffee, that he wished only to see the white hunters leave, to stop killing the buffalo that belonged to the Pawnees. His words cut at Clay. *White hunters!* Was that what he had become? Clay translated Wolf Tail's response for Ty and the others.

"This is ridiculous," Virgil said impatiently. "Oscar, tell this redskin we're here to hunt buffalo, and that we don't intend to leave until we've killed every damn shaggy on the plains."

Chuckling gleefully, the old man started to comply, but Ty cut him short. "Hold it, Oscar." But before he could add any more, the Pawnee started to speak, following with his hands.

"When your men make trouble, you call them bad and hunt them down. But when our men make trouble, you say Indian, and blame us all. When we kill the white man's cattle it is called a crime and we are punished by the blue coats, but when the white men kill our buffalo they are not punished. Your black robes and your agents give us tools and tell us we must give up war, but by that they ask us to become women. Would the white man

wear skirts and learn the magic of the loom? Would he spread his legs during copulation? This is the question that I ask the white men. He made the sign for being finished, then swung onto his pony and popped its hip with his quirt, riding north toward the trees along Tornado Creek. The woman followed compliantly, not once having spoken or looked at any of them. Clay stared at her as she rode past, wishing for her to return his gaze, to understand that his hands were tied, and that there was nothing he could do. But the woman kept her eyes on the Pawnee's broad shoulders, heeling her pony into a trot when he did, and never looking rearward.

"Whewee," Oscar said, pushing his hat back and scratching his forehead as he watched the Indians ride off. He gave a rough interpretation of the Pawnee's speech, then added, "That was a mouthful all right, and most of it true, too." He glanced at Clay, smirking. "All except that part about only white men killin' their buffler, eh, boy?"

"Damn," Ty said, hooking his thumbs behind the buckle of his gunbelt. "I'd hoped to convince him to bring his people back in the spring with robes and pelts. Or horses. I'd trade for horses or mules."

"Ty," Virgil said peevishly. "You ain't never

learned to listen, have you? You couldn't do it as a kid, and you're no better at it now. That red buck wasn't about to trade shit for anything you've got stowed away in your cabin."

"A man's gotta try," Ty replied.

"The hell with that," Virgil said, then spun on a heel and headed for the corral.

"Where are you going?" Ty called after him.

"I'll bet I've got something that redskin can't refuse," Virgil flung over his shoulder. "I want to see if I can't trade it for that woman. You chickenshits never did ask him what he'd take for her."

"Leave him be, Virg," Ty hollered. "Just let 'em go."

"Kiss my ass, Tyler. I'm your partner, not your darky."

They watched in heavy silence as Virgil saddled his horse and led it out of the corral. Oscar went over to hand him his rifle as he rode past, leaving only Jonas and Ty and Clay standing beside the wagon. The Indians had already disappeared up Tornado Creek when Virgil spurred after them. As the sound of Virgil's mount faded, Ty said, "One of them's going to end up dead, aren't they?"

"Looks that way," Clay agreed spiritlessly.

Sadness shadowed Ty's face as he turned away. "Come on," he said. "Let's get this wagon unloaded. We've got another long day ahead of us tomorrow."

Wolf Tail left the Creek Where the Trees Had Blown Down — what the white-eyed buffalo hunters had dubbed Tornado Creek — about halfway to its source. He guided his pony into an arroyo coming in from the west, and soon topped out on the sloping land that led to the divide separating the Smoky Hill and Big Creek drainages. From here he had a good view of the rolling prairie that stretched away in every direction; only the broken lands directly below him, along the Smoky Hill, remained hidden.

Wolf Tail was fairly certain that at least some of the white hunters would follow him. He had seen it in their eyes as he left their camp, a lust for the woman that had manifested itself differently in each man. The black white man felt sorry for her, and wanted to set her free. The man with so much anger in his heart was either jealous or resentful of Wolf Tail's possession of so valuable an object, and wanted her for himself, as he would have wanted a fine rifle or horse or fancy knife. The old one's feelings were more primal, yet in its own way, more pure; he coveted the woman simply for his blankets, perhaps seeking in copulation a temporary reprieve from his own ebbing manhood, a reminder of days past.

Such misdirected desires brought only contempt to Wolf Tail's mind, yet he would have bet his fastest pony that one or another of them would act upon their feelings.

Wolf Tail reined his pony toward the higher ground of the divide. He had never fought a white man before, and was looking forward to the encounter, as well as adding some more unique scalps to his collection. Wolf Tail's father, Stands Alone, had made war against the white-eyes numerous times as a younger man. Wolf Tail, when a boy, had listened in rapt attention to his stories of the glory days of the Pawnee Nation, in that time before the Great White Father in the East had sent his agents and black robes and missionaries to infest their lands.

Now it would be Wolf Tail's time to fight the white men, and he vowed to teach them the same lessons his father had taught them a generation earlier — that the Pawnees would not stand idly by while pale-skinned interlopers destroyed their land, their buffalo, and their heritage.

Wolf Tail rode twice as far as a good rifle

could shoot, then dismounted and handed his single, jaw-line rein to the Kiowa woman. Kneeling on the cold ground, he removed the blanket coat and buckskin war shirt he had taken from the Kiowas, then set out his paints, grease, and small mirror. Carefully, yet ever-conscious of his pursuers, Wolf Tail applied fresh paint to his face, torso, and limbs, touching up the designs he had originally put there on the morning he'd left the Pawnee hunting camp. When he finished, he returned the items to his possibles bag and set it aside. Next he brought his fusil across his lap and flipped open the frizzen, blowing out the old powder and replacing it with a fresh charge from the buffalo horn he carried on a strap over his shooting bag. With the smooth-bore ready, he laid it aside, then slid half a dozen arrows from his quiver and meticulously checked the fletching, the notched shafts for straightness, and the sinew that held the tin arrowheads in place. Placing these arrows on the grass beside him, he was in the process of extracting another handful from his quiver when he sensed his pony lifting its head behind him. Looking up, Wolf Tail saw a single rider top out of the arroyo he and the Kiowa woman had exited only a short while before. There was a moment's disappointment that only one man, the one with the angry heart, had followed him. Were the whites so confident in themselves that they thought one man would be enough? he wondered. Or had only this one, this man driven by raging demons, sensed the silent challenge Wolf Tail had issued to them all?

Without haste, he returned the arrows to his quiver, replacing them one at a time and in such a way that when he pulled his first arrow free he wouldn't drag the rest out with it. From time to time, he glanced up to study the solitary horseman watching him from the edge of the arroyo. Wolf Tail considered it his good fortune that it was one of the younger hunters who had come after him, rather than the old man with the thin, greasy hair. Even covered by a broad-brimmed felt hat, Wolf Tail could tell that the angry man's hair, falling below his shoulders in back, was thick and luxurious, and would make a fine trophy to hang inside his lodge.

Calmly, Wolf Tail rose to his feet, cradling the smoothbore in his left arm. Angry Man still waited at the head of the arroyo, regarding him with what must have been surprise and suspicion. He had not counted on this, Wolf Tail knew. He had expected a lone

Pawnee to run, or try to hide. A cruel smile twisted Wolf Tail's lips as he remembered a saying among his peers. *White-eyes are unpredictable except in their arrogance.*

Angry Man nudged his horse to a walk, his rifle butted to his thigh. Without taking his eyes away from the approaching enemy, Wolf Tail ran his thumb lightly over the edge of the knapped flint clamped in the jaws of his fusil's hammer. The sharp-edged black stone cut a shallow, bloodless trough across the ball of his thumb, reassuring him that the weapon was ready. Curling his thumb around the hammer's jaw screw, he slowly cocked it. A feeling of admiration for the white man's cool courage as he kept his fine black gelding moving forward at a leisurely pace touched Wolf Tail. Surely, he thought, a man who rode such a horse would also carry a good rifle. He hoped so. For a long time now he had wished to own a better weapon than the old, awkward-to-fire flinter he currently owned.

Spreading his feet wide, Wolf Tail slowly let the fusil slide down his arm into his hands, where it would be easier to snap to his shoulder. He kept it low, though, not wanting to frighten Angry Man away before he came into range.

But Angry Man fooled him. He stopped

his horse well out of the fusil's reach, then dismounted and dropped to one knee, letting his horse wander free. Wolf Tail watched in puzzlement as Angry Man shouldered his rifle. Did he not know he was still too far away? Did he not also realize that no rifle, not even a good Leman or J. Henry or Deringer, could shoot that far?

Wolf Tail watched the puff of gun smoke mushroom from the muzzle and heard, a heartbeat later, the dull boom of the report. Then a white-hot ball of fire blossomed in his chest, knocking him back with enough force to spin him in midair, so that he fell face first to the ground.

For a moment, he couldn't move. Then, dizzily, he lifted his head a few inches. His cheek was numb where it had struck the earth, his lips flecked with dead grass and a frothy pink spittle. Then the pain came like a steel band drawn agonizingly tight across his chest, and he realized he had been shot in the lungs, close to his heart.

Wolf Tail had not expected this, had not thought a man, even a white man with his many wonderful inventions, could do what this angry young white-eye had just done. Yet it had happened, and there was no denying that his own disdain for the white race, his refusal to take more precautions, had inadvertently contributed to it.

With difficulty, Wolf Tail pushed to his hands and knees. The Kiowa bitch stood with the horses, unmoving and unmoved. Wolf Tail's expression was grim as he searched for his fusil. He found it lying several feet away, a dark scar on the tan grass. Ignoring the growing sense of suffocation, he began to crawl toward it. From the lower slope he could hear the pounding of the black gelding's hooves as Angry Man raced toward him. Fighting back waves of light-headedness, Wolf Tail increased his effort, dragging his knees across the grass now, rather than try to lift them. He reached the fusil and managed to get his hands over it, then discovered he was too weak to pick it up. He let his head loll, his arms trembling from the strain. Angry Man was close now, already slowing his mount. Wolf Tail forced his fingers around the dinged cherrywood stock, struggling to pull it toward him. But there was no strength left, and with a muffled cry of futility, he fell forward, sprawled across the long gun with the side of his face pressed to the cold, hard ground. He listened to the jingle of spurs as Angry Man dismounted and came to stand over him. The fusil was jerked from beneath his body, knife and tomahawk yanked from his belt. In a hoarse, croaking whisper, Wolf Tail began his death chant, informing the heavens that he would soon begin his journey, asking the spirits for their help in guiding him there.

Angry Man's toe slid under his ribs, and Wolf Tail was rolled onto his back. He was grateful. He wanted to see the sky again, to focus on that faraway place where his father's fathers, resided. He was still conscious when Angry Man knelt over him with a butcher knife, but the pain had left him. The tug of the white man's blade sawing roughly through the flesh and muscle of his stomach seemed distant and unimportant. It pleased him to know Angry Man would be denied this pleasure, that the deep incisions he carved into Wolf Tail's body would elicit neither physical nor emotional responses. He glanced a final time at the white man whose heart was consumed by rage, then peacefully closed his eyes.

TWENTY-FIVE

Rounding the last bend in the trail, Clay drew up. Through the falling snow he could just make out the box-like shape of Sam Dooley's trading post, the sturdy adobe structure plugged in the center of its west wall by a square patch of beckoning lamplight, the long L of the warehouse hidden from this angle. In the gathering dusk, the post looked warm and inviting, a haven from the frigid winds sweeping down out of the northwest.

It was the middle of December, according to Jonas, who had announced in the same breath, and with more than a trace of wistfulness, that Christmas was less than two weeks away.

The coming holiday meant little to Clay. Ty had promised that they'd take it easy that day, and that maybe he'd rustle up a turkey or venison or raccoon, as they were all growing weary of buffalo meat, but Clay doubted if they would do anything else. The mood at the hunter's ranch had been strained from the beginning, but it had deteriorated rapidly after Virgil's return with the Pawnee's scalp and the Kiowa woman.

Twisting in the saddle, Clay watched Jonas guide the freighter with its five yoke of oxen into view. Jonas was riding Ty's dappled gray, bundled up in a buffalo robe against the growing storm. Pulling up alongside Clay, he said, "I was beginning to wonder if we'd make it tonight."

They had been on the trail for two days, the weather windy and overcast the whole time, but the snow had held off until sunset tonight. Now it fell in gusting flurries, lodging in the grass like grains of white sand, but sticking, too, and showing signs that it might accumulate overnight. Although Clay didn't voice it, he was as glad to see the trading post as Jonas. He hadn't looked forward to another cold night sleeping under the wagon.

As the oxen pulled even with the horses, Jonas tapped the flank of the near leader with the tip of his whip and said, "Haw," in an authoritative voice. Obediently, the team swung toward the adobe post, perhaps sensing that beside its protecting walls awaited the end of another day.

Clay and Jonas rode in together. The front door opened as they quartered into the yard, and Sam Dooley stepped outside with a double-barreled shotgun in his hands.

"Take the wagon around to the lee side," Clay instructed Jonas. "I'll be out in a minute to help you unhitch."

"I can handle it," Jonas assured him.

"All right, but be sure to snub ol' Brownie up tight. A night like this, she'd be halfway to Riley by morning if she got the chance."

"I can handle Brownie, too," Jonas said resentfully.

Clay nodded and veered away, guiding the pinto toward the hitching rail in front of the trading post, calling out his name and Ty's as he did. Dooley waved and let his shotgun sag. Clay stepped from the saddle and wrapped his reins around the rail. Hauling his rifle from its loop on the saddle horn, he approached the burly trader.

"Well'n be damn, but ye never know what a strong wind'll blow in out here," Dooley said with a grin, pumping Clay's hand. "Come on inside, young fella, where there be some heat." He led the way, slamming the door shut behind Clay.

"How are you, Sam?" Clay asked, brushing the snow from his coat.

"Middlin', Clay, middlin'." He inclined

his head toward the counter. "Belly up there, mon, and I'll fix ye a shot o' somethin' hot tae chase away ye chill."

Clay leaned his rifle against the wall, then moved to the counter. The post was empty save for himself and Dooley and the sounds of someone in the kitchen. "Where are your hands?" Clay asked.

Dooley made a sound of disgust. "Deserted me, the hoary bastards. Lit out for Cherry Creek near a month ago. 'Tis just me and Emerson now, though he be a good mon, and fair company tae boot."

"I expected to find two or three outfits hanging around, this time of year."

"Well, we be on the edge here, Clay, and nae that many hunters wantin' tae range this far out yet. But next year'll be different, I'm thinkin'. I figured me first year would be skinny, but come spring I'll be humpin' it to keep up, ye mark me words on that. Especially once the rush starts for Cherry Creek."

"Gold?"

"Aye, gold. Fact is, there's already been more'n a few pass through. I've got some coloreds squattin' out behind me in dugouts right now."

"Coloreds?" Clay looked up curiously from where he had been watching Dooley

470

pour a shot of whiskey from his private jug into a tin cup.

"Aimin' tae get a jump on it next spring, they be. Or maybe they was just afeared tae tackle the plains this late in the season. Not that I'd blame 'em much, if that was the case. The weather out here'll turn on a man quicker'n a buff'lo bull, he ain't careful."

Clay accepted the cup Dooley pushed toward him, lifting it to sniff suspiciously at the contents. The liquor smelled raw and fiery, and made his eyes water just holding it close.

"Go ahead," Dooley urged, grinning. "It'll nae bite, though it might blister a wee bit."

Clay took a sip and grimaced. Dooley's grin stretched wide as he corked the jug and set it aside.

"I see ye ain't a heavy drinker."

"I reckon not," Clay acknowledged.

"There be a pot o' elk on the stove, spiced with red peppers tae bring a good sweat tae ye brow, if that be more tae ye likin'."

"It sounds good, for a fact," Clay said, before trying another sip. Already the whiskey was sliding through his veins like an uncoiling snake, climbing the back of his skull, warming his cheeks. "So who are these colored folks you mentioned?" he asked huskily.

"Bunch o' 'em in from Nebraska Territory. Maybe ye'd know 'em. I mean, I ain't forgettin' ye be Choctaw, Clay. I remember that right enough, and respect it, tae. But, considerin', I thought ye might know 'em."

"I've met a few Negroes along the way," Clay said without animosity. "One of 'em wouldn't be an old man with white hair, would he?"

"Ol' Plato," Dooley said, brightening. "Sure, him and 'is daughter."

"Daughter?"

"Aye, Jenny, but there be others, tae. Jesse and Minnie and George Simms and 'is wife. A bunch o' 'em. Seventeen, countin' the younguns." He wagged his head sadly. "Good folks, all, but poor. Half starved and barely enough shot a'tween 'em tae bring down a jackrabbit. I've loaned 'em some, but they won't take much. Says they're doin' all right, but I figure 'tis naught but a damn lie. Just too proud to accept help, they are. I admire 'em for it, but 'tis foolish, tae, especially with children. A man hadn't ought tae get so proud 'is small ones go hungry, I say."

"I've got some cured hams and tongues on the wagon," Clay said. "Maybe they'd accept some of that."

"They might, you bein' . . . well, dark and all."

"It's all right, Sam," Clay said, smiling appreciatively. "My adoptive daddy was Choctaw, but I've seen a mirror."

"Well, if ye say so. I remember ye bein' touchy aboot it, is all."

"Sometimes," Clay agreed, "just sometimes," then changed the subject. "We've got hides, meat, and some tallow outside that we're wanting to ship east before the snows shut down the roads. Ty says he talked to you about it?"

"Aye, he did. Phillips, over tae Salina, had contracted for a couple o' wagons worth o' supplies, and he said he'd send 'em on out around the first of the year tae pick up whatever I had on hand."

"We've got just shy of a hundred skins, around eighteen hundred pounds of meat, and about three hundred pounds of tallow, wrapped in sacking. It's not a big load, but Ty figured we ought to take advantage of a passing freighter. He wants to send everything to Lobenstein."

Nodding agreeably, Dooley said, "Sure, t'will be nae problem a'tall. We'll figure out the paperwork after supper, as soon as ye skinner gets in."

Clay took another sip of his drink, then

set the cup aside. "We'll do that," he agreed. "In the meantime, I think I'll mosey over and see Plato. I didn't expect to find him here." He indicated the cup with a nod of his head. "Save that for me."

"Sure, it'll be sittin' right here when ye get back. The coloreds got their soddies built intae the side o' the hill on t'other side o' the trees."

Clay nodded his thanks and headed for the door. He remembered the steep-sided hill from the last time he was here, and thought he could find it easily enough. Leaving his rifle against the wall, he went outside and mounted the pinto, riding around the west side of the building.

At first he couldn't see anything in the swirling storm. He let the pinto pick its own trail through the trees, feeling ahead with his hand for low-hanging branches. Then he caught a whiff of wood smoke, and a moment later spotted the wafer-thin bars of light spilling from a loosely fitted doorjamb. Dismounting in the shelter of a small wagon, he hitched the pinto to a wheel, then made his way to the door. His knock on planks that had once been the sideboards of a wagon caused a stirring from within, followed by a raspy voice that brought a smile to his face.

"Who that?"

"Open up, old man," Clay shouted above the wind. "There's a half-wild Choctaw out here who's ready to lift that mangy piece of nap you call a scalp."

"Clay!" The door swung inward on leather hinges, the bottom dragging at a dirt floor. Then Plato stepped into the night, wrapping his arms tightly around the younger man's shoulders. "By the Lord," he said tearfully, giving Clay a hard shake, "Ol' Clay Little Bull. That truly be you, son?"

"It's me, dad. I came to pay you a call."

"My, oh, my. Well, come on in, come on in. Lordy, but you look froze right through."

Clay laughed with a happiness he hadn't felt in weeks as he ducked through the low door. Although Dooley's whiskey still coursed through his blood, he felt an added warmth now, something more subtle, and infinitely more genuine.

He stepped aside as Plato shouldered the makeshift door back in place, his gaze roaming swiftly over the tiny room. He had seen worse lodgings in his life, but not many. The soddy had been dug into the hill, and was about eight feet wide by twelve deep. There was a small cookstove in the middle of the room with a rusted pipe running through the ceiling; a pair of pallets against the rear wall served as beds. Someone had taken the seat off the wagon, springs and all, and set it close to the stove. A worn-out patchwork quilt hung from the ceiling to partition off a corner of the room for dressing and bathing. An empty twenty-gallon keg with broken staves functioned as a table, while a wooden box at its side held a meager collection of cooking utensils. Atop the keg, a homemade betty lamp with a rag wick threw off a feeble, smoky light.

Jenny stood partially hidden in the shadows behind the stove, her expression cautious as she watched Clay pull off his hat and shake the snow onto the floor. Then her face hardened, and she said, "That'll be mud in another minute. Most folks know 'nough to shake the snow off 'em 'fore they comes into a person's home."

"Hush, now," Plato chided. "Clay here be our friend, and it's been a spell since we seen him, so don't go barkin' at him right off." He looked at Clay and smiled. "How you doin', son? How you been farin'?"

"I've been doing well, dad. Holding my own most days, making a little progress on others." He moved closer to the stove, holding his hands out to its warmth. But it was cold in the dugout, even with the fire. "How about you two? Damn if I didn't think you'd be nearly to Mexico by now."

Jenny huffed some kind of reply and came forward to take Clay's hat and coat, muttering under her breath about keeping such wet things away from the heat, where they would soon go to stinking.

"Well now, we got us a start for Mexico, we surely do," Plato said. "Onliest trouble is, this here whole wagon train's caught itself a touch of gold fever. Ever'body's wantin' to go out to that Cherry Creek and get theyselves a bucket full of nuggets to take with 'em. Was all het up for it and on the way, too, 'til Jesse's wagon busted a axle coming down that hill to Mr. Dooley's. We had to hole up here while Jesse went back to find hisself a length of hardwood for a new axle, us not wantin' to trust no cottonwood for somethin' that important. Then the dern weather turned uglier'n a overseer with a splinter up his bum, so we decided right here was the place to nest. I reckon the Lord was lookin' over us kindly when we made that decision, cause this here ol' storm would'a caught us out in the middle of nowhere if we'd'a gone on. We'd've been sorry pickles then. Ain't that right, Jenny?"

Jenny gave him a withering look, then returned to her place behind the stove and sank to her knees on a pallet.

Plato chuckled without offense. "Jenny don't agree with ol' Plato yet that folks of color has got to stick together."

"Stuck, is what you mean," Jenny replied tardy. She looked at Clay. "You rich yet, Mr. Little Bull red Injun? You kill you all them buff'lo what's gonna make you the richest nigger in Kansas?"

"From what I've seen of Kansas," Clay replied solemnly, "a ten-dollar gold piece would just about do that."

Jenny grunted, but seemed satisfied with his answer.

Plato motioned toward the wagon seat. "Have yourself a rest, Clay. My, oh, my, you come in all the way from that place you all's got out there on the prairies?"

"You know about it?" Clay asked, shunning the wagon seat to fold down cross-legged in front of the stove.

Yes, sir. Mr. Dooley tolt us 'bout it. I figured it was you. They can't be that many Clay Little Bull's roamin' these here parts, I figures." His smile shrank as he eased onto the wagon seat, the old leaf springs squealing rustily above the popping of his knees. "Fella named Dunlap came through here couple weeks 'go, driving hisself a mighty nice team of mules and a small wagon. Said he was headin' back to civilization 'fore the snows set in. Tolt us about that Virgil fella, what he done to that Injun."

Clay nodded soberly. John Dunlap had renounced his partnership with Virgil soon after the latter's return with the Indian woman, keeping only the wagon and mules for himself. Although Dunlap hadn't offered any reason for the breakup, Clay had formed his own opinion regarding the matter.

"That man as mean to that girl as Dunlap says?" Plato asked.

"They keep pretty much to themselves," Clay replied carefully. "Nash and Dunlap had started a dugout kind of like this one before the buffalo came back. Once he had the girl, Virgil finished it by himself, and the two of them moved in there. Virgil still hunts, but not as much as he could. The woman skins for him, and takes care of the hides."

"It true she ain't nothin' but a whore?" Jenny asked bluntly.

"Jenny!" Plato rebuked. "What kind of talk be that, comin' from a lady like yourself?"

"Shoo, I ain't no lady. I was born a slave, same as you. But I never let no white man have his sport with me. I'd a clobbered him upside his head with a skillet 'fore I done that."

"Some have that option," Clay said pointedly. "Rain Dancing On Water doesn't. Virgil would kill her if she tried it."

"Better dead than some white boy's whore," Jenny countered.

"I dunno," Plato mused. "I dunno 'bout that a'tall. But that Nash fella, he don't sound like much of a man, you ask me. Treatin' a woman like that. And killin' a man to get her, too."

Clay considered telling them about Virgil's brother, Wade, and the things the Cheyennes had done to him over on the Saline River the previous fall. Yet he knew that as horrible as that must have been to those who had found him, it mattered only to Virgil now, and changed nothing for Rain Dancing. "Virg is Virg," he said finally. "So far, we've stayed out of it."

"Easiest that way, huh?" Jenny asked sarcastically.

"It ain't always so simple, Jenny, gettin' messed up in 'nother man's business," Plato said in Clay's defense.

"Meanin' that Virgil Nash's business, not the Injun gal's."

Clay looked at her in exasperation. "What would you have me do, kill Virgil to free her?"

"That's what I'd do. I'd kill that Virgil

480

Nash with a rock upside his head."

"Or a skillet?"

Jenny's dark eyes flashed angrily. "Skillet works just fine, ain't no rock handy."

"Well, you're welcome to it," Clay said with sudden heat. "Just follow our tracks back to the ranch. Virgil's dugout is on the east side of the creek. Just waltz in there and crack his skull like it was an egg, then send the woman home."

"Now, now," Plato soothed. "Ain't no call for you two to be snappin' at one 'nother. Ain't nothing ever settled that way."

"I reckon," Jenny said starchily, "I'll go visit with Minnie Harper a spell." She rose and yanked her coat off a peg driven into the wall, flinging it over her shoulders without bothering with the sleeves. When she was gone, Plato offered Clay an apologetic smile. "She be sassy, for a fact."

"Bullheaded, is more like it."

"Some might see her that way, but not me." He gave Clay a conciliatory look. "You know she was headed for them gold fields by her lonesome when Ezra roped her down and dragged her in with the rest of us, don't you? She heard 'bout it eavesdroppin' on some white folks in St. Louie, where she was a house nigger in a hotel. Listened in while she was makin' up the bed with fresh

481

sheets. Bunch of dirty, bearded old miners she said looked like they hadn't touched a chunk of soap in ten year, but there they was, sleepin' on clean sheets and eatin' two dollar suppers and smokin' fifty cent seegars." He chuckled. "So little Jenny, she ups and decides her days of nigger work is over. Her masser had gone up to Chicago last winter where he had him a sick mama, and left the hotel in charge of a lazy partner who didn't give no hoot 'bout how it was run. That's what decided Jenny. She knows ain't no one gonna say nothing 'bout her goin', and that lazy partner ain't gonna bother huntin' her down. So Jenny takes what she needs from the pantry and toolshed and loads it into a wheelbarrow, and off she takes for Cherry Creek, bold as you please."

"From St. Louis?" Clay asked incredulously.

"All the way, and a pushin' a wheelbarrow, too."

Clay laughed. "She would," he agreed.

"Now, don't you go makin' sport of her," Plato admonished. "You don't know little Jenny the way I's come to know her. She ain't a gal to laugh at. After Sammy Lee left us, Jenny was ready to go her own way, too, back the way we'd come." The old man's eyes twinkled with merriment as he recalled her stubbornness. "She aimed to fetch her wheelbarrow from where Ezra had dumped it in some bushes, and by damn, she done it."

"No!"

"Yes, sir, she did. 'Course by that time we'd talked a little more and decided them horses we was riding was a mite too fancy for black folks. So we traded 'em to a Injun for a wagon and a couple rundown mules. It was a poor trade, maybe, but that Injun said he'd have a rocky time sellin' those horses, too, so we allowed we'd done all right. But Jenny wouldn't let go of her wheelbarrow. No, sir. She says them mules ain't got more'n another year or two left in 'em, but she aims to have that wheelbarrow 'til the day she dies. And you know what?"

"She'll have it?"

"I think she will, one way or t'other."

Clay smiled. "You might be right, dad."

"Dern tootin' I'm right. That Jenny has got spunk. And she's sweet on you, too."

"On me? You're crazy, old man."

"Ain't. Oh, she wouldn't admit it, not if you took a hammer to her toes, but I seen it in her face the day you left us there on that Santy Fe Trail. That was a hard day for our little Jenny."

"You sure she hasn't taken a skillet upside

483

your head lately? You're talking nonsense now."

"No, I just knows her some. You think on that, Clay. A fella could do a lot worse than a gal like Jenny."

"I reckon not," Clay replied dryly.

Plato was quiet a moment, thinking. Then he changed the subject, his voice going low and a little mournful. "They found them bodies, you know?"

"Captain Carry and them? I heard about it in Leavenworth."

"Ever'body knows it was niggers kilt 'em. They just don't know which niggers yet."

Clay nodded gloomily. "I guess I'd hoped I'd left that behind me when I came out here."

"That be a ghost won't ever go to rest in these parts," Plato prophesied. "Just one more reason you oughta come with us to Mexico. It be behind us certain sure, was we there."

Clay shook his head.

"Mexico be the onliest place a black man is gonna find hisself any real freedom," Plato insisted. "Don't know why you can't see that, don't know why them others can't see it, either. I'm havin' the devil's own time convincin' 'em Mexico is our bodily salvation."

"Maybe that gold fever you mentioned has bit down too hard. Money's a scarce thing for a black man."

"Huh!" Plato sniffed, then let it drop. Clay reached for his hat, sliding his pipe from its band. He filled the bowl with tobacco and lit it with flint and steel and a piece of char, then puffed contentedly for several minutes. A smile twitched at the corners of Plato's mouth as he watched the younger man. "I 'member Jenny tellin' me how you smoked that thing Injun fashion, the day me'n Sammy Lee caught up with you after getting shet of the Captain. She said you pointed it in all four directions, then at the ground and up to the sky. I'd always heard Injuns did that, but I never knew why."

"Prayer, I guess."

"Injun prayer?"

"Is there a difference?"

"Some folks say so. White folks, mostly. They gots a right strong fear of African prayer, it seems. Always tryin' to stomp it out in the quarters, but they never do."

"No," Clay said, thinking of the Seminoles, whose heritage was so tightly interwoven with that of Africa, and whose religion was so different from their Choctaw neighbors. "I suppose not."

"Do you believe in it, that Injun prayer, I mean?"

"Simon didn't always follow the traditional ways. He said he liked to look around and see what other religions were doing. He told me I needed to find my own way, my own medicine, he called it. He said I already had some African medicine running through my veins, and some Kiowa and Choctaw, too, and through him a smidgen of Christianity. But I'm not sure how it's all mixed together yet."

"Your daddy sounds like a wise man."

"Simon? He wasn't really —"

"Sure he was. A daddy ain't always him what sleeps with your mama, Clay, what sires a child like some randy ol' stud horse sires a colt. No sir, a daddy is him what be there when times turn weedy, what teaches you to find your own path, and guides you when you needs it. Like that ol' Simon did."

"Then I guess he was my daddy," Clay said. "At least for a part of my life."

"You still think 'bout them wild tribes out there, like you did when we was ridin' together for the Santy Fe Trail?"

"Some," Clay admitted. "I've thrown in with Tyler Calhoun now, and I'll see that through to the end of the season, but I can't stop thinking about the Kiowa, either. I keep remembering what it was like when I lived with them, how I used to feel like I belonged there. I sure as hell haven't felt that way lately."

"What you mean, son?"

"I mean this is a white man's country, dad, and I'm Indian. Maybe you don't see it that way, and maybe no one else does, but it's all I've ever known. The only time in my life I ever really felt like a Negro were those days in Captain Carry's chains. The rest of my life has been lived as an Indian, one tribe or another, though it's a tough road, red or black. Sometimes, out on the buffalo range with Ty and Jonas, I'll forget for a while that I'm different, but sooner or later Oscar Garrett or Virgil Nash will say something to bring those days with Carry rolling back. Maybe I can't return to the Nations, but the Kiowa aren't very far from here. Their land starts around the Arkansas River."

"Why you want to go back to them people what made you a slave as surely as me or Jenny ever was?"

"I wasn't a slave," Clay argued. "I lived a good life with the Kiowa."

"You was a boy then, a future warrior. Now that you be a man, you think they'd even 'member you?"

"They'd remember," Clay said, but he was unable to conceal some doubt.

Hearing it, Plato grunted knowingly. "I thought as much. Them Injuns, son, that was a long time ago . . . so long ago they ain't gonna 'member no little nigger child tooken away —"

"I'm not a nigger," Clay snapped, the brittle clay stem of his pipe clacking against his teeth.

Plato reached out to tenderly lay a hand on top of Clay's knee. "Son, you ain't pure black, even I can see that. You got them green eyes, and your hair ain't kinky like mine, though I 'spect it might be, was it cut short. But that don't take away the things you is, either. That buckskin shirt or them mokkysons or that feather in your hatband, ain't none of them changes a thing."

"Maybe, but you said yourself that Simon Little Bull was my father. Simon was Choctaw, and my uncles are Kiowa."

"What were their names?" Plato queried gently. "Them uncles what be Kiowa you is all the time talkin' 'bout. You never mentioned their names."

A pang of sorrow stabbed Clay's breast. He lowered his head, taking the pipe from his mouth and holding it cupped in both hands, the heat from the bowl warming his

488

palms. Plato lightly squeezed Clay's knee, then let his hand slide away.

"Sometimes, Clay, them things we 'member from way back, they ain't always the way it really was. Not the whole of it."

"I was free, dad. I remember that," Clay said in a strained voice.

"Mebbeso you was free," Plato conceded. "And mebbeso, was you to go back, you'd be free agin, but I ain't certain sure of it, Clay. I 'member my daddy and his African ways. He was brought over here a boy, but he never lost all his notions, his 'stitions, my mama called 'em. You once pointed that pipe of yours all around the sky, but I always wondered, did you mean it, son? That there Kiowa uncle of yours, now he'd mean it, was he to do it. It'd touch something deep inside of him, the way hearin' spirituals do to me. But does it do that for you, Clay? Does pointin' that pipe at the sky touch anything inside of you? 'Cause if it don't, then mebbeso you ain't meant to go back to them Kiowa."

Clay sucked in a ragged breath. "I don't feel black," he said quietly.

"What's that mean?" Plato asked, scowling. "What's it mean, you don't *feel* black? What's *black* feel like?"

Clay shrugged.

"You feel white?" Plato asked.

"No."

"You feel Injun?"

"Yeah." But after a pause, he amended, "No, I guess not."

"Then what is it you do feel like, son?"

"Just . . . me, whatever that is."

Plato smiled. "I don't rightly know what that is, either," he admitted. "But I do know *I* don't feel black. Even if I *am,* I don't feel it. Doubt if any African does much, comes right down to it. Don't reckon a white person *feels* white, or an Injun person *feels* Injun. A body ain't a color, Clay. A person is hisself, what he's seen in life, what he's done. What he feels. Ain't no color in that. You was raised a whole lot different'n me, and that's why you ain't nothing *like* me. Ain't sayin' you ain't black, but you be a different kind of black. Like Sammy Lee, raised up there in Canada where it gets so cold. He be black, too, but he ain't nothin' like you or me."

"There wasn't a whole lot of difference between us when we were dragging along in Carry's chains," Clay pointed out bitterly.

"No, no there weren't, and that be a fact, certain sure. Weren't much difference a'tall 'tween you'n me or me'n Jenny. But it wasn't *color* made us the same back then,

490

son. It was *fear,* and I don't reckon a white person or a Injun person would feel much difference, was they in the same sit'ation, and facin' what we was facin'. It's our experiences set us apart, Clay, them things we survive and learn from, not color. You take them slaves your Kiowa band had, that Mexican they nutted, and that crazy white woman. How much different you think they be, livin' there amongst them Kiowa? Not so much, I figure. Shoot, Clay, we all be the same color, anyway, just different shades of it."

Clay sighed. "I can't go back to the Choctaw, dad."

"You in trouble down there, Clay? Trouble with the law?"

"Something like that, although I'm not exactly sure how it all came about."

Plato nodded shrewdly. "I reckon you ain't the first man — black, red or white — what's been in that pickle, but it do cull down your options some."

Quietly, Clay told Plato about Moses Gray, and the reward on his head from the Choctaw Council. He also told him about Abner Bell and the whore, Dee Dee, and of the conversation he'd had with the Leavenworth constable, Bob Ripley, regarding the deaths of Carry and his men, and how he'd fled afterward and not been able to stop until well past Topeka. When he finished, Plato shook his head in awe.

"You been attractin' trouble like that all your life, Clay, or has you just recent like fallen into a trouble hole and ain't found your way out yet?"

Clay laughed but didn't reply. In the recounting he had stirred up some old memories; now grief stung him like a freshly drawn wound, a sense of loss for a life he had valued greatly but would never live again. It surprised him a little, too, that he had confessed as much as he had, but he realized he'd always been more open with Plato, allowing him access to places within himself that no other man or woman had ever visited.

"Well, I don't reckon it matters," Plato said after a while, "though some would say you been attractin' trouble since you was a snapper, what with gettin' yourself kidnapped by a bunch of wild Injuns when you weren't nothin' but a tyke." With a note of admiration, he added, "Clay, you done lived more of life than most folks do by the time they's cotton-topped, and you not much more'n a sprout yet. Someday somebody's gonna write a book 'bout you. Call it, *The Adventures of Clay Little Bull,* they will."

"If they don't hang me first."

"Well, that's true, but that's just one more reason for you to go to Mexico with me'n Jenny. These here United States and Territories of America ain't what they's cracked up to be for freedom. Not for black folks, anyway."

"Do you even speak Spanish?"

"I can learn, boy, I can learn." Plato lowered his voice confidentially. "That Tyler Calhoun sounds like a decent sort, but he be white, too. What you figure he'd do, was he to find out what happened down there on the Neosho?"

"I figure he already knows," Clay replied.

"He knows! And them others, that Oscar Garrett and Jonas Sands and Virgil Nash! They all knows?"

"No," Clay admitted. "I don't think so."

The relief on Plato's face was plain, and for a moment Clay's resolve weakened. Would it be so wrong to throw in with a party of Negroes, he wondered, to give up this pigheaded notion of his that he could someday live among the white-eyes as an equal? He couldn't help speculating about how it would be very different among Plato's people. Could someone like Jesse or Minnie Harper, or George Simms — strangers all — be trusted any further than Ty or

Jonas when the law came sniffing around, just because of the color of their skin?

"Sometimes a man has to make a stand, dad," he said, shoving to his feet and sliding the now cold stem of his pipe back through his hatband. Glancing at the old man, Clay's features softened. "I have to get back," he explained. "Dooley and I have some business to take care of, but I'll drop by again before I leave. I have some hams and tongues on the wagon that we probably won't sell, so I'd just as soon give them to you as see them go to waste." He would pick up some beans, coffee, flour, sugar, and maybe a little tobacco from the trader, and drop those off as well, he decided.

"Shoot, they ain't no call for that," Plato protested, rising stiffly. "We be gettin' 'long just fine. That Mr. Dooley is a generous man, and I gots some snares set for rabbits'n such. Thankee kindly for the offer, Clay, but we don't need no buff'lo meat. That be money outta your pocket, I reckon."

"Naw, it wouldn't be that much. I'll drop it off in the morning, before we head back." He pulled on his mackinaw and hat, then dragged the door open.

Grabbing an old coat and ratty muskrat cap with earflaps, Plato followed him outside. "Lord, I shore is glad we didn't try to make it to Cherry Creek," he said, as he stepped into the full blast of the storm.

"It gets pretty rough west of here," Clay acknowledged. They walked around the wagon, and Clay loosened the pinto's reins. But Plato stopped him with a hand on his arm before he could mount.

"I gots to say it, Clay. I know you don't want to hear it, but I gots to try one more time."

"I ain't going to Mexico with you, dad. I wish you luck, but my life is here."

"Son, I know you had yourself a good daddy, that Simon Little Bull. I admire him for that, and I admire the boy he raised to be a man. *But you ain't Choctaw, Clay.* A white man looks at you, all he's gonna see is another African, and that ain't no life for you, son. You be too proud to live like that. Sooner or later it'd get you kilt. Or else you'd die on the inside, a little at a time. But that be a bad way to go, too. Worser'n any bullet, I 'spect. But they's the onliest ways you gonna get along out here, Clay. One way or another, body or spirit, you gots to die."

Clay looked across his saddle into a wall of falling snow. "I ran from the Choctaw Nation," he said, so softly he wasn't even sure Plato would hear him. "I ran from

Carry and his men, and what we did down there on the Neosho. And I ran from Bob Ripley, in Leavenworth. I can't keep running, dad. It doesn't feel right."

Plato's grip tightened on Clay's arm. "Runnin's all you got now, Clay. Onliest thing left. Sooner or later, white men'll be comin' to make you pay for that day on the Neosho. Gonna come sure as the sun shines in summer."

"Then I reckon they'll come."

A single tear trailed down the old man's wrinkled cheek. He took his hand away from Clay's arm and swiped at it, sniffing loudly. "You a good man, Clay Little Bull. Damn if sometimes I ain't as proud of you as if you was my own flesh and blood." Backing off a couple of paces, he forced a smile. "You go on now, take care of that business you got with Mr. Dooley. But you come see ol' Plato 'fore you head back to them buff'lo ranges, you hear? You come see this old man one more time, 'fore you go."

"I'll do that," Clay promised. "You bet on it." Gathering his reins, he brushed the snow from the seat of his saddle and mounted. But when he looked again, Plato was gone.

TWENTY-SIX

"Let me get this straight," Colonel Douglas J. Carry said coolly. "You questioned the Negro in regard to the Neosho killings, you even had a flier for his arrest from the Indian Nations, and yet you still let him slip through your fingers?"

Sitting behind his cluttered desk, Sheriff Bob Ripley flushed a deep red. "I sometimes get a dozen fliers a week," he returned stiffly. "I didn't know Little Bull was a wanted man until well after he'd flown the coop, and I still haven't received anything official on him for the Neosho killings. Have you reported your suspicions to a federal marshal?"

Colonel Carry made a dismissing gesture. "That's irrelevant. I'm more concerned with the murderer's escape."

"Goddamnit, so am I," Ripley snarled. He leaned forward to brace both hands against the edge of his desktop. The two men were sitting in the sheriff's office at the back of the Leavenworth jail. In the corner a medium-size coal stove crackled and popped, emitting waves of heat that distorted the air around it, yet barely reached the opposite corner of the room. Both Carry and Ripley were wearing heavy coats against the chill, and the window behind the sheriff was laced with ice.

"Can I assume you've furnished the surrounding communities with a description of the killer?" Carry asked in a tone that clearly indicated he didn't.

Ripley's flush became splotchy, which was always a bad sign, but he struggled to keep his anger in check. "No, I didn't," he replied. "Until you showed up I'd considered it an Indian matter, which I don't normally make a priority."

"So you didn't make any effort to locate Little Bull?" Carry persisted.

"I made some inquiries," Ripley allowed grudgingly. His fingers closed into fists, the flesh over the knuckles turning white. "These things take time, Colonel. I'll ask you to remember that this is a legal matter, and not something I figured needed interference from the private sector."

"Meaning you didn't want the citizens of Leavenworth to learn you'd allowed a killer to escape?"

"Meaning," Ripley replied stridently, "that had I known he was involved in a killing, especially of white men, I would have handled it differently, but as far as I know you're the only one claiming Little Bull was a participant at the Neosho." He took a deep breath and forced himself to sit back, to fake composure. It galled him to have a man like Carry show up out of the blue with his condemnations, particularly after he'd already questioned the suspect and dismissed him as a fugitive of only minor importance, not worth the paperwork involved to make an arrest. Damnit, how was he to know the bastard was likely involved in the Neosho Massacre? Little Bull had acted so damn cool that day in the Hamilton and Finn wagon yard that he'd thrown Ripley off completely. And now he had this pompous ass from Tennessee raking him over the coals like he was some slack-jawed jayhawker, instead of an outspoken Southern sympathizer. Ripley had to remind himself that Carry was a man of considerable influence, and used to getting his own way. Although that in itself failed to impress the sheriff, he wasn't ignorant of the assistance a man of Carry's status could offer a struggling politician, were he so inclined.

For that reason alone, Ripley was willing to subdue his growing ire toward the man.

The problem was, Carry seemed unswayed by the sheriff's willingness to co-operate. The Tennessean had blown into Ripley's office twenty minutes earlier like a blast of winter wind, having already learned of Little Bull's stopover in Leavenworth, and even of Ripley having questioned him in the lee of a broken down freighter. No doubt that was Jimmy Flannigan's doing, Ripley thought with annoyance; the damn Irishman hadn't even been nearby when Ripley talked to Little Bull, but it was obvious he'd clouded Carry's opinion of the encounter.

So be it, Ripley decided suddenly. If Carry thought he was an incompetent buffoon, then he would just have to prove the snobbish bastard wrong. Leaning forward to fold his blunt-fingered hands over the desk, he said, "There's not much I can do about Little Bull and the Neosho affair without some kind of official paperwork, but if I were a man unhampered by legalities, I'd take a ride up to Nebraska."

Carry arched his eyebrows. "Why is that?"

"There's a town full of Africans up there called Blackbird Creek. That ain't its real name, but you ask for Blackbird Creek and folks'll know what you're looking for."

"You have reason to believe Little Bull might be hiding there?"

"Well, no, but I have heard there're some hardcases up that way, so it'd be a place to start. It'd be where I'd go, if I was looking for Little Bull and not tied to my duties here."

For a moment the Colonel looked almost pleased. "Where exactly is Blackbird Creek?"

"Just follow the road north to Nebraska City, then turn west. It's about fifty or sixty miles out that way, on a branch of the Big Blue River. I hear there's a road of sorts that'll take you right to it, but you'd have to ask the sheriff at Nebraska City how to locate it. He's a friend of mine. Just tell him I —"

"I'll find it," Carry interrupted. He stood and marched to the door, pausing there with a hand on the knob. "One more thing, Sheriff. If you do locate Little Bull before I do, hang onto him this time. He belongs to me now. Is that understood?"

The red splotches on Ripley's cheeks spread and burned, and his pulse thundered in his ears. Swallowing hard, he managed, "If Little Bull comes back, I'll hold him as long as I can on that trouble down in the

Nations. I'll hold him until hell freezes over if you can get a murder warrant on him."

"There won't be any warrant," Carry informed him curtly. "I don't want legal interference in this matter, Sheriff. I just want you to hold him until I return. Lose the paperwork, if you must, but hold onto him. Can you do that?"

Ripley nodded stiffly.

"Good," Carry said, then yanked the door open and disappeared down the hall.

Ripley took a long, ragged breath, then rose to follow Carry through the main office. He went to the barred front window where the westering sun had melted off the ice and peered through the dirty pane to observe Carry mounting a long-limbed thoroughbred. The Colonel jerked savagely on the horse's reins, then drove a pair of cavalry spurs into the animal's ribs. He took off at a lope — a reckless gait considering the frozen ruts that scored the broad street. Nearly half a dozen hard-bitten men on weary mounts galloped after him. Ripley watched until they were out of sight, then stepped away from the window. The high-pitched voice of his jailer, coming from the stairs, startled him.

"I will tell you one thing," old Moss proclaimed loudly. "If I was Little Bull I'd start sayin' my prayers, 'cause that Carry feller ain't gonna rest until he's dead."

Ty was up before dawn on Christmas Day, awakening everyone as he rustled a fire and clattered pots and pans about in his search for the griddle.

Jonas lay in his robes and tried not to think of home, of the afternoon meal his mother would be preparing even then, and the scent of holly and pine that would waft through the house. Presents would be laid out along the mantel in the parlor — gifts of clothing and necessities wrapped in thin tissue and brightly colored bows. His father, always an early riser, would be reading the morning newspaper in his den, his head crowned by a blue wreath of tobacco smoke from his favorite ironwood pipe, while Jonas' sisters would be in the kitchen helping their mother set the table for a light breakfast, before their guests started arriving later that morning for a day of feasting and caroling.

He recalled the frolicsome atmosphere of Christmas the year before — the rowdy shouts of his siblings and cousins as they played a game of keep-away ball behind the carriage house, the lively conversations of his father and uncles around the long dining-room table that, by meal's end, resembled nothing so much as a miniature battlefield. The reserved voices of the women as they gathered in the kitchen afterward came to him now as warm and secure as a fire on an autumn eve. For not the first time since coming west, Jonas asked himself what he was doing out here, how he could have been so stupid as to leave home over such a trivial matter. He longed to tell someone, but if he had learned anything in the nearly three months that he'd been with the Calhoun and Little Bull outfit, it was that a man kept his past to himself and shared only the superficial things, the ones that never really amounted to anything.

I ran away from home because my mother caught me smoking a cigar, and threatened me with a switching.

That was it. His sole reason for leaving. Feeling too old for such childish punishment, he had run away from home to show the world he wouldn't tolerate it any longer. Thinking about it now sometimes made him want to laugh, but most of the time it made him want to cry. Yet he had come too far to stop now; even if he returned home, it could never be the same.

Fighting tears, Jonas threw his robe back and sat up. On the opposite side of the tiny cabin, Oscar Garrett was scratching his crotch through his woolies; against the south wall, Clay sat cross-legged on top of his bedroll, lacing on his heavy winter moccasins.

"It's about time you lazy birds rolled out," Ty said cheerfully as he pulled a sheet-iron griddle from a trunk. "I was beginning to think you were going to sleep all day."

"I can see why you were worried," Clay replied dryly, eyeing an oblong piece of buffalo intestine stretched tautly over a crude window hacked out of the chinking; not even a sliver of light showed through the yellowish gut, the first rays of the sun having yet to breach the horizon.

Laughing good-naturedly, Ty said, "It'd be light if it were June, instead of December."

"June, December, it don't mean squat to me," Oscar grumbled, then spat against the wall.

Silently, Jonas pulled on his grimy clothes, stomping into his boots last. He felt a faint stirring in his armpit but ignored it. He had nearly scratched himself raw after first contracting lice, until Clay advised him to learn to live with it. "A man can't skin the curlies and not end up with a few graybacks," he'd told Jonas. "Best leave 'em be.

You'll get used to them soon enough."

Although Jonas was still waiting for that day to arrive, he had quit scratching except when absolutely necessary, and only picked off the lice he saw outside his clothes, or those that wandered down the side of his face or up from the collar of his shirt, bound for the struggling fuzz along his cheeks.

"I'm fixing hotcakes, in honor of the day," Ty announced. "Jonas, there's a little pint crock of sorghum in those packs in the corner there, if you want to dig it out."

"I'll go see to the stock," Clay said. He glanced at Oscar. "Give me a hand."

Oscar scowled, but followed him outside without comment. Jonas fetched the crock and set it by the fire to warm, then gathered up the coffeepot and water bucket and headed for the door. He would take the ax, too, and chop through the ice over Tornado Creek to pail up water for their meal, and to scrub the dishes afterward. As he started outside, Ty said, "See if Virgil's awake, and tell him and Rain Dancing to come over for some grub, if they are."

Jonas hesitated, then went on out. There was no point in telling Ty that he was afraid of Virgil, and dreaded the thought of knocking at his door. That was another lesson Jonas had learned since coming to the frontier, to keep his mouth shut and do what he was told. Oscar Garrett had taught him that. Although the old man hadn't been as difficult to get along with since the day of the fight, Jonas knew Oscar harbored a grudge against him that time would never erase. Through Garrett, Jonas had learned that a man needed a hide as tough as a bull's to survive out here. For that same reason, he'd come to the conclusion that he didn't have one. That was why he was so certain he wouldn't live long enough to ever go home again.

After chopping through the ice over Tornado Creek, Jonas filled the bucket and coffeepot, lingering to listen to the sound of bubbling water from the slush-filled cavity. When he had postponed the inevitable for as long as he could, he set the pot and bucket and ax aside and crossed the ice to the east bank. A well-beaten path led to the door of Virgil's soddy, and smoke curled from the stubby stone chimney. Taking a deep breath, he rapped loudly at the slab-wood. The door rattled under his knuckles, seemingly flimsy enough to collapse if struck too hard. From inside, a hoarse voice bellowed, "Who the hell's out there?"

"Jonas. Ty's fixing hotcakes, and wants to

know if you and Rain Dancing would like some."

"Get out of here, asshole."

Jonas flinched and moved back a step, glancing around to see if anyone had overheard. Screwing up his courage, he hollered, "It's Christmas. We thought maybe you'd like to have some breakfast with us."

Virgil guffawed. "Go away, kid. I'm opening my present now."

Jonas blushed and backed off several more paces. He wished he could help the Indian woman. Sometimes he daydreamed of bringing her a horse and gun and enough supplies to get her safely back to her people. Occasionally he even fancied himself standing up to Virgil and telling him that what he was doing was wrong, and that he had to stop, to let the woman go. But he knew the crazy young hunter would probably kill him if he ever tried anything so bold.

Retrieving the bucket, coffeepot, and ax, Jonas returned to the cabin. As he approached, Oscar and Clay came around the corner. Clay pulled a rope off a peg driven into the chinking on the front wall and hung it over Jonas' shoulder. "Brownie slipped her hobbles," he said. "Go see if you can run her down. Her tracks were heading for the Smoky." He took the coffeepot and bucket from Jonas' hands. "Go on. We'll save you some hotcakes."

Jonas glanced at the sky, hanging overhead like a dirty gray blanket, then shrugged and turned toward the Smoky Hill. He found Brownie's tracks before reaching the ford and turned downstream, following them eastward. The ox was heading for the breaks that pinched down close to the river below Tornado Creek, an area of broken hills, steep clay banks, twisting arroyos, and a few small, widely spaced groves of trees. Jonas had explored portions of the breaks on his own earlier that fall, but the terrain was too rough for a wagon, and Ty and Clay never hunted there.

It felt even colder along the river than it had near the cabin. Hoarfrost cloaked the alders and cattails along the banks, and the frigid air needled his lungs with every shallow breath. His toes, wrapped in thick wool socks inside his oiled boots, quickly began to ache from the cold as he tromped through the ankle-deep snow. Pulling the collar of his heavy winter coat tight around his chin, then shoving his mittened hands into the pockets, Jonas cursed the wayward ox. He'd gone perhaps a quarter of a mile when the tracks veered sharply toward the river, as if the ox had been spooked. Puzzled, Jonas

509

came to a standstill to examine the broken country around him. He saw nothing out of the ordinary — barren dirt banks, broken hills, and stunted trees, and in the river a long, low island covered in tall rushes. Brownie's prints led straight to the river, the trail there marked by broken ice; they appeared again on the island's shore, only to vanish once more into the rushes.

Shelter from the wind, Jonas thought irritably. *The damn bitch.*

He looked once more at the river, the black water sliding past the broken trail Brownie had left in her flight across the narrow channel, and cursed. He knew the water was just deep enough to pour in over the tops of his boots if he tried to follow her. After briefly considering returning to the ranch for a horse, Jonas decided to risk crossing above Brownie's path. If the ice over narrow Tornado Creek was thick enough to hold his weight, maybe this would be, too. And if it cracked too loudly, or threatened to break under him, he could always back off and fetch a horse then.

Resolutely, Jonas made his way to the river. He could hear the flow of water under the ice, and remembered some of Oscar Garrett's more morbid tales of plainsmen stumbling into camp on frozen feet or with frozen hands, of digits amputated and men — strong men, experienced men — crippled for life on the high, frozen wastelands of the plains.

"You old whore," Jonas shouted at the rushes. He took a cautious step onto the ice, then another. Step by careful step, he edged across the frozen channel, breathing shallowly until he reached the island.

At the point where Brownie's prints emerged from the river, Jonas stopped and frowned. It seemed obvious now that something had frightened her badly. Her tracks were scrambled — as if she'd stumbled coming out of the water, then taken off in a lumbering, heavy-bodied run — but he saw nothing in the snow to indicate she was being chased. Perhaps she'd scented something, he decided, a panther or a wolf. Once more, Jonas studied the tumbled hills surrounding him. There was no sign of danger, but when he sniffed the air, he caught a faint whiff of something pungent yet familiar . . . blood, perhaps, or the sickly sweet odor of freshly exposed meat.

A shiver ran down his spine. He put his hand on the butt of his pistol, belted around the outside of his coat, and wished he'd thought to bring the Sharps, as well.

Instead of following Brownie's trail blindly

into the rushes, Jonas walked along the bank next to the river, peering into the thick growth for some sign of the strayed ox. He'd gone perhaps fifty paces when he heard a rattle of limbs from the island's interior and jerked to a stop. Standing on tiptoe, he was just able to make out a patch of light brown hide near the center of the island. "There you are," he murmured. He scraped aside a patch of snow to uncover a pair of fist-size stones, then took careful aim and chucked them one after the other into the rushes. The first rock sailed too high, but the second struck the animal squarely on the flank, drawing a grunt.

"Goddamnit, get out of there!" Jonas shouted. Kicking at the snow, he quickly disclosed several more suitable stones. Hefting the largest in his right hand, he threw it with all the force he could muster. "Come on, Brownie," he commanded. "Get out of there!"

On his fifth throw he must have struck a tender spot, for the animal jumped and whirled. With a squawk, Jonas staggered backward, his heart leaping wildly in his chest. Fear came full-blown, and suddenly it all made sense — the abrupt change in Brownie's trail, the sharp odor of a freshly butchered carcass. He had seen pictures before — paintings, and woodcuts in books — but no one had ever told him a bear could be as big as an ox, or explained how deathly terrifying a snarling grizzly could be.

The bone-like rattle of dried stalks sounded deafening as Jonas watched the bear plow through the rushes toward him. Desperately, he shook the mitten from his right hand and pulled his Colt. The bear was less than thirty feet away when it emerged from the rushes, advancing like a slow-chuffing locomotive, more irritated at this point by the pummeling stones than truly angry. But Jonas couldn't have known that, as inexperienced as he was. With a childlike whimper he took aim at the bear's low, broad forehead and began to fire, working the hammer and trigger with an instinct governed by fear.

At this range it was almost impossible to miss, although he knew he did with a couple of his shots, so violently did his hands tremble. Yet at least two of the slugs ripped into the flesh of the grizzly's face, causing the hump-shouldered beast to rock back on its haunches, swiping the air around its head as if slapping at bees. Then it let out a roar that echoed off the bluffs. Blood and saliva flew in every direction. Jonas saw the yellowish fangs that were like small skinning knives, the pale pink tongue, the shiny, twitching nose, and lost his courage. Flinging the pistol away, he spun and raced for the river, splashing through the icy waters along Brownie's backtrail and up the opposite bank where he stumbled and almost fell before getting his feet under him and turning toward the cabin, screaming at the top of his lungs now — screaming in a mindless, gut-wrenching terror.

TWENTY-SEVEN

Clay looked up as the cabin door swung inward. Although expecting Jonas, he wasn't surprised to see Virgil Nash duck inside, a smirk warping the tall hunter's thickly bearded face. Virgil's smirk had become a fairly common feature of late, further broadening the gulf that already separated him from the others. Yet if his status as an outsider bothered him, he never allowed it to show. Heeling the wooden-framed rawhide door shut, he sniffed loudly and exclaimed, "Damnation, Ty, that smells almost good enough to eat."

Ty looked up from where he was pouring batter onto the greased griddle. "Where's the woman?" he asked.

Virgil's smugness faded. "Don't fret over her," he said curtly. "She'll eat."

"Jerky?"

"If that's what she decides to fix."

Pushing more than was normal, Ty said,

"There's plenty here, Virg. Go fetch her. She might enjoy something besides buffalo meat for a change."

"I said she's fine where she's at."

"What's the matter, boy?" Oscar cackled. "You afraid we'd get us an idea or two, was she here?"

"An idea's about all you'd get anymore," Virgil returned, but the smirk was back, and he slipped out of his coat and tossed it over a nearby crate. Going to the fireplace, he knelt and helped himself to a cup of coffee. To the room in general, he added, "Ol' Oscar traded women for booze a long time ago. Ain't that right, old man?"

"You think what you want, but I've made the wimmen's eyes shine in my day, and could do 'er again, was I so inclined."

Virgil laughed and took a seat on Jonas' bedroll. "Is that a fact?"

"You damn tootin' that's a fact. I've made 'em squeal, or I wouldn't say so. White gals, nigras, greasers, squaws, you name it."

"Sheep?" Virgil asked innocently, sipping his coffee.

Oscar's face darkened. "You had potential, once a time, but you ain't worth shit now."

"Careful," Virgil warned, though still smiling. "I've seen you nipping cups outta my whiskey keg. Let that mouth of yours run too fast and I'll bung those kegs tighter'n a preacher's ass." He laughed. "You'd wither up like a weed before you got your next drink."

Ty scowled. "You stay out of Virgil's whiskey," he ordered the old plainsman. "The last thing I need is you lopping off a finger with a skinning knife."

Oscar snorted. "That'll be the day."

"Did you see Jonas?" Clay asked Virgil.

"I didn't look for him. Is he lost?"

"No, but Brownie is."

"Ty, you should've shot that crazy cow last summer."

"Brownie's all right in yoke," Ty replied. "She's a good leader, too. Better than Janey."

"You've wasted more time lookin' for her than she's worth. Why don't you shoot her and get yourself another leader?"

"That yeller steer with the crooked horn shows promise," Oscar interjected.

Clay pushed to his feet, feeling suffocated by the mindless bickering of the men. "I think I'll go look for Jonas," he said. "Maybe Brownie's bogged down in the ice."

"If she is, leave her," Virgil recommended.

Clay pulled on his coat and hat and went outside. He paused at the corner of the cabin to take a deep breath. The cold air bit at his lungs, and suddenly he dreaded the thought of going out again, of trying to make a kill under such bitter conditions. *We were fools to buck this kind of weather,* he thought, *fools, maybe, to even he out here at all.* His thoughts flashed back to that night in the grove of trees where he'd made his first camp after escaping from the Captain's chains. He remembered the turmoil stirring within him as he'd dropped the heart and liver of the rabbit he'd killed for supper into the embers of his fire — appeasement to the spirits for his taking of a life to sustain his own, he'd thought at the time. The irony of his present occupation was not lost on him.

How the hell does any man alone for this? he wondered, eyeing the ricked hides below the cabin.

At the corral he bridled the pinto, then led him to the lean-to beside the cabin where they kept their tack. He was tightening the cinch when he became aware of the door to Virgil's dugout creaking open. Looking up, he discovered Rain Dancing On Water peering at him from the soddy's entrance. Her boldness surprised him. She'd been like a mouse ever since her return with Virgil, and although they'd all tried talking to her at one time or another, she'd always shied away as if they were yelling at her. Only Clay, speaking the few words of Kiowa he still recalled, had been able to draw more than a sideways glance from her.

Lowering the rawhide-covered stirrup of his saddle, Clay was debating whether to make another attempt at communication when he heard a string of shots echoing over the breaks along the Smoky Hill. Swinging into the saddle, he heeled the pinto toward the river. As he passed in front of the cabin the door flew open and Ty ran out with his Hawken. Spotting Clay and sensing what he was up to, Ty tossed him the rifle.

"Go on," he shouted. "I'll be right behind you."

Clay slammed his heels into the pinto's ribs. The horse jumped into a run, kicking up a shower of snow as it raced toward the river. Although daylight had swept the open prairie above, the bottomland along the Smoky Hill was still shrouded in a misty, deceptive light. Entering the breaks, Clay was forced to slow his horse to a running jog until, rounding a bend, he yanked hard on the reins. A chill, colder than the icy air along the river, seized him.

Like Jonas, Clay had never seen a live grizzly, although he had had the opportunity to examine a few silver-tipped hides brought back to the Nations from the western plains. The huge robes had always awed him, and he would try to imagine what a living, breathing grizzly would look like compared to the blackies he hunted around Red Creek. But nothing his mind had conjured up could have prepared him for the sight that greeted him now.

Jonas was running a serpentine path along the bottoms, and at first Clay couldn't figure out what he was up to. It only became apparent when the youth veered toward the river, leaping onto the slick ice and scurrying to the far bank. The bear — a big sow with a torn and bloodied face, her muscles rippling under thick layers of fat, her wet belly hair clattering with miniature icicles — switched directions in the same instant, but as soon as she hit the ice her paws skidded out from under her and she went down with an enormous force, breaking through to flounder in knee-deep water littered with razor-edged shards of ice. Although she quickly regained her feet, pouncing after Jonas like a fox after a mouse, her best efforts proved futile. With every yard gained the ice cracked, bowed, then gave with a crash that dumped the bear into the frigid stream.

Jonas gained ten precious yards in the time it took the bear to break through to the other side, sprinting upstream with the heart of a thoroughbred. Clay felt a flash of admiration for the boy's pluck. Those who knew said a full-grown grizzly could outrun a horse over a short distance. Had Jonas not used his head, he likely would have been dead by now, torn into bloody chunks by the grizzly's claws.

The pinto was throwing a fit, tossing its head and wanting to buck. Clay swore and jumped free, letting the horse bolt back upstream, holding its head sideways to avoid the trailing reins.

"Jonas!" Clay waved wildly, motioning the younger man toward him. The bear was closing fast now, making up in seconds the time it had lost crossing the river. *"Over here!"*

Jonas was still fifty yards away when he spotted Clay, close enough for Clay to see the look of relief that crossed his face. He was terrified, and so was Clay. In tossing him the Hawken, Ty had neglected to include his powder horn and shooting bag. That meant Clay had only one shot with the rifle, one slim chance to drop an enraged, charging quarter ton grizzly. He knew the odds were against him. There wasn't one man in twenty who could make such a shot. But he had to try. Either that or watch helplessly as the bear slaughtered his friend.

Jonas was on the south bank when he spied Clay. Changing direction, he scrambled onto the ice, skating awkwardly across with his arms spread wide for balance. His movements taut but sure, Clay checked the cap on the rifle's nipple, then dropped to one knee and brought the iron buttplate to his shoulder. The bear raced onto the ice after Jonas without hesitation, breaking through as she had before, then lunging up and forward and through again. Blood splattered her chest where jagged pieces of ice slashed the flesh, infuriating her all the more.

"Clay," Jonas gasped, his face red as an autumn apple. His arms flapped and his knees buckled.

With all the calmness he could muster, Clay snugged the Hawken to his shoulder, whispering a curse when the sights came in line with Jonas' swaying torso. Lowering it an inch or so, he yelled, "Jonas, get down, you're blocking my shot! Jonas!"

But Jonas was too far gone. Reeling from fear and exhaustion, he stumbled forward on weakening legs while the bear plunged up the near bank in a spray of water.

"Goddamnit, Jonas, *get down!*"

Jonas came to a wavering stop, his chest heaving; sweat ran down his cheeks and dripped from the end of his nose. He stood slack-limbed for a moment, staring at Clay. Then his knees gave out and he fell flat on his face.

Clay snapped the rifle to his shoulder. The silver-tip was almost on top of Jonas when he found the grizzly's chest in his sights. Without taking time to use the set trigger, he squeezed off his shot. The Hawken must have been heavily charged. It slammed back against Clay's shoulder. Through the roiling powder smoke he saw the great bear catch herself in mid-stride, then stumble sideways. Clay lowered the rifle, breathing a long sigh. He knew his shot had been true, yet even as he watched, the grizzly caught her balance, remained standing. She took a hesitant step forward, then another, gaining momentum despite the thumb-sized chunk of lead that had to lie close to her heart.

Rage kept her alive, kept her dragging toward her prey.

"*No!*" Clay shouted, lunging to his feet and flinging the Hawken away. He stumbled through the snow, shouting, waving his arms, trying to draw the bear's attention away from the boy.

It worked. Clay was no more than seventy feet away when the bear stopped and lifted her head to sniff out his scent, her own inherently poor eyesight further diminished by the bullets that had ravaged her face.

"Here I am!" Clay bellowed, drawing the Kerr and snapping off a shot that smacked the bear in the shoulder. She reared back on her haunches, then rose to her hind feet, towering a good eight feet into the sky; her throaty roar seemed to ripple the air in the same way a pebble rippled the surface of a still pond. Clay's scalp crawled, but he couldn't turn back now. He pressed forward, pausing every few feet to thumb another round at the grizzly's neck. With a loud *whuff,* the sow dropped to all fours and lunged toward him, passing Jonas's unconscious form without even a pause.

Clay skidded to a stop. Less than twenty yards separated them now, and despite her many wounds, the bear was coming on strong. Coming on like a she griz in the prime of her life.

"You silver-backed whore," Clay whispered. He lifted the revolver, aimed, fired. The ball struck the bear between and slightly above her eyes, tearing away a strip of hair and flesh to expose the hard white skull underneath. The blow stopped her for a moment, causing her to fall back on one hip. Then she climbed to her feet and lumbered forward, weaving but undaunted. Standing firm, Clay cocked the Kerr and pulled the trigger once more, but this time the hammer snapped on an empty chamber.

"Oh, shit," he murmured, and let the pistol fall. Drawing the coffin-handled bowie, Clay braced himself for the grizzly's charge.

The bear never slowed. At ten feet, she lunged forward to swipe at him with her right forepaw. Although Clay tried to dodge the club-like limb, he was incapable of matching the bear's speed. The blow lifted him like a leaf and tossed him limply aside, her long claws shredding the thick fabric of his mackinaw and the leather of his shirt as if they were made of paper.

Clay hit the snowy ground hard, but rolled quickly to his knees. Blood flowed down his left arm and shoulder, and the cold air stung the four parallel gashes that cleaved his back. He shook his head and tried to stand, but the grizzly pounced before he could gain his feet, flattening him without effort. Instinctively, he jabbed upward with his knife, opening a fresh wound along her head that pared away a section of her tiny, rounded ear. But the bear seemed beyond pain now. She roared in his face, her hot breath like something wet and rotting against his cheeks. He plunged the knife into the bear's throat even as her jaws closed over his mangled shoulder, shoving with everything he had as he probed for the sow's jugular. His shrill scream rived the frosty air. From a long way off, he heard the boom of a rifle. The huge bear shuddered, but it was too late now. Her jaws tightened, and she reared back with Clay dangling brokenly from her mouth. His shoulder snapped like a brittle twig, and his body convulsed. The battle was over, the bear had won, yet Clay wouldn't give up. With a last, herculean effort before unconsciousness claimed him, he drove the knife another inch deeper into the bear's throat. . . .

There was no pain or discomfort, just a peculiar sensation of buoyancy, a lack of encumbrance. He saw Ty and Jonas and Oscar sitting morosely around the cabin. Flames blazed in the hearth, although he felt neither heat nor cold. Vaguely he recalled the bear's attack — the teeth like serrated steel, claws sharp as skinning knives, breath reeking.

Those things he remembered, but little else.

He tried to move and was surprised to find it

so easy; like dust motes dancing in a shaft of summer sunlight, he glided effortlessly toward the rafters. Ty's voice came to him as if over a great distance, the words soothing as he spoke to Jonas, but unintelligible. Below him he saw the supine body of a black man lying on a pile of robes close to the fire, his long, loosely curled hair fanning out under his head, his chest and shoulders swathed in bandages. There was something familiar about him, but unimportant, too, and in the next instant he was outside the cabin with the moon gleaming off the snow and the stars like flakes of crystal sprinkled across the heavens. He could hear the sounds of the creek and river from under the ice, could sense the weight of the snow on grass that yearned for spring. Then he was moving toward the corral, where the pinto munched hay in a corner, and after spending some time there he slid across the creek and into a cave-like structure where Virgil Nash sat in front of a smoky fire cleaning his rifle. At the rear wall, Rain Dancing On Water was cutting strips of buffalo meat to be dried into jerky. He spoke to her but there was no sound, no voice. Yet there must have been something, for she looked up, startled at first, then frightened, her eyes wide as they darted about the cramped soddy. He spoke again, reassuring her in Kiowa, and after a moment her features relaxed and a smile came to her lips. He felt the good will that radiated from her like warm sunlight. There were no words, but her voice was clear and strong as she wished him a good journey along the Hanging Road to the Other Side. Then he was gone, back over the creek with a pain that was faint but steady. Wearily, he entered the cabin, angling toward the still body of the black man, where the pain was sharper for one quick flash of time, before sweet darkness overtook him once more.

To Jonas, Clay's recovery seemed agonizingly slow. For days he lay unconscious, sometimes barely breathing. At times he would thrash weakly, as if still doing battle with the bear. Occasionally he tried to speak, but the words never made sense — the ravings of a man locked in fever-induced nightmares.

Twice in those first days after his duel with the bear, Jonas was sure Clay had died. His breathing would slow, then seem to stop altogether, and his lips would take on an odd, bluish cast. Each time, Jonas would feel the fear rise up in him. He would rub Clay's body vigorously, shaking his good shoulder, slapping his face. And each time Clay responded, the color returning to his lips, his breathing becoming deeper, steadier than before.

Jonas blamed himself for Clay's injuries. He knew that if he hadn't been such a tenderfoot, none of this would have happened. That conviction made him even more miserable than his longing to return home. In all his time on the plains, Clay was the only real friend he had made, and he remained constantly at his side, leaving only to relieve himself or catch a few hours' sleep.

Ty also stayed close. Although he rarely spoke, his somberness and unpredictable temper explosions attested to his worry.

Even Oscar Garrett seemed subdued. The old man kept to himself much of the time, and seldom spoke except to announce that a meal was ready, or that he'd go fetch more firewood or care for the livestock. But Jonas knew it was Clay's encounter with a grizzly this far east, more than the seriousness of his wounds, that had spooked the older man. Although grizzlies often wandered the high plains, Oscar claimed he'd never heard of one venturing this far from the Rockies. "It ain't *natural*," he had declared that first night, clearly unsettled by the incident. "Especially this time of year. She should'a been *hibernatin'*, fer Christ's sake."

It was Oscar who had taken charge of the bear's remains, hanging the choicest cuts of meat in a rear corner of the smokehouse to cure, and taking extra care with the hide, which he promised to tan into a robe as soon as the weather warmed up.

Only Virgil appeared unchanged by the event. He had come over that first day — Christmas Day — to silently observe their efforts to treat Clay's wounds, but after that he'd gone back to hunting as if nothing had happened, leaving early each morning with the Indian woman and not returning until late. Without the wagon John Dunlap had commandeered, Virgil was forced to rely on the horses he'd taken from the Pawnee, Wolf Tail, to pack his meat and hides back to camp. Rain Dancing went along to skin and butcher the buffalo he shot, and he often chortled that she was much better at it than Dunlap had ever been. But without a wagon, his daily harvest remained small.

Not that Jonas gave a damn about Virgil's problems. He was preoccupied with caring for Clay, keeping him warm and clean, dabbing the sweat from his face and chest when chills racked his weakened body. Several times a day he warmed up a broth and forced some between Clay's lips with a spoon.

The fever broke on the fourth day. It was Ty who noticed that Clay seemed to be resting easier, and that his breathing, which had been erratic earlier, had leveled off and deepened. Jonas placed the inside of his wrist against Clay's forehead, as his mother had done for him during his childhood bouts with illness. When he looked up, it was with a weary but welcome grin. "I think you're right," he said to Ty. "I think he's asleep, rather than unconscious."

"Sleep's what he needs most," Ty said. "As long as he wakes up from time to time to eat something solid. He'll starve on broth, sooner or later."

He already looked emaciated, Jonas thought. Earlier, pulling Clay's robes back to sponge the sweat from his body, he had been appalled at the gauntness of Clay's frame, the way his ribs and hips protruded like charred limbs and knobs.

"That nigra's got the hair of the b'ar in him, or I wouldn't say so," Oscar declared unexpectedly. "I'm bettin' he'll pull through."

"It'll be a while, if he does," Ty answered. "He'll be lucky to be walking in a month."

"Lucky or tough," Oscar countered. "I say tough. Hell, another month and he'll be huntin' agin."

"I doubt it," Ty replied somberly. Staring at Clay's wasted form, Jonas was inclined to agree.

Toward evening, while Oscar checked on the livestock, Ty started a supper of buffalo meat and biscuits and a fresh pot of coffee. Although there were a few wrinkled potatoes left in a gunny sack, all gone to eyes and grown soft, and some dried peas and canned tomatoes, they'd taken to avoiding the extras in anticipation of the day Clay began to eat solid foods again. Even Oscar agreed that a few vegetables might aid in his recovery, although he was quick to amend that they weren't absolutely necessary.

"Many a coon's wintered out here with nuthin' more'n hump meat'n rose hips to fill his paunch," he'd said.

After supper, they settled down to another long evening. Jonas could tell that the waiting was starting to gnaw at everyone's nerves. That was why Oscar announced a couple of hours later that he was going out to check on the oxen a final time before turning in, even though they all knew it wasn't necessary. Jonas yawned and stretched as he watched the older man pull on his coat and hat, then duck outside. Clay was still sleeping soundly, and his fever hadn't returned.

Jonas was considering warming up some more broth when he heard Oscar's footsteps squelching the snow outside, returning hurriedly. Ty grabbed his Hawken, and Jonas threw a glance at his revolver, the gunbelt hanging from a peg above his bed. Then the door flew open and Oscar stooped inside, his faded eyes running with tears brought on by the cold air.

"What's up?" Ty asked quickly.

"Buffler's movin' out, sonny, that's what be up."

"Moving out?" Ty looked puzzled.

"Come on, I'll show you."

Ty and Jonas exchanged glances, then both men scrambled to their feet and pulled on their coats. They followed Oscar into the frigid darkness, latching the door behind them.

"Are you sure?" Ty asked, turning his collar up around his ears.

"Sure as it's cold enough to freeze the balls off'n a bull," Oscar returned gleefully. "You boys listen to ol' Oscar. He's seed it afore."

"Seen what?" Jonas asked. They were walking away from the cabin, trying to keep up with Oscar's lengthy strides.

"Buffler talk, boy." The old man stopped and threw up a mittened hand. "Listen to

533

'em. Hear it?"

They grew silent. Jonas gave his full attention to the distinctive grunts and bellows of the wide-ranging herd, but could distinguish nothing out of the ordinary. The sounds of a winter's night on the prairie — the creak of snow, the cud-chewing of the oxen, the calls of the buffalo, and the melancholy chorus of prairie wolves — all seemed as before.

"Where will they go?" Ty asked after several minutes, clearly accepting the old plainsman's say so.

"Who the hell ever knows what runs through a buffler's noggin? They's notionable critters, here one day, then gone the next like a puff'a smoke."

"I've been out here two years," Ty said. "I've never known a herd this size to just vanish."

"I been out here most of my life," Oscar asserted calmly. "I've seed it happen many a time."

Ty drew a long breath. "Then we'll have to follow them."

"Yeppers, be the onliest way, you wanna make hides'n meat."

"What about Clay?" Jonas asked quietly.

Ty sighed heavily. "I guess we'll worry about that tomorrow," he replied. He tucked his hands under his arms as if for warmth, staring up at the brittle black sky. Almost to himself, he added, "We'll worry about Clay once we've seen which way the buffalo's gone."

TWENTY-EIGHT

Ty didn't feel any surprise when he halted his horse on top of the high bluff overlooking the valley of the Smoky Hill. Yesterday the snowy plains flanking the valley had been dotted with buffalo, more than a man could count, scattered into hundreds of smaller bunches. Now, except for the churned tracks and the dark platters of dung, the land was empty, not even a slinking wolf remaining. It was spooky, in a way. Although he'd seen the land emptied like this before, he'd never seen it happen so swiftly, or with such a large herd.

Movement on the trail behind him caught his eye. A few minutes later, Virgil came over the top, his black gelding kicking up clumps of hoof-shaped snow. Virgil drew up as he viewed the empty plains, then reined over to Ty's side. "The old man told me this morning that the buffalo'd pulled out, but by damned, I didn't believe him," Virgil said.

"He's a hard pill to swallow sometimes, but he ain't often wrong when it comes to the shaggies."

"No he ain't, and that's a fact. So what now?"

"I want to follow them, see which way they went. They won't be hard to track in the snow."

"Then what? You figure to go after them?"

"Maybe."

Virgil gave him a calculating look. "What about Clay? Me and Rain Dancing can just pack up and go if we wanted to, but Jonas ain't smart enough to handle a man tore up that bad." He laughed without humor. "And Oscar, hell, that old drunk's liable to get a notion to hike over to Dooley's for a cup of whiskey, and say to hell with the nigger."

"Don't call him that," Ty said.

"Don't call who what? Clay a nigger, or Oscar a drunk?"

"Don't call Clay a nigger. I'm getting tired of the word."

A look of hurt flashed across Virgil's face. "You think more of that damn darky than you do me."

"Don't call him a darky, either. He's Choctaw."

"Choctaw! If he's an Indian, my granny was an Egyptian princess." He shook his head in puzzlement. "What's come over you, Ty? You act like you'd like to kick my ass half the time, anymore."

"More than half, I reckon," Ty admitted. He lifted the bay's reins. "Come on, let's see if we can figure out which direction these buffalo took."

"Upstream, I'd say." Virgil spurred his mount after Ty. "Buffalo graze into the wind," he added.

"Most of the time, but not always."

Virgil gave him an aggrieved look. "What the hell are you so contrary about, all of a sudden?"

"You beating that woman, Virg?"

Virgil's expression turned to stone. "That woman is my business. You stay out of it."

"I just asked if you were beating her. I thought I heard her cry out a few nights ago, like she was hurt."

"But you didn't check it out, did you?" Virgil taunted.

Ty felt a twinge of guilt, and didn't reply.

"That woman's mine, Ty-boy, bought and paid for in redskin currency to do with as I please. Wade ought to have proven that, even to you."

"Wade's death doesn't justify slavery, or rape."

Virgil grunted. "Another goddamn bleeding heart abolitionist. Let me share a little secret with you, Tyler, something you might not know about me."

"That you support slavery," Ty said gruffly.

Virgil gave him a sharp look. "How'd you know that?"

"You'd have turned that girl loose if you didn't."

"The hell with that. I need a skinner, and she's the best I've ever seen. And what we do under the robes ain't your concern."

"No, I reckon it isn't," Ty agreed sadly. He touched his horse's ribs with his heels, putting it into a lope that left Virgil several yards behind.

They rode west without speaking for the rest of that morning. At noon, Ty turned toward a tiny grove of trees with the intention of taking a breather. Virgil caught up with him there, and they built a fire for warmth, chewing on jerky and ash cakes to fill their stomachs. Ty estimated they'd come twenty miles since leaving the cabin, and he was convinced Virgil had been right that morning — the buffalo had gone west, with the wind in their faces. The question would be: How far west would they go before stopping again? Another twenty miles? A hundred? To the foothills of the Rocky Mountains? The range of the great herds was vast, but Ty knew there was a limit to how far he could safely take an outfit after them. Although trading posts dealing in furs and Indian-tanned buffalo robes had been doing a lucrative business all over the plains for decades now, there was no steady market for green hides or meat closer than Leavenworth. But as much as he wanted to break into the robe trade — it was why he'd brought along so many trade goods this trip — he wasn't ready to take on the larger outfits to the west just yet. The Indian robe trade was a big business, but it was also a cutthroat business, with small interlopers like himself easily swallowed by the larger companies.

"You gonna eat that jerky, or just chew it to death?" Virgil asked.

Ty stirred self-consciously and swallowed. "Guess my mind was wandering."

"Racing, is more like it. You still figure to follow 'em?"

"What other choice do we have?"

"Wait until they come back. Another bunch'll probably blow in with the next blizzard."

"When will that be?"

"Hell, it's damn near January. We could be butt-deep in snow by the time we get back tonight."

"Maybe, but it ain't likely," Ty said. He bit off another piece of jerky and chewed thoughtfully. "What about you, Virg? Are you going to follow the herds?"

Virgil was quiet a moment, then he said, "I don't hardly see how I can. That goddamn Dunlap stole my wagon. I'd have to haul so much gear on my packhorses there wouldn't be any room left for hides." He gave Ty a crafty look. "Unless I claimed my share of the outfit by borrowing the schooner."

"Uh uh. I'll need that wagon. The freighter's too big to take where we'll have to go. That's mostly for hauling the hides and meat back in the spring, anyway."

"Then I guess I'll have to sit on my ass, won't I?" Virgil said.

"You could throw in with us."

"Huh! How's that?"

"I won't pull out until Clay's better, but he's coming around. His fever broke last night and he's resting easier. But it'll still be weeks before he's on his feet again, and I can't wait that long. I've been thinking about this all morning, and I figure our best bet, yours and mine, is to leave Jonas and the Indian woman at the cabin —"

"No!"

"Hear me out."

"Ain't nothin' to hear out. The woman stays with me."

"You aren't worried about Jonas, are you, Virg?"

He guffawed. "She'd take a knife to the kid and Clay both, and ride out of there free as a bird."

"She wouldn't if we took the horses with us," Ty argued. "Like you said, it's damn near January. She wouldn't try to hoof it back to her people this time of year, not with just what she could carry on her back."

Virgil seemed to think that over. Before he could worry it too much, Ty went on.

"Oscar could tell her in sign what would be expected of her. The three of us would hunt until we filled the wagon, then come on back. Rain Dancing could look after Clay, while Jonas took care of the rest."

Virgil hesitated, then shook his head. "No, I won't do it," he said, and went to his horse.

Ty kicked snow over the fire, dousing the small flame. "Think about it," he urged as Virgil swung into the saddle. "We'd be working as a team again, hunting and skinning our own kills. Half of what we made would be yours."

"And if I still say no?"

Ty shrugged. "I can't hunt alone. There's just too much work involved to make it profitable. And I'd need at least two people at the ranch, one to care for the hides and meat and oxen we leave behind, and the other to stay with Clay until he's further along."

"Then it looks like we're both shit outta luck, don't it?" Virgil said caustically.

"It doesn't have to be that way. Think about it, Virg. Hell, Rain Dancing doesn't mean that much to you, does she?"

"It doesn't matter what she means to me," Virgil said. "The answer is still no." He yanked his horse around and rode out of the trees at a gallop, heading back toward the ranch.

Clay was awake when Ty got in that night. After setting aside his rifle and shucking out of his hat and coat, Ty went to hunker at his side. "How're you feeling, pard?"

"Kind'a weak and runny, like the old man's soup." He nodded toward Oscar.

"That was broth, you pile of black buffler shit," Oscar growled. "The soup's for supper." He scowled fiercely, but it was plain that Clay's joking pleased him somehow. Ty smiled at Oscar's feigned gruffness; it was the first he'd seen it since Wade's death last fall. Not that Oscar had ever been what you'd call gregarious, but he'd had his lighter moments, back in the early days.

"I swear, Oscar, you've got dead men complaining about your cooking now," Ty said, smiling.

"He's not dead," Jonas said quickly, giving Ty a warning look.

"Aw, I was just joshing Oscar some. It's been so long since I've seen him smile, I thought he'd forgotten how."

"Just see that you're smilin' when I serve up this here tongue soup," Oscar said, stirring a bubbling concoction in the cast-iron kettle hanging over the fire. "Figured Clay needed somethin' light tonight."

"Soup sounds fine," Ty said. He looked at Clay. "It's good to see you've come around. I was afraid we were going to lose you."

"Close," Clay whispered, but didn't elaborate.

"He's been sleeping a lot," Jonas added. "And his fever's back, although it's not as high as it was before."

Oscar chortled. "Ol' Clay woke up this afternoon talkin' tongues. 'Bout had the kid spooked outta his wits, till I tolt him it was only Kiowa." He leaned back, tapping the rim of the kettle with a long-handled wooden spoon. "Supper's ready, if'n anyone's hungry. They's some bigger pieces of tongue in there, for them that wants to dig 'em out."

Ty got his deep-bottomed plate and spoon from the stack of gear they called the kitchen, and Jonas handed him a coffee cup. "Smells good, old man."

"Chilled through to the bone, ain't cha?" Oscar asked shrewdly. "And nary a sign of buffler, I'm bettin'."

"Plenty of sign, but that's all." He sat back cross-legged and began spooning Oscar's thick, rich soup into his mouth. The old man had seasoned it heavily with peppers, and Ty could feel it warm his stomach like a chug of good whiskey. He ate three full plates of soup and drank four cups of coffee before wiping his mouth on the sleeve of his shirt and belching contentedly.

Afterward, smoking his pipe, Ty rehashed in his mind the proposal he'd made to Virgil that morning. It had been fermenting in his thoughts all day, but coming in tonight and finding Clay awake and even joking around a little had sparked a new sense of urgency. After weighing the pros and cons for an hour, he finally decided it was the only way that wouldn't waste precious weeks of hunting, time they could ill afford to lose if they wanted to come out of the season with a profit.

Putting away his pipe, Ty stood and

slipped into his hat and coat. Clay was sleeping again, but Oscar and Jonas looked up curiously. "Think I'll take a walk," Ty said nonchalantly.

He crossed the frozen creek to the soddy and rapped loudly at the splintery slabwood door. "Virgil, it's me. Open up."

There was a muted command from within, and a second later Rain Dancing opened the door. She was wearing her greasy buckskin dress, and had a blanket draped over her shoulders against the soddy's chill.

"Come on, damnit," Virgil called. "You're letting all the cold air out."

Ty stepped inside but kept his coat on, his hands plunged into the pockets. "Christ, Virg, it's like an icehouse in here."

"Glad you like it," Virgil replied sarcastically. Rain Dancing shut the door and moved back to a folded robe at the rear of the soddy. "It ain't the palace you're used to, but it suits me'n the missus," Virgil added.

Ty took a seat on a pile of green hides and put his back to the dirt wall. Whiskers of frost clung to the roots of grass on the west wall, and his breath came out in quick, vaporous clouds. "Clay's awake," he began uncertainly.

"Good for Clay."

"Good for all of us," Ty replied curdy. "Have you given any thought to what we talked about this morning?"

"What did I tell you then?"

Ty smiled and shook his head. "The hell with you," he said, standing. But at the door he hesitated, his hand on the latch. "We'll be pulling out in two or three days, as soon as I'm sure Clay's definitely on the mend. I guess it'll be me and Oscar, and Jonas will have to do the best he can. If you change your mind, you'll be welcome to come with us. Just remember that if you do, the girl stays here."

Virgil's face clouded in anger. "You're mighty damn bossy for a matter that ain't none of your concern."

"I'll tell you straight, Virg, I don't need another hunter. I can shoot enough buffalo to keep me and Oscar busy. What I do need is someone to look after Clay while Jonas takes care of the hides and meat. There's over two hundred hides out there, not to mention the smudge we need to keep going in the smokehouse. It'd be a chunk of work by itself. It'll be damn near impossible if he has to spend half his time looking after Clay."

"That does put your nuts in a grinder,

don't it?"

"It's nothing I can't handle, Virg," he replied softly. "It'd just be easier the other way. You think about it." He lifted the latch, but before he could open the door, Virgil stopped him.

"Wait!"

Ty paused, his hand on the latch.

Virgil rubbed his jaw with the palm of his hand, glaring at the wall. Then he said, "I get half of everything, right, hides and meat?"

"That's the deal."

His voice grating, Virgil said, "All right, I'll go. But I ain't staying out for more than a month."

"A month, maybe six weeks, should just about do it."

Virgil brought his gaze to bear on Ty, the tendons in his throat taut as bow strings. "If she ain't here when I get back, someone's gonna die."

"Don't make threats, Virg."

"It ain't a threat. If Rain Dancing is gone, I'll kill both of 'em, Jonas and Clay. I'll kill you, too, if you try to stop me."

For a moment Ty was too unnerved to answer. He had never seen the promise of such violence on Virgil's face before. Nodding stiffly, he said, "All right, Virg, then you'll have to kill me, too."

They were ready to pull out two days later. Ty ordered four yokes of oxen hitched to the prairie schooner, in anticipation of the rough country they would travel through, and had Jonas tie a couple of extra head behind the wagon so they could switch off from time to time. They would take with them only the basics — food, bedding, and ammunition, plus the wall tent and a small stove to cook on, in the event they were caught by a blizzard. They would take along a few trade goods, too — a case of knives, a few hanks of beads, a package of arrowheads — items that wouldn't take up a lot of room, but might pacify any Indians they encountered. And Virgil was taking his whiskey, at least a keg of it; for medicinal purposes, he alleged.

Ty saddled his bay. He was letting Oscar ride the dappled gray so he could handle the oxen from horseback. Virgil had shown up earlier with his own horse and the two Pawnee mounts in tow, then tied Clay's pinto on at the end of the string. It was a farce, Ty thought as he eyed the queued horses, but, like the whiskey, a necessary concession to Virgil's paranoia.

Ty hadn't seen much of Rain Dancing

since Clay's run-in with the bear, but Virgil brought her over that morning, and with him watching and Oscar translating, Ty had explained what he wanted her to do. Rain Dancing had nodded her quick comprehension. After Ty had shown her the salves they were rubbing on Clay's wounds and the bolt of cotton calico they used as bandages, she'd asked only a handful of questions — did they have this root or that herb? — and when Ty shook his head, she announced that she would go down to the river later and see if she could find some under the snow. Ty started to protest, but Oscar quickly shushed him. "Let 'er do her stuff, boy. Injuns has been doctorin' b'ar maulin's long afore white man's medicine showed up."

Receiving a consenting nod from Clay, Ty relented. "Tell her to do what she thinks best," he instructed Oscar.

Although Clay was still unable to sit up under his own power, and had to use a bucket for a chamber pot and another man's help to get on it, he was clearly improving. He could speak for longer periods without becoming fatigued, and his eyes would follow the flow of conversation from man to man around the cramped quarters of the cabin, rather than fading off into oblivion. His appetite was increasing, too, although he still favored bland foods.

Ty's biggest concern had been that — after Clay had hung on for the first twenty-four hours following the attack — infection would set into the wounds. It had been over a week now, with no sign of poisoning yet. Clay was on the mend, and the mood of everyone except Virgil seemed lighter because of it.

To the east, the sun was just pulling free of the horizon. They were ready to go, waiting only for Virgil, who stood beside the cabin door with Rain Dancing as if saying good-bye to his fiancée. Repelled by the image, Ty turned away. Jonas waited beside the corral, and Ty walked over, leading his bay. "You'll be all right," he said, sensing the youth's fears. "Watch the hides and keep the smokehouse going. The woman will probably take care of the rest."

"What if someone comes for her?" Jonas asked quietly. "Her people, I mean."

"Don't stand in their way."

"Virgil said he'd kill me if she's gone when he gets back."

"Don't worry about Virgil. He'll have to get through me first."

"I've never seen him so serious about anything as he is about Rain Dancing,"

Jonas said. "I think he loves her . . . sort of."

"Yeah," Ty grunted. "Sort of." He hooked a toe in the stirrup and heaved into the saddle. After settling himself, he added, "If she tries to leave on her own hook, let her go. It's not your responsibility. Other than that, use your own judgment."

"Sure," Jonas said. "I'll take care of things."

But Ty could see the doubt in the younger man's eyes. He tried to think of something to say, then decided to hell with it, and reined his horse around. Giving Oscar a nod, he said, "Take 'em across. We'll stay south of the river today."

The old man spat in reply and lifted his whip, cracking it over the backs of the oxen like a gunshot, yet disturbing not a hair. "Hey, *up,*" he shouted. "Git on there, girls! You, Janey! Haw, girl, haw!"

The oxen eased forward, drawing the chains taut. The wagon groaned and swayed as it broke free of the snow and ice that had bound it tightly to the ground in the time they had laid up with Clay. It lurched forward with bits of ice and frozen sod clinging to the iron rims of the wheels. Oscar jogged forward on the dappled gray, crowding the leaders. "*Haw,* damn you.

Turn, ya stupid idjits."

Virgil came away from the cabin with an expression as dark as a thundercloud. Stalking to the corral, he came to a halt about ten feet in front of Jonas and put his hand on the butt of his pistol. "You remember what I told you, kid. You lay one hand on that bitch and I'll cut your balls off and feed 'em to the wolves."

Jonas took a deep, ragged breath, then squared around to face the larger man. "I don't intend to touch Rain Dancing," he said in a quavering voice. "But I don't intend to let you cut off my balls, either, no matter what else happens. I'll put a bullet through your brain the second I think you're about to try it."

Virgil scowled and blinked, and Ty laughed. "You'll do, Jonas," he called, grinning. "We'll see you in a month or so. Come on, Virg, I'll help you line out that pony herd of yours." Touching the bay with his heels, he trotted off.

TWENTY-NINE

Jacques Peliter rocked back on his heels and wiped the hand-forged blade of his hunting knife clean on the bedspread. It took some looking to find a dry spot on the quilt, but he finally located one on the corner at the foot of the bed. After sheathing the knife, he stood back to survey his work. He didn't know the woman's name. She was black and somewhat plump, and she had been attractive until she refused to answer his questions. She'd finally told him everything she knew — little enough, to be sure, but another piece of a puzzle that was becoming more complete every day.

Moving to the wall, Jacques picked up his rifle, then slipped the straps of his shooting bag and powder horn over his shoulder. It was late, very late, and the saloon was quiet. Outside, the street was dark and deserted. Jacques knew he could exit through the window and make the twenty-foot drop to the frozen ground without anyone being the wiser, but something stayed him. Cocking his head to one side, he sniffed the air, but the blood scent was too strong. Twisting his head at a different angle, he focused all of his concentration on his hearing. The wind whispered softly under the eaves, scraping against the sun-blistered lumber of the building like a piece of fine silk drawn slowly over a stubbled cheek.

He closed his eyes, breathing shallowly. It was almost as if he could hear the building itself giving up its little secrets, making them known to him in small ways — a woman's ways, he would have said, had he felt inclined to articulate it. Then he leaned his rifle against the wall and glided silently to the door. *Sacré,* the building *had* spoken to him, in a voice so faint it was more touch than sound, like a gentle puff of air against his eardrums, and he knew, without knowing how he knew, that he was not alone.

He pressed his ear to the door under an iron hinge, where the integrity of the wood would be at its weakest. As he listened, a beam cracked in the rafters; another popped somewhere on the floor below him. He dismissed these sounds as the normal settling of the roughly constructed saloon, but when he felt a floorboard press upward ever so slightly through the sole of his pucker-toe moccasin, he knew someone was in the hall on the other side of the door.

Jacques Peliter could not have explained this special harmony he shared with his surroundings. For a long time, growing up in the St. Lawrence River Valley just across from New York state, he had often felt annoyed with the other members of his family who had been unable to hear the things he heard or feel the things he felt. He thought they feigned ignorance merely to irritate him. It wasn't until he was twelve or so that he began to understand that he *was* different, and that the people he'd once considered family and friends viewed him as an oddity. He had been hurt at first, then angry, the anger metamorphosing over time into alienation and aloofness.

It was this newfound detachment that allowed Jacques to observe with nothing more than curiosity the discomfort of others. It was as if their very emotions created disturbances in the atmosphere that only he could feel. A freak, Jacques soon came to realize, might be tolerated only so long as he acknowledged his strangeness with shame or meekness, or ignored it. But when it became apparent that young Peliter was actually embracing his peculiarities, it proved too much for the simple farmers of the village where he had been born, and they turned their backs on him as they would a coward, shunning him completely.

At seventeen, Jacques left the St. Lawrence Valley to become a trapper in the deep forests west of the Great Lakes. There his special attunement to the world around him became even more acute. He began to accept not only his uniqueness, but also his superiority.

It was an attitude that could not long be tolerated by the rough-hewn woodsmen of the Old Northwest country. Before the year was out he had killed two men, and been forced to flee the rainy woods of the north as a murderer. He went south, and killed again.

It was in New Orleans, when he was but twenty-years-old, that a prominent plantation owner offered him nearly a year's wages to slit the throat of a gambler he thought had cheated him. Jacques had taken the job without conscience, slaying the gambler on a warm spring evening when the air was thick and humid, imbued with the fragrance of blooming magnolias.

Although he'd left New Orleans immediately afterward to escape the law, he couldn't elude his reputation. By the time he was forty, he had killed more than thirty-five men and women. Twelve of the men and seven of the women had been murders for hire, the money netting him enough funds to live the life he loved most — traveling often by horseback, but always returning to the rolling mountains of northern Arkansas, the eastern fringe of the Indian Nations, and northeastern Texas.

Jacques Peliter was not a celebrated man. He did not live a flamboyant life. He had never sipped champagne or tasted a truffle. He was a true *homme du bois* — a man of the woods. He lived with Indians when he could, and had wives among the Cherokee, Creeks, and Alabamas. He liked to roam the hills and valleys of his adopted homeland, a gaunt, bearded ghost who was seldom seen but whose presence was occasionally, and sometimes ominously, felt. He was not a bounty hunter, although he killed for money; nor did he consider himself a thief, even though at times he did steal. But he never hunted down a man who had run afoul of the law merely to enrich himself, just as he had never stolen for profit or want. His was a purer purpose, an art that, no matter how beautiful the form, still required periodic financial inflows.

Although many men called him an assassin, Jacques preferred the simpler definition of *hunter* — one who killed not for greed or pleasure, but for subsistence alone.

He was living with his Creek wife, Marie, when a white whiskey peddler brought word that the Choctaw known as Moses Gray wanted to hire his services. Before Jacques even offered the messenger a cooling drink of water, he ordered Marie to saddle his horse. At that point it had been more than a year since he'd hunted his last human being, and his soul was hungry.

The deal with Moses Gray had been struck quietly in the slightly odorous study of Gray's home in Red Creek. Gray offered five hundred dollars in advance, and promised an additional five hundred when Jacques delivered the head of the renegade Negro, Clay Little Bull, to Gray's study. Jacques accepted without haggling. Although he wouldn't have committed to the hunt without payment, he was as unimpressed by the amount as he was by Gray's reasons to have Little Bull executed. What mattered most, the only thing that ever really did matter for Jacques, was that he would soon begin the delicious process of the stalk, of matching wits with the only animal that had ever provided him a true challenge.

Clay Little Bull's trail wasn't difficult to untangle, but it did take time — especially in Kansas, where for a while it disappeared altogether. Through persistence, Jacques was able to sort it out. The trail, several months old by now, had brought him to this town they called Leavenworth, and finally to a black whore in shanty town, in a saloon called Abner Bell's.

Jacques moved his ear away from the door, glancing down at the white porcelain knob just as it rose slightly under the touch of a hand on the outer knob. Slitting his eyes, Jacques could sense the pressure exerted on the cool porcelain, could almost see its slight warming through the mechanism as the hand on the other side tightened, then slowly began to turn. He pulled his knife and waited. The latch clicked softly as it slid off the striker plate, and the door sagged inward no more than a thirty-secondth of an inch. He smiled as he felt the room's quick change, the readjustment of air as a new entry was granted. The door edged slowly open — a half inch, an inch, then two. Jacques raised his free hand. The door creaked ever so slightly as the hinges bit into the tender wooden grain of the frame. When it opened another inch, he calmly reached around and grasped the hand behind the wrist, yanking the intruder inside.

It was a man, clutching a pepper-box pistol in his right hand. Jacques threw him against a chest of drawers. His knife flickered leaflike, and the pistol clattered to the floor alongside a spurt of blood. Then his elbow twitched and the door swung shut as if on its own accord.

He recognized the man instantly. It was the bartender, Abner Bell, whose name also belonged to the building. Abner Bell was a lanky black man with suspicious eyes. Those eyes were wide now as Jacques pushed the cutting edge of his knife against his throat.

"Hey," Abner Bell squawked. "Easy with that thing. Easy, now."

"What for you come snooping around here, eh?" Jacques demanded. Although he harbored no qualms about killing anyone who got in his way, it wasn't a thing he did lightly, either.

"I . . . I thought . . . the light was on, you see . . . and I saw it under the door . . . and I thought —" His gaze traveled to the bed, to the butchered woman lying on top of it, and his voice suddenly failed.

"You lying to me," Jacques said impatiently.

"No, no, I'm not," Abner Bell gasped, but

before he could say more, Jacques increased the pressure of the blade against his throat.

"Sure, you lying. You tell me what you know about Clay Little Bull damn quick now, all right? You know Clay, huh?"

"C . . . Clay? Uh uh, I never —"

"Listen, you, pretty damn soon I gonna cut you throat, so you tell me about this Clay, maybe you live a few minutes more."

"Oh, God," Abner Bell moaned, his knees trembling so violently the chest of drawers started to clatter. Jacques could tell that Abner Bell knew he was going to die; he could see it in the black man's eyes. "Look, I don't care what you did to Dee Dee," Bell said tremulously. "Maybe she tried to rob you or —"

Jacques moved his knife ever so slightly, knowing that Bell would feel the trickle of blood running down his throat and shut up without being told to do so. "I got no more time, barman. You tell me ever'thing now, all right?"

Tears welled suddenly in Abner Bell's eyes, spilling down his cheeks. He tipped his head back, wailing, "Oh, God, I don't want to die!"

"Sumbitch," Jacques murmured. He stepped back, lowering his knife. "Too bad you make so much noise, barman. Bad for business, you know?"

Bell stared at him uncomprehendingly, but when he tried to reply, he couldn't. He made a gargling sound in his throat, then grasped it with both hands. Blood pulsed out between his fingers, soaking the white linen front of his shirt. Jacques put his hands under Bell's arms and helped him to the floor, watching impassionately as death glazed the black man's eyes even before he was all the way down.

"Too damn bad," Jacques sighed, wiping his blade clean on Bell's trouser leg. "Maybe you would have told Jacques something new, eh? Another piece for the puzzle." He shrugged philosophically and rose, returning the knife to its sheath. Then, picking up his rifle, he moved to the window and opened it as gently as he could, apologizing to the wood when it shrilled in protest. A moment later, he was gone, leaving the ragged curtains flapping in the breeze.

Rain Dancing On Water paused at the cabin's door to watch the young man called Jo-Nas toil at the pegging ground. His clumsiness in carrying the unwieldy hides to a nearby stack of frozen skins never failed to puzzle her. Did he not know there were easier ways? Had not the women of the

People been handling hides for untold generations? Yet not once had he come to her for advice. None of them had. As contrary as badgers, they insisted on doing everything their own way, as if they could force their will over even the Mother, the earth.

They were an enigma, these white-eyes who came to slaughter the buffalo. That their medicine was strong, none of the People would deny. Their guns and knives, their items of steel and iron and glass, all bespoke favor from Man Above. Yet how could such a powerful people be so comical in their attempts to survive in a land He had blessed with such plenty? Like awkward and unenlightened children, they plundered the land, seemingly lacking any consideration for tomorrow, or the tomorrows of their offspring.

It was for that reason the white-eyes frightened Rain Dancing, for in their heavy-handed ignorance she foresaw the eventual destruction of her own people.

She continued to watch as Jo-Nas struggled with the stiff buffalo hide, knowing that the trickster, Wind, would have something to say about that. She wondered briefly why Jo-Nas did not use Wind's strength to assist him, but she could see the thought had not occurred to him. Still, she did not laugh when Wind caught the hide and whipped it around, as she knew it would, tripping Jo-Nas and nearly causing him to fall. She had learned well to keep her emotions to herself.

Pulling the leather drawstring that lifted the latch inside the cabin, she shoved the door open with her hip and entered. It was warm inside, but not cozy in the way of a well-kept lodge. Elbowing the door shut, she quickly crossed the close-packed room to lower her armload of firewood beside the hearth. It was only then that she glanced at the bed where the black white-eye called Clay lay sleeping. Her moccasins barely whispered as she crossed the hard-packed dirt floor to his side, dropping to her knees and placing the palm of her hand against his chest. He felt cool to the touch, and his breast rose and fell with the deep, even rhythm of slumber. Lightly, Rain Dancing caressed the taut black flesh, marveling at its color and texture, its contrast to the pale, clammy epidermis of the man called Virg-El. Of all the men who inhabited this lonely outpost, it was Clay who puzzled her most.

She recalled the night his wandering soul had visited her in the dugout. Why had he come? What had drawn him to her that evening?

And what drew her to him now?

Reluctantly, she pulled her hand away. As she did, Clay's eyelids fluttered, then opened. Meeting her gaze, he smiled.

"I awakened you," she said guiltily.

"No, I have only been dozing." He spoke in Kiowa, the language of the People, which had been returned to him following his encounter with the bear.

"What is the time?" he asked. A smile flitted across Rain Dancing's face; a larger one appeared on Clay's. "Where does Sun stand in the sky?" he amended.

"Sun is ready to retreat behind the mountains, so that it may sleep. Are you hungry? Jo-Nas will come soon."

"I am always hungry."

"Like the bear." Impulsively, she touched his shoulder. "Its spirit has marked you."

"Its claws and teeth marked me. I do not know about its spirit."

Rain Dancing felt a moment's vexation at his dismissal of something so portentous. How else could he explain his sudden remembrance of the Kiowa tongue, or his visit to the dugout she shared with Virg-El, if not aided by the powerful spirit of the great, silver-tipped bear? Or why had the bear journeyed so far from its rugged western homelands, if not to impart its medicine upon him?

She had asked him these questions many times, and although he readily acknowledged his inability to answer them, he refused to accept her explanations. Yet his protests were always voiced in such a wry manner that she was never certain if he was serious about them. Sometimes Rain Dancing suspected he only denied her logic to tease her.

He did that a lot. Not in the same way as Virg-El, who sometimes threw frozen disks of buffalo dung at her, or while sitting quietly in the soddy after an evening meal, suddenly jump and shout at her just to see her recoil. Nor was he like the Pawnee, Wolf Tail, who had taken great delight in shaking the buttons of a rattlesnake in her ear when she least expected it, or while she slept. It was different when Clay teased her. He was gentler, almost affectionate, reminding her of a brother more than a master. Clay was unlike any man Rain Dancing had ever known, and although she retained a certain guarded caution in his presence, she couldn't deny a growing fondness for his company.

She started to rise, but Clay caught her wrist. "I want to talk," he said.

"About the People?"

"Yes."

It was a subject he seemed never to tire of, and as time went on it became obvious he was recalling more and more of his years with them. Sometimes when they spoke of the Kiowa, his face would take on a faraway cast and his eyes would light up and a smile would come to his lips. At those times Rain Dancing wanted to smile, herself, for watching Clay was like watching the face of a child when the men returned from a successful hunt, their travois laden with tons of fresh meat that meant feasting and celebrating far into the night, and the next several nights to come.

Rain Dancing seldom smiled, though, even with Clay. Her distrust of white-eyes — *all* white-eyes — was too deeply ingrained.

"There is something wrong?" Clay asked, sensing her withdrawal.

Hesitantly, she said, "I miss my village. I fear I will never see it again."

Clay's jaws worked as if chewing on something tough and unpalatable. Finally he turned away, teeth clenched.

Rain Dancing's eyes widened fearfully. "I have made you angry? It is all right. Virg-El is a good man, a good hunter. He —"

Clay spoke rapidly in the white man's

tongue, swinging back to face her. Then he switched to Kiowa. "Virgil is not a good man," he said. "He is a coward who grows strong only when preying upon those who are weaker than himself."

"Virg-El is a warrior. He has taken me from the Pawnee, so that I am his, as the horses he took from Wolf Tail are his. Is this not the way of the land?"

"Yes," Clay answered bitterly. "It is the way of these lands, at least, where the strong devour the weak."

"As it is with the People. Many slaves have been brought to my village, but few live. Yet you were a slave, and when you became strong, you became free."

"Free." He spat out the word. "Here, on the plains away from the villages of the white-eyes, I am free, but only as long as I remain strong. From where Sun rises each morning, in that land I would not be free."

"But is that not also true of the bravest warrior of the People, who cannot journey into the land of the Osage?" Her fingers tightened on his shoulder. "You are a warrior. This I know. When you faced the great silver-tipped bear to save the life of Jo-Nas, when you killed that bear with your knife, yet lived yourself so that you might tell of it, these are the deeds of a brave man, a strong man. None among the People could claim more."

Clay shook his head in frustration, and although Rain Dancing could sense his anger, she could not understand it.

"I see now that I have never been truly free," he said. "Not in the way I was when I lived among the People."

Rain Dancing nodded. This, she understood. "The People are the one True People, whom Man Above created in his image and smiled upon."

"Maybe," Clay said slowly, "it is time that I returned."

"To the People?"

"Yes, to become Kiowa again."

For a moment Rain Dancing did not reply. It seemed so foolish that this black white-eye would think that all he had to do to return to the People was to go back, and he would be accepted as one of them. Taking a shallow breath, she ventured, "We would go together, you and I?"

Clay nodded. "I would need your help to convince the People that Night's Son, who was taken from them long ago, has come home."

"There are no horses," Rain Dancing pointed out.

"I am too weak to travel, anyway. But I

grow stronger each day, as you have seen yourself. When Ty returns with the horses, then we will go."

"And of Virg-El? You will purchase me from him?"

Clay was silent a moment, thinking. Then he shook his head. "Virgil would never give you up, not even for white man's money. We will have to leave without his knowing of our plans."

Rain Dancing's heart soared. She had thought the same thing, that the man called Virg-El would never sell her, that her worth to him was twisted up in his own rage. But if Clay thought they could slip away without Virg-El's knowledge, if they could gain just a small lead, then perhaps they could make it.

Taking a quick, tentative breath, Rain Dancing nodded assent. "It is good," she said in a voice barely above a whisper. "I would like to see my sisters again."

THIRTY

The tiny hamlet sitting on the west bank of
Blackbird Creek, Nebraska Territory, had
been christened New Hope City just a little
over two short years before. With a bottle of
cheap champagne and a rousing cheer, its
eighty-one citizens, all of them black, most
of them former slaves, had announced the
town's inauguration to the world.

Only the birds roosting along the creek
heard. Inevitably perhaps, word reached
New Hope that the citizens of Omaha, the
territorial capital, were already calling the
town Blackbird. Six months later, when a
trader on his way west to barter with the
Sioux for robes and furs paused long
enough to empty both barrels of a ten-gauge
shotgun into the sign at the edge of town,
obliterating most of *New Hope, Founded,*
and *1856,* it seemed to doom any expectation of the original name enduring. And
when Mayor Jenkins closed up his combina-

tion saloon and barber shop at the end of the year to make the trip to Omaha to request a post office for the new town, he had been met with blank stares until one of the New Hope delegates accompanying him mentioned that some folks might know the place as Blackbird; it was only then that the territorial post master's eyebrows had arched in recognition, although he'd still denied them their request for a post office. Mail bound for Blackbird would be delivered only as far as Omaha, he'd asserted, where it would be set aside in a box until someone from Blackbird made the one hundred and twenty-odd mile round-trip to pick it up.

And that, according to Mayor Jenkins, was that.

Late one wintry afternoon toward the end of January, 1859, the outlaw Sammy Lee sat alone at a small round table in the New Hope City Saloon and Barber Shop, listening only halfheartedly to Mayor Jenkins' story of his trip to Omaha. The New Hope was a dimly-lit, low-ceilinged room with a sod roof and a single window flanking the front door. If not for a sign above the door and a pair of hitching rails out front, the building might well have been mistaken for some settler's home.

Besides alcohol and haircuts, the town offered the services of a livery and blacksmith, a harness maker who also cobbled shoes, and a general store with a three-room sod addition in the rear that doubled as a hotel when the need arose. An even dozen homes, set out in no particular order, completed the burg, and there were several small farms within an hour's ride.

Taken as a whole, Blackbird looked like a community on the verge of extinction, and that suited Sammy Lee just fine. He was glad to be out of the cold wind that had dogged them all the way from Kansas, and equally grateful for the chipped blue willow plate that only moments before had been heaped with hominy, green beans, steaming chunks of sidepork, and a thick slice of bread.

Buford Hart and Ross Lake stood at the bar, eating on their feet and enduring the mayor's story at close range. Jenkins was a short, shriveled up husk of a man with a hacking cough and gummy eyes shielded behind a pair of wire-rim spectacles. His Christian name was Lucas, and he had been suffering from the croup since November, to hear him tell it, although Sammy Lee was more inclined to believe he was running out his string under the delusion of a minor illness, and that the town of Blackbird would be looking for a new mayor before spring planting.

Sammy Lee shoved the last bite of bread into his mouth and leaned back to chew it slowly, savoring its taste. He had been as hungry as a stray dog, and that was a fact. He and Buford and Ross had just come up from Leavenworth after selling some stolen horses to a livestock dealer named Bramberg. The horses had come from the Oto Reserve, but Sammy Lee had a forged a bill of sale that the portly horse trader accepted without question. After collecting their money, they'd hit the trail for Nebraska.

Selling stolen horses in Leavenworth had been the boldest move yet by the Hart gang, and they had been anxious to put the town behind them. By they time they rode into Blackbird seventy-two hours later, Sammy Lee wasn't sure whether he was too tired to eat or too hungry to sleep. After entering the New Hope Saloon and smelling hominy and sidepork already cooking on the stove, the question became irrelevant. Now, with food in his belly and a shot of whiskey under his belt, he was ready to go to the hotel and wrap up in his blankets for a week — maybe longer, if it was still this blustery when he woke up.

The trouble was, before he could go to bed he had to take care of his horse. That in itself wasn't a problem, but he lingered over his second whiskey because he knew that as soon as he made a move toward the front door, Buford would order him to see to his and Ross' mounts, too, and Sammy was damned if he wanted to get roped into stable duty while these two slugabouts loitered at the bar swilling Mayor Jenkins' whiskey.

Sammy Lee was debating how to exit the saloon without attracting Buford's attention when he heard a horse nicker in the distance. His head came up quickly, and a muscle in his cheek twitched. Buford and Ross also heard the nickering, and exchanged questioning glances.

"So we decided we'd go back next summer and try again," Mayor Jenkins was saying, still in a postal vein. "Ain't no reason we can't put a little cubicle in the general store to handle —" He shut up when Buford lifted a hand. "What?" he asked, looking at their plates. "You want some more side-pork?"

"I want you to be quiet," Buford said.

"Say —" Jenkins started to protest, but before he could continue, Ross slipped a pistol from his belt and pointed it at the mayor's head.

"Shh," Ross breathed.

Buford and Sammy Lee moved to the single window. The view was to the south, along the rutted road from Nebraska City. Beyond the grime and distortion of cheap glass, Sammy Lee saw a group of horsemen jogging toward the saloon.

"White men," Buford said in a strained voice. "This ain't good news, boys."

"It can't be a posse," Sammy Lee whispered, soft enough that Jenkins wouldn't overhear. "Even if they left Leavenworth right behind us, they couldn't have sorted out our trail that fast."

Buford pondered Sammy Lee's argument for a moment, then said, "Maybe you're right, but this is still a nigger-town, and those are white men, armed to the teeth. That's trouble, no matter how you crack it."

"Maybe they're slavers," Sammy Lee said, feeling a sudden hitch in his stomach.

"Be my guess," Buford agreed.

Jenkins started to come out from behind the bar to see for himself, but Ross waved him back with his pistol. "Stay put, bardog." He looked at Buford. "How do you want to play this, Buf?"

Buford stepped back from the window as

the horsemen drew close. To Jenkins, he said, "Is there a back way out of here?"

The mayor shook his head. His eyes, magnified by his spectacles, looked as big as an owl's.

"It's no use, anyway," Sammy Lee said. "They're too close, and our horses are still out front."

He looked past the horsemen to the snow-covered prairie that stretched away in rolling, treeless hills. It struck him that he was tired of winter, of the cold and snow and the constant wind. But mostly he was tired of the overcast skies. It had seemed like a hard winter, even for someone who had grown up in Canada, and he missed the warm sunshine of summer. He wondered what it would be like here in the spring, with the grass shooting up green as emeralds and the hills splotchy with wildflowers. How would it feel to turn back the rich prairie sod with a plow and smell the moist, black earth? Stepping away from the window, he crossed to the bar and ordered a whiskey.

Sammy Lee could hear the *chink* of spurs and the stomp of hooves as the men dismounted. He didn't look around when the door swung open, but listened to the sound of men shuffling into the room and fanning out. A chill settled in his stomach like a chunk of ice. No one came to the bar.

"Is he here?"

"No, but that's one of 'em, there at the end of the bar."

There was a roaring in Sammy Lee's ears as he set his glass down and turned to face the room. There were six of them, the leader a tall man with graying hair and a stiff military bearing who looked vaguely familiar. But it wasn't until Sammy Lee spotted Hog Waller and Jake Jacobs standing near the door that he made the connection.

"What the hell is this?" Buford grated to Sammy Lee.

"Well, well," Sammy Lee said loudly. "If it isn't my old friends, Jake and Hog." He looked at the leader. "You must be Colonel Carry, of Tennessee."

"Is that the one?" Carry asked.

"That's Sammy Lee," Hog confirmed.

Carry was silent a minute, studying him. Then he said, "Come here."

Sammy Lee stepped away from the bar, brushing his coat back to reveal the ivory-handled Colts that had once belonged to the Colonel's brother.

"Don't be a fool," Carry snapped, his brows furrowing. "Drop those pistols and come here."

"Go to hell," Sammy Lee replied leadenly.

He wrapped his fingers around the cool ivory grips of his right-hand Colt and pulled it upward, but the man on Carry's right had entered the saloon prepared, his pistol drawn but hidden under his coat. Sammy Lee's revolver hadn't even cleared leather when the Colonel's lanky gunman fired.

Sammy Lee was hurled into the bar, the wind driven from his lungs. He looked down to see a dark hole drilled through the coarse fabric of his white shirt, and around it a crimson stain like a small, embroidered flower newly sewn to the trail-worn material. A message snaked down from his brain to his right hand, urging him to bring the Colt up, but before he could respond a second bullet struck him in the chest. The log walls and low ceiling of the New Hope Saloon flashed before Sammy Lee's eyes as he slid to the floor and died.

Jake Jacobs stood flattened against the wall of the saloon. Gray clouds of acrid powder smoke swirled on the eddying breeze that drifted in through the open door. On the floor in front of the bar the three black gunmen lay like crumpled wads of paper, the two in longcoats heaped together in a pile, the third, Sammy Lee, lying face down several feet away. Of them all, only Sammy

Lee had managed to free his gun from its holster. The Colt lay inside his bent elbow, its ivory grip resting in a puddle of blood.

Behind the bar a frail-looking old man was trembling so violently Jake thought he might pass out. His arms were thrust over his head, his palms pressed flat to the low plank ceiling.

For perhaps a full minute, nobody moved or spoke. Jake's eyes were locked on the Colonel, who stood just inside the door with his shoulders bunched in anger. "The damn fool," he finally said. "The damn, selfish fool."

Jake had no idea what the Colonel meant by that. He glanced at Bill and Boyd and Quint, standing with their smoking pistols still drawn. Hog had also pulled his pistol, but he hadn't fired a shot; he stood with the muzzle pointed toward the floor, his narrow face pallid as a sheet. Of the six, only Jake and the Colonel hadn't touched their weapons — the Colonel because that was why he'd hired men like Bill and Boyd and Quint, and Jake because it had all happened too fast, and because he'd never killed a man in his life, and didn't ever want to.

Bill Hawkes barked an order, and Boyd and Quint stalked to the rear of the room, where they kicked open a door and ducked into the lean-to beyond. They reappeared in seconds, and Boyd gave a negative shake of his head. "Just a bunk and some clothes and stuff."

"Mr. Waller," the Colonel said mildly, staring at Sammy Lee's body.

Breathing hard, Hog edged forward. "Y-yes, sir?"

"I believe those are Eugene's pistols lying beside that dead Negro. Kindly retrieve them before any more blood stains the grips."

"Yes, sir." Hog holstered his own weapon and hastened to Sammy Lee's body.

As Hog laid the bloodied Colt on the bar and began his tussle with the gunbelt, the Colonel turned to Jake. "Well, Mr. Jacobs, what do you think?"

Jake stared at the Colonel uncomprehendingly. Finally, his voice raspy with exasperation, the Colonel said, "Do you concur with Mr. Waller? Is that man, or are any of these men, the Negroes who participated in the murder of my brother and his associates?"

Jake nodded dumbly.

"*Damnit, man!* Don't just stand there bobbing your head like an idiot. Go examine them. I want to be sure."

Jake moved toward the corpses on legs that felt more like oak than flesh and blood.

He paused above the two gunmen in long coats only a moment, then walked over to Sammy Lee just as Hog rose, holding up the Captain's gunbelt as if it were a dead snake. "Got it, Colonel," Hog announced triumphantly.

"Take the pistols and belt outside and wrap them in a piece of cloth for protection, then put them on the packhorse. And Mr. Waller, be sure all the blood is cleaned off before you put them away."

"Yes, sir." Hog stepped over Sammy Lee's body and hurried outside.

Jake looked up. "This here's Sammy Lee, all right, Colonel, but I ain't never seen those other two."

"Neither is Clay Little Bull?"

"Uh uh."

The Colonel glanced at Bill. "You know what to do?"

Bill nodded, and he and Boyd and Quint went outside, keeping their pistols in hand.

The Colonel turned to Jake. "Mr. Jacobs, I would suggest you draw your weapon and start earning your pay. I want you to start showing some gumption."

Jake pulled his pistol, held it awkwardly for a moment, then pointed it at the bartender.

Colonel Carry walked to the bar, speaking

to the tiny black man behind it. "I'm looking for three Africans — an old, white-haired man called Plato, a girl of breeding age called Jenny, and a young man called Clay Little Bull." He pulled the flier on Clay from an inside pocket of his coat and placed it on the bar. "Do you know these people, or do you recognize this man in particular?" He tapped the wanted poster with a finger.

The bartender leaned forward without taking his hands off the ceiling. "No, suh, I ain't never seen that fella, and them names don't ring no bell, neither."

"Think very hard," the Colonel encouraged gently, as if speaking to a child. "If they are here, my men will find them, and if you've lied —"

"No, suh! No, *suh!* On my life, I ain't never seen nor heard of any of them folks."

"And these three?" The Colonel gestured toward the dead men.

"Them two in the long coats, they been here before, though they never give me no names. That one your man called Sammy Lee, this is the first I ever seen him. They come riding in no more than half an hour ago. I swear to that on my life." He looked at the empty plates still on the bar, as if to draw attention to them without lowering his hands. "They just rode up and asked for

584

some food, so I give 'em some. But they ain't friends or nothing. They was gonna pay, like regular customers."

"Mr. Jacobs," the Colonel said, folding the wanted poster and returning it to his pocket. "Escort this man outside." He indicated the bartender with a nod of his head. "I suspect Mr. Hawkes will be collecting the others in front of the general store. Take him there."

Jake looked at the bartender. "You heard the Colonel. Let's move."

The bartender released his grip on the ceiling, though he kept his hands above his head. They walked to the door, where both men paused to look back. The Colonel was standing over Sammy Lee's body, unfolding a clasp knife. "Jesus," Jake breathed, and quickly poked the bartender's ribs with his pistol. "Hurry up!"

They stepped out into a cold blast of wind, and Jake sucked in a mouthful of air.

"That . . . that ain't right," the bartender said. "What he's figuring to do in there, that ain't Christian."

"Best you just hush up," Jake said, "before he decides to do the same to you."

Silently, the bartender led the way around the saloon and across the empty street. The Hawkes brothers and Quint had already gathered a number of people in front of the general store — men, women, children, even babes in arms. Bill Hawkes stood on the top step of the porch smoking a cheroot, while Hog rode herd at the rear of the group. Boyd and Quint were nowhere to be seen, but Jake figured they were checking out homes and businesses, looking for hide-outs.

"Get in with the rest of 'em," Jake told the bartender. "Don't cause no trouble, and chances are the Colonel'll ride outta here without hurtin' anyone."

"Anyone *else*," the bartender reminded him emphatically.

"The Colonel wants those three mighty bad," Jake admitted. "And he's got a short temper right now. You keep talkin' like you are and you're liable to rile him into lynchin' someone. I've seen him do it, too, so don't think he won't." He gave the wizened old man a shove. "Go on now." He waited until the bartender had joined the others, then walked over to the foot of the steps.

"Where's the Colonel?" Bill asked without removing his cigar.

"You wouldn't want to know."

"Goddamnit, if I didn't want to know, I wouldn't have asked."

"He's with Sammy Lee."

586

Bill hesitated, then chuckled. "I reckon he's still wanting that conversation with him. Was he using his knife?"

"Yeah," Jake said hollowly.

A woman screamed from one of the houses at the north end of town; a second later she came flying out of the front door to land sprawling on the frozen ground. Quint followed, aiming a kick at her backside. The woman yelped and scrambled to her feet. Quint shouted something the wind whipped away, and pointed toward the general store. Gathering her skirts, the woman came on at an awkward run, while Quint ducked back inside. After several minutes he reappeared emptyhanded and made his way to the next building.

Jake watched Quint disappear. He looked at the saloon, where the Colonel was apparently still attending to his grisly task. He looked at the sky and the prairie and the widely spaced buildings — the majority of them constructed from sod — that made up the town. He glanced once at Bill, leaning against the storefront with a bored expression. And when he couldn't look anywhere else, he just stared out over the heads of the townspeople as if they didn't exist. He knew that many of them were watching him, but he was too ashamed to meet their eyes. Some of them hadn't even had time to grab their hats or shawls or top coats. Jake felt even worse for the children, although he'd noticed that most of them had been shepherded toward the center of the crowd, where there was some protection from the elements.

After a time the Colonel appeared from around the front of the saloon and strode purposefully toward the general store. At the same instant, Boyd and Quint exited the last house at the end of the winding street, spoke briefly together, then also headed for the general store. Bill straightened and moved to the edge of the porch. His cheroot was smoked down to a stub, but he kept it in his mouth, his left eye closed to the smoke that curled up under his hat brim. Moving like a man who had just completed a hard day's work, Colonel Carry mounted the wooden steps of the general store and turned to face the townspeople. Coming close, Boyd called out, "That's it, Colonel. They're all here."

Without raising his voice, the Colonel said, "Walk among them, Mr. Jacobs, Mr. Waller. I want you to be sure."

Jake nodded, and with Hog coming in from the far side, moved slowly through the crowd. He looked at the men, women, and older boys, and wondered what he would do if he saw one of them. Would he tell the Colonel, just so he could hang them? Or would he keep his mouth shut and hope that Hog did the same, risking his own neck in the process?

It was a tough decision, but one he fortunately didn't have to make. After walking through the crowd twice in a circuitous pattern, Jake breathed a sigh of relief and headed for the porch. "They ain't here, Colonel. I'm sure of it."

"Mr. Waller?"

Looking disappointed, Hog concurred. "Nary hide ner hair," he said.

"Very well, then." Colonel Carry looked at the crowd. "Who is in charge here?"

For a couple of minutes, no one replied. A few men near the front began to fidget nervously under the Colonel's ice-hard glare, until finally the bartender stepped forward. "I reckon I am, Colonel."

"Your name." It was a demand, not a question.

"Lucas Jenkins, suh. I'm mayor of this here town."

The statement seemed to amuse Colonel Carry. He looked at Bill and said, "We have a politician with us, Mr. Hawkes."

Bill's eyes narrowed as he studied the

scrawny bartender. "Beggin' your pardon, Colonel, but he looks more like a honey dipper than a politician."

The Colonel chuckled. "Well, you know how it is in a small town, Mr. Hawkes. A mayor's duties never end."

Bill and Boyd and Hog laughed loudly; even the stoney-faced Quint allowed a flicker of a smile to cross his face. But none of the citizens of Blackbird laughed or smiled, and neither did Jake.

"Come inside, Lucas," the Colonel commanded. He entered the general store, and after a moment's hesitation, Jenkins followed. The door closed behind them, and Jake was left standing with the others, shivering in the cold.

The Colonel and Jenkins were inside for about twenty minutes. When they came out, Jenkins joined the others without comment, and the Colonel handed Bill a sheet of brown paper with a map drawn on it in pencil. "There are seven small farms in the immediate vicinity that contain Negroes, perhaps twenty-five in all. Take Hog and Quint and check them out. If you run into anyone who even remotely resembles the Africans we're looking for, bring them in."

Bill nodded as he studied the map, then looked to the northeast, as if taking a bearing on the first farm. "Quint, Hog, grab your horses!" He jumped off the porch and headed for the saloon, where their mounts were still hitched.

Jake shifted his weight from one foot to the other as he watched the three men disappear around the saloon; soon they reemerged, riding hard toward the first farm. Jake looked at the people standing in front of the general store, then at the Colonel. Apprehensively, he cleared his throat.

"Yes, Mr. Jacobs?" the Colonel said without looking at him.

"Well, I was just thinking —"

"A novel experience, I would imagine."

"Uh, well, uh, these folks have already been cleared, so to speak, and they're cold, especially them little ones. Shoot, I'm kind'a cold myself —"

"Don't make a habit of it, Mr. Jacobs," the Colonel said shortly.

"What?"

"Don't make a habit of thinking. You aren't very good at it, and a man shouldn't avail himself of something he isn't good at." Raising his voice so that all could hear, the Colonel added, "If anyone here is too frail to survive these chilly conditions, Mr. Jacobs, perhaps we should shoot them now, and save them the pain of prolonged suffering. That goes for anyone, black *or* white."

"It was just a thought," Jake mumbled.

"I would suggest you concentrate instead on your charges, Mr. Jacobs," the Colonel added in a more moderate tone. "I suspect a similar laxness occasioned my brother's death. You might also keep in mind that I doubt if any Negro here would hesitate to cleave your head with an ax, were he or she given the opportunity."

"Yes, sir, you're probably right."

The Colonel seemed to grow angrier. He looked at Boyd and said, "Keep a weather eye out, Mr. Hawkes, and don't hesitate to shoot anyone who attempts mischief."

"Sure, Colonel," Boyd said, grinning at Jake. "I'll keep 'em in line, black *and* white."

Abruptly, the Colonel turned and went inside, slamming the door behind him. Minutes later, a fresh column of black coal smoke chuffed into the sky from a metal chimney. Looking at Jake, Boyd laughed.

It took Bill and Quint and Hog more than three hours to make the circuit of farms surrounding Blackbird. It was mid-afternoon when they returned, coming in alone from the south. Bill reined in at the hitch rail in front of the general store, but before he could dismount, the Colonel stepped outside, letting the door hang open behind him.

Bill shook his head. "No sign of 'em, Colonel. I'm sorry."

"How many individuals did you examine?"

"Twenty-five on the nose, with Hog standing right there beside us. We searched the buildings real good, too. I don't think they were hiding anyone."

"Well," the Colonel said, glancing at the saloon, "our trip wasn't an entire loss, but I still want Little Bull, gentlemen. More than any of the others, I want the man who led the insurrection that killed my brother."

"We'll get him, Colonel," Boyd said, drifting up. "It don't look like he came north, but he wouldn't go east, either, and he'd be a damn fool to go back south with a reward on his head."

"Then that leaves only one direction left," Colonel Carry said softly. "He went west, back to the plains where he fled from the Choctaw last spring."

"West is a mighty big place, though," Boyd said uncertainly. "Hell, Canada to Mexico, and all the way to California."

"I disagree," the Colonel replied thoughtfully. "He was last seen in Leavenworth, and in all likelihood he went west from there. That's where we'll find him, gentlemen. Somewhere west of Leavenworth."

THIRTY-ONE

To Jonas, it seemed pretty clear that Clay and Rain Dancing were falling in love. Not that that bothered him. The truth was, it gladdened his heart to see Rain Dancing coming out of her shell like she was, her eyes taking on a sparkle that had been absent before, her expression looking far less pinched from pain and fear. But it worried him, too, remembering Virgil's threat, and the malevolence that had twisted his face on the day of his departure.

Looking back, Jonas figured Virgil was probably insane. Maybe not raving mad, the way he'd always imagined a lunatic to be, but definitely irrational and dangerously unpredictable, and probably capable of killing. Jonas didn't know what would happen when Virgil returned, but he reckoned all hell would break open in some manner. Clay wouldn't let Rain Dancing go back to him, and Virgil would never give her up without a fight.

Jonas found himself wishing Virgil would die on the plains, which would settle everything. Lord knew the weather had been hazardous enough. Even Clay had voiced his concern about the hunters when a blizzard in the middle of January had dumped another eight inches on the already snow-covered ground, and the temperatures had plunged below zero for days.

But Jonas knew he couldn't count on weather to stop Virgil Nash. It would take more than that, and he guessed what it came down to was a bullet. Jonas had never killed a man, but he'd learned a few hard lessons since coming to the frontier, one of them being that life was cheap out here, cheaper than he would have ever imagined possible back East, and as January waned, he began to realize that if the situation warranted it, he could probably kill another human being. He could do it for Clay, and what's more, he was pretty sure he could do it for Rain Dancing.

The frightening part was that Jonas was also fairly certain that no matter what he tried, Virgil would best him at it. The others thought Virg was a coward, and maybe he was in his own way, but to Jonas he was just a tough, mean son of a bitch who might pause to consider the odds against someone like Clay or Ty or Oscar, but would swat Jonas like a fly against a window pane. Yet when Jonas fantasized about facing Virg, he never had to remind himself that Clay was his friend. Some things, he had come to realize, were worth fighting for, and if need be, dying for.

The deep freeze that had gripped the prairies since December broke in early February, and the wind that had blown almost constantly out of the west and northwest switched hard to the southwest, bringing with it the warm, moist air from the Gulf of Mexico.

The shifting winds awakened Clay sometime before dawn. He lay quietly for several minutes, trying to identify what had roused him, before he realized the wind had a different sound — a softer, less insistent hum as it moved through the crooked eaves of the roof and probed the cracked chinking in the walls. It was a subtle change, to be sure, but it had been enough to penetrate his dreams, to let him know something was out of kilter. He listened to it for a couple of minutes, then pushed back a corner of his buffalo robe and slid naked from his bed.

Last evening's fire had burned down to a

handful of ash-dusted coals. Clay laid several pieces of kindling over them, then bent carefully to blow at the base of the coned nest. A twinge of pain shot through his left shoulder as he leaned forward, but it wasn't enough to make him stop. He blew again, and was rewarded with a thread of smoke; moments later a small tongue of flame licked greedily at the wood. Clay rocked back to watch the climbing flames, absently rubbing his aching shoulder. A stirring in his bed caught his attention, and Rain Dancing sat up. The flickering firelight shone off her raven-colored hair, illuminating the bare, coppery curve of her shoulders and back. She looked at him questioningly. "There is something wrong?" she asked in a whisper, conscious of Jonas' light snoring from across the room.

"The wind has shifted. Can you hear it?"

Rain Dancing cocked her head to one side, and a smile played across her face. "Winter Man has finally released his hold on the land."

"The time of the grass greening is still a long way off," Clay reminded her.

"It is true that there will be more storms and more cold, but is it not also true that for a while the air will turn warm and the snow that covers the earth will leave?"

"My people call it a January thaw," Clay said, coming back to sit at the side of the bed where he could admire the full swell of her breasts, the cherry-dark nipples taut in the chilly air.

"Your people?" Her nose crinkled as she made a face at him. "Do you not yet know that your people are the same as mine?"

"All right. The Choctaw call it a January thaw. So do the white-eyes." He didn't add that it was actually February, by the white man's calendar; he could tell she was confused enough as it was.

"I do not understand this word, Jan-U-Wary."

"The Moon when the Cold Grows Deep," Clay explained. He wasn't sure what the Kiowa term for it would be — it seemed as if every tribe had its own unique description for the different moons, the passing months — but he knew Rain Dancing would understand.

Her smile broadened and a mischievous glint appeared in her eyes. Straightening her shoulders until her breasts were in full view, she said in a teasing voice, "I thought perhaps it meant the moon when a man's penis grows long and hard."

Clay laughed and slipped under the robe with her, wrapping himself tightly around her body, their legs entangling. "That would be every moon," he whispered in her ear.

"Every sun of every moon."

"Every day of every month," Clay repeated in English. He touched her back, tracing the ridged spine with his fingertips to the dimpled cleft at the top of her buttocks. Rain Dancing squirmed closer, putting her arms around him. They cuddled like that for a long time, their hands roaming lazily as they explored one another's body. But there was no urgency in their movements. They had made love twice during the night, and both felt sated.

After a while Clay rolled onto his back. Rain Dancing slid her hand over his chest to feel the puckered scar tissue on his shoulder, the healing tooth marks like shallow craters. Gently kneading the stiff muscles, she asked, "Does it still pain you?"

"Not when you do that."

Rain Dancing smiled, but then her expression changed and she looked at the wall as if she could see beyond it. "Listen. Already the snow starts to drip."

"It will be good to feel the ground under my moccasins again," Clay confessed. "I have grown weary of the snow."

But Rain Dancing had something else on her mind, and after a couple of minutes, she said, "He will come now."

Clay took a deep breath, then let it go slowly. He knew of whom she spoke. "They are probably on their way now."

"Without the snow, we could —"

Clay put a finger to her lips. "It is too far to walk, even without the deep snow. And you said yourself that Winter Man hasn't left for good, he has only loosened his hold for a few days."

Rain Dancing's voice took on a note of despair. "Virg-El's heart is bad. He is like my husband-who-was-killed. Sometimes he causes pain to others just for the pleasure it brings to him."

"But no more," Clay promised her. "You are my woman now."

"As you are my man. But Virg-El will not let me go. He will fight, and you are too weak to defeat him."

Clay mocked a scowl. "What are you saying, woman? That I am no match for him?"

Rain Dancing buried her face in the shaggy hair of the buffalo robe.

"She's right, Clay," Jonas said from across the cabin. "You can't fight Virgil in the shape you're in. He'd kill you."

"Ho, so you've been eavesdropping?"

Jonas laughed. "If you two don't slow down, I'm going to take my bedroll outside.

600

It might be colder, but it wouldn't be nearly so noisy."

"Your time will come, pard, your time will come."

Jonas rose on one elbow. "Listen, Clay, I don't understand Kiowa, but I recognized Virgil's name, and I know how Rain Dancing feels about him, so I can guess. Virgil's going to explode like a powder keg when he finds out what's been going on here. He'll try to kill you, sure as hell."

"If I remember right, it was you he said he'd kill."

"Both of us, then. He's crazy enough."

Rain Dancing had been watching this quiet exchange between the two men without understanding a word, but as Jonas had earlier, she sensed its content, and her fingernails began to dig unconsciously at the flesh of Clay's shoulder. Pushing her away, Clay slid out from under the robe and padded barefoot to the fire. He added more wood, building up a blaze, and a light that spread throughout the cabin.

Rain Dancing said tentatively, "We could steal some ponies. In the direction of the morning sun there is a white-eyed trader. Virg-El told me of him."

"Dooley's," Clay said.

"What about Dooley?" Jonas asked.

"Rain Dancing wants to steal some horses from him." Clay stood and pulled a blanket around his shoulders, unaware of the image it created. "Likely you've already guessed, but I've decided to go back to the Kiowa with Rain Dancing."

Jonas was quiet a moment, staring at the ceiling. Then he shrugged and said, "Well, I don't suppose I'm all that surprised, at least that you two were planning to run off together. Short of killing Virg as soon as he rides up, it's about the only way out. But going back to the Kiowa, ain't that pretty risky? To hear Oscar talk, they're about the meanest tribe on the plains, them and the Comanches."

"I've heard the same," Clay admitted. "But I was raised among them. Maybe it won't be too bad. At least I'd be my own man."

"I know it's tough being a black man in this country, Clay, but it's been all right out here, hasn't it? Nobody's given you any trouble?"

"Out here is about the only place a black man can find a little freedom," Clay said bitterly.

"It's none of my business, but I'll say it anyway. I don't think you can go back to the Kiowas, Clay. You just don't seem *Indian* enough. I think it's been too long."

Clay gave him a curious look. "Where the hell'd you get so much wisdom?" he asked.

"It's not wisdom, it's just that plain to see. It would be to Ty and Oscar, too. Rain Dancing knows it. *You* know it."

"I don't know anything of the kind," Clay replied shortly.

"Don't get mad. I just don't figure you've got the temperament to live that kind of life anymore."

"What the hell would you know about it?" Clay said with unexpected anger. "What the hell would you know about being Indian or black or . . ." He let the words trail off. Across the cabin, Jonas stiffened.

"I guess you're right. What the hell would I know?" He lay back, pulling his robe over his shoulders.

Clay's jaw knotted in regret, but he kept his mouth shut. In his heart, he knew there was truth in Jonas' words, maybe more than he wanted to admit. But if he couldn't live a free man with the Kiowa, if he couldn't survive among the white-eyes or go back to the Nations, then what the hell could he do? In frustration, he went back to bed, tossing the blanket aside as he slipped under the robe with Rain Dancing. "What is it?" she asked, casting Jonas a suspicious look.

603

"What did he say that upset you?"

Clay shook his head. "He didn't say anything."

After a pause, she asked, "He is our friend still?"

"Yes," Clay replied, dropping his head to the rolled-up blanket that served as their pillow. "He is our friend."

The southerly breezes continued, and in the afternoons the temperatures rose into the forties. The snow melted under the warmth of the sun, and the ice in Tornado Creek and the Smoky Hill started to rot. New streams appeared, tumbling down old gullies that had been dry since the previous spring, filling the sinuous paths of the buffalo trails. After a few days, patches of short, tan buffalo grass began to emerge from the snow on the south-facing slopes, like scabs on the wrinkled white flesh of some giant, slumbering beast.

A week passed, and still the hunters did not return. Daily, Clay or Jonas, or sometimes all three would climb the highest hill on the near side of the river to scan the surrounding countryside. Although there were better vantage points along the bluffs south of the Smoky Hill, the ice was too treacherous to risk now.

The buffalo returned with the warming weather. Not the great herd that had made the earth tremble with its arrival in the fall, but smaller bunches of a few hundred here, a score or more there. Soon there were shaggies grazing in every direction, but Clay didn't hunt. Although he felt strong enough, having recovered rapidly in the seven weeks since the bear's attack, he'd lost his heart for the slaughter. Money didn't matter anymore, at least not the bloodied money of butchered buffalo. Nor could he generate any excitement for his partnership with Ty, for all that he wished him the best of luck. He helped Jonas and Rain Dancing stack what hides they could into the freighter to keep them as dry as possible, and oversaw the construction of a makeshift platform of cottonwood poles that they piled the rest of the hides on. But he didn't add to the tally. He left his rifle in the cabin, and sometimes didn't even wear his pistol.

It was hard work for a while, especially caring for the hides that had frozen before they could dry, but they made the best of a bad situation until there came a time when all of the hides were either cured or stacked above the runoff to be dealt with later, the hams smoked and wrapped in salted bags of burlap, the tongues smoked or brined in barrels. After that, there wasn't much to do at all. Sometimes Jonas took an ax and whipsaw up to the cottonwood grove to cut firewood, but it was a chore designed more to kill time than anything else. They already had enough firewood to last until summer.

Often, when Jonas was away, Clay and Rain Dancing would retire to the cabin to make love. It should have been a wondrous time for them, the weather mild and the work minimal, but Clay sensed a growing anxiousness in Rain Dancing. Finally, ten days after the switch in the weather, she once again broached the subject of leaving. This time, she didn't let Clay put her off.

"But what will you do when he comes?" she insisted.

"I do not know. Wait and see what happens."

"He will kill you."

"Others have tried."

"Virg-El is different. His anger is swift, like the strike of the rattlesnake."

"Virgil is a coward. I am not afraid of him."

Rain Dancing took his face in both her hands, gritting her teeth in frustration. "We must go now, before it is too late. We must walk if you will not steal ponies from the man called Dooley. But we cannot be here when Virg-El returns."

"I want my pinto," Clay answered lamely. He didn't add that, more than anything, he was tired of running, of sneaking off like a thief in the night, the way he'd done in the Nations, and again in Leavenworth.

"My father will give you a hundred pintos," Rain Dancing argued.

"I don't want your father's ponies," Clay said. "I like the one I have." He threw the robe back and reached for his trousers.

"Where are you going?" she asked.

"To walk," Clay replied. "I need to think."

"I have angered you?"

"Damnit," he snapped in English. "I said I'm going for a walk. You stay here." He motioned toward the kettle, sitting on the hearth. "Get some supper started."

"You are hungry?"

Clay shook his head, then yanked the worn leather shirt that Rain Dancing had mended for him over his head. Bending to grab his moccasins, he switched to Kiowa. "I will hear no more of this. What is to pass between Virgil and myself will pass. I will not run."

Then the door swung open and Dancing Rain shrieked.

"What the hell?" Virgil Nash exclaimed. He saw Rain Dancing, naked on Clay's bed, and Clay with his moccasins still in his hands. Then Virgil's expression changed to a murderous rage, and a chill skittered down Clay's spine. "You sonofabitch!" Virgil roared, his hand reaching for the pistol holstered at his waist. "You dirty, stinking, black-skinned sonofabitch!"

THIRTY-TWO

Clay didn't even attempt a response. He threw his heavy-soled moccasins into Virgil's face, then lunged forward as Virgil batted them away. He drove his shoulder into the woolly hunter's stomach, and they stumbled outside together, falling and rolling away and scrambling to their feet as one. Clay swung savagely before he was all the way up, his fist catching Virgil on the jaw and staggering him backward. Clay followed like an enraged bull, connecting twice more before Virgil managed to get an arm up in defense, deflecting Clay's next punch so that his fist skidded across his cheek and into empty air.

That was all the opening Virgil needed. He leaped forward, trying to wrap his long arms around Clay's shoulders, to drag him to the ground. But Clay was too slippery. He twisted free of Virgil's hold and drove two hard, vicious jabs into the taller man's solar plexus. Virgil reeled as if drunk, his chest heaving as he tried to pull air into his starving lungs. Then Clay swung a final time, putting everything he had into a perfect uppercut. Virgil's head snapped back, his eyes rolling loosely. He teetered on the rundown heels of his boots for a moment, then dropped like a rock.

Clay stood over Virgil's sprawled form, breathing hard. His shoulders were hunched, his fists knotted like chunks of black iron. He remained that way for a long time, barefoot in the slush and mud, unaware of the cold, or the renewed throbbing in his injured shoulder.

"Wow."

Clay looked up. Jonas stood at the corner of the cabin with a wrist-thick length of firewood gripped in both hands, staring astonished at Virgil's battered face.

"I saw him ride up," Jonas explained, "so I came down to help. I see you didn't need it." He looked at Clay with awe. "Damn, he never had a chance."

"He had his chance," Clay said shortly. He straightened, forcing himself to relax as the fog cleared from his brain. "Give me a hand," he said. "We'll drag him inside and tie him up."

"Ty's on his way," Jonas informed him,

tossing his makeshift club onto a pile of firewood beside the door. "They're bringing the wagon down off the bluffs now."

Stooping, Clay grabbed one of Virgil's boots and started to drag him toward the cabin. Jonas grabbed the other foot, and together they hauled him inside. Clay glanced at Rain Dancing, crouched fearfully against the rear wall fastening her dress. "Get some rope," he said in Kiowa.

Rain Dancing came over with a length of hemp, and Clay and Jonas quickly bound Virgil's wrists and ankles. When they were through, Clay licked his dry lips. Rain Dancing touched his arm. "Your hand bleeds. Are you hurt badly?"

Clay glanced at his fingers. The knuckles on his right hand were indeed dripping blood, probably cut on Virgil's teeth. He shook a few drops onto the floor just as a horse trotted up outside. Saddle leather creaked, and soon afterward Ty ducked through the low door into the cabin. He stopped when he saw Virgil lying on the floor, trussed and unconscious, his face already swelling. He looked at Clay and Jonas and Rain Dancing, his expression grim. "You and Rain Dancing?" he asked Clay.

"We're pulling out, Ty. I'm giving you and

Jonas my share of the hides to split between yourselves, but Rain Dancing and I are going back to the Kiowa."

"I wondered on the way in . . ." Ty said softly, then let the thought drift off. He nodded resignedly. "Take whatever supplies you'll need. I'll get your horses — your pinto and the pony Rain Dancing rode in on." He turned to go.

"Ty," Clay called. Ty paused at the door. "This isn't what we had in mind," Clay said with a twinge of guilt.

"I know," Ty said gently.

Clay's shoulders sagged. Turning to Rain Dancing, he said, "Get your stuff. We're going home."

It didn't take long to pack what they'd need. They could reach Rain Dancing's village in two weeks if the weather held, and carry enough supplies for such a short trip in their saddlebags. Ty and Jonas saddled the horses as Clay and Rain Dancing rolled their heavy bedroll. Clay packed all of the powder and shot he could carry, while Rain Dancing concentrated on food — jerky, flour, some beans and coffee and sugar, plus a small tin kettle to cook in. They were ready within a quarter of an hour.

Ty and Jonas waited outside with the

horses, while Oscar unyoked the oxen and turned them loose to graze. Seeing the animals that had made the mid-winter journey over the plains startled Clay. He was struck by how thin and exhausted they looked, compared to the cattle that had remained behind.

The hunt had taken its toll on the men, too. For the first time Clay noticed the gauntness of Ty's face, the wind-honed flesh and hollow eyes. Dirt and grime darkened his features, and his hair and beard were long and unkempt. His clothing was in worse shape, spotted with old blood and fat and mud, and worn nearly through in places. But the wagon, Clay noticed, fairly sagged under its load of hides and meat.

"Looks like you had a rough time of it," Clay observed.

"We managed."

"Maybe someday we'll get a chance to talk about it."

"I hope so," Ty said. He smiled wearily and put out his hand. "Good luck, Clay."

Clay gripped Ty's hand hard, in appreciation of their time together, and of the confidence the friendly white-eye had put in him. He couldn't help feeling that he was betraying that trust, but if Ty shared his sentiment, he hid it well. Clay turned to

Jonas. "Pard," he said, shaking the younger man's hand as well. "You've been a good friend. I've been proud to know you."

"I feel the same way," Jonas said, his voice catching. "You watch yourself."

"I will."

Jonas looked at Rain Dancing, already mounted and eager to be off. He spoke her name in Kiowa.

"Jo-Nas," Rain Dancing replied, and flashed a grateful smile.

Taking the pinto's reins, Clay affectionately scratched the rangy gelding's neck. The horse swung its head around to rub its headstall familiarly against Clay's shoulder. Gathering the reins, Clay stepped into the saddle.

"I'll keep Virgil tied up another hour or so," Ty promised. "That's about all I can give you."

"It'll be enough," Clay said. Virgil had regained consciousness about ten minutes earlier, and was ranting now for someone to cut him loose. He was fighting mad yet, his voice already going a little croaky from hollering, but Clay figured he'd settle down some in another hour.

"He'll come after you, you know?" Ty said.

"It'll be dark in a couple of hours. He'll have to stop for the night, but Rain Dancing and I won't. That ought to turn him back."

"I wouldn't count on it," Ty replied gravely.

"Well, if it doesn't, I'll just have to deal with him when he catches up." He touched the brim of his hat without enthusiasm. "Good-bye, Ty, Jonas."

"Good-bye, Clay."

He glanced toward the meadow where Oscar was standing alongside the prairie schooner, watching from a distance. But as soon as Clay met his gaze, the old plainsman wheeled around and started fiddling with one of the ropes holding the load in place. Smiling, Clay reined the pinto away, walking it out of the yard. Rain Dancing followed, keeping her pony in the pinto's tracks. They crossed the Smoky Hill where the wagon had already broken through the ice and climbed the trail to the top of the bluff. There Clay paused only long enough for Rain Dancing to come up beside him. Then they struck out due south at a trot. Neither of them looked back.

"So the nigra run off with Virgil's woman, did he?"

Ty looked up from where he was sliding a rawhide-laced hide sack of meat onto his shoulder. He paused with the bottom of the sack resting on the wagon's tailgate. "I don't want you using that word around me anymore."

Oscar scowled. "Don't be talkin' at me like I'm some buffler-witted schoolboy, Ty. I won't put up with that shit."

"I don't like that word, Oscar, and the more I hear it, the less I'm inclined to tolerate it."

"You're gettin' as touchy as a sore-titted sow anymore," Oscar grumbled, "but I'm thinkin' you'd best be gettin' used to the word. Virg'll be usin' it a lot in the next few hours."

Jonas came out of the smokehouse, his glance darting between Oscar and Ty.

"Not around me, he won't," Ty said. He hoisted the sack onto his shoulder and took it inside, flopping it atop a dozen others already stacked against the east wall. They would cut the meat free tomorrow and begin the smoking process. Ty had already decided he would leave Oscar in charge of that, while he and Jonas delivered a wagonload of hides and meat to Dooley's.

He went back outside, stepping aside as Jonas passed with an eighty pound sack balanced over his shoulder. Oscar already had another one waiting on the tailgate.

"When you gonna cut him loose?" the old man asked.

Ty glanced at the cabin. Clay and Rain Dancing had been gone an hour now, and Virgil's cries had tapered into silence some time ago. "When we're finished here, I guess."

"Be closin' in on dark by then."

"That's what I was thinking," Ty admitted.

"You know that ain't gonna stop him. There'll be a good moon tonight, with enough light to track 'em if he takes the notion."

"You just keep quiet about tracking by moonlight, and maybe he won't think of it."

"Oh, he'll think of it, all right. He's thinkin' 'bout it right now, I'd wager. Hell, boy, we'll be lucky he don't shoot us all for this."

Ty took the sack from the old man's hands and tipped it outward, ducking his shoulder under it. "That's a possibility," he said, straightening his knees under the load. "But I doubt it. He'll be too mad at Clay to think much about us. Besides," he grinned a little, just to nettle the older man, "there's three of us. I doubt if he'd kill more than two before someone got him."

"Smartass," Oscar growled, going after another sack. "You mark my words, Ty, that

617

boy's gonna be madder'n that griz what nearly kilt Clay. He could shoot us all in our sleep."

It was still light when they finished unloading the meat, but the sun had dropped below the horizon and the shadows were beginning to pool in the low spots. The patchy snow turned from white to blue-gray, and the muddy ground in between started to freeze. Standing in front of the smokehouse, Ty said, "We'll pull the hides off tomorrow."

"Won't hurt nuthin', leavin' 'em another night," Oscar agreed. He threw a leg over the sideboards, found the iron rim of the wheel with his toe, and clambered down. Wiping his greasy hands on the seat of his trousers, he gave Ty a calculating look. "Now what, sonny?"

Ty sighed. "You and Jonas take care of the stock. I'll get supper started."

"You gonna cut him loose?"

"Yeah."

"He'll kill you."

"Maybe." Ty shrugged into his coat, chilled now that he'd stopped working. "Go see to the livestock, Oscar. Virgil is my worry."

He walked to the cabin, stomping the snow from his boots at the stoop, then entering and shutting the door behind him.

"It took you long enough," Virgil said quietly. Ty had to squint to make him out in the shadowy light, still bound and lying on the floor, but rolled closer to the fireplace, where it was warmer. "I hope to hell it was that nigger holding you at gunpoint that kept you away."

"Don't call him that," Ty said, moving to the hearth, although he knew he was wasting his breath with Virgil.

"Cut me loose, Ty."

"Give me a minute. I need some light."

"You don't need any goddamn light!" Virgil shouted. *"Cut me loose!"*

"I've been outside," Ty parried. "I can hardly see my hand in front of my face." He squatted at the hearth and added kindling to the coals, gently fanning it with his hat. A blaze kicked up, growing rapidly.

"Don't think I don't know what you're up to," Virgil accused. "You're trying to give Clay and Rain Dancing a good lead, thinkin' I won't follow 'em after dark, but you're wrong, Ty-boy. I'm gonna catch 'em, you can count on that. Then I'm gonna cut that nigger's balls off, right before I kill him."

Ty stayed by the fire, watching the flames. "Why don't you just let 'em go, Virgil? Rain

Dancing doesn't belong to you. She never did."

"You're on their side in this. I never should've gone with you. I should've stayed here."

"What's done is done. Let it go."

"Cut me loose, Ty. Or do you plan to keep me staked out till spring?"

Sighing, Ty rose and went to Virgil's side. "Naw, it wouldn't do any good. You'd just chew your ropes off."

Virgil laughed harshly. "Now you're talking." He held up his bound wrists. Ty pulled his hunting knife. Taking a firm grip on Virgil's forearm, he paused. "Let them go, Virg. For old time's sake."

"Cut the ropes, Tyler."

Slipping the blade between Virgil's wrists, Ty sawed upward. Virgil jerked his hands apart, then pulled the rope free and threw it into the fire. Plucking the knife from Ty's hands, he jackknifed into a sitting position and quickly severed the bonds at his ankles. Tossing the knife aside, he got to his feet and grabbed his gunbelt off a nearby crate. He strapped it on, then checked the loads. Ty retrieved his knife, then moved to the door. He stood there with his shoulders hunched, breathing hard. "I can't let you go, Virg."

Virgil looked up. "What the hell are you talking about?"

"I can't let you go after them."

"You think you're going to stop me?" Virgil asked, laughing.

Ty brushed his coat back, putting his hand on the butt of his pistol. "I'm going to try."

Virgil eyed him humorously. "You're going get yourself killed, is what you're going to do. We've been friends a long time, and I ain't hankering to do it, but by God I will if I have to."

"Why don't you help me get some supper started? We can talk this over after we eat."

Virgil's expression hardened. His Colt was still in his hand, and he curled his thumb over the hammer, cocking it slowly, deliberately. The cold, metallic click of the sear locking into place sounded loud in the close confines of the cabin. "Get out of my way, Ty."

Drawing in a deep breath, Ty started to draw his Colt. Virgil lifted his pistol and pointed it at Ty's chest.

"Move that shooter another inch and I'll pull the trigger," Virgil warned.

"Shit," Ty breathed, feeling suddenly light-headed. He wanted to laugh, but didn't. He knew Virgil meant exactly what he said. What Ty hadn't realized was how calmly a man could face death, to know it would happen if he did a certain thing, but to go ahead and do it anyway. It all seemed so unreal.

Ty yanked upward on the Navy, but the holster's grip was too snug and the pistol snagged. He saw the bright yellow spit of muzzle flash from Virgil's revolver, deafening at that range, and was slammed backward by the slug. His head rapped against the cabin's wall; darkness fluttered at the edges of his vision. He saw Virgil's pistol jerk again, and felt his body twist under the impact of the .36 lead sphere. Then he was falling, plummeting head first into a bottomless black abyss.

THIRTY-THREE

Jonas had been expecting the shots, listening for them without really being aware that he was. There were two, coming in rapid succession. Before the echoes of the first one had died over the pegging grounds, Jonas was sprinting for the cabin. Virgil stepped through the door just as he rounded the corner and skidded to a halt. Glancing at the revolver in Virgil's right hand, Jonas cursed and started for the door.

"Stay back!" Virgil commanded, his voice harsh and wild.

Jonas slowed, then stopped. "You killed him, didn't you?"

"Drop your pistol, then go saddle my horse."

"Saddle your own damn horse."

Virgil brought his revolver up. "Do what I say, kid. I swear to God I ain't bluffin'."

"He tried to stop you, so you shot him?"

A muscle jumped in Virgil's cheek. "Just

do what I say, before I do the same to you."

Jonas shook his head. "No."

"You bastard," Virgil whispered. "You'll all against me, aren't you? You, the old man, Ty — every last one of you." Although his hand trembled with rage, he never let the muzzle drift away from Jonas' chest. "But you ain't gonna stop me. Not you or anyone. Now go saddle my goddamn horse."

Jonas' heart thundered in his ears. Virgil cocked his pistol, his eyes wide and flighty. Then Jonas heard the hard crunch of boots on the half-frozen ground, and knew Oscar had followed him down from the pasture.

"Easy, boy," Oscar said, as if speaking to a frightened horse. "Ain't no one gonna git in your way."

"You sure as hell ain't, old man."

"Naw, sonny, I ain't even gonna try," Oscar replied, sidling closer to Jonas.

"He's killed Ty," Jonas said tautly. "We've got to stop him."

"It's too late to stop him," Oscar said, still in that low, soothing voice. "Too damn late."

Jonas caught a glimpse of something long and dark slicing through the air toward him. He tried to duck it, but was too slow. Pain exploded above his right ear. He folded to his hands and knees like an empty bellows, hearing only dimly the sound of Oscar's shout, the blast of Virgil's pistol. His hands started to slide through the mud, as if the earth itself were pulling him down.

When he awoke it was as if no time had passed at all, but he knew it must have. He was lying on top of his bedroll, his head throbbing in time to his pulse. Firelight danced across the low ceiling, and he could hear the wooden tapping of a spoon against the rim of the cast-iron kettle they kept by the fire. Gingerly, he moved his hand up to explore the side of his head.

"You're alive," Oscar grumbled defensively. "That's what matters. Come a time, you'll know that."

"You hit me," Jonas said, fingering the oblong lump above his ear.

"Saved your mangy hide, is what I done." Oscar hove into view, spoon in hand. "You ain't gonna puke, are you? If you do, you can damn well clean it up yourself. I ain't your mama."

"Where's Virgil?"

"He lit out after Clay and the girl. Got hisself a good start by now, too."

"What about Ty?"

A pleased expression came to Oscar's face. "He's alive, by God. I wouldn't've bet a nickel on it, seein' the look in Virgil's eyes when I found you two squared off like a couple'a bulls. I figured ol' Ty was wolf bait for sure, but he ain't. Got hisself a bullet through the shoulder and another through his side, but I've seen worse. Both of 'em passed clean through, like shit through a goose."

Jonas pushed himself up on one elbow to look across the room. Ty was lying in his bed, tucked under a shaggy buffalo robe. His eyes were closed, but he was breathing easily.

"I cleaned 'im up and doctored his wounds," Oscar said proudly. "He'll be all right."

Carefully, Jonas swung his legs around and sat up. He remained that way for several minutes, waiting for the dizziness to pass.

"I reckon you'll live, too," Oscar said. "I whomped you a good one, but kids has generally got tough heads."

"You could've backed me up. We might have stopped him if you had."

"Got both ourselves kilt, is what we'd'a done," Oscar returned scornfully. "I've seed people like that afore, boy. Ol' Virgil was gonna plug anything got in his way. Hell, after I whacked you, he took a shot at me. Was my good luck he was so worked up he missed." He shook his head in disgust. "Damn fool drank near a whole keg of whiskey out there on the buffler ranges, frettin' over that squaw the whole time. Wouldn't share any, either, though I slipped me a cup or two when I could. It must'a addled his brains, though. That boy is downright spooky anymore."

"How much of a head start does he have?"

"Virgil?" Oscar went back to the hearth where he could keep an eye on the kettle. "Forgit that notion, sonny. Even if you was to catch up, he'd just shoot you dead. Naw, let Clay handle Virg. He'll know what to do."

"I'm going after him," Jonas said. "I owe Clay that much."

"*Owe 'im!* Boy, you don't owe that buck a damn thing."

But Jonas was adamant. "I'll take Ty's bay. There's enough snow left on the ground that I ought to be able to track them."

"You'll end up lost and froze to death afore dawn, you damn green-ass colt."

"I've got to try."

Oscar snorted and turned away. When Jonas thought he could move around without passing out, he knelt beside his bedroll and rolled it into a bundle. Oscar spooned up a bowl of stew and sat back to eat. He watched Jonas with a contemptuous expression, grease dribbling down his whiskered chin. "Ever track a critter afore?" he asked casually. "Asides from ol' Brownie, that time you run onto that grizzle b'ar?"

"I'll find them," Jonas replied. He finished lashing his bedroll together, then fetched Ty's saddlebags and dumped their contents onto a case of trade goods. He began stuffing them with his own gear — ammunition for the Sharps carbine and Colt, a change of dry clothes with extra socks and mittens, hard oil to waterproof his boots, some bandages and salve just in case, and food — mostly jerky and ash cakes that Rain Dancing had made the night before. When he was finished, the saddlebags bulged.

"You got enough grub there to last you to Texas," Oscar noted drolly.

"If that's how far I have to go, I'll do it," Jonas said. He pulled on his coat, then tugged his hat down carefully over the lump above his ear.

Oscar's spoon slowed. "You're serious, ain't cha?"

Jonas picked up a rope and went outside without answering. He studied the sky before going to the corral. Clay had tried to teach him how to tell time by the position of the stars, but he'd never been very good at it. He guessed it was close to midnight, which meant Virgil had a good six-hour lead. Grim-faced, he circled the cabin and crawled through the rails. He was going to have to ride hard and not make any mistakes if he wanted to catch up in time.

It took only a few minutes to saddle Ty's bay. When he led it back around the cabin, Oscar was standing at the door with Jonas' bedroll and saddlebags under one arm, the Sharps held in his free hand.

"Go grab yourself some stew," Oscar growled. "If you're set on gettin' yourself kilt, you might as well do it on a full stomach."

Jonas hesitated. Although he was anxious to push on, he knew Oscar was right. It would take only a few minutes to wolf down a bowl of stew, but the warmth the greasy food created in his belly would last the rest of the night. Grudgingly, he handed Oscar the reins. "Thanks," he said.

"Don't thank me, you dumb shit," Oscar snapped.

Jonas went inside, veering past Ty's bed. Ty was still asleep and snoring lightly, a sign Jonas took as good. He went to the rear of the cabin and squatted beside the fire without taking off his hat or coat, and began eating straight from the kettle, spooning up heaping mouthfuls of stew that burned the roof of his mouth as he swallowed it. Oscar came in a few minutes later, shaking his head at the sight.

"Anybody you want me to write?" he asked sarcastically. "Your ma or pa, so's I can let 'em know you're dead?"

"I ain't dead yet," Jonas replied. "Besides, you can't write."

"And you think you're better'n me 'cause you can?" the old man flared. "Think you're better'n me 'cause it ain't me goin' after Virgil like some goddamn do-gooder saint?"

"No," Jonas said, startled. "Hell, Clay was my friend, not yours."

"You're goddamn right about that," Oscar replied huffily. "Clay weren't nuthin' but an uppity nigra, far as I'm concerned. Down south they'd'a hung him for sure, but up here I had to swaller it whole."

Jonas stood, tossing his spoon to the floor. "I'm going now," he said flatly. "Don't try to stop me."

Oscar snuffed. "Good riddance, I say."

Jonas went outside. The bay was hitched to the top rail of the corral. Jonas tightened the cinch, then double-checked the saddle-bags and bedroll. The Sharps was carried in a loop fastened to the horn, so that it would ride across his thighs when in the saddle. Everything seemed secured. He hooked a toe in the stirrup and hauled himself up.

When he rode back around the cabin he half-expected to find Oscar standing on the stoop, but the door remained shut, and there was no sign of the cantankerous old plainsman. Taking a deep breath, Jonas gigged the bay toward the Smoky Hill crossing.

Clay didn't call a halt until the moon went down, around four in the morning. He and Rain Dancing hobbled their horses, then rolled up in their robes to catch a few hours' sleep. Dawn was a pale steel band of color across the eastern horizon when they awoke, and frost covered their robes like mold. They readied their mounts in the hazy predawn light and pushed on. The sun hadn't yet come up when they came to a low saddle between two ridges, and drew up. To the south a valley opened before them like a shallow trough scraped through the hills, stretching toward a nameless creek several miles distant, the land rising again on the far side, low but far-reaching. Closer, near the head of the valley, was a rocky outcropping with a gulch curving around its near side, a lightning-struck cottonwood at its mouth. It was the cottonwood that caught Clay's attention. It stood about twenty feet high, its crown splintered and scorched, its sheered top crashed across the mouth of the gulch.

Rain Dancing looked at him questioningly.

Twisting in the saddle, Clay studied their backtrail. The tracks of their horses were clear in the rotting snow, stippled lines that disappeared a hundred yards behind them in the pewter light. Buffalo grazed in the distance, patiently watched over by large gray wolves — the only signs of life he saw. It worried him some, their tracks being so clear. A man determined enough could probably have followed them through the night. It was that which helped him make his decision. Swinging back, he said, "We will build a fire here, and eat a bite."

Rain Dancing's eyes widened frightfully. "But he will see our smoke, and come all the faster."

"There will not be any more wood between here and the Arkansas. We should warm ourselves, and have some food."

"Sun will warm us," she argued. "We can wait for Sun."

Clay motioned toward the broken cottonwood. "Make a good meal. I will stay here and watch."

Biting her lower lip in deference, Rain Dancing reined toward the gulch. Clay turned the pinto sideways to the trail and dug out his pipe and tobacco.

It was cold here in the low pass, but not unbearably so, not after the frigid temperatures of last December and January. And the wind was still, as it often was around the dawn hour. Clay filled his pipe and lit it with flint and steel. Cocking a knee around his saddlehorn, he smoked thoughtfully, watching the plains to the north.

He knew Virgil was coming after them. He could feel it as surely as he did the cold, or the harsh bite of the tobacco on the back of his throat. He knew also that he'd been mighty lucky last night. Virgil, in his surprise at finding Clay and Rain Dancing together, had been no match for Clay. But it would be different next time. If Virgil caught up before they reached the safety of the Kiowas, then one of them would surely have to die.

The thought didn't bother him as much as it once might have. Something had changed for him since his near death encounter with the grizzly. Or perhaps it had been changing all along, and he just hadn't noticed it. He kept remembering Ty's reaction the night before when he'd told him that he and Rain Dancing were leaving. Not the calm acceptance that was so like Ty, but the quick, unfathomable expression that had so briefly shadowed his eyes. Nor could he shake the odd feeling that had come over him since then, a foreboding that had dogged him through the lonely hours of the night.

I'm still running.

He had sworn to Plato on that snowy night behind Dooley's trading post that he would never run again, that he would never allow himself to feel what he'd felt about himself after fleeing the Choctaw Nation, Captain Carry's slavers, and Leavenworth's pompous sheriff. Yet here he was, doing it all over again, this time from a loudmouthed rapist and bully.

The sun crept above the horizon, throwing its rays across the gentle swells of land, sparkling brilliantly off the snow. From below, Rain Dancing called his name. The meat she had put on would soon be ready, she announced, and the ash cakes were done; he should come and eat, so that they could push on as soon as he was finished.

Slowly, Clay straightened in the saddle. He knocked the dottle from his pipe and slipped the stem back through his hatband.

As he started to rein off the low pass, a flicker of movement caught his eye. He pulled up, staring. A distant speck of color had appeared on the northern rim of the horizon, like a dot of black India ink at the upper edge of a clean sheet of foolscap. "I knew you'd come," he said under his breath. "I knew we'd finish this someday."

After breakfast, Rain Dancing stowed their gear and tightened the cinch on her horse. Clay kicked sand and snow over the fire, but made no move toward the pinto. Holding her reins in hand, Rain Dancing watched puzzledly as he stared out across the valley to the south. "We must hurry now," she insisted after several minutes. "Soon Virg-El will come."

"Virgil is already coming," Clay told her. "I saw him before I came down here to eat."

Rain Dancing caught her breath. "Then we must make our ponies run. My village is still far away."

Clay was quiet a long time, then he nodded and went to the pinto. "Let's go."

They rode away from the gulch at a gallop, and didn't stop again until they came to a low bluff overlooking the valley of the Arkansas, several hours later. Clay reined up at the top of a buffalo trail cut into the steep bank, and let his gaze sweep the broad, flat valley all the way to the tree-lined river.

"The Crossing Where the Vultures Roost

in Spring," Rain Dancing explained. She pointed toward a jumbled heap of rocks that was part of a sandstone ledge running away to the east; the ground around the rocks was bare for several feet, the snow melted back from the sun-warmed stones like brown skirting. "It was here that the Pawnees waited for the others of their raiding party to catch up."

"Did they?"

"No. It was also here that Wolf Tail tired of waiting for them, and came on with me."

"Straight into our camp."

"And Virg-El's gun." She glanced over her shoulder. "He draws near."

Clay looked back. Virgil was pushing hard now, with his prey in sight. He had closed the distance to about a mile, but he would be much closer by the time Clay and Rain Dancing reached the river, for Clay had refused to punish their horses the way Virgil had his. He was about to turn away when something else caught his eye. Twisting in the saddle for a better view, he scowled. "Someone's following Virgil."

Rain Dancing wheeled her horse, spotting the far-off mote of color immediately. "Jo-Nas," she said, after a moment's pause. "He comes to help."

"Jonas! Are you sure?" Clay squinted

636

against the snow's glare, but the harder he tried to make out anything specific, the more blurred the figure became.

"Who else would come?" Rain Dancing asked simply.

"The damn fool," Clay grated. "Come on."

They put their horses over the edge of the bluff and rode to the bottom, the ponies' hooves slipping dangerously in the softening mud of the south-facing slope. At the bottom, Clay lifted the pinto to a trot, looking ahead for a place where he could make his stand.

They were about halfway across the broad flat when Clay heard Rain Dancing's quick gasp. He looked back, wondering what had startled her. But Rain Dancing was not watching behind her. She was looking ahead, beyond the Arkansas. Following her gaze, Clay felt his stomach lurch, and hauled the pinto to a stop. Across the river, silhouetted against a bright blue sky atop low, rolling sand hills, was a line of horsemen at least fifty strong. They were still several miles away, but in the clear prairie air they were etched sharp as cut glass.

Rain Dancing let her pony range alongside Clay's as she silently contemplated this new obstacle. Then her face broke into a wide smile. "The People!" she exclaimed. "They have come for me."

The People. *Her* people.

"I do not yet know if they are warriors from my village," Rain Dancing went on excitedly. "But they are surely of the People. See the decorations on their ponies, the way they wear their hair?"

Clay took a deep, steadying breath. He hadn't counted on this, hadn't wanted to even think about it after making his decision back at the gulch that morning. Staring at the line of horsemen across the river, he felt an old fear return, the fear all Choctaws felt when confronted by their ancient enemies — the Kiowas.

"We must hurry," Rain Dancing said. "They will help us kill Virg-El."

"No," Clay replied. "You go on, back to your people. I will stay here and stop Virgil."

Rain Dancing looked confused. "*Our* people," she said uncertainly. "We will go back together, you and I."

Gently, Clay said, "It is true that we talked of my returning with you to the People, but I know now that cannot be. Is it not true that to your tribesmen I would be only a black white man, no different than any white-eye except for the color of my skin?"

638

Rain Dancing searched his face, then looked across the river to where the Kiowas were already coming down off the sand hills toward the Arkansas. She lifted her reins. "You will not stop me?" she asked tentatively.

"No. Go back to your people, Rain Dancing On Water. Be happy there. I will wait here for Virgil, and if I live, I will go back to the white-eyes."

Rain Dancing hesitated only a moment, then heeled her pony toward the river and quirted it into a run.

Clay watched her go, intrigued by his own lack of sadness or regret. He had thought he loved her, and that through her he might reclaim a life that had seemed almost too good to be real. But he realized now that love had never been a true factor, not for either of them. He'd reached that conclusion that morning at the gulch, and had come this far only to see Rain Dancing safely across the Arkansas.

Calmly, Clay turned to face his backtrail. Virgil had reached the edge of the bluff and was starting down, pushing his black gelding at a reckless pace. Clay held his breath as he watched horse and rider negotiate the treacherous course. Twice he thought the black was going to fall on the slick trail, and knew that if it did it would roll all the way to the bottom, crippled or dead. The same fate would likely await Virgil, but each time Clay thought it would happen, the black got its feet under it and plunged daringly on. Finally they reached the bottom in a shower of slushy mud. Virgil yanked savagely on the black's reins, raking its ribs with his spurs.

Clay slid his rifle free of the leather loop on the saddlehorn, stripped away the elk-hide case, and cradled the long gun in his left arm. He pried the old cap off with a thumbnail and replaced it with a fresh one. Then, resting the rifle across his saddlebows, he pulled the Kerr and replaced the caps on that. When he looked up, Virgil had brought his lathered mount to a stop less than a hundred yards away.

Clay dropped his reins over the pinto's neck and tapped the animal with his heels, guiding it with his knees. He had returned the pistol to its holster, the rifle to the crook of his left arm. He kept his right hand on the long gun's wrist, close to the hammer and trigger. Virgil carried his own rifle butted to his thigh, the muzzle pointed skyward. As Clay drew nearer, the expression on Virgil's face became more distinct — a look of madness, of rage and hatred beyond reason.

When less than fifty yards separated them, Clay halted the pinto. Virgil let his rifle swing and drop until he held it in both hands. Drawing a ragged breath, Clay slid his thumb around the hammer, slipped his finger inside the trigger guard. Lifting his voice, he said, "This is crazy, Virgil. Rain Dancing is gone. Look behind me, across the river."

Virgil looked, then shook his head. Clay glanced over his shoulder. The Kiowas had disappeared behind the trees and alders along the Arkansas. Only Rain Dancing remained in sight, running her pony hard for the shelter of the trees, the protection of the warriors approaching from the opposite shore.

"She's mine," Virgil shouted. "I won't let you take her away from me."

"She was never yours, Virg. Let her go back to her people, where she belongs."

"I'm gonna kill you, Clay." His voice sounded high and oddly cracked.

"Damnit, Virgil, there's fifty Kiowa warriors behind those trees. We have to get out of here."

"You want her for yourself, but I won't let you have her." With that, Virgil lifted his rifle and fired.

Clay flinched involuntarily as the ball

passed close to his face. Virgil's movements had been so swift that, even half-expecting it, Clay hadn't had time to react. But now Virgil faced him with an empty weapon, and Clay's thumb hesitated on the hammer. Before Clay could make up his mind, Virgil threw his rifle to the ground and pulled his pistol. With a hoarse shout, he slammed his spurs into the black's ribs. The startled horse lunged forward with a squeal and a buck, then flattened into a run.

"Jesus Christ," Clay breathed. He shouldered the rifle. Virgil rode straight at him, presenting a target Clay knew he couldn't miss. But at the last instant he lowered the rifle, shouting, "Damnit, Virgil, stop this nonsense!"

He doubted if Virgil even heard him. At thirty yards, Virg fired his first shot from his Colt. The bullet whizzed past Clay's left shoulder, coming dangerously close for a revolver fired from the back of a running horse. When Virgil fired a second time and the pinto snorted and jumped as if bee-stung, Clay swung from the saddle and went to one knee, leveling his rifle on Virgil's hunched form.

"Virgil!"

But Virgil couldn't be stopped now. Blood lust glowed triumphantly on his face as he fired his third round. The ball kicked up a geyser of snow at Clay's knee.

Swearing helplessly, Clay cocked the big-bore rifle and brought the sights down on Virgil's chest. Virgil was less than thirty feet away when Clay pulled the trigger. The rifle bucked against his shoulder, and through the blossoming powder smoke he saw the look of astonishment that crossed Virgil's face as the .53 caliber lead sphere hammered him from his saddle.

Virgil hit the ground hard, his Colt flying from his grasp, his body rolling and skidding through the snow, coming to rest less than half a dozen feet from where Clay knelt.

Clay took a deep breath, dragging in a mouthful of powder smoke. His hands were trembling as he lowered the heavy rifle. Virgil lay face up before him, his eyes wide open, staring sightlessly into the cold winter sky.

THIRTY-FOUR

Clay reloaded his rifle, then found Virgil's Colt and reloaded that, too, before shoving it in his belt. He went to stand beside the pinto, his eyes on the trees along the Arkansas, but the Kiowas remained hidden. Staring at the Crossing Where the Vultures Roost in Spring, where Rain Dancing On Water had already disappeared, it would have been easy to imagine that there wasn't an Indian within a hundred miles, so tranquil was the wintery scene.

When twenty minutes had passed, Clay decided the Kiowas weren't going to show themselves. He could only conclude that Rain Dancing had spoken on his behalf, urging them to leave him alone. After a while, he walked over to Virgil's body, staring numbly at the corpse while the events of the past twenty-four hours played through his mind. It seemed strange, adding it all up; it was only last evening that he'd said good-bye to Ty and Jonas, yet it seemed like a lifetime now.

Wearily, he slid his rifle through the loop on the horn. An oblong patch of pink skin ran across the gelding's left shoulder where one of Virgil's bullets had nipped the hide, but there was no blood, nor cause for concern. Clay caught Virgil's black without trouble and led it over to the body. Virgil had been Ty's friend once; it seemed only fitting that Clay take him back to the ranch to bury.

It took some effort to get Virgil's body draped over the black's saddle and lashed in place. Clay kept a wary eye on the trees as he struggled with the corpse, but didn't see so much as the flash of color from a horse. Still, he wouldn't risk stopping now, no matter how exhausted he or the horses were. Swinging onto his own mount and dragging the trail-worn black after him on a lead rope, Clay put his back to the Arkansas.

It was a hard climb to the top of the bluff, and Clay hauled up there to let the horses blow. In the far distance he spotted a speck of color that brought a frown to his face. If that was Jonas, then he was a lot farther away now than he had been when Clay first spotted him. It was a puzzle, but one he was too tired to try to figure out now, and after a short rest, he heeled his horses north to meet him.

From the gap in the rocks overlooking the Crossing Where the Vultures Roost in Spring, Jacques Peliter watched his long sought after prey pass out of range. He lay curled on his side, one bearded cheek pressed flat to the sandy soil, and regarded the shrinking figure of the black man with a philosophical calm. Although he harbored no animosity toward Little Bull for his escape, there was a keen sense of regret for a job not finished, a goal unmet. Yet the fault for this failed opportunity rested solely upon his shoulders, and no one else's.

The mistake wasn't his first, of course. Even a man of such extraordinary talents as his occasionally erred. *Sacré,* but that was life. Yet to fail in this way, to lose his life over so trifling an oversight, rubbed hard at his pride.

Jacques had been well-pleased with himself when he finally located Little Bull, for the trail had been long and complex, and had covered a lot of country. But his tenacity had paid off in the long run, leading him to the hunter's ranch along the Smoky Hill River, and the drama that was unfolding even as he arrived.

At first, reconnoitering the ranch from the breaks to the east, it had been difficult to figure out just what was happening. Even as he slipped into position atop a nearby ridge, a man and woman — an Indian woman, judging from her dress — were passing from sight beyond the bluffs to the south. But Jacques hadn't been able to get any closer to the cabin until dusk, and it wasn't until then that he learned the identity of the man and woman, and of the rage that consumed the one called Virgil.

Jacques didn't care about the particulars of Little Bull's relationship with the others at the ranch, so he hadn't hung around. Even before Virgil reached the top of the bluff south of the river, he was spurring his horse out of the breaks to follow him. He had no plan other than to stay as close to the wild-eyed white hunter as possible. At the pace Virgil set, Jacques knew it wouldn't take long to catch up.

He dogged Virgil's trail all night, though falling back some at first light. When they came to the bluff overlooking the Arkansas, he left the trail altogether, reining eastward into this tangle of sun-warmed stones.

From here, he'd been able to look out over the flats to where Clay waited alone for Virgil's assault, the Indian woman having

already crossed the river to rejoin her kins-
men. Jacques watched with interest as Clay
faced Virgil, silently cheering not only his
calm performance, but also his skill with a
rifle. There had been a few tense moments
afterward, with Jacques keeping as close an
eye on the distant Kiowas as Little Bull, but
the Indians left soon after Virgil fell, staying
close to the river as they filed upstream.

When Little Bull began to struggle with
Virgil's corpse, Jacques knew his own moment with the black man would soon be at
hand. He backed away from the rocks and
quickly led his horse into a nearby coulee,
where he dropped the reins, commanding
the well-trained mount to stay in place with
two sharp, downward tugs on the curb.
Then he hurried back to the rocks with his
rifle. Clay was still watching the trees along
the river, unaware from his lower position
on the flat that the Kiowas had already
departed. Jacques angled toward a cleft in
the rocks that would offer him a clear view
of the flat, dropping to his hands and knees
to crawl the last few yards. From here he
had a perfect field of fire, and as he brought
the rifle up, using his folded winter coat as
a rest, he decided he would kill Little Bull
just as he reached the foot of the bluff. At
that point Clay would be about two hundred

yards away — a long shot for a muzzle loader, but within the range of an experienced marksman.

The faint, dry scraping against the stone on Jacques' left warranted hardly a glance. He'd seen the shallow pocket under the rock when he crawled up there, and the scent had confirmed that this was a snake's den. That they were stirring so early in the year was unusual, but not unheard of. Although the wind was still sharp and snow patched the tawny grass, the rocks radiated a warmth from the sun's rays that was like the flesh of a woman snuggled under a man's robes. But Jacques had not thought the snakes would leave their den, and that had been his mistake. He could not have known about an old bull whose buttons had been hacked off, or that the angry, rotting flesh of its silent stub might goad the snake to go where others of its kind would not venture for several more months.

The snake struck him above the hip with a force that was like a fist slammed into the soft flesh over his kidneys. Jacques grunted in surprise, his body wrenching involuntarily. Drawing his knife, he killed the snake by cutting off its head, then pried the dripping fangs from his side and flipped the head away even as the rattler's body writhed about his legs. He pulled his shirt away from the twin puncture marks, then sliced the wound awkwardly with his knife, but he wasn't able to twist around far enough to suck the poison from the bruised flesh, and in the end the old rattler had had its revenge.

Perhaps, Jacques reflected now that it was too late, he should have called out to Little Bull for help, or fired his rifle into the air as a signal that Clay in all probability would have answered. But he had been too stubborn. He had come here to kill Clay, not beg him for his own life.

A convulsion racked his body, and the nausea suddenly worsened. Sweat beaded his forehead and ran into his eyes. His limbs were stiff, and it was becoming harder to swallow with every shallow beat of his heart. He tried to smile, but his constricting muscles would not allow even that. Well, it didn't matter, he reasoned. He had made a mistake, and for that mistake Clay Little Bull would live and he, Jacques Peliter, would die. He looked at the sky, ringed now with a rapidly funneling darkness, and smiled inside, where the snake's venom had not yet touched him. He had ridden many trails in his life. Now he faced a final journey. He looked forward to seeing where it would take him.

It was mid-afternoon when the two horse-men met. Jonas took one look at the grisly load strapped to the black's saddle and quickly averted his gaze. "Are you all right?" he asked Clay.

"Yeah."

"You're looking a mite peaked. How's the shoulder?"

"I'm tired," Clay said. "What are you do-ing here?"

"I came to stop Virgil, but I see I'm too late again. Where's Rain Dancing?"

"She went back to the Kiowas," Clay said. "I'm taking Virgil to the ranch to bury."

It wasn't much of an explanation, but Jonas didn't ask for more. They rode north at a walk, and Jonas told Clay of the events at the ranch after he and Rain Dancing left. "I didn't get a peek at Ty's wounds," he confessed, "but Oscar said they weren't bad."

"He'd know," Clay said. "He's a trying old bastard, but he's savvy."

They made camp in a draw that night that offered some shelter from the wind, and were in the saddle again by first light. It was coming onto dark when they reached the bluffs overlooking the Smoky Hill. At a glance, Clay knew something was wrong. Although most of the oxen and all of the horses were in sight, grazing on rich bluestem freed by the mid-winter thaw, there was no smoke curling from the cabin's chimney, nor was the prairie schooner anywhere to be seen.

"You think the old man ran off with some of the meat and hides?" Jonas asked with concern.

"Naw, he's got too much pride for that. Maybe he took Ty to Dooley's, or Salina."

They rode down to the ranch. The horses, Clay discovered, had been turned loose to fend for themselves, although they appeared to be staying close to the oxen. There was no note, but Jonas discovered several sticks laid out in the shape of an arrow beside the cabin door, pointing east.

"I'll bet that's what happened," Clay said. "Oscar's taken Ty to Dooley's."

"Then what are we waiting for?" Jonas asked.

Clay glanced at the sky, already softening into twilight. "There's no sense riding through another night," he said. "Besides, I've handled this long enough." He jerked a thumb toward Virgil's corpse. "We'll leave him in the dugout. It'll be cool enough in there for a while. Then tomorrow we'll switch to fresh horses. These ponies are fagged."

Although it was obvious Jonas was anxious to push on, he yielded to Clay's logic. They led the black across the creek and deposited the corpse in the cave-like soddy, wrapped tightly in a buffalo robe. Clay latched the door, then propped the heavy, foot-trundled grindstone against it to keep wolves and other varmints from forcing their way inside. Afterward, he and Jonas went out to the pasture to check on the oxen and haze the horses back to the corral. By the time they finished, it was full dark. Jonas kindled a blaze in the fireplace and got supper started, while Clay pulled the loads in his rifle and pistol and cleaned each weapon thoroughly. He did the same with Virgil's rifle and pistol, reloading the Colt afterward as if to keep it handy.

They were on the trail again by dawn, Jonas riding the dappled gray and Clay using the gray-whiskered dun that had belonged to Wolf Tail. Without a wagon they made good time, reaching Dooley's late that afternoon. Rounding the last bend, Clay spotted the oxen Oscar had used to pull the schooner grazing with Dooley's herd, the wagon itself parked close to the adobe trading post. He took that much in with a glance, then let his gaze shift to the crude village of dugouts behind the post. The Negroes were still there, the wagons and carts scattered haphazardly across the flat between their rough-built winter homes and Dooley's snug post, their stock filling out nicely on the newly exposed grass. Several children were running between the wagons, and chickens pecked at the bare ground in front of the soddies. Clay laughed at the sight, and said, "That'll give Red Elk's Cheyenne something to ponder when they come in to trade this spring."

"Likely these folks will be gone by then," Jonas reminded him. "Dooley says they're set for Cherry Creek to dig for gold."

"Well, I hope they find it," Clay replied, but in his heart there was a heaviness he hadn't expected.

Oscar appeared at the door as Clay and Jonas dismounted and tied their mounts to the hitch rail. He gave Clay a chary look, but made no comment on his return.

"How's Ty?" Jonas asked.

"He'll live." Oscar sniffed and stepped into the sunlight, squinting in its glare. "I didn't expect to see either of you two agin," he went on petulantly. "I'd'a stayed back to the ranch if I'd'a knowed you was comin' back."

Clay didn't reply. A party of horsemen had appeared on the ridge trail to the east. Seeing them, Oscar spat. "More damn fool gold seekers, I reckon. Dooley says they been comin' through regular as clockwork the whole winter."

Clay placed a hand on the dun's hip, watching as the riders began their descent. "They're traveling awfully light for miners," he observed.

"Hell, they been comin' through afoot is what Dooley says, some of 'em with barely enough grub to last another week. But they won't quit. No, sir, they gotta git on to Cherry Crik like they was driven."

Jonas came to stand at Clay's side, eyeing the distant horsemen. "Is something wrong?" he asked.

"Naw, go on in and see Ty. I'll be along directly."

Jonas went inside. Oscar stood at the door a while longer, his hands thrust into the pockets of his trousers, then he also disappeared into the trading post. Clay lowered his hand from the dun's hip and unbuttoned his mackinaw, freeing access to the Kerr. A few minutes later, when the horsemen reached level ground and lifted their mounts to a jog, he dug Virgil's Colt from his saddlebags and shoved it into his belt.

As the horsemen drew closer, one of them urged his mount to the fore of the group and lifted an arm to point at Clay.

Hog!

The name popped into Clay's mind like the crack of a bullwhacker's whip, and for a moment an icy panic swept through him, his throat constricting as if by one of the Captain's iron collars, drawn too tight. Then the fear vanished and he reached across the saddle and slid his rifle from its loop. At the same instant, the six horsemen spurred their mounts forward, racing across the flat. Clay walked into the yard, away from the horses. As he did, the six men slowed cautiously, fanning out to advance the rest of the way at a walk. Holding his rifle in both hands, Clay cocked it with a deliberate slowness.

"I wouldn't do that," a gray-bearded man in the center of the group called gravely. "Brashness is a fool's courage."

Clay's heart beat a little faster when he saw the gray-bearded man's resemblance to Captain Carry. A brother, perhaps? The infamous Colonel Douglas J. Carry, of Tennessee?

The horsemen drew up about twenty feet away, and the gray-bearded man looked at Hog Waller, then at a second man leading a packhorse — Jake Jacobs. "Is this him?" he queried brusquely.

"That be him, Colonel" Hog said excitedly. "That there's Clay Little Bull."

Clay's finger stroked the rifle's trigger as he studied the tall, lean-figured man on the leggy thoroughbred. He had the same dark, emotionless eyes, Clay thought, the same gaunt sharpness as his brother, and he decided then that he would take this one first. He might die here today, but he intended to wipe away a parasite that had fed off the misery of others for too many years.

"Put the rifle down, boy."

Clay looked at the man on Carry's right, slim and hard-bitten, with menacing gray eyes.

"I told you to put that rifle down," the hard-bitten man repeated. "I don't generally tell a nigger twice."

"Nigger," Clay breathed, his anger blossoming sudden and full-grown. Raising his voice so that Carry's men could hear, he said, "I'm getting tired of that word, and the way your kind like to use it, like it was a clod of dirt to step on, or kick out of the way."

A sardonic grin came to Colonel Carry's face. "You have spunk, son, which can bode well on the auction block with the right crowd. Nothing brings up the price like an African that thinks he can't be broken. It's a shame we won't have the opportunity to teach you differently."

Before Clay could reply, the door to Dooley's trading post swung open. Clay didn't dare take his eyes off the six gunmen, but he could tell by the tread that it was Jonas. "Go back inside," he called. "This doesn't concern you."

"Sure it does," Jonas replied casually, moving closer.

"Get out of here," Clay snarled. "Get your goddamn white ass back inside with the others."

"Shoot, Clay, you ought to know that won't work on me."

"Get!" Clay barked.

"Naw, I think I'll stay," Jonas replied, halting about halfway between Clay and the trading post.

Colonel Carry's expression hardened. "I would suggest you follow this Negro's advice, young man. Loyalty to a pet is an admirable quality in a boy, but it hints of weakness in a man."

Jonas laughed. "Go kiss a skunk's ass," he replied cheerfully.

Carry blanched, his lips compressing into a thin, bloodless line. He started to turn to the gray-eyed man at his side, but then Dooley's door opened once more, stopping the Colonel cold. This time, Clay risked a peek. Tyler Calhoun limped into the sunlight, clutching a revolver in his right hand. He moved only far enough away from the door to allow Sam Dooley room to step out with his double-barreled shotgun.

Colonel Carry let his breath out in an exasperated rush. "I had heard the interior of Kansas crawled with nigger lovers, but by God I hadn't expected to find so many in one place."

"Ye ain't wanted here, Carry," Dooley said loudly. " 'Tis a free territory, this, and soon enough the vote will show that the majority o' its citizens want it tae be a free state, tae boot. Go back to Tennessee, and take ye man killers with ye."

"Colonel," Jake said tautly, nodding toward the row of dugouts where half a dozen black men had appeared. They were approaching warily, Plato in the lead, and Clay's heart swelled with an unexpected pride. Most of the Negroes carried rifles or shotguns, but a few also had pistols holstered at their waists or thrust into their belts. The children had disappeared, but some of the women walked with the men, and Clay smiled to see Jenny striding angrily at Plato's side.

"There's another one of 'em," Hog said. "That there white-haired nigra out front. The gal, too. That's Jenny, sure as hell."

Colonel Carry took a deep breath. "Then it appears our quest has neared its completion." He turned to Clay with a look of deep satisfaction. "So, you've banded together for protection, like the settlers at Blackbird."

"Colonel," Jake said. "We're outnumbered here."

"Control yourself, Mr. Jacobs, unless you would prefer to join the larger force."

"To tell you the truth," Jake said, tossing aside the lead rope to his packhorse. "I ain't hankering to mix up in this here ruckus, anyway. You wanted me along to identify the men who killed the Cap'n. Well, I done that. Now I'm leavin'." He yanked on his mount's reins, pulling the animal out of line.

"Stand your ground, Jacobs," Carry commanded. His face, pale only moments before, was now livid with rage. "All of you stand your ground. I'll shoot the first man who attempts to desert." He glanced at the contingent of blacks, huddled uncertainly at the corner of the trading post. It was obvious only Plato and Jenny had any inkling of what was going on, but they all seemed to sense that it was important, that it could easily affect them all. Jake Jacobs had halted his horse at the Colonel's threat, but he hadn't reined it back in line; he looked as if he wanted to run, and probably would as soon as the shooting started. All eyes were focused on Colonel Carry, waiting in expectant silence.

A look of impatience crossed Carry's face. "Boyd, I want you and Mr. Quint to kill the Negroes standing beside the trading post. Bill, shoot the trader and the man with him. I will attend to Clay and the boy." He turned to Hog. "Mr. Waller, as soon as Mr. Jacobs attempts to flee, I want you to shoot him down. Is that understood?"

For a moment Clay thought Hog might refuse, but then his courage failed and he nodded glumly. "All right."

"Ye be makin' a mistake," Dooley called edgily. "Ye can't just waltz in here and gun down a bunch o' white men like ye was shootin' rats in a barn."

"You are the one making the mistake, sir, by siding with armed Negroes," Carry responded. "Stand aside if you do not wish to suffer the consequences."

"I think it's you who's made the mistake," Clay said quietly. He nodded toward Plato and the others. "We have you outgunned."

"*Negroes* have me outgunned," Carry corrected scornfully. "I count one white man the equal of any ten shuffling black brutes."

"I don't know, Colonel," Quint said uneasily. He was watching Plato and the others, who had finally spread out some. At least half of them were carrying shotguns, weapons that would cut a wicked swath at such a close range. "Maybe we ought to back off today."

"Ain't nobody backing off from a bunch of darkies," Bill Hawkes growled. "Once the shooting starts, they'll scatter."

"I don't think so," Clay said, his gaze on Quint.

"I got no 'tention of scatterin'," Plato interjected, taking a step forward. "We done decided a long time ago, Colonel, that we be stickin' together, them of us what's here. Come hell or high water, or even a bunch of Tennessee gunmen."

"Enough of this foolishness," Carry said tautly. "Little Bull, throw down your weapons!"

"I reckon not."

Carry's eyes narrowed. "Then your time has come." He turned to the grim-faced man at his side. "Kill them," he ordered in a voice that resonated with hatred. The command given, Carry slid his pistol from its holster and leveled it at Clay.

Clay swung his rifle around, snapping off a shot from the hip that tumbled Carry from his saddle. Then all hell broke loose, and Clay hardly knew what was going on. He found himself moving instinctively away from the post, clawing for his pistol. The reports of shotguns and rifles created a deafening roar behind him. Buckshot whistled through the air; horses whinnied in pain and terror; pistols cracked, and clouds of gunsmoke twisted through the yard like dancing wraiths. He saw Carry sitting hatless on the ground with his legs extended before him. Blood colored the Colonel's shoulder and spotted his right cheek like war paint, yet he still gripped his pistol, still fired, the revolver jumping in his hand, the reports lost in the din of the battle.

A slug took Clay in the ribs and spun him around. He lost his footing and fell to his knees, but managed to thrust the Kerr toward Carry and snap off a wild shot. Carry fired again, and Clay's head snapped back as if struck by a fist. Pain coursed down his neck and into his shoulder, a white-hot streak of fire laid against the side of his skull. He brought the Kerr up for a second shot, but its sights wavered horribly, and when he fired, the recoil yanked the pistol from his weakened fingers. Yet through a mushrooming cloud of powder smoke he saw the Colonel knocked backward, his arms flailing.

Then the sound of gunfire died and an unearthly silence came over the meadow. Clay stared stupidly at his empty hands and wondered what had become of his pistol. Jenny was at his side then, lowering him to the muddy ground. "It's over," she whispered in his ear. "It's all over."

THIRTY-FIVE

Clay's eyes fluttered open to stare at a rough plank ceiling. For a few minutes that was all he could do — just stare vacantly while his thoughts skittered in different directions. After a time he managed to turn his head. Ty was sitting motionless in a rocking chair beside the bunk, his arm in a sling, his face haggard. He looked up when Clay stirred, and a smile wormed its way through his beard.

"How're you feeling?"

"My head hurts."

"I don't doubt it."

Clay reached up to explore the bandage wrapped snugly around his skull, wincing as he probed the tender flesh. "What happened?" he asked.

"What do you remember?"

Clay rummaged backward through his memory, dredging up a hodgepodge of images that flashed like tintypes in his mind.

"Colonel Carry," he said finally. "And . . . others . . . Jake . . . Hog . . ." Then he said, "Jonas! Is Jonas all right?"

"He's fine. One of Plato's men, George Simms, took a bullet in the leg, and one of Dooley's oxen was shot in the spine by a stray bullet and killed. You took a crease across your ribs and another one alongside your head, but neither is serious."

"And Carry?" In Clay's mind was a picture of the slaver's body being thrown backward by the Kerr's slug, but he had to be sure.

"Colonel Carry is dead. They're all dead."

"Even Jake?"

"Even Jake," Ty said flatly.

Clay relaxed, sinking back into his pillow. "Then we did it," he said, not bothering to hide his surprise.

"Yeah," Ty said quietly. "We did it." He pulled a wrinkled envelope from the pouch on his belt and handed it to Clay. "Dooley gave me this," he said. "A freighter brought it in around Christmas."

Clay turned the envelope over in his hands, taking note of the smudged ink and torn corners. The wax seal had been nearly worn away by handling, although enough remained to protect the contents. It was addressed to: *Clay little Bull, car of C Lobinstin,*

Levenworth Kansas Ter. He didn't recognize the handwriting.

Hooking a finger under the flap, Clay ripped open the envelope and shook out a single sheet of paper, torn from a ledger book. He checked the signature first, then slowly read the contents.

Deer Clay.

Hope you ar fine I am well So is Weed. Charges agaist you ar droped by choctaw counsil on acount of Sally Gray shot Moses in the hed and killed him. they ar going to try her in Jacks fork in the spring but probly wont hang her on acount of everbody nos what Moses was doin with them womin slaves of his at his plantashun. folks figured it was her all along that shot him in the elbow but i don't no about that. Counsil sez you ar stil a fugitiv on acount of being blak and steeling them things off the farm, but folks think you could beat them charges easy was you to come back on acount of everbody here liks you a lot and nos Simon gave all his blaks there freedom. Me and Weed is deputys agin, cause we was fired a while back but hav ben reenstated by the counsil. if you come back I will speak for you at the counsil. so will weed. yor friend, Lyn.

"I'll be damned," Clay murmured, staring at the paper.

"Good news?" Ty asked.

Shrugging, Clay returned the letter to its envelope. "Old news, I guess," he said, then crumbled it and let it drop to the floor.

Ty shoved to his feet. "It's late," he said. "I'm going to bed, but there's someone outside who's been waiting to see you."

"Plato?"

Ty smiled and left the room. A moment later Jenny came in, her eyes reddened as if by the wind. "Well," she said briskly, coming to his side. "They say you gonna live, after all."

"I'll be fine by morning."

"Huh! I wouldn't go countin' on that," she replied. "You got whomped upside your head pretty good."

"It wasn't you who whomped me, was it?" Clay teased.

"Don't be sassin' me, Mr. Clay Little Bull. That be my blouse all cut up and wrapped 'round your head."

A frown crossed Clay's face. "What are you doing here?" he asked. "Is Plato all right?"

"What be so wrong with my bein' here?

You want me to leave, you jus' say so."

"I didn't say I wanted you to leave. I was just wondering if Plato was all right."

"That old man be fit as a fiddle," she replied in a scornful voice. "Crowin' like some ol' rooster 'bout what we all done." She settled in the rocker Ty had vacated a few minutes before, pushing back with her toes. "That Dooley feller, him and Ty and Jonas, they say they's gonna take all the blame for killin' them white folks. Say ain't no lawman gonna come 'round botherin' us for that."

"They're good men," Clay agreed. "If they say they'll do it, they will."

"Ain't never knowed me no good white men afore, but Plato say they's some, here and about. Me, I don't trust 'em much. Sooner we lights a shuck for Cherry Creek, the sooner I be happy."

"Still set on panning for gold?"

"Gonna need it, we all go to Mexico like Plato wants. You coming?" She asked it casually, as if the answer didn't matter one way or another, but Clay noticed she'd stopped rocking while awaiting his reply.

"I guess I'll stay here," he said. "I promised Ty I'd see it through to the end of the season, if he still wants me."

"Well, that be jus' fine then. You jus' stay

here." She got to her feet. "I thought maybe that bullet upside your head might'a done some good, but I see it didn't." She left the room, slamming the door after her. Clay winced at the bang, then closed his eyes. He didn't feel sleepy, but when he opened them again Plato was sitting where Ty and Jenny had sat the night before, and the candle lantern that hung from a spike in the adobe wall had been snuffed. Daylight crept into the room around a shuttered window high on one wall.

Plato's face crinkled into a smile when he saw that Clay was awake. "Thought you was gonna sleep all day," he said.

"What time is it?"

"Near 'bout noon, I reckon. How you feelin', son?"

"Hungry," Clay said. He pushed his robe back and swung slowly out of bed, the muscles across his ribs stretching painfully.

A look of alarm crossed Plato's face. "Now, you just settle back there, Clay. Ain't no cause for you to be movin' 'bout. I fetch you a bite to eat, you be hungry."

Clay ran his hand lightly over the bandages covering his ribs. The flesh immediately surrounding the wound was bruised, and his whole side felt hot and sore, but there was nothing distressing enough to keep him in bed. He saw Plato eyeing the scars across his shoulder, where the grizzly had mauled him last Christmas. It kind of surprised him to discover that the jagged furrows were still a deep, angry shade of pink; the bear's attack seemed so long ago now that it was odd to remember that it had all happened only a couple of months ago.

"My, oh, my," Plato murmured. "That boy, Jonas, he tolt me 'bout you tanglin' with ol' Mistuh Bear. Said you near 'bout got yourself kilt."

"Been a real interesting winter," Clay admitted. "I reckon it's behind me now, though." He looked around the room. There wasn't much to see — the bunk with its mattress of rope and robes, a brass-bound leather trunk sitting against the wall with some clothes stacked on top of it, the rocker where Plato sat. The adobe walls were smooth save for the lantern, the floor hard-packed earth. "Where are my clothes?" he asked.

Plato picked up the stack of clothing from the trunk and set it on the bed at Clay's side, along with his winter moccasins. There was a new pair of underwear, socks, trousers, and a red wool shirt. "Jenny be washin' and mendin' your old clothes," Plato told him, "though she allowed that buckskin shirt of yours needed burnin', it was so rag-gedy."

Clay looked up sharply. "She'd better not. I'm partial to that shirt."

"Well, it got punched up some by the Colonel's bullet, and some bloody, too, but maybe she'll mend it for you."

Clay took his time dressing, pulling on his moccasins last. Then he and Plato walked through the trading post and outside. The sun was shining bright as polished brass in the sky, but the wind was out of the west again, sharp as a thorn.

"Storm brewin'," Plato predicted, button-ing his coat. "My knees tell me so."

"Feels like it," Clay agreed.

At the warehouse, Oscar Garrett and a couple of Negroes hired by Dooley were loading baled hides into a blue and yellow freighter from Leavenworth. Dooley stood to the side with a manifest, checking off each ten-hide bale, oaken keg of tongues, or sack of meat as it was wrestled into the wagon. Ty stood with him, his arm in a sling, but watching the proceedings closely.

"Where's Jonas?" Clay asked, looking around.

"Him and Jesse went back to fetch Virgil Nash's body. Ty wants to bury him here. I reckon he ain't plannin' on stayin' at that there ranch forever, and figures Virgil'll get into less trouble here, where Sam Dooley can keep a good eye on him."

Clay didn't smile. "I reckon Virgil's caused all the trouble he's going to in this life, and that was a hatful."

They walked away from the trading post, and in their wandering came to the banks of the Smoky Hill. The snow was deeper under the trees, and although the breeze was keen, it had a clean, fresh smell, free of the stench of death that surrounded the hunter's ranch back on Tornado Creek. Clay reached for the pipe he carried in his hatband, feeling a moment's embarrassment when his hand encountered Jenny's blouse instead. He pulled the bandage off and shoved it into the big right-hand pocket of his mackinaw.

Plato chuckled knowingly. "Jenny tolt me what you said 'bout stayin' with Ty. He be a good man, Clay, or so he seems to me."

"He's a good man."

Plato turned to face Clay. "You gots yourself a choice here, son, a sure-'nough 'tunity, what only a handful of folks get in they life. You want, I figure you can follow that Injun gal, and she'd likely get you into that Kiowa tribe, like you was always talkin' 'bout.

"Same time, that Tyler Calhoun'd keep you on as a partner, if that be what you wanted. Mebbeso you could find yourself a life out here amongst these white folks.

"But you gots yourself a third choice, too, Clay. Was you to change your mind 'bout it, you could come on down to Mexico with me'n Jenny and the others, make ourselves a little community down there. I'd be proud to have you, son, you know that. So would Jenny. Whether you believe it or not, I 'spect she'd be right proud to have you come live with us in Mexico.

"That be all I got to say, Clay. I won't ask agin."

Clay sighed, looking off across the rolling hills to the north. "I'm tired of running, dad. That's why I came back. Part of the reason, anyway."

"I wondered," Plato said softly. "That Oscar Garrett, when he come in with Ty all banged up, he said you'd lit out for the Kiowa country with that Injun woman. I was some surprised when I seen you was come back, till young Jonas told us how you'd turned 'round after makin' sure that gal got back to her folks."

Clay laughed. "Is that what people think?"

Plato smiled. "You let folks think what they wants, son. Ain't your place to go med-

674

dlin' in that." He paused a moment, then added, "Clay, you gots to know the difference a'tween runnin' from something and runnin' to it. What these folks gots in mind," he nodded toward the dugouts, "that's runnin' *toward* somethin', and they ain't nothin' wrong in that."

Following the direction of Plato's nod, Clay saw Jenny talking to a woman he'd never seen before who was tending a big, cast-iron kettle hung over a fire. As he watched, the woman minding the kettle said something, and both of them laughed. Then Jenny looked up and caught Clay watching her, and her laughter faded.

"We gonna start us a new life," Plato went on. "Gonna go where slavery's been outlawed a long time and make us our own place. Not just for us, but for our children, and they's children, and anybody else what wants to come and help us build up a community. Ain't gonna be easy. They's Injuns down there in old Mexico, and bandits, and the Lord only knows what else. But they be freedom down there, too, and warm winds to soothe an old man's bones. A man what's got that, got his freedom and his old joints don't creak ever step, then ain't nothin' gonna stop him. It what you call p'spective. Now you take a man or woman what gets they's freedom after not havin' it, then ain't nothin' gonna be hard on them ever agin. You see what I mean?"

Clay nodded. "Yeah, I see."

"Mebbeso you do, son, mebbeso you do."

"I've been doing a lot of thinking about what you said the last time I was here."

"Said me a lot of things, Clay," Plato reminded him.

"I guess you were right when you said I wasn't Choctaw or Kiowa. I'm black, same as you, same as Jenny —"

"No," Plato interrupted gently. "You ain't black. Not all the way, you ain't. You just ain't all the way Injun, either. You a'twixt and a'tween, and I reckon that be a mighty confusin' road sometimes. But you can take the best outta both worlds, son, and out here on these prairies you just might make it. With folks like Sam Dooley and Ty and Jonas, you might."

"Yeah, I might at that," he said, but the thought brought him no joy.

"And if you don't, you can always come to Mexico and look us up. I 'spect we'll be 'round down there somewheres."

"Maybe I'll do that."

Plato started to walk off, but stopped after a few strides, turning and smiling. "You come down to see Jenny, too. I gots me a hunch she'll be lookin' for you. Be watchin' that backtrail for quite a spell, she will."

Clay laughed. "With a wheelbarrow full of rocks, more'n likely."

"Don't think so, Clay, I surely don't." He started off again, adding over his shoulder, "Come on over to the soddy in a few minutes. I'll tell Jenny you be hungry, and we'll see what she whips up. Somethin' scrumptious, I'll bet."

"She's too damn bullheaded," Clay said, lifting his voice for Plato's benefit. "And you're too damn easy to see through."

"Shoo, look who be callin' that kettle black. You come on over, Clay. Spring be a ways off yet. A man can change his mind a dozen times a'tween now and then."

Clay looked past him to the dugout where Jenny was squatting beside the fire, fussing with the flames. "Hey, old man," he called. "They got buffalo down there in Mexico?"

"Why, I don't rightly know, son, but if they ain't, they oughter have somethin' a hunter could hunt."

"If I was to come down there next summer, just sayin' *if,* mind you, do you think you could quit using that damn slave talk? It grates on my nerves."

Plato was quiet a moment, looking south and west as if he could see the free air over

Mexico from here. Then he said, slowly and deliberately, "Old habits die hard, Clay, but if you were to come," he smiled, "just saying *if,* mind you, then I might see what I could do about that."

Clay laughed, watching the old man walk away. A couple of minutes later, he followed him toward the soddy.